John G. Edgar

Sea Kings and Naval Heroes

A book for boys

John G. Edgar

Sea Kings and Naval Heroes
A book for boys

ISBN/EAN: 9783337214296

Printed in Europe, USA, Canada, Australia, Japan

Cover: Foto ©Andreas Hilbeck / pixelio.de

More available books at **www.hansebooks.com**

SEA-KINGS

AND

NAVAL HEROES.

A Book for Boys.

BY JOHN G. EDGAR,

AUTHOR OF

"HISTORY FOR BOYS," "BOYHOOD OF GREAT MEN,"
"FOOTPRINTS OF FAMOUS MEN," "WARS OF
THE ROSES," &c., &c.

ILLUSTRATED BY C. KEENÉ AND E. K. JOHNSON.

NEW YORK:

HARPER & BROTHERS, PUBLISHERS,

FRANKLIN SQUARE.

1863.

PREFACE.

THE propriety and policy of directing the attention of English boys of the nineteenth century to the achievements of men who, at various periods of modern history, have made their names known to fame as "Sea Kings and Naval Heroes," will be questioned by few in the present circumstances of Europe. Under an impression that such is the prevailing sentiment, I have ventured on writing the following biographical sketches, with the object of interesting my juvenile readers in the careers of the principal personages among their ancestors, who, from the time of Rollo and Hasting to that of Nelson and Collingwood, figured conspicuously as maritime warriors; and I have endeavored to give variety to the work by narrating with care the enterprises, the battles, and the adventures in which they took prominent parts.

In a historical point of view, the advantage of such a book for boys will not be lightly es-

timated by any one capable of comprehending
the importance of history as a branch of education, and able to appreciate the benefits to be
derived by boys, in after-life, from obtaining,
at an early age, adequate ideas of great events
and clear conceptions of renowned personages.
But apart from the question of historical intelligence, I would fain hope that a knowledge of
what our English heroes have done and suffered in the cause of duty and patriotism—leading brave lives in times of their country's trial,
and dying glorious deaths in the hour of their
country's need—may not be altogether without its influence in inspiring some of the rising
generation with a noble ambition to emulate
the heroic valor and rival the patriotic devotion so often displayed by their progenitors.

J. G. E.

CONTENTS.

LIST OF ILLUSTRATIONS.

SEA KINGS AND NAVAL HEROES.

ROLLO THE NORMAN.

AT the time when Alfred the Great reigned in England, and when the heirs of Charlemagne occupied the throne of France, both countries were perpetually menaced by the piratical adventurers from the coast of Norway and the islands of the Baltic, who are celebrated in history as Sea Kings and Vikings.

Of all human beings these grim Northmen were the most enterprising. They highly prided themselves on not sleeping under the smoke-dried roof, or emptying the brimming can by the chimney-corner. They regarded the ocean as their home; they called the tempest their servant; they guided their ships through the waves as a skillful rider does his steed; and, when the storm raged, and the sea ran high, they disdained the thought of fear. "Blow where thou wilt, O wind!" they were in the habit of exclaiming on such occasions; "whithersoever thou takest us, the land is ours."

As invaders, the sea kings made themselves pe-

culiarly formidable. Hoisting their mystic banners, and launching their ships, whose gayly-
painted sides were hung with bucklers of polished steel, and whose prows were ornamented with
figures of lions, bulls, and dolphins, they dashed
over the blue waters in search of prey. Impel-
ling their fleets with oars and sails, they entered
rivers, landed to plunder the banks as they ascended, and when a bridge interfered with their
progress, they drew their vessels on shore, placed
them on rollers, conveyed them beyond the obstacle, and then proceeded with their predatory
voyage. In the day of battle their enthusiasm
soared high, and they delighted in conflict and
carnage. Nor did they feel any fear at the approach of death; for they saw, in imagination,
goddesses beckoning them to the halls of Odin,
and infinitely rejoiced in the prospect of passing
to their Valhalla, or paradise of heroes, where
they expected to indulge, morning after morning,
in the luxury of cutting each other to pieces, and,
evening after evening, to feast at a great banquet-
table, and to quaff draughts of beer out of cups
of horn.

While the sea kings were ravaging every coast
where plunder was to be obtained, a king named
Harold resolved, about the close of the ninth century, to form a single kingdom out of the petty
states into which Norway was divided. In order
to strengthen his resolution, Harold vowed not to

HAROLD HARFAGHER.

cut his hair until his object was accomplished; and as the operation occupied him for several years, his fair locks grew so long and thick that he acquired the surname of "Hirsute." At length, however, the Norwegian king deemed that his vow was fulfilled; and, repairing to the house of a Jarl named Rognvald, he took a bath, and ventured to comb and trim. This having been done, the improvement in Harold's appearance was such that the Jarl could not refrain from expressing his admiration. "King," said he, "your hair is now so beautiful that, instead of being surnamed 'Hirsute,' you must be surnamed 'Harfagher.'"

It happened that Rognvald had a wife, named Hilda, of noble blood and high spirit, and several sons, all noted for their prowess and valor. Of these the most remarkable was Rollo. He was tall, and of large bulk; and being unable, on account of his stature, to ride any of the horses of the country, he became generally known as "Rollo the Walker."

Rollo, being a Norman of high birth, naturally had a liking for the salt water. From his youth he accustomed himself to the life of a sea king, and was constantly in the habit of cruising in the Baltic. But after he reached manhood, new ideas came into fashion, and the occupation could not be pursued without considerable risk. In fact, Harold Harfagher had set his face decidedly against piratical adventure, and passed the most severe laws to prevent his subjects from interfering with the property of their neighbors.

Nevertheless, Rollo, in whom the spirit of the sea king was strong, one day, when returning from a cruise, had the imprudence to shorten sail off the coast of Wighen, and to exercise a privilege long enjoyed by sea kings of impressing provisions. The consequences proved somewhat serious; for Harold Harfagher happening at the time to come into the vicinity to administer justice, the peasants immediately complained loudly that Rollo had seized their flocks; and the king, without regard to the rank of the offender, summoned a council to try the son of Rognvald according to law.

The probability of Rollo escaping sentence of banishment now appeared slender. But the spouse of Rognvald, moved by maternal tenderness, determined to make an effort on her tall son's behalf. Going, therefore, into the royal presence, she endeavored to soften Harold Harfagher's heart.

"King," said Hilda, "I ask you to pardon my son."

"It is impossible," replied Harold; "the laws must be respected."

"Ha! has the very name of our race become hateful to you?" exclaimed she, rearing herself to her full height, and speaking in a tone of menace: "you expel from the country and treat as an en-

emy a man of noble race. Listen, then, to what
I tell you. It is dangerous to attack the wolf.
When once he is angered, let the herd in the for-
est beware."

In spite of this vague threat, and the high place
Rognvald occupied in the king's esteem, Rollo
was sentenced to exile; and, finding himself without a country, he collected vessels, sailed to the
Hebrides, and there found many Norwegian chiefs
banished by Harold Harfagher. With these exiles Rollo took counsel, formed an alliance, and
resolved on some great enterprise. Being all
men of rank, all warriors and sea kings from boyhood, they agreed that there should be perfect
equality among them, and that Rollo should have
no advantage over his comrades. With this un-
derstanding they cut their cables, and, as they
expressed it, gave the reins to their great sea-
horses.

It appears that Rollo had been directed by a
dream to seek a home in England, and that a
Christian priest, whom, pagan as he was, he consulted, advised him to obey the warning. Accordingly, he made an attempt to land in England; but the English treated him as an enemy;
and finding the country strongly fortified, and
the coasts guarded against invaders by the fleets
of Alfred, he was forced to retire. Making for
the French coast, however, he, in September, 876,
entered the Seine, pillaged both banks of the riv-

er, and ere long anchored his ships at Jumièges,
five leagues from Rouen.

When rumors of the ravages committed by the
Normans reached Rouen, a city then surrounded
by woods and forests, the inhabitants were overwhelmed with surprise and terror. Expecting
no succor, and entertaining no hope of defending
their walls against such foemen as the Normans,
they wrung their hands and gave way to despair.
Fortunately, however, the Archbishop of Rouen
was a man of prudence and presence of mind;
and, taking upon himself the task of saving the
city by capitulation, he repaired to Jumièges,
spoke, by an interpreter, to the Norman chiefs,
and, after much trouble, negotiated a treaty. By
this the archbishop consented to admit Rollo and
his comrades into the city; and the Normans, in
return, promised to commit no acts of violence.

Matters having thus been arranged, Rollo and
his grim comrades sailed up the Seine to Rouen,
and moored their vessels near the Church of St.
Morin. Landing peaceably, they walked through
the city, surveyed the quays, the ramparts, and
the fountains, and, finding every thing to their
liking, resolved on making the place their capital.
Having thoroughly examined Rouen, the Normans felt anxious to see more of a country which
they destined as their home, and leaving a band
of warriors to keep possession of the city, they
continued to ascend the river till they reached

that point where the Seine receives the waters of the Eure. Learning, however, that a French army was on its march to encounter them, they landed, formed a fortified camp, and, with little apprehension as to the issue of a conflict, awaited the approach of their foes.

At that time, Charles the Simple, a descendant of Charlemagne, occupied the French throne, but swayed the sceptre with a feeble hand. On this occasion, however, he did make an effort to save his realm. Assembling an army, he placed it under the command of the Duke of France, and sent it forth to do battle with the Normans. Reaching the right bank of the Eure at a short distance from the Norman camp, the French held a council of war; and, after long deliberation, they resolved, before risking a conflict, to hold a parley with the invaders.

With this object, three French chiefs, who understood the northern tongue, were dispatched to ascertain the views of the sea kings; and appearing on the right bank of the Eure, and halting exactly opposite the Norman camp, these emissaries entered into conversation with the invaders, asked them to submit to King Charles, and tempted them with offers of lands and honors. But the Normans all cried, "We will submit to no one;" and the three messengers, going back to the Duke of France, informed him that their mission had been in vain. On hearing the result of the parley, the French determined to force the Noman camp, and advanced with that object. But they found foes much more formidable than they had anticipated. After a struggle, the French were repulsed, and the Duke of France, who had undertaken the task of putting Rollo down, fell by the hand of a fisherman of Rouen, whom the son of Rognvald had pressed into his service.

Rollo, after his victory, was at liberty to navigate the Seine; and, sailing up to Paris, he laid siege to the city. But at this stage he met with a check. One of the Norman chiefs was taken prisoner by the French; and the great sea king, in order to redeem his comrade, was under the necessity of making a year's truce with Charles the Simple.

But Rollo was not a man to waste the year in inaction. He employed the time in ravaging the northern provinces, which had ceased to be French; and having, on the expiration of the truce, returned to Rouen, he proceeded to surprise Bayeux, a city governed by a count named Beranger, who had a fair daughter. After killing Count Beranger, Rollo sacked the city, and, as his share of the plunder, took possession of the count's daughter, Popa, whom he married after the rites of his religion and the laws of his country.

Soon after the sack of Bayeux, the Normans

made themselves masters of Evreux and other places; and Rollo, whom they now elected as their king, found himself reigning as a conqueror over the greater part of the territory known as Neustria. But he perfectly comprehended the position which he occupied. He made himself popular with the inhabitants; and though he was a pagan, and the Neustrians were Christians, they could not help respecting him for the powerful protection he afforded, and the peace they enjoyed under his government.

While such was the state of affairs, Rollo formed a league with the Scandinavians occupying the territory at the mouth of the Loire; and having agreed with them to pillage simultaneously the whole territory between the Loire and the Seine, he commenced a systematic war against the French. The consequences were most disastrous to the subjects of Charles the Simple; and the French, continually annoyed and plundered, ere long began to complain, and at length loudly to demand that an end should be put to the war.

"Do we not see in every place churches burned and people killed?" some asked.

"Yes," replied others. "By the fault of King Charles and his weakness, the Normans do as they please in the kingdom. From Blois to Senlis there is not an acre of corn, and no man dares to labor either in the fields or in the vineyards."

"It is true," cried all; "and till this war is finished we shall have dearth and dearness."

When such murmurs pervaded his kingdom,
Charles the Simple had sufficient sense to perceive that something must be done to conciliate
the Normans; and, convoking his peers and prelates, he laid before them the complaints of the
people. These being recognized as just, the Archbishop of Rouen was employed to negotiate with
Rollo; and, willingly undertaking the mission, he
sought the presence of the sea king.

"Rollo, son of Rognvald," said the archbishop,
"King Charles offers you his daughter, Gisla, in
marriage, with the hereditary seigneury of all the
country situated between the River Epte and the
borders of Brittany, if you consent to become
Christian, and to live at peace with the kingdom."

"The words of the king are good," replied
Rollo, gravely, "but the land he offers is insufficient. It is uncultivated and impoverished. My
people would not derive from it the means of living in peace."

"What say you to Flanders?" suggested the
archbishop.

"Flanders," answered Rollo, "is a poor country, muddy, and full of swamps."

"Then," said the archbishop, "King Charles
must give you Brittany in conjunction with
Neustria."

"That will suffice," said Rollo, smiling grimly.

Affairs having reached this stage, preparations were made for ratifying the treaty in the most solemn manner. St. Clair, a green village on the Epte, was selected as a fitting place for the ceremony; and on a summer day, Rollo and the Norman chiefs pitched their tents on one side of the river, and Charles the Simple, with the French lords, on the other. At the hour appointed, Rollo, crossing the Epte, approached Charles, and, standing in front of the chair of state, placed his hands between those of the king, and pronounced the formula.

"Henceforth," said the son of Rognvald, addressing the heir of Charlemagne, "I am your vassal and your man, and I swear faithfully to protect your life, your limbs, and your royal honor."

After Rollo had taken the oath of fealty, Charles the Simple gave him the title of count, and the Norman concluded that the ceremony was at an end. Indeed, Rollo was about to retire, when the French lords informed him that there was one custom too important to be neglected on such an occasion.

"It is fitting," said they, "that he who receives such a gift of territory should kneel before the king and kiss his foot."

"Never," exclaimed Rollo, with undisguised contempt. "Never will I bend the knee be-

fore a mortal; never will I kiss the foot of any
man."

"It is a remnant of the etiquette formerly used
in the court of the French emperors," urged the
lords.

Finding himself thus pressed, Rollo, with an
affectation of simplicity, made a sign to one of
his comrades to kiss the king's foot, and the Norman obeyed. Ridiculous was the result. Instead
of kneeling, the Norman stooped without bending
his knee, and attempted to raise the king's foot
to his mouth. But, ere that could be accomplished, the heir of Charlemagne fell on his back, and
lay sprawling on the ground, while the French
raised their hands in horror, and the Normans
burst into shouts of laughter.

For a few moments every one was in confusion;
but fortunately the ludicrous incident produced
no serious quarrel. Order having been restored,
arrangements were made that Rollo's conversion
and Rollo's wedding should take place at Rouen,
and thither many French lords formally escorted
the royal bride. Every thing went smoothly;
and Rollo, having received baptism and the hand
of the princess from the archbishop, commenced
life anew as a Christian and a count.

While in process of conversion, Rollo listened
to the Archbishop of Rouen with the utmost do-
cility, and no sooner was he baptized than he
manifested a laudable zeal for Christianity. On

leaving the baptismal font he earnestly inquired the names of the most celebrated churches and the most revered saints in the country, and the archbishop repeated the names of seven churches and three saints—St. Mary, St. Michael, and St. Peter.

"And who," asked Rollo, "is the most powerful protector?"

"St. Denis," answered the archbishop.

"Well," said Rollo, "before dividing my land among my companions, I will give a part of it to God, to St. Mary, and to the other saints you have named."

The old sea king was as good as his word. During the week in which he wore the white habit of the neophyte, he delighted the archbishop by the eagerness he displayed to keep his promise. Each day, while applying himself to religious duties, he bestowed an estate on one of the seven churches that had been indicated as most worthy of his gifts.

On the eighth day after his baptism Rollo laid aside the white habit, and, resuming his ordinary dress, devoted his attention to secular affairs, and to the partition of Neustria among the companions of his exile from Norway. Every thing was done in the most systematic manner. The country was, according to the Scandinavian mode of mensuration, divided out by the cord; and all the lands, having been taken possession of without regard to the feelings of the natives, were shared among the Normans. Important, indeed, were the consequences of this settlement. Becoming seigneurs of towns and rural districts, the comrades of Rollo, having changed the name of the province to Normandy, polished their manners, refined their language, and, as time passed on, became, from a band of grizzly adventurers, the foremost, most religious, and most chivalrous race in Christendom.

Rollo the sea king, metamorphosed into Rollo a count of France, proved himself eminently qualified for the position he had won. His administration of affairs in Normandy was characterized by wisdom and vigor; and, tempted by the security felt in the districts subject to his sway, artisans and laborers flocked from other parts of France, and established themselves under his government. His name gradually acquired a wide celebrity, and became famous all over Europe as that of the most energetic and successful justiciary of the century.

At length, in 927, when fourscore years of age, Rollo, worn out, and incapable of governing, resigned Normandy to his son, and disappeared from the public eye. After surviving his abdication for five years, the aged hero gave up his soul to God, and his mortal remains were laid in the Church of Nôtre Dame, in Rouen.

HASTING.

ABOUT the time when Rollo the Norman was leaving his country and his kindred to find a new home in a land of strangers, a body of grim adventurers, manning a fleet of corsair vessels, made their way up the Seine, plundering and ravaging as they proceeded, and doing their work so thoroughly that where they had passed hardly even a dog remained to bark at the solitude. At the head of this piratical expedition was a man of dauntless courage and extraordinary energy. His name was Hasting; and he had long been renowned as the sea king who caused most terror throughout Christendom.

Hasting, however, was not by birth a Scandinavian. Indeed, he is said to have been the son of a peaceful peasant near Troyes, and to have been tempted from his home by the Danes during one of their incursions. No sooner, however, had he set his foot on the pine plank than he began to take kindly to Northern customs; and gradually learning to regard piratical enterprise as the chief end of existence, he outdid his masters in all they had to teach, ate horse-flesh, sacrificed to Thor, and at length became one of the most formidable of sea kings. Adopting, as the southern poets expressed it, the ocean for his home, Hasting passed his life in sailing from Denmark to the Orkneys, from the Orkneys to Gaul, from Gaul to Ireland, from Ireland to England.

In fact, Hasting soon filled Europe with his fame; and when, standing on the prow of his ship, he blew an ivory horn which hung round his neck to collect the vessels of his corsair fleet, the sound was more awful to men following peaceful pursuits than the noise of thunder. Some of his expeditions have been recorded by chroniclers as among the most remarkable enterprises of the ninth century. One of these was to Italy, the other to England.

It appears that, about the year 857, Hasting, having heard of the wealth and grandeur of Rome, resolved on paying a visit to the eternal city, and bringing off whatever he could in the way of plunder. Accordingly, he mustered his ships and sailed for Italy. But, instead of finding his way to Rome, he reached Luna, an ancient city on the left bank of the Magra, when the inhabitants were celebrating the festival of Christmas.

The error was somewhat unfortunate. But Hasting, having landed his men and formed a camp on the Magra, acted on the principle of making the best of circumstances. Finding that Luna was well prepared for defense, he thought it politic to use stratagem rather than force. Instead, therefore, of commencing operations with fire and sword, he sent some of his men to inform the Count of Luna that he wished to repair his shattered fleet, and to inform the bishop that, being weary of a sea king's life, he felt desirous of becoming a Christian, and of finding within the bosom of the Church the repose for which his soul had long sighed.

The Count of Luna, knowing what manner of men sea kings were, listened to the message of Hasting with suspicion. He resolved, however, to adopt a middle course; and while careful not to admit the Northmen within the walls, allowed the inhabitants to supply them with such provisions as they required. But the bishop, deceived by the professions of Hasting, went to the camp of the Northmen, baptized the grim sea king, and returned to the city, rejoicing in the idea of such a pagan having been brought to repentance.

Many men would, at this stage, have abandoned their object, left Luna in peace, and fared forth in quest of new adventures; but Hasting had no such intention. Bent upon plunder, he pretended to be sick unto death, and while his camp resounded with lamentations, intimated his wish to leave all he possessed to the Church. He declared his anxiety, however, to be buried in consecrated ground, and that his remains should be interred in one of the churches of Luna. Not

suspecting any fraud, the bishop readily consented to such a condition ; and a rumor having soon
after been spread that Hasting was no more, several of the most valiant of the Northmen bore a
coffin through the gates of the city, and on to the
cathedral.

The bishop was present to celebrate the sacred
office for the repose of the soul that had departed, and proceeded in all due form with the solemn
ceremony. But suddenly Hasting sprung out of
the coffin, brandished his sword, and gave the
signal for carnage by slaying the bishop. The
Northmen thereupon drew their blades, and after
having massacred those assembled in the cathedral, sallied into the city, cut down all who crossed their path, made themselves masters of Luna,
and, after exhibiting the utmost ferocity, set fire
to the houses. Hasting then had the booty carried to his ships, and "not forgetting to take with
him the handsomest woman in Luna," he sailed
for Denmark, to secure his plunder and muse over
new projects.

At this period, England, after being long infest-
ed by the Danes, was enjoying something resem-
bling repose under Alfred the Great. Moreover,
the country was so fortified that an attempt at invasion could hardly be successful. Hasting, however, was not dismayed. Landing, he was joined
by the Danes of the Humber and the Danes of
East Anglia ; but he found the Anglo-Saxon king

prepared to encounter him as an enemy, and not
to submit to him as a conqueror. In several engagements Hasting had decidedly the worst; and
his wife and children, whom he had left in a fortress erected by him at Beafleet, fell into Alfred's
hands. But Hasting, having sued to the royal
Saxon, was granted peace on engaging on oath
to w'thdraw from England; and Alfred, with
characteristic generosity, restored to the baffled
invader his wife and children.

Notwithstanding this check, Hasting immediately prepared for new enterprises. Sad, but not
desperate, the sea king took to his ships, crossed
the English Channel, and ascended the Seine.
Terror preceded him wherever he appeared, and
the inhabitants fled trembling at the sound of his
horn. At the dread blast, the serf, quitting the
field, made for the recesses of the forest; while
his master, the French lord, hardly less alarmed,
hurried to his castle, raised the drawbridge, examined his defenses, and buried his treasure deep
under the floor of the vault.

As time passed on, however, Hasting grew
tired of piracy. Forsaking the pine plank for the
peaceful hall, this old sea king received baptism
from the priests, and the dukedom of Chartres
from the King of France; and when Rollo and
the Normans invaded France and sailed up the
Seine, he appeared as a duke and a Christian, and
displayed his banner and arrayed his men among
the nobles of Charles the Simple.

When the Duke of France resolved to hold a parley with the Normans before giving them battle, Hasting, with two Frenchmen who understood the Norman language, set forward on this mission. Following the course of the Eure till he reached the place opposite that where the Normans were encamped, Hasting halted, and, raising his voice so as to be heard, addressed them in their own tongue:

"What ho! my brave warriors," cried he, "what is the name of your lord?"

"We have no lord," replied the Normans; "we are all equal."

"For what purpose do you come into this country?" asked Hasting.

"To drive out the inhabitants, or subject them to our power," answered the Normans, "and make ourselves a home."

"Ha!" exclaimed Hasting, with a gesture which made the Normans stare.

"And who," inquired they, "are you, who so well speak our tongue?"

"Who am I?" said Hasting. "Have you never heard of Hasting, the famous sea king, who scoured the seas with so many barks, who did injury to so many kingdoms, and the blast of whose ivory horn the Gauls called thunder?"

"Ay," replied the Normans, "we have heard of Hasting, who began so well and ended so il'—who began like a lion and ended like a lamb."

"Well," asked Hasting, "will you submit to

King Charles, who, on condition of faithful service, offers you lands and honors?"

"By no means," answered the Normans; "we will submit to no one; and over all that we win by our arms we will assert dominion. Go and tell this, if thou wilt, to the king whose messenger thou art."

Having failed in his object, Hasting returned to the French camp; and the Duke of France, on learning the answer of the Normans, called another council of war. A long consultation was then held as to the expediency of attacking the invaders in their camp; and the French lords were divided in opinion.

"For my part," said Hasting, gravely, "I advise you not to make the attempt."

"Not make the attempt!" cried a count named Roland, starting up; "that is the counsel of a traitor."

"It is the counsel of a traitor," shouted several others, repeating Count Roland's cry.

On hearing the charge of treachery from so many tongues, Hasting was cut to the heart. Looking around with an indignant frown, he rose, left the council, mounted a horse, and rode away from the French camp. Whither he went none could tell. But it was not to Chartres. He abandoned his dukedom, departed from France, and never again appeared in the haunts of men with whom he was familiar.

SWEYN, KING OF DENMARK.

AMONG the Northmen who rendered the tenth century memorable, and who, in their piratical adventures, associated their names with the history of England, Sweyn, King of Denmark, was one of the most remarkable.

Sweyn was the son of that King Harold who carried on a long war with the Emperor Otho. In 980, on the death of his father, Sweyn—a sea king from boyhood—succeeded to the sovereignty of Denmark, and soon after, while fighting with the Jutes, had the misfortune to be taken, and cast into prison. But the love with which the Danish king had inspired the fair-haired ladies of his kingdom opened his prison doors. In fact, all the women of rank in Denmark came generously forward, expressed their determination to set their young king free, threw their gold and silver ornaments into a heap, and thus collected such a sum that his ransom was paid. Sweyn was accordingly freed from captivity, and, on being restored to his capital, evinced his gratitude to his benefactresses. Forthwith he passed a law granting the women of a family the privilege of sharing their father's property on equal terms with the men, instead of having a right, as previously, to nothing beyond a very small sum of money.

For some time after having, with the aid of the ladies of Denmark, recovered his liberty, Sweyn remained in his northern home, governing his subjects, gratifying his tastes, and cruising in the Baltic. In 994, however, he was seized with a desire to invade England, where Ethelred the Unready then reigned, and speedily resolved upon an expedition in company with Olaf, King of Norway. Eager for carnage and plunder, the two Northmen collected a fleet of eighty-eight ships of war, embarked for England, gave their sails to the wind, and made their way up the Thames. In token of taking possession of the country, the invaders planted one lance on the bank of the river, and threw another into the current; and then, landing from their tall ships, endeavored to seize London, then a small, rude city, with houses built mostly of timber. The attempt, however, proving abortive, they entered rural regions, carried fire and sword through Kent, Sussex, and Hampshire, and rendered themselves so formidable to the Saxons that Ethelred, in despair of opposing the invaders with success, offered to hand them over a large sum of money on condition of their retiring.

Tempted by the gold, the Northmen accepted Ethelred's terms; and Olaf of Norway, before his

departure, not only took an oath never more to
molest England, but even asked to have the privilege of receiving baptism. The admission of the
Norwegian king into the Christian Church took
place in the cathedral of Winchester; and many
of the Northmen, impressed with the grandeur
of the ceremony, felt their wonder rise.

"It is marvelous!" they exclaimed to each
other.

"Tush!" said an old Dane, contemptuously,
"I have gone through that process twenty times
without its producing the least effect."

Olaf of Norway, however, faithfully kept his
promise; and, during his reign, England was not
troubled by the Norwegians. But Ethelred and
the Anglo-Saxons had not seen the last of King
Sweyn. About three years after having received
the English gold, the Danish king entered the
Severn, and commenced the most fearful devasta-
tions on all hands. But fortune interfered to
save England at that time from farther ravages.
Summoned to aid Richard, Duke of Normandy,
the heir of Rollo, in some of his wars, Sweyn
drew off his men, embarked in his ships, and left
England, for a time, at peace. In 1001, however,
he again appeared on the coast, plundered the
Isle of Wight, ravaged Cornwall, Dorsetshire, and
Hampshire, and made continual incursions into
the neighboring counties. Ethelred, in despair,
and seeing no means except bribery of getting

rid of such a foe, agreed to pay yearly to Sweyn an immense sum, which was levied under the name of " Dane-gold."

Having exacted this satisfactory tribute, Sweyn took to his ships and returned to Denmark. Many of the Danes accompanied their king; but those who remained in England were sufficient in number to be formidable to the Saxons, and conducted themselves with all the insolence of conquerors. They lived at ease and in plenty, while the Saxons toiled to raise the tax; and wherever they went, they without scruple made free with the property of the Saxons. Besides, they behaved as if England had been their own; and the Anglo-Saxons, half in fear, half in derision, described them as "Lord Danes."

Day by day the Danes in England became more odious, and ere long the Anglo-Saxons were ready for any effort, however desperate, to rid themselves of such unwelcome guests. At length extermination was resolved upon; and Ethelred, who had just married Emma, sister of the Duke of Normandy, and who felt secure in his alliance with the heir of Rollo, weakly and rashly gave his consent to a general massacre. The 13th of November, 1002, the day of St. Brice, was appointed for executing the barbarous project; and on that day, the Saxons in all parts of England had orders to be ready.

The project was executed with vindictive fury.

Nothing, indeed, could have exceeded the cruelty exercised on the occasion. Men were slaughtered without mercy; and many women were put in holes dug in the ground, buried up to the waist, and then torn to pieces by mastiffs, which seemed to partake of the ferocity of their masters.

At that time there happened to be living in England a sister of King Sweyn, who had been converted to Christianity, and married to an Anglo-Dane of high rank. During the massacre on St. Brice's day this lady did not escape. Notwithstanding her earnest and constant efforts to promote peace and good-will between Saxons and Danes, she was exposed to the bitterness of seeing her children killed, and she was then beheaded with every circumstance likely to excite the indignant horror of her countrymen.

Intelligence of the barbarities perpetrated in England speedily reached Denmark, and Sweyn vowed vengeance. Without delay, he gathered an armament to invade England; and three of his sisters prepared a mystic standard, in the centre of which was a black raven with open beak and outspread wings. It was worked in one night, with magic songs and gestures, and, according to Scandinavian ideas, was a sure pledge of success to the invaders. With his confidence much increased by his banner, and with a certainty of victory, the Danish king went on board his ship, which from its being of the elongated form of a serpent, was called the "Great Dragon."

At the same time thousands of Danes embarked for England. Their ships had all distinctive badges. One had at the prow the figure of a lion, in gilt copper; another, of a bull; a third, of a dolphin; and some had at their mast-heads birds spreading their wings, and turning with the wind; while the sides of all were painted various colors, and hung with bucklers of polished steel, in rows. Almost every Dane on board these ships was noble or free, and all were eager for battle and revenge. Among these grim sea kings figured the ancestors of many of the best and bravest men of whom in later ages England has had to boast. It is probable that among them might have been found the progenitor of Nelson. Eight centuries later, when that great hero destroyed the armament of Denmark at Copenhagen, a Danish poet consoled his countrymen in the day of defeat by this reflection, that Nelson, as his name inferred, was of Danish origin, and that his actions were therefore to be ascribed to Danish valor.

Having put to sea with his fleet of tall ships, King Sweyn appeared off the coast of Cornwall, and the Danes, landing from their vessels, marched to Exeter, put the inhabitants to the sword, and reduced the country to a smoking desert. The progress of Sweyn and his comrades was rapid, and their course was marked by blood and devastation. In every place where they halted, they forced the Saxon host to give them the best of cheer; devoured with boisterous mirth the repast set before them; and, on taking their departure, slew the host and set fire to the house.

During their king's career of conquest the Danes reached Canterbury, and, after killing nine out of every ten of the townsmen and the monks of St. Augustine, seized the archbishop with the object of making him pay an enormous ransom. On this point, however, they were deceived. The archbishop bore his captivity with serene patience, and refrained even from offering the smallest sum to purchase his freedom. At length the Danes, who from motives of policy had kept silent on the subject, became eager for a settlement, and mooted the question.

"Bishop," said they, "we will give you liberty on condition of paying us three thousand gold pieces, and counseling King Ethelred to pay us four times that amount."

"I have no money of my own," replied the archbishop, "and I will not deprive my ecclesiastical territory of one penny on my account. Neither will I counsel my king to do aught that is contrary to the country's honor."

"It will be better for you to do as we wish," said the Danes, significantly.

"You urge me in vain," replied the archbishop,

with mild decision; "I am not one who will furnish Christian flesh for pagan teeth to tear."

After having met the demand of his jailers with firmness, the archbishop was allowed for some time to remain at peace. It was only, however, for a brief period. One day when the Danes, seated on large stones in a circle, were celebrating their victories with full cups, they ordered the archbishop to be brought from prison, placed on a miserable hack, and led into the midst of them.

"Gold, bishop," cried they, "give us gold, or we will cause thee play a game shall make thee noted through the world."

"I offer you the gold of wisdom—that ye renounce your superstitions and be converts to the true God," calmly replied the archbishop. "If you heed not this counsel, know that ye shall perish as Sodom, and shall take no root in the land!"

No sooner had the archbishop uttered these words, which the Danes regarded as a threat, than they rose with one accord from their seats. Some pelted the archbishop with the bones of the oxen on which they had feasted; others threw stones at him; and many took aim with their axes. Felled to the ground, wounded and bleeding, the venerable man attempted to kneel and pray. But the Danes rushed in a body upon their victim, and, by completing the murder, released him from his sufferings.

Ere this, Ethelred had begun to rue the rashness of which he had been guilty in sanctioning the massacre on the day of St. Brice. In his desperation, however, he attempted resistance, and intrusted the command of his forces to Edric Streone, Earl of Mercia; but, finding himself betrayed by that unprincipled chief, he sent his wife and son to Normandy, and, following soon after, left Sweyn master of England.

Sweyn, now without a rival, was proclaimed King of England, and in a position to do almost as he chose. In the plenitude of his power, he laid a heavy tax on the Saxons, to raise money sufficient to reward the companions of his victory. But he did not live long to enjoy possession of the country which he had conquered. Hardly had he worn the crown of England more than a year, when he was summoned from the scene of his carnage and conquest.

One day, after having threatened to spoil the monastery of St. Edmund, Sweyn was at Thetford carousing among his chiefs, and indulging somewhat freely in the intoxicating cup. Suddenly he felt as if he had received a violent blow, and his face underwent a rapid change.

"Oh!" cried the Danish king, giving way to superstitious fear, "I have been struck by this St. Edmund with a sword."

"Nay," replied the Danish chiefs, who sat drinking around, "there is no St. Edmund here."

Nevertheless, the career of King Sweyn was evidently drawing near its close. Death, in fact, was written in his face, and horror took possession of his mind. After three days of indescribable torments, he breathed his last at Thetford; and his son, having, after a struggle with Edmund Ironside, made himself master of the English throne, rendered himself famous as Canute the Great.

HAROLD HARDRADA.

AMONG the heroes of Europe in the middle of the eleventh century, the most remarkable was Harold Hardrada, King of Norway. Even his personal appearance excited wonder and awe. His stature was almost gigantic; indeed, he appears to have much exceeded seven feet in height: his face was fair; his eyes blue; his yellow hair was parted over a brow of marvelous intelligence, and so disposed as to flow in profusion over magnificent shoulders. Moreover, Hardrada was regarded with curiosity as having seen infinitely more of the world than any prince of the age, and as being "the most valiant of the Scandinavians, and the last among them who led the adventurous life whose charm had vanished with the religion of Odin."

Harold Hardrada was son of Sigurd, and younger brother of Olaf, King of Norway, who by force of hand converted the Norwegians to Christianity, and whose banner, on which he was represented in full armor trampling on a dragon, was long preserved in the principal church of Ladvig to commemorate his triumphs over paganism. Hardrada, however, was not destined

to win fame as a champion of Christianity. He
early imbibed that passion for war and song
which distinguished the old sea kings; and in
his teens, as in his ripe manhood, he appeared to
the world as a warrior and a scald.

At the battle of Stiklestad, where King Olaf
fell, Hardrada, then only fifteen, signalized his
warlike prowess, and did not leave the field till
all was lost and his body covered with wounds.
Escaping with some choice spirits to the forest,
he took refuge in the cottage of a woodman, and
there lay concealed till his wounds were cured.
With his health restored, and his soul glowing
with visions of future triumphs, Hardrada, attended by a band of brave comrades, left the
woodman's cottage, and, passing through Sweden
and Russia to the East, he chanted extempore
verses breathing high hope. "A day," he sang,
"will come, when my name will be great in the
land I have now left."

Having halted at Constantinople, Hardrada
viewed the capital of the Emperors of the East
with admiration, and not, perhaps, without some
vague ambition of one day making it his own.
Meanwhile he took service, with his comrades, in
that celebrated body known as the Varings, who
acted as guard to the Emperor of Constantinople, stood on duty at the door of the imperial
chamber, kept the keys of the town in which they
were quartered, and, at critical periods, had the

custody of the imperial treasury. Most of the
Varings, being Scandinavians, wore their hair
long in the Northern fashion, and stalked about
carrying axes with double blades on their right
shoulder. The Greeks described the Varings as
barbarians, but trembled instinctively at the sight
of their large limbs and huge axes.

In this body Hardrada and his comrades en-
rolled themselves. Though the brother of a king,
he kept guard with the axe on his right shoulder
at the gate of the palace. But Hardrada was
too remarkable a person to be insignificant in any
position. Such a man could hardly fail to excite
the jealousy of men and the admiration of wom-
en; and, ere long, he became an object of antipathy to the Greek chief of the imperial forces, and
of affection to no less exalted a lady than the
Empress Zoe.

The quarrel with the Greek general resulted in
Hardrada withdrawing from Constantinople, and
repairing, with a Varingian force, to seek enterprise in Africa and Asia. The plunder of castles
and towns, stormed and won by his band, rewarded his exertions; and, after fighting his way to
Jerusalem well-nigh a century before Peter the
Hermit rode thither on his mule, he bent his
strong knee in adoration at the Holy Sepulchre,
and bathed his stalwart limbs in the waters of the
Jordan. No sooner, however, had he returned
to Constantinople, than he heard news which in-

spired him with an eager desire to return to his native land.

It would seem that Olaf, Hardrada's brother, albeit forcing Christianity on the Norwegians, was not quite prepared to obey the Christian priests who admonished him to have only one wife. One result of the warrior-saint's disobedience was the birth of an illegitimate son named Magnus; and, during Hardrada's absence, Magnus not only recovered Norway from King Sweyn, the successor of the great Canute, but was occupying himself with attempts to seize Dermark also.

On hearing of the success of Magnus, Hardrada felt that it would better become him than his illegitimate nephew to retrieve the honor of his country, and immediately resolved to leave Constantinople and return to Norway. This, however, proved no easy business. The Empress Zoe had no wish that the warrior who had won her heart should leave the capital of the East; and to perplex matters still farther, Hardrada had a strong affection for Maria, the empress's niece. The consequence was that, instead of being allowed to depart, Hardrada was seized and thrown into prison.

The prospects of the Northern hero were now rather gloomy. But a Greek lady, moved by a dream, resolved to effect his liberation. By lowering ropes from the roof of a tower in which

Hardrada was confined, she enabled him to escape; and Hardrada, rousing his Varings, went to the palace of Maria, bore off the princess to his galley, and soon left the Bosphorus behind.

But the adventures of Hardrada were not ended. Putting to sea, he cruised along the coast of Sicily, and won great wealth by his piratical enterprises. When his ship was becalmed on a long voyage, he amused himself with celebrating in verse his successes and his hopes, and sang how he had led his vessel afar, the terror of peasants, his dark vessel filled with grim warriors.

On one occasion, while besieging a town of Sicily, the houses of which were thatched with straw and reeds, Hardrada, finding the walls somewhat strong, and despairing of taking the place by force, resolved to seize it by stratagem. With this view, he ordered fowlers to catch the birds that had nests in the town, and flew during the day to the neighboring forests in quest of food for their young. The birds being secured, he caused splinters of inflammable wood, incased with sulphur and wax, to be fastened to them, and in the evening set them at liberty. The birds, finding themselves free, immediately made for their nests under the thatched roofs of the houses, and the straw and reeds instantly caught fire. The town was, of course, soon in a blaze, and the inhabitants, opening the gates in alarm, rushed out, and threw themselves on the mercy of the besiegers. Hardrada and his Northmen entered, extinguished the fire, and took possession of all the wealth the place contained.

On another occasion, when Hardrada was besieging a town of Sicily, with little hope of succeeding by force, he resolved on a stratagem similar to that practiced by Hasting at Luna. Suddenly he contrived to become ill, and his sickness seemed such that his life was despaired of. His men, turning the circumstance to account, demanded a parley with the besieged, stated that Hardrada was dead, and begged that the clergy would allow the body to be brought into the town and buried in one of the churches. Readily consenting, the clergy, with cross, shrine, and reliquary, repaired to Hardrada's camp to attend the corpse, and found the Northmen ready with a splendid coffin. Preceded by the monks chanting hymns, a chosen band of warriors carried the coffin under a canopy of the finest linen, and marched solemnly toward the town. But no sooner were they admitted than, setting the coffin down in such a position as to keep the gate open, they drew their swords, sounded trumpets, and made a signal for their comrades to enter. Having been joined by Hardrada's whole force, they made themselves masters of the town, set upon the male inhabitants, " and," says the chronicler, " cut down every one around them, priest and layman without distinction."

D

After a variety of piratical enterprises, Hardrada landed in Norway, raised an army, and made war on Magnus. But the nephew proved a more formidable adversary than the uncle had anticipated. Resolutely did Magnus defend his prize; and Hardrada, at length perceiving the difficulty of conquering, made peace, shared his treasure with Magnus, and received half of the territory that Magnus had wrenched from the Danes.

Magnus, however, did not long survive the treaty; and Hardrada, becoming king of all Norway, continued to fight with Sweyn for the possession of Denmark. Wealthy, wise, daring, and experienced above his compeers, Hardrada was regarded as one of the most flourishing kings of Europe; and he was occupied with a project for adding Scotland to his dominions, when, one day in the year 1066, there anchored on the coast of Norway some ships, which formed the fleet of a banished Anglo-Saxon named Tostig, son of the powerful Earl Godwin.

For some time Tostig held the earldom of Northumberland. But the Northumbrians, revolting against his tyranny, banished him from York; and leaving England, he betook himself to the court of Baldwin, Count of Flanders, whose daughter he had married. No sooner, however, did Tostig hear that his brother Harold had succeeded Edward the Confessor as King of England, than he hastened to Rouen, and incited William, Duke of

Normandy, to invade England. Not having patience, however, to await the Norman duke's preparations, Tostig got together some ships, and, sailing to Denmark, craved aid from King Sweyn. But the royal Dane gave Tostig no satisfaction; and the banished Saxon, again embarking, sailed for Drontheim, where Harold Hardrada kept his rude northern court.

Hardrada was now too experienced and wary to be easily entrapped into any expedition. But Tostig, not unaware with what manner of man he had to deal, approached him with soft flatteries. "The world knows well," said the son of Godwin, "that there exists not on earth a warrior worthy to be compared to thee. Thou hast only to will it, and England will be thine."

After some manifestations of reluctance, Hardrada allowed himself to be persuaded; and, having promised to sail as soon as the annual melting of the ice set the ocean free, commenced preparations on a scale commensurate with the grandeur of the enterprise. Tostig, however, was too impatient to wait. With a few ships, manned by adventurers collected in Flanders, he put to sea, reached England, and, after plundering the Isle of Wight and the Hampshire coast, sailed up the Humber, pillaging as he went. But Edwin and Morkar, the grandsons of Leofric and Godiva, united their fleets, and, pursuing Tostig, compelled him to sail to the Scottish coast. Failing to secure the alliance of Malcolm Canmore, who then reigned in Scotland, Tostig retreated to the Orkneys, and there awaited the coming of Hardrada.

Nor was the patience of Godwin's son put to any very severe test. In due time, Hardrada collected several hundred vessels of war and transports, and, summoning the fighting men of his kingdom, encamped on the coast, where multitudes of grim warriors assembled. But the expedition did not take place under the most joyous auspices. While the fleet lay for some time at anchor, vague impressions of gloom pervaded the Norwegian host. One man dreamed that the fleet had sailed, that he saw flocks of crows and vultures perched on the masts and sails, and that a witch wife, seated on an island, holding a drawn sword in her hand, cried out to the birds, " Go, and go without fear ; ye shall have plenty to eat, for I go with you." Another man dreamed that he saw his comrades landed in England, that they were in presence of an English army, and that a woman of gigantic stature rode on a wolf, to which she gave human bodies, which it held in its jaws and devoured one after another. Hardrada dreamed that he saw his brother, St. Olaf, and that the warrior-saint warned him, in vague words, that the expedition would terminate in disaster.

But Hardrada was far too bold of heart to be daunted by dreams and visions. On the day ap-

pointed he embarked with his son Olaf, his black
steed, and his raven banner, which was known as
"The Ravager of the World." It was remarked,
not without terror, that when Hardrada placed
his foot in the royal galley, the weight of his body
pressed it farther down in the water than usual.
But Hardrada, despising presages which his companions regarded as threatening, sailed without
delay.

At the Orkneys, Harold Hardrada was joined
by Tostig, with two chiefs and a bishop; and the
fleet, coming in sight of the shores of England,
touched at Cleveland. Driving the inhabitants
before them, the Norwegian king and the Saxon
earl took possession of all they could find. Bearing the plunder to their ships, they sailed into
Scarborough, and fiercely attacked that place.
Finding the townsmen bent on resistance, the
Norwegians took possession of a high rock that
commanded the town, and, rearing up an enormous pile of stubble and wood, set fire to the
mass, rolled the fire down on the houses, and
availed themselves of the confusion to force the
gates.

Again carrying the booty to their ships, the
Norwegians sailed up the Humber and the Ouse,
and landed near York, to please Tostig, who was
eager to regain the capital of his earldom. Morkar, the new earl, mustered his fighting men, and
came to drive back the invaders. But Hardrada

mounted his black steed, unfurled his raven banner, and, after a brief conflict, chased the English into York.

It was by this time the middle of September, 1066; and the citizens of York, closely besieged, and seeing no hope of success unless in the event of Harold, the Saxon king, leaving the south exposed to William of Normandy, and coming to their rescue, consented to surrender the city. On the morning of the 25th of September, Hardrada and Tostig left their camp at Stamford Bridge, on the Derwent, and, with a part of their force, rode toward York. It was a warm autumn day, and the Norwegians, not expecting enemies to combat, had left behind their coats of mail and other defensive armor, and only wore helmets and bucklers. Suddenly, as Hardrada and Tostig approached York side by side, they perceived through clouds of dust something glittering in the sun like steel, and soon horsemen and footmen appeared in sight.

"Who are these men?" asked Hardrada.

"They can only be Northumbrians coming to ask our pardon and implore our friendship," answered Tostig.

"An enemy! an enemy!" cried the Norwegians, as the advancing mass, becoming more distinct, proved to be an army in battle order.

"It is Harold the king!" exclaimed Tostig, in amazement.

"Unfurl my standard!" cried Hardrada.

While "The Ravager of the World" was raised on high, the Norwegians drew up in a long line curved at the extremities, and, pressing against each other, stood with their lances planted in the ground and the points turned toward the foe. Mounted on his black charger, Hardrada rode through the ranks singing extempore verses. "Let us fight," he sang. "Let us advance, though without our cuirasses, to the edge of the blue steel. Our helmets glitter in the sun; that is enough for brave men."

At this stage, and while three Norwegians were spurring back to Stamford Bridge to bring up the men from the ships, twenty riders, men and horses clad in steel, came forth from the Saxon ranks, and approached the Norwegian lines.

"Where is Tostig, son of Godwin?" asked the foremost.

"Here," answered Tostig.

"If thou art Tostig," said the Saxon, "thy brother greets thee by me, and offers thee peace, friendship, and thine ancient honors."

"These are fair words, and very different from the insults I met with in other days," said Tostig. "But if I accept these offers, what will be given to the noble King Harold Hardrada, son of Sigurd, my faithful ally?"

"He," answered the Saxon, "shall have seven feet of English land, or a little more, since his height passes that of other men."

"Then," said Tostig, scornfully, "tell my brother that he may prepare for battle; for none but liars shall ever have it in their power to relate that the son of Godwin deserted the son of Sigurd."

Without farther parley, the battle began; and, at the first shock, Hardrada, pierced in the throat with an arrow, tossed up his arms, disappeared from his black steed, and fell lifeless upon the ground. Tostig then took the command, and a fierce conflict ended in the Saxons obtaining a victory. But the Norwegians encamped on the other side of Stamford Bridge still held out, and Harold the Saxon found them obstinate foes. One grim Norwegian, probably one of the warriors who had accompanied Hardrada to the East, fought by his side on the way to Jerusalem, and shared in his victories at sea, posted himself on the long wooden bridge, the site of which, with one remaining buttress, has often, in the nineteenth century, been pointed out to the curious traveler, and contested the passage with obstinate valor. Even after all his companions had fallen, this warrior, defying the press of numbers, defended the bridge with his single arm, killing forty men with his own hand.

Of course, the hardiest Saxon recoiled from the axe of a man who seemed to have supernatural strength, and to bear a charmed life. At length, however, one of the Saxons, leaping on board a boat, floated under the bridge, and, thrusting a long spear through the planks, pierced the Norwegian to the heart. After his death the camp was forced; Tostig having fallen in the conflict, and Olaf, the son of Hardrada, having made peace with the victors, sailed to Norway with the survivors of the expedition.

But scarcely had the Saxons obtained the victory when news arrived that William of Normandy had landed, with a mighty army, at Pevensey. The Saxons, under the necessity of marching immediately to meet this new foe, had no time to bury the slain; and the bones of the Norwegians long after whitened the field, and marked where Harold Hardrada fell, and where his raven banner sunk to be unfurled no more.

SIR ROBERT MORLEY.

ABOUT the close of the thirteenth century, when Edward the First was king of England, a knightly Anglo-Norman, named William de Morley, was inhabiting moated castles in Norfolk, making a considerable figure, maintaining baronial state, exercising feudal functions, and recreating himself with such sports as hunting and hawking. At one time William de Morley might have been seen riding up to London to attend the Parliament at Westminster; at another, journeying toward Carlisle to accompany the king in an expedition against the Scottish insurgents. It does not appear, however, that he did any thing deemed particularly worthy of record, and he owes the preservation of his name from oblivion to the fact of having been the father of a son who won a place for himself among the naval heroes of England.

Robert de Morley was born toward the close of the thirteenth century, and was in all probability a native of Roydon, in that county which in later times produced Cloudesley Shovel and Horatio Nelson. When Morley was still a child, England was alarmed by rumors of a French invasion; and, the French having landed and burned

Dover, the great Edward fitted out three squadrons to protect the property and persons of Englishmen. Of these squadrons, one, under John de Battletort, was stationed at Yarmouth. It is therefore probable that, when a boy, Morley constantly heard stories of the wonderful ships which the king had placed to guard the Norfolk coast; and it is even possible that, as years passed on, he saw service at sea on board the squadron of which Battletort had the command.

But, however that may have been, Morley, when a youth with auburn hair and aquiline features, succeeded in 1304 to his father's castles and manors in Norfolk. Being still under age, he was placed under the guardianship of a baron who figured as Marshal of Ireland; and he was soon after united in marriage to Hawise Marshal, the daughter of his guardian. The alliance proved fortunate in a worldly point of view; for, on the death of William de Marshal and his only son John, during the unfortunate reign of Edward the Second, Hawise became their sole heiress. Morley, as the husband of Hawise, acquired the barony of Rhie, with the castles and manors of the Marshals in Norfolk, Herts, and Essex, besides the office of Marshal of Ireland, and estates in that country which were probably more extensive than valuable.

It was not an age in which a man, enjoying such possessions as Morley, was allowed to pass his time flying his hawk, hunting his deer, or feasting in his halls at Morley, Rhie, or Hingham. Besides, England was on the eve of the great war between Edward the Third and Philip de Valois for the crown of France; and when, in 1338, the King of England formed an alliance with the Flemings, sailed from the Orwell, and appeared in Flanders at the head of an army, Englishmen of rank perfectly comprehended that they must sharpen their swords and buckle on their armor.

No sooner, indeed, had Edward declared war, than Philip de Valois ordered his admirals, Sir Philip Quiriel and Sir Peter Bahucet, to make a descent on England; and these "master corsairs," approaching the coast with a fleet manned with Normans, Picards, and Spaniards, commenced hostilities by sailing into Southampton one Sunday. Being in church at the time, the inhabitants were quite taken by surprise; and the French proceeded to slaughter men, violate women, pillage the houses, and set fire to the town. Having carried the booty to their ships, they fell down with the next tide, made sail for Normandy, and landed triumphantly at Dieppe.

But Quiriel and Bahucet were by no means content with the plunder they had acquired and the mischief they had wrought. Week after week they appeared on the English coast. One day they were at Sandwich; on a second at Winchelsea; on a third at Rye; on a fourth at Dover;

on a fifth at Portsmouth. Every where they were guilty of fearful violence; and they succeeded in capturing several English ships, among which were the "St. Edward," the "St. George," the "Black Cock," and the "Christopher," a magnificent vessel, built by the king at great expense, and laden with warlike stores for Flanders. All the men on board the "Christopher" were put to death; and the French, in that spirit which has always characterized their nation, boasted loudly of their prize.

Soon after this, King Edward, leaving Queen Philippa at Ghent, embarked at Antwerp, and sailing into the Thames on St. Andrew's day, was welcomed with great joy by his subjects. In truth, he looked a king of whom any subjects might well have been proud. He was then in his twenty-eighth year, and in the very flower of youthful manhood, with a noble presence, a figure six feet in height and magnificently proportioned, long-drawn and thoughtful features, a high nose, an intellectual brow, and in his eye some sparks of the genius and the patriotism which had glowed in the brain and heart of his grandsire. He was not, indeed, the great king his grandsire had been, but he enjoyed over his contemporaries a degree of superiority which his people felt with pleasure and proclaimed with pride. It was natural, therefore, that much loyalty should have been manifested on his return from Flanders. But loud

above all loyal expressions rose complaints of the
ravages committed by the French, and fierce burned Edward's wrath as he listened to the story of
his subjects' wrongs.

"Oh king," cried the populace, "our towns have
been burned, our homes pillaged, our maidens de-
flowered, and our young men slain."

"Be patient," said the king; "and be assured
that when it comes to my turn, I will make your
enemies pay dearly for all they have done."

It now became Edward's great object to fit out
fleets for the defense of the coasts, and he spared
no exertion with that view. Ships were built;
men were mustered; every port became the scene
of excitement and enthusiasm; and Morley, appointed admiral from the mouth of the Thames
northward, began to cruise with a fleet which,
had it existed a year·earlier, Quiriel and Bahucet,
with all their boasting, would perhaps rather not
have encountered.

Meanwhile the French were busy with preparations for naval warfare. In fact, Philip of Valois had collected hundreds of vessels; and Quiriel
and Bahucet, stationed with a formidable armament on the coast of Flanders, had peremptory
orders, on peril of their lives, not to allow the
King of England to set foot on continental soil.

It was the summer of 1340, and Edward was
at Ipswich, preparing to sail from the Orwell with
forty ships, when thither in haste came the Arch-

bishop of Canterbury with intelligence of great import.

"Philip of Valois," said the archbishop, "having had notice of your intended passage, has, with as much diligence and privacy as the nature of the thing would permit, assembled a great fleet in the port of Sluys in order to intercept you."

"Nay," said the king, looking angrily at the archbishop, "I can not believe that. At all events, I am resolved to sail."

After reflecting, however, the king adopted a more prudent course. Having sent for Morley and a seaman of mark named Crabbe, Edward commanded them to inquire into the truth of the matter. Embarking in swift ships, Morley and Crabbe soon made the inspection, returned without delay to Ipswich, and, on being admitted to the king's presence, confirmed what the archbishop had stated.

"Ha!" cried Edward, looking upon the admiral with suspicion, "you have agreed with that prelate to tell me this tale in order to stop my voyage."

"Sir," said Morley, "you do us grievous wrong."

"But," continued Edward, not noticing the interruption, "I will go; and you, who are afr
where there is no ground for fear, m
home."

"Sir," said Morley, with becomi
dignity, "we are ready to attend

death; but Philip of Valois has set a price on your head, and we will stake ours that, if you persist in sailing with your present force, you will be destroyed."

The words of men so wise and valiant as Morley and Crabbe were not lost on Edward. "The king having heard them," says the chronicler, "sent for the archbishop, and, with abundance of kind speeches, prevailed on him to receive the great seal into his care, after which the king issued orders to all the ports both in the north and south, and to the Londoners likewise, for aid, so that, in the space of ten days, he had a navy as large as he desired."

Every preparation having been made, Edward, on Thursday, the 22d of June, accompanied by the Earls of Derby, Huntingdon, Pembroke, and Northampton, and by Sir Walter Manny and many warriors of fame, sailed from the Orwell. Next day, Morley, with the northern fleet, joined the armament; and, after having been welcomed with a thundering cheer, the admiral placed himself in the van, and, in his own good ship, led the way toward Flanders.

On the morning of Saturday, the 24th of June, othe English approached the coast. It seems they King ot near to Sluys without seeing the French It was the 1 doubtless began to think he had at Ipswich, prep. s to the preparations made to opforty ships, whei denly, however, the man who kept a look-out from the admiral's ship cried that he saw masts; and the impression was quickly conveyed through the fleet that they were in presence of an enemy.

"Who will they turn out to be?" asked Edward, addressing the captain of his ship.

"Doubtless," was the answer, "this is the armament kept at sea by the French, under the admirals who have done England so much harm, and who took your good ship the ' Christopher.' "

"Well," said Edward, "I have, for a long time, wished to meet these men, and now, please God and St. George, we will fight with them; for, in truth, they have done me so much mischief that I will be revenged on them if it be possible."

Every man was now on the alert; and orders having been sent through the fleet to form in order of battle, the strongest vessels were placed in the van; those with archers were posted on the wings; and between every two vessels with archers there was one with men-at-arms. Some ships were detached as a reserve to support those that might most require aid; and the king ordered that the vessels, on board of which were many ladies of rank going to the queen at Ghent, should be carefully guarded by five hundred archers and two hundred men-at-arms. Observing, however, that they had the sun in their faces and the wind against them, and, moreover, "that the French ships were linked together with chains, and that

F.

it was impossible to break the line of battle," the English hoisted their sails, and, standing a little out to sea, soon got the sun and wind as they wished.

While this was going on in the English fleet, Quiriel and Bahucet, having a hundred and twenty large ships and forty thousand men under their command, and the orders of Philip of Valois not to allow King Edward to land, felt quite disinclined to shirk a conflict. Indeed, the French admirals, being "expert and gallant men on the seas," were somewhat confident of victory, and were in high spirits as they set their ships in order; and, as if to exasperate the English, placed the "Christopher" in their van to begin the action.

"But what are these English doing?" cried the French, as Edward's fleet, under the direction of Morley, tacked to gain the weather gauge.

"Oh," was the answer, "they are turning about for fear of meddling with us. But never mind, they can not escape," the French added joyously; "and, as their king is on board, we will make them fight, whether they will or not."

It soon appeared that the French were not to be balked of an opportunity of proving their superiority as naval warriors. The English, having now the wind in their favor, sailed gallantly forward to the encounter; and Morley, in his own ship, coming to close conflict, auspiciously commenced the action by recapturing the " Christopher." Clearing her decks of Frenchmen, he contrived, with rapid dexterity, to place English archers on board, and sent her, amid the cheers of the fleet, to fight with the Genoese, on whose crossbows the French much relied.

Meanwhile the Earl of Huntingdon, closely following Morley, and closely followed by the Earl of Northampton and Sir Walter Manny, and many other of the English, came almost hand to hand with the foe, and the battle assumed an aspect of excessive fury. Quiriel and Bahucet, being able and determined men, exerted themselves to the utmost, and having the advantage of numbers in the proportion of four to one, pressed hard upon the English. But, undismayed by the odds against them, the English fought dauntlessly. Edward, in spite of being wounded by an arrow, performed many deeds of prowess; and Derby, Pembroke, and the other warriors, animated by the king's example, strove to signalize their valor.

For some time the combat was bravely maintained. But at length, after the battle had raged for many hours, victory so decidedly inclined to the English that the French lost heart and hope. Perceiving that all was over, and only animated by some vague hope of saving themselves, some began to leap from their ships, and the example thus set proved so contagious that more Frenchmen perished in the waves of the sea than by the weapons of their foes. The victory was perfectly decisive, and for centuries afterward it was remembered as one of the most complete in the annals of naval warfare.

It was seven o'clock on Saturday evening when this great battle off Sluys came to a close, and the king anchoring, celebrated his triumph with sound of trumpets. Next morning, however, Morley got the fleet into the harbor of Sluys, and the victorious king, landing, set off on foot with his knights on a pilgrimage to " Our Lady of Ardembourg." This ceremony over, Edward mounted his horse, and, riding to Ghent, where Queen Philippa had just given birth to her son, afterward renowned as John of Gaunt, he wrote to inform the Archbishop of Canterbury of his success at sea, and to request that a public thanksgiving might be appointed in gratitude for so great a victory.

At this time Philip of Valois was making war on the Count of Hainault; and, when news of Edward's victory reached the French camp, not a knight was bold enough to tell their king that his fleet had been destroyed. This delicate duty was therefore left to the court jester, who entered upon his business with some abuse of the English, and gradually roused Philip to a sense of the loss he had sustained.

" Cowardly English," said he, repeatedly, and with bitter emphasis.

" What do you say?" asked Philip.

"Cowardly English!" exclaimed the jester. "Dastardly English! False-hearted English!"

"Why do you call them so?" asked Philip.

"Because," said the jester, "they durst not leap out of their ships, as our brave men did, when they fought at the battle of Sluys."

"Ah!" exclaimed Philip, with a sickly sensation as he began to comprehend; and, on learning the whole truth, he flew into one of his violent rages, retreated toward Arras, and broke up his army. Edward, eager for a meeting, sent an offer to decide their disputes by a single combat; but Philip declined on the ground that the message was not addressed to the King of France, but to Philip de Valois, and could not, therefore, be intended for him.

After the battle of Sluys, Morley continued King Edward's admiral, and took part in several of the great enterprises that rendered the period memorable. In 1341 he sailed with his fleet and other ships of the Cinque Ports for Normandy, where he burned eighty ships, four sea-ports, and made himself terrible to the French; in 1346 he sailed from Southampton with the king on that great expedition which resulted in the victory at Cressy; and in 1347, he, at the king's summons, suddenly transported himself, with all the men he could raise, not staying even to take horses on board, and repaired to the king, who was then before Calais, and apprehensive of Philip of Valois coming with a mighty army to the relief of the town.

It would seem, however, that the navy of France had been so completely destroyed at Sluys, that any idea of contending with the English at sea for the present was abandoned by Philip. Morley's occupation was therefore possibly believed to have gone; and in 1347, after the capture of Calais, his commission as admiral having expired, he returned to Norfolk. Having lost Hawise, the wife of his youth, he consoled himself with a bride in the person of Joan, daughter of Sir Peter de Tye, and probably indulged in the idea of enjoying the repose he had so well earned. But the valiant hero, whose seamanship had been so admirably displayed at Sluys, was soon recalled to scenes of strife. In fact, about 1348, King Edward found that England was exposed to the attacks of a new enemy. It was then that the Spaniards, whose navy was formidable, began to infest the coasts of England, and English merchants loudly complained of the injury done to their commerce. Edward then called upon Morley to resume his post as admiral, and prepared to inflict signal chastisement on the Spaniards.

"For a long time," said the king, "we have spared those people; but, instead of amending their conduct, they have yearly grown more insolent, and do us much harm."

"Yes," said his lords, "they must be chastised."

The king soon had an opportunity of castigating the Spaniards. A Spanish fleet happened to put into one of the harbors of Flanders : Edward at once sent them notice that they should not be allowed to return home without rendering satisfaction to the English; and having ordered his ships to be in readiness, he summoned the chief knights and barons to attend him, and proceeded to the coast near Dover, where he was joined by the Black Prince, the Earls of Warwick and Hereford, Lord De Roos, Sir Walter Manny, Sir John Chandos, and other brave warriors; and thither also, before the king embarked, came the Lord Robert de Namur. Having heartily welcomed and appointed him to the command of a ship named the "Salle de Roi," Edward embarked, and putting to sea, kept cruising for some days between Dover and Calais.

In the mean time, the Spaniards had received Edward's warning, but without manifesting any of that alarm which the king supposed it would create. "They knew that they should meet the English," says Froissart, "but were indifferent about it; for they had marvelously provided themselves with all sorts of warlike ammunition, such as bolts for cross-bows, cannon, and bars of forged iron to throw on the enemy, in hopes, with the assistance of great stones, to sink him. When they weighed anchor the wind was favorable for them. There were forty large vessels, of such a

size and so beautiful that it was a fine sight to
see them under sail. Near the top of their masts
were small castles, full of flints and stones, and
a soldier to guard them; and there was also the
flagstaff, from which fluttered their streamers in
the wind, that it was pleasant to look at them.
If the English had a great desire to meet them, it
seemed as if the Spaniards were still more eager
for it. Intending to engage the English fleet,
they advanced with a favorable wind until they
came opposite to Calais.

On that day, Edward, wearing a black velvet
jacket and a beaver hat, and looking well and
joyous, was lounging about the deck of his ship.
The minstrels, to amuse him, were playing a German dance recently introduced by Sir John Chandos, and that gallant knight was greatly delight-
ing the king by singing with the minstrels, when
suddenly the man who kept a look-out from the
castle on the mast uttered a cry, which attracted
Edward's attention, and silenced the music.

"Ho!" cried the man. "I spy a ship, and it
appears to me to be a Spaniard."

"Are there more than one?" asked the king.

"Yes," answered the man, "I see two, three,
four, and so many that, God help me! I can not
count them."

When this occurred the hour of vespers was
approaching. Nevertheless, Edward resolved at
once to give battle; and, as he drank with his

knights and put on his helmet, the Spaniards drew near. Having the wind in their favor, they might have escaped. But, confident in their superiority, they determined on engaging, and as they offered battle in the most handsome way, the English could not but acknowledge that they were well-appointed foes.

"Lay me," said the king to the master of his ship, "lay me alongside the Spaniard who is bearing down upon me, for I will have a tilt at him."

The king was obeyed. The master ran the ship against the Spaniard, and the two vessels met with such a crash that their masts came into contact; and while the castle of the Spaniard was whirled into the sea, the king's ship was so damaged that the water poured into her hold.

"Grapple my ship with her," cried the king, unaware of his danger, "for I will have possession of her."

"Nay," said the knights, "let her go; you shall have better than her."

Accordingly, the Spaniard was allowed to sail away; and another of the enemy, bearing down upon the king, was grappled with hooks and chains. A fierce struggle then began; and the king's crew, after an arduous conflict, succeeded in boarding and taking their adversary.

Meanwhile the ship of the Black Prince was grappled by a huge Spaniard, and ere long so disabled that the leaks could not be stopped. Aware of their danger of sinking, the prince and his company made desperate efforts to conquer. But the Spaniard was "so large, and excellently well defended," that she defied their most vigorous attempts, and the consequence would have been fatal if the Earl of Derby, perceiving their peril, had not came to their aid with a shout of "Derby to the rescue!" and laid his ship on the other side of the Spaniard. This wrought a change; and the action, after great valor had been displayed on both sides, resulted in the Spaniard being taken. But it was not a moment too soon. The prince, with his friends, had just time to spring on board the enemy, when their own vessel went down.

By this time night was rapidly closing over the scene. It was nearly dark; and the Spaniards, having lost sixteen of their ships, and abandoned all hope of victory, bethought them of flight. In desperation, however, a Spaniard of great bulk endeavored to carry off the "Salle de Roi," and grappling that vessel, began to tow her away. In vain Lord Robert de Namur attempted resistance; in vain, as he was tugged past King Edward, he shouted loudly, "Rescue the 'Salle de Roi!'" The Spaniard had decidedly the superiority in force, and in the confusion and darkness he was neither heard nor seen. But suddenly the tables were turned. One of Lord Robert's men, climbing on board the Spaniard with his

sword drawn, severed the large cable which held
the main-sail, and cut four other ropes with such
dexterity that the sails fell on the decks, and the
ship, rendered unmanageable, stopped in her
course. Lord Robert and his men, then boarding vigorously, put the crew to the sword, and
took possession of the vessel.

The fight being now over, Edward caused
trumpets to sound a retreat. Sailing back to
England, the fleet, a little after nightfall, anchored at Rye; and the king, having taken horse, rode
to a mansion in which the queen was lodged, passed that night in celebrating his victory, thanked
his friends next day for the service they had done
him, and courteously dismissed every man to his
own home.

When this victory over the Spaniards was won,
and when a coin had been struck to perpetuate
the memory of it, Morley was no longer young,
and it is likely he returned gladly to his estates
in Norfolk, and to the company of his spouse,
Joan de Tye. But he continued ready, as he had
ever been, to exert himself in defending the coasts.
In 1352, when the French threatened an invasion,
Morley was joined in commission with Robert de
Ufford, Earl of Suffolk, for arraying the men of
Norfolk and Suffolk; in 1355, when there was
again danger, he was appointed admiral of the
fleet; and in 1359, when Edward went to France
in that expedition which terminated in the treaty

of Bretigny, Morley, leaving the decorous Joan, accompanied the king in the hope of fighting the French once more.

But the days of the old hero were numbered. In 1360, while still attending Edward in France, Morley's once strong frame gave way to time and fatigue, and about mid-Lent he died, commending his soul to God, and conscious, at least, of having faithfully done his duty to his king and his country.

THE EARL OF PEMBROKE.

One day in the summer of 1372, when Edward the Third, then a gray old man, with threescore years on his head, was keeping the feast of St. George at the castle of Windsor, Sir Guiscard D'Angle arrived at the English court and besought the king to send one of his sons to be governor of Poitou.

"But," said Sir Guiscard, "if you can not send one of your sons, the Poitevins entreat you to send your noble son-in-law, whom they know to be a good and hardy knight."

"John, my fair son," said King Edward, turning to a young man of noble features and patrician figure, "I ordain and institute you governor of Poitou. You will therefore accompany Sir Guiscard."

"My lord," said the young nobleman on bended knee, "I return you my warmest thanks for the high honor you have conferred on me. I am willing to act for your majesty beyond seas as one of the smallest of your marshals."

The personage whom King Edward, at the instance of the Poitevins, nominated governor of Poitou, was an Englishman of great name and high rank, who had scarcely attained his twenty-fifth year. His name was John Hastings, and he was Earl of Pembroke.

The ancestor of the Hastings family, according to genealogists, was that famous old sea king who, after being the terror of the French and English coasts, became toward the close of his life Duke of Chartres, and disappeared under circumstances so mysterious at the time when Rollo the Norman sailed up the Seine. From the time of the Conquest, the chiefs of his family occupied a conspicuous place among the Anglo-Norman nobility, and at length one of its members espoused Isabel, the sister and heiress of Aymer de Valence, Earl of Pembroke. This marriage proved favorable to the fortunes of his line; for when Aymer de Valence breathed his last without male heirs, Laurence Hastings, a grandson of Isabel, was declared Earl of Pembroke. After enacting an honorable part in the wars of his time, and sharing in the great naval victory obtained under the auspices of Morley at Sluys, Laurence departed this life in 1348. About a year before that date, however, he had espoused Agnes, daughter of Roger Mortimer, Earl of March, and, by that lady, left an infant son to inherit his earldom and his possessions.

John Hastings, second Earl of Pembroke, though deprived of his father at an age so early, was carefully nurtured, and doubtless educated in

all the accomplishments which, in that era of English chivalry, were deemed essential to men of
blood and nobility. While still young, he was
united in marriage to Margaret, one of Edward's
daughters, and regarded by the old king with as
much affection as any of his own sons. As years
passed over, Pembroke went with his brother-in-
law, the Earl of Cambridge, into Aquitaine, where
the Black Prince was then struggling with enemies and disease, and while on the Continent,
proved his mettle in a series of adventurous enterprises, which Froissart has faithfully chroni-
cled. Finding himself, on his return to England,
deprived by death of his youthful spouse, he married Anne, only daughter of Sir Walter Manny;
and the lady had just inherited her patrimonial
estates and become mother of an heir to the earldom of Pembroke, when the mission of Sir Guiscard D'Angle to the English court led to the appointment of her young husband as governor of
Poitou.

It did not appear that there was any particular
danger in the expedition upon which Pembroke
was bound, and it was in a gay mood that the
earl and his companions, having caused ships to
be fitted out and men to be mustered, rode from
their castles to embark at Southampton. At first
their voyage was unpropitious. After waiting
fifteen days, however, for a fair wind, they were
favored with one to their heart's content, and set

sail for the coast of Poitou. Recommending themselves to God and St. George, they left the shores
of England, and on the day preceding the vigil of
St. John the Baptist's day they approached Rochelle.

But at Rochelle Pembroke found himself face
to face with enemies on whose presence he had
not calculated. In fact, the King of France, informed by spies of all that had taken place at
Windsor, had resolved that the earl should have
a warm reception, and, with this object, prevailed
on Henry of Castile to send such a fleet to the
coast of Poitou as should prevent the English
from landing. Eager to avenge the defeat in-
flicted on them many years before by King Edward, the Spaniards fitted out forty ships and
thirteen barks, well furnished with towers and
equipped with seamen and foot-soldiers, who had
cross-bows, cannons, and large bars of iron, and
staves loaded with lead. This armament, placed
under the command of Ambrosio de Balequer,
Cabesso de Vaccadent, Rodrigo de Rosas, and
Hernando de Leon, sailed for Rochelle, and, anchoring before that town, awaited the coming of the
English. On seeing Pembroke's little fleet approach, the Spanish admirals ordered their large
ships to make sail so as to gain the wind, and
bring their towers to bear with full force on the
enemy, whom they had destined to destruction.
When Pembroke saw so many huge ships

standing high above the water, with the flag of
Castile flying from the mast, ready to dispute the
entrance to Rochelle, he must have felt surprise
of no agreeable kind. His vessels were small
and his men were few compared to his adversaries, and he had so little the advantage in seamanship that he did not quite comprehend the
object of the Spaniards in getting the wind in
their favor. It was a time at which the English
might have exclaimed, "Oh, for one hour of old
Morley!" But Morley slept with his fathers, and
there was no hope for the English except in the
exercise of superhuman valor and endurance.

Nevertheless, Pembroke was undaunted. Encouraging the English and Poitevins to do their
utmost, he prepared for battle, posted archers on
the bows of his ships, and gave the signal for action. Ere long, the English and Spaniards met
with loud shouts on both sides. Fierce was the
shock, terrible was the conflict. The English attacked with the fury of lions; and the Spaniards,
hurling huge bars of iorn and masses of rock upon
their assailants from the towers and ramparts of
their ships, did fearful execution. Therefore,
though Pembroke and his comrades fought with
the utmost chivalry and prowess, the missiles of
their foes proved so formidable that many men
were killed; two vessels were sunk with all on
board; and the earl must have experienced a feeling of relief when darkness brought the conflict

F

to a pause, and the two fleets, separating for the
night, cast anchor hard by each other, with the
intention of renewing the carnage at daybreak.

It was clear, however, to the Rochellers, who
witnessed the fight from the shore, that Pembroke, with his small fleet, could not cope successfully with the Spanish admirals; and Sir John
Harpedon, at that time governor of Rochelle, began to tremble for his friends. All night, while
the Spaniards, by means of fire-ships, were destroying the English vessels, he employed himself in attempting to persuade the mayor and
townsmen to go to Pembroke's aid; but the Rochellers were unmoved by the governor's elo-
quence.

"Embark in the vessels and barges lying along
the shore," said Sir John, "and let us assist our
fellow-subjects, whom we have seen so gallantly
defending themselves against odds."

"No," answered they, "we have our town to
guard. Besides, we are not seamen, nor accustomed to fight at sea, nor with the Spaniards."

Finding that nothing could be done to rouse
the Rochellers to action, Sir John Harpedon and
four other knights rose at daybreak, put on their
armor, summoned their men, and, embarking in
four vessels, made for the English fleet.

"Welcome," said Pembroke as they came alongside.

"But," said Sir John, "we come alone. You

must not expect any assistance from Rochelle. The townsmen positively refuse to come."

"Well," said Pembroke with resignation, "we must trust to God and to our best efforts;" and he added laughingly, "A time may come when the Rochellers will repent of their refusal."

But Pembroke and Harpedon had little time for conference. When it was day, and the tide flowed full, the Spaniards weighed anchor, formed a line of battle, and getting the wind in their favor in the hope of inclosing Pembroke's fleet, bore down, full sail, upon the English. The four Spanish admirals led the van, and on coming to close quarters, flung out grappling irons, and, lashing the English ships to theirs, commenced an engagement of the most murderous kind. On both sides the prowess exhibited was remarkable. But the English, though superior in close conflict, suffered much more severely than the Spaniards.

Indeed, by nine o'clock in the morning Pembroke had decidedly the worst of the sanguinary struggle. Many warriors of rank were lying corpses on the decks of their ships; the vessel in which King Edward had sent the money to pay the fighting men of Poitou was sunk; Sir Odo Grandison, after a brave combat with Rodrigo de Rosas, was overpowered and made prisoner; and both the English and their Continental allies, finding fortune in favor of the Spaniards, fought no longer for victory, but for life.

Pembroke, in the mean time, was doing all that in the circumstances a brave man could. Fighting in front of twenty-four knights, " who united good inclinations to tried valor, and who vigorously defended themselves with spears, swords, and other weapons," the earl continued to resist with all the energy of despair. But vain was the struggle. Four large Spanish ships, filled with men-at-arms, and commanded by Cabesso de Vaccadent and Hernando de Leon, making a deadly attack on Pembroke's vessel, grappled her with a determination there was no mistaking. After meeting with an obstinate resistance, which cost many a life, the Spaniards fought their way on board, killed most of the earl's company, among whom were Sir Robert Beaufort, Sir John Grimstone, and Sir John Curson; overpowered and took Sir Simon Whitaker, Sir John Martin, Sir John Touchet, and Sir Thomas St. Aubin; and, in the end, the man on whom their heart was set —bruised, wounded, and overborne by numbers —John Hastings, Earl of Pembroke.

All that day the Spaniards remained at anchor before Rochelle, celebrating their triumph with riotous joy. But this, of course, had an end; and on the afternoon of St. John the Baptist's day, having sounded trumpets and beaten drums, they weighed anchor, gave their sails to the wind, and with their captives departed. After being detained some time at sea, the ships entered the port of St. Andero; and the Spaniards, taking Pembroke and Sir Thomas St. Aubin ashore, conducted them to a strong castle, placed them in a secure prison, and made matters safe by fastening them with iron chains.

Scarcely did Pembroke find himself in this unfortunate plight when he was exposed to an unexpected insult. A man, who appears to have had a Celtic imagination and an imaginary pedigree, who called himself heir of the ancient princes of Wales, and enjoyed the confidence of the King of France, and whose natural audacity prosperity had increased, presented himself to the captive earl with the air of a dispossessed sovereign.

"Pembroke," said he, in insolent accents, "are you come into this country to do me homage for the lands you hold of me in the principality of Wales, of which I am the heir, and of which your king has deprived me, through the advice of evil counselors?"

"Who are you that address me in such words?" asked the earl, in a tone that would have brought the blush to the cheek of Evan, if the Celt had been capable of so much decorum.

"I!" cried the Welshman; "I am Evan of Wales, the son of Edmund, Prince of Wales, whom your king wrongfully and wickedly put to death. But I may, perhaps, with the aid of my dear lord, the King of France, be enabled to ap-

ply a remedy to this, and I will certainly then
do so."

"Evan of Wales," said Sir Thomas St. Aubin,
standing forward in spite of his chains, "if you
mean to say that my Lord of Pembroke owes
you any homage, or any thing else, throw down
your glove, and you will find one ready to take
it up."

"No," replied Evan, thinking perhaps he was
carrying his imposture too far, "you are a prisoner, and I can gain no honor in calling you out;
but when you are at liberty, I shall speak more
boldly, for things can not remain as they now
are."

Higher words would have ensued; but at this
point, some Spanish knights, shocked at the
Welshman's insolence, interfered. Soon after,
the Spanish admiral conveyed Pembroke and his
companions to Burgos, where the King of Castile
then resided. On their arrival, that monarch received them with much courtesy; and, ordering
them to be honorably treated, sent them to different castles throughout his dominions.

For well-nigh two years Pembroke remained
in captivity. In 1374, however, negotiations
were opened for ransoming the earl and those
who had been taken with him at Rochelle. A
large amount was demanded for Pembroke; but
at length the sum of a hundred and twenty thousand francs was agreed on; and the Lombards

of Bruges, having covenanted to pay the money, he, under the protection of a passport, commenced his journey through France, rejoicing in his freedom, and in the prospect of ere long being in England with those whom he best loved. But, alas for the earl's anticipations, on the road he was attacked by a fever, which gradually became so alarming that he was fain to travel in a litter to the city of Arras, where, far from his country and his family, he lay down to struggle with his malady.

It soon appeared, indeed, that Pembroke had no reason to indulge in hopes of recovery. The fever daily grew worse; and on the 16th of April, 1374, not without suspicion of having had slow poison administered to him by the Spaniards, the earl, at the age of twenty-seven, drew his last breath in sorrow and sadness. His body, having been brought to England, was first laid at rest in the church at Hereford. It was afterward removed to London, and buried with becoming state in the church of the Gray Friars.

THE DUKE OF BEDFORD.

In the autumn of the year 1390, Mary de Bohun, wife of Henry of Bolingbroke, Earl of Derby, already mother of two promising boys—Henry, afterward Henry the Fifth, and Thomas, afterward Duke of Clarence—gave birth, in the castle of Lancaster, to a third son, destined to be known to fame as Duke of Bedford. Meanwhile, as grandson of John of Gaunt, and born within the walls of "Gaunt's embattled pile," the royal infant was distinguished as Prince John of Lancaster.

When the Prince John came into the world his prospects were bright. But clouds soon gathered around his boyhood. He was scarcely four when the Countess of Derby died; and he was not ten when the Earl of Derby, exiled by his cousin Richard the Second, left England, and took refuge in France. However, Prince John and his brothers, when thus deprived of father and mother, found a careful protectress in their grandmother, the old Countess of Hereford, and passed safely through the perils that surrounded them till 1399, when their father, returning from exile, raised the banner of Lancaster, dethroned the second Richard, and ascended the English throne as Henry the Fourth.

When Henry of Bolingbroke thus became King of England, his sons were brought into notice. Soon after his father's coronation, Prince John was appointed Constable of England; and, as years passed on, he gave such proofs of wisdom and discretion, that Englishmen could hardly help expressing a wish that he had been the eldest of the king's sons and heir to the crown.

It certainly was not wonderful that such sentiments should have prevailed among the wise and prudent. While Prince John, with a decorum and dignity that commanded general respect, was attending to public affairs, watching the progress made by his politic sire in strengthening the English navy, and obtaining the knowledge of trade which led to his subsequently forming large and clear views on that important subject, Henry, Prince of Wales, was making merry in taverns, talking to tapsters and hostesses with ridicule of his exploits against Hotspur at Shrewsbury, expatiating in comic phrase on his adventures when fighting Owen Glendower in Wales, and breaking jests, not perhaps the most decent, at the futile attempts of his father to provide him with a suitable bride. Nor was this the worst. Nothing, indeed, could exceed the heir-apparent's recklessness. One day he took part in a street fray; another day he aided to rob the officers of the

Exchequer on the highway; and on a third, when staying with some riotous comrades at the manor of Cheglesmore, he played such outrageous pranks that the Mayor of Coventry was under the necessity of taking him into custody.

At length a circumstance brought the Prince of Wales into collision with one of the most eminent judges of the period. It appears that one of the prince's dependents was brought before the Court of King's Bench, and, the prince entering, attempted to rescue the culprit. Chief Justice Gascoigne expressed his indignation, and the prince so far forgot himself as to strike that judge. But Gascoigne, who was a gentleman of Norman blood, instantly ordered Henry to be arrested, and the prince, yielding quietly, was conducted to prison. At the same time, the Prince of Wales was deprived of his seat at the Privy Council, and Prince John was nominated to take his brother's place at the board.

But a great change was at hand. In the spring of 1413 Henry the Fourth breathed his last, and, when the Prince of Wales succeeded as Henry the Fifth, every body predicted the worst. His conduct, however, frustrated all prophecies; and when he had settled the affairs of England in a way that excited universal admiration, he revived the claims of his great-grandsire, Edward the Third, to the crown of France, gathered an army, sailed in the summer of 1415 in a ship

which had purple sails embroidered with gold,
and, anchoring near the mouth of the Seine, laid
siege to Harfleur, a sea-port commanding all that
part of the Norman coast.

Prince John, who now figured as Duke of Bedford, did not accompany the young king on his
expedition to France. At home, however, he
was not idle. During the absence of his brother
he governed England as regent, and he was exercising his viceregal functions with signal success, when tidings arrived that the English king,
after taking Harfleur, had marched toward Calais,
and that, on the way, near Agincourt, he had, with
his handful of men, totally routed a mighty army,
led by the Constable D'Albret, and composed of
the chivalry of France. Though not privileged
to share in the glory of Agincourt, Bedford ere
long had an opportunity of facing his country's
foes on that element on which his countrymen
have ever been triumphant.

It happened that Henry had no sooner returned
to England after taking the town of Harfleur and
winning the battle of Agincourt, than Sigismund,
Emperor of Germany, visited the courts of France
and England with the object of making peace between the kings. Neither objected to treat on
reasonable terms; and the emperor was rejoicing
in the prospect of success, when the French bethought them of making an attempt to recover
Harfleur, which had been left under the auspices

of the Duke of Exeter. Accordingly, while the Count of Armagnac attacked Harfleur with an army on the land side, Viscount Narbonne, a French admiral, appeared with a formidable fleet —composed of ships built by the French, and borrowed from Castile, and hired from Genoa— to attack the town from the water. On hearing this, King Henry was greatly enraged. "Now," he exclaimed to the emperor, "I can hearken to no treaty till I'm on the soil of France with my sword in my hand and my army at my back."

Meanwhile the necessity of relieving Harfleur was recognized, and for that purpose ships were hastily got together. At first, Henry expressed his intention of taking command of this fleet; but, at the emperor's instance, he gave up the idea, and the Duke of Bedford was appointed admiral. Embarking at Rye, with the Earls of March, Oxford, and Warwick, Bedford put to sea with a fleet of two hundred sail, and, " with a prosperous wind and a fresh gale," soon reached the mouth of the Seine.

Viscount Narbonne was not alarmed at Bedford's coming. The French admiral, having a naval force infinitely superior in number, felt assured of victory, and looked with complacency on the Genoese ships, which were so large and magnificent that it was thought the English would not have the courage to attack them. No sooner, therefore, did he hear of the approach of the English fleet, than he came boldly out of the harbor to offer battle. But Bedford was not daunted by this display of force. Having rapidly reminded the English of the superiority exhibited by their ancestors at sea over Frenchmen and Spaniards in the days of King Edward, he sent on several large ships to commence the encounter, and then, gradually moving forward the whole fleet to their aid, came hand to hand with the French in a terrible and sanguinary struggle.

On both sides the action was fought with remarkable valor, and the victory was long disputed with desperate obstinacy. But the English, inspired with the memory of great triumphs, fought with the prescience of a successful issue, and, after the engagement had lasted for many hours, the skill of Bedford and the energy of his men proved irresistible. Narbonne, completely defeated, yielded to fate. Most of the French vessels were sunk or destroyed, and among them several of the Genoese ships, the very sight of which the French admiral had flattered himself would frighten the English out of their propriety.

But the danger of the English was not over. In fact, Bedford had scarcely congratulated his companions upon their victory when the English ships were becalmed. For three weeks they remained in this predicament; while the French, availing themselves of this circumstance, used their galleys to annoy the English, and made

earnest endeavors to burn the English fleet with
wildfire. At length, however, a breeze sprang
up; and, while Armagnac beat a retreat from
Harfleur, Bedford, ordering sails to be set, entered the harbor and relieved the town.

After this triumph, Bedford returned with the
fleet to England, and met with an enthusiastic reception. The Emperor Sigismund, surprised at
the whole affair, desisted from his attempts to
bring about a peace, and paid a high compliment
to the king and people of England. "Happy,"
said the German Cæsar, "are subjects to have
such a king, and happier still is the king who has
such subjects."

It soon appeared, however, that the French had
yet to learn that on the sea they were no match
for their English foes. A new fleet was without
delay fitted out; and, having been strengthened
by some caracks of Genoa, it was placed under
the command of the Bastard of Bourbon, and
posted at the mouth of the Seine to prevent any
thing in the way of succor going from England
to Harfleur. But some English ships, returning
to scour the coast, encountered the French, won
a decisive victory, took the Bastard prisoner, captured three magnificent caracks of Genoa, in one
of which was a large sum of money, and, clearing
the mouth of the Seine thoroughly of enemies, returned in great triumph to Southampton.

Many long years elapsed ere the French again

tried their fortune in an engagement at sea, and
Bedford had no farther opportunity of signalizing
his prowess as a naval warrior. He was destined,
however, to a career of high distinction. When
Henry the Fifth, after having made himself master of France, died in 1422 in the midst of his
glory, Bedford was appointed regent. In that
capacity he displayed high powers as a ruler, nobly sustained the honor of England on the Continent, and won a great battle over the French
and Scots at Verneuil. But no man is wise under all circumstances; and an impolitic matrimo-
nial alliance, into which this brave and good duke
rushed after having passed the age of forty, led
to the destruction of his own peace of mind, and
to many of the misfortunes experienced by England at home and abroad during the fifteenth
century.

It appears that, soon after becoming regent,
Bedford espoused Anne, sister of Philip, Duke of
Burgundy, and cemented that alliance on the per-
manence of which the interests of England on the
Continent mainly depended. In 1432, however,
the Duchess of Bedford died at Paris, and the
duke, after appearing for some time the most dis-
consolate of widowers, was captivated by the fair
face and elegant form of Jacquetta of Luxem-
bourg, daughter of the Count St. Pol. With a
rashness which he had not hitherto displayed,
Bedford, in the beginning of 1433, espoused this

damsel, and Jacquetta, then seventeen, became
wife of a man who was as old as her father.
This marriage, so hastily contracted, was most
disastrous in its results. The Duke of Burgundy, who was tiring of the English alliance, pretended to be highly offended; represented that
Bedford's sudden marriage was a slight on his
sister's memory; indignantly complained that,
without his consent, the Count of St. Pol had
ventured to dispose of a daughter; and finally,
going to Arras, gave his hand in friendship to
Charles the Seventh.

The reconciliation of France and Burgundy
was celebrated throughout the country with
transports of joy, and Bedford experienced such
annoyance at the thought of having lost England
so powerful an ally that he gave way to the most
poignant regret. After much suffering the great
warrior-statesman expired at Paris on the 14th
of September, 1435; and scarcely had his mortal
remains been conveyed to Rouen, and laid at rest
in the cathedral, when his widow, still under
twenty, forgetting him and all dignity, made a
clandestine marriage with an obscure squire
named Woodville. Living with this man at her
manor of Grafton, Jacquetta became mother of
Elizabeth Woodville, who was afterward, under
romantic circumstances, elevated by Edward the
Fourth to the position of Queen of England.

Meanwhile the news of Bedford's death, when

carried to England, caused profound grief; and
while the English people mourned the hero as
"one of the best warriors that ever blossomed
out of the royal stem of Plantagenet," the French
king held his memory in reverence as that of a
mighty foe. When Charles the Seventh gained
possession of Rouen, and his nobles proposed to
destroy the monument of black marble over Bedford's tomb, the French king shook his head,
and gravely rebuked the proposal. "No," said
Charles, "let him repose in peace, and let us be
thankful that he does so repose; for, were he to
awake, he would make the stoutest of us tremble." Even Louis the Eleventh had too much
generosity to disturb the hero's ashes. When
advised to deface Bedford's tomb as that of a foe
of France, he treated the idea as unworthy of being entertained. "What honor should it be to
us," asked Louis, "to break the monument and
pull out of the ground the bones of him whom, in
his lifetime, neither my father nor your progenitors were ever able, with all their puissance, to
turn one foot backward, and who, by his prowess,
policy, and wit, kept them all out of Normandy
for so many years? Wherefore," continued Louis, "I say, God save his soul, and let his body now
lie at rest, who, when he was alive, would have
disquieted the proudest of us all."

G

SIR ANDREW WOOD.

EARLY in the sixteenth century there stood hard by a canal in the parish of Largo, in the county of Fife, a strange old-fashioned mansion, surrounded by a moat, and fortified with a circular tower. In other days this castellated edifice had been a jointure-house of the queens of Scotland; but it was now inhabited by an old man with white hair, a face browned by exposure to sun and wind, with a person somewhat the worse for many years of toil and fatigue, and with the air of one who had surmounted many difficulties and passed through much danger. As he walked abroad muttering to himself, or was rowed on the canal in a barge manned by mariners almost as old as himself, the peasantry gazed on him with interest and respect, for the old hero had won a name as by far the greatest sea-captain of whom his country could boast.

Andrew Wood appears to have been a cadet of a family long settled in Angus, and to have been a native of Fifeshire. He is said to have been born at the old kirk town of Largo, on the Frith of Forth. It was probably while wandering in boyhood about the shore, watching ships at sea, and rowing in frail boats in Largo Bay, that he imbibed that love of salt water and of adventurous enterprise which afterward conducted him to fame and fortune.

In early life Wood became a merchant trader, and in that capacity sailed between Scotland and various parts of the Continent. At that time such a man, of course, played a very different part from a person engaged in commercial affairs in our days. Wood not only bought and sold, but commanded his own ships, carried guns and other weapons for defense, fought his way from port to port, and held his own against pirates, Easterlings, English cruisers, and foes of every description. The career of a merchant was, in that age, one of constant peril, and bore little resemblance to that of the man who spends his days at the desk or on the Exchange, and passes his nights with his head on a pillow, and his property secure under protection of recognized laws. He fed with his faculties on the watch, and slept with arms by his side, ready to start up and encounter any emergency.

During the fifteenth century Leith was rapidly rising into importance, and Andrew Wood, when ashore, made that sea-port his home. On such occasions, however, he must have reminded his friends of a fish out of the water. His real home was the deck of the " Flower" or the " Yellow Carvel," or some other of the vessels which he had built, and with which he traded to Holland and the Hanse Towns. Nevertheless, he was often mentioned as "Andrew Wood of Leith," and regarded as an enterprising man, who sailed to strange lands, who studied navigation and gunnery, and who had allured into his service foreign sea-captains of great experience.

As time passed on, and his reputation as a seaman extended, Andrew Wood attracted the notice of James the Third, who then reigned in Scotland. A weak prince, but not without redeeming qualities, James prided himself on being the patron of men devoted to art and architecture, and naturally evinced his appreciation of such a navigator as Andrew Wood. Accordingly, the king, having appointed the gallant captain as royal pilot, granted him the lands of Largo on condition of his always keeping the "Yellow Carvel" in readiness to take on board James and Margaret of Norway, his young queen, when they wished to go on a pilgrimage to the chapel of St. Andrew, in the Isle of May; and Wood, besides directing the attention of James to naval architecture, well repaid the monarch's favor by his loyal fidelity in the hour of need.

It would seem that the preference shown by James to artists and architects was far from agreeable to Scottish magnates. Indeed, the Homes, Douglases, and Hepburns expressed the most intense disgust with the minions the king patronised; and finally, in 1488, forming a strong league, they indicated their determination to hurl him from the throne. Aware of his danger, the king resolved to repair to the north, where the chiefs continued comparatively loyal, and with that object summoned Andrew Wood, who at the time had a vessel ready to sail for Flanders. Without in the least considering the consequences of offending the barons, the captain hurried to the rescue of his sovereign, conducted him on board, set him ashore in Fife to proceed to the northern counties, and afterward bringing him back, landed him at Blackness. Soon after James attempted to seize the castle of Stirling, but the governor, refusing him admittance, gave up his son James to the insurgent lords. The ill-starred king, instead of taking refuge on board of Wood's vessels, resolved on risking an engagement at Sauchie Burn. At first the king's men charged with such vigor that the main body of the baronial army gave way. But the fortune of the day quickly turned. Lord Home and the Earl of Angus, bringing up the Borderers with their long spears, swept away the royal army as the wind scatters leaves, and deprived the king's adherents of all hope.

Meanwhile James had fled from the field. On learning that his son was with the lords, and seeing his own banner displayed against him, the poor king lost heart, turned his horse's head, and galloped from the scene of action. But he was not destined to escape. His horse, starting at a woman carrying a pitcher of water, threw the royal rider violently on the ground, and, having been carried into a mill, he was assassinated by one of his pursuers, who pretended to be a priest.

For some time the baronial chiefs remained in ignorance of the king's fate, and, being uncertain whether or not he had perished, experienced considerable perplexity. Moreover, young James, having passed from the field of Sauchie to Stirling, and heard the monks in the chapel royal bewailing the king's death, was seized with the most painful remorse. Both prince and barons were therefore eager for intelligence; and learning that Andrew Wood, with the "Flower" and the "Yellow Carvel," was "travishing up and down the Forth," that boats had taken wounded men out to these vessels, and supposing that the king might have escaped on board, they hastened to Leith, and sent messengers to summon the captain to appear before the council.

At first Andrew Wood hesitated; but, after arranging that Lord Fleming and Lord Seton should be sent on board as securities for his being allowed to return in safety, he consented. He then placed his ships under the command of his brother, with orders to hang up the hostages in the event of any treachery being practiced; and having taken these precautions, he entered his boat, went ashore, landed at Leith, and entering the council chamber, presented himself to young James and the assembled lords.

"Sir," said James, who appears to have fancied that the sea-captain was the king in disguise, "are you my father?"

"No," said Wood, as the tears rolled down his cheeks, "I am not your father, but I was your father's true servant, and shall be to his authority till I die, and an enemy to them who were the occasion of his down-putting."

"But," cried the lords, "tell what you know of the king, and where he is."

"I know nothing of the king, nor where he is," was the reply.

"Then," asked the lords, "who were they that came out of the field and passed to your ships in the fleet boats?"

"It was I and my brother," answered Wood, "who were ready to have laid down our lives in the king's defense."

"Is he not in your ships?" again demanded the lords.

"No," answered Wood, "he is not. But would to God he were there safely! I should defend and keep him scathless from all the traitors that have cruelly murdered him. And I trust to see the day that will see them hanged and drawn for their demerits."

It was doubtless well for Andrew Wood, when

he used such language, that he held Lord Fleming
and Lord Seton as security for his safe return.
As it was, the delay somewhat irritated his
friends, and the two lords began to tremble for
their necks. After considerable suspense, however, Wood's boat was observed to leave the
shore, and the captain appearing on board, relieved the hostages from their unpleasant predicament. But the baronial leaders were the reverse of easy at the idea of so stanch a friend
of the departed king being at large; and resolving on sacrificing him to their resentment and
apprehensions, they summoned all the skippers
and mariners at Leith, in the hope of finding some
Scottish sea king bold enough to execute their
project.

"We are ready," said the lords, "to furnish
artillery, men, and money to your contentment, if
you will sail against Wood and lay hold of him."

"Ay," said all the skippers; "but that is more
than we will venture to attempt."

"My lords," said the celebrated Captain Andrew Barton, "the fact is, there are not ten ships
in Scotland that would give Andrew Wood's
two ships the combat; for he is so well practiced
in war, and has such artillery and men, that it is
hard dealing with him by sea or land."

Finding no seamen ready or willing to undertake their commission, the Scottish lords left
Wood at liberty to navigate the sea, while they,

proceeding to Edinburgh, crowned young James
as king. This led to results hardly anticipated.
The young monarch, horrified at having partici-
pated in the rebellion against his father, and
eager to atone for his fault in every possible way,
was inclined to treat Wood with the highest consideration. But, whatever his feelings, James
would have had little choice in the matter.
Scarcely, in fact, had he ascended the throne as
James the Fourth, when the services of the Scottish sea-captain became absolutely necessary for
the country's defense.

In fact, the Scots had not quite recovered from
their surprise at the mysterious disappearance of
James the Third and the sudden triumph of the
Homes and Douglases, when five large English
ships appeared in the Frith. Pretending to be
pirates, though dispatched, as was suspected, by
Henry Tudor, who then unworthily wore the
crown of the Plantagenets, the seamen not only
seized and plundered many Scottish vessels, but
landed and committed the most daring outrages.
The ferocity of these invaders caused general
fear. Such, indeed, was the terror they inspired,
that for some time no captain in Scotland durst
go out to fight them. The young king was naturally mortified; but, ere long, Andrew Wood
came to the rescue. Entering the Frith with the
" Flower" and the " Yellow Carvel," Wood fell
in with the English before the Castle of Dunbar.

A desperate battle immediately began, and for some time lasted with great obstinacy on both sides. But Wood's naval skill proved irresistible; and, after a severe struggle, he succeeded in defeating the English, capturing their ships, and towing them in triumph to Leith.

After reaching Leith with his prizes and prisoners, Andrew Wood took the English captain to Holyrood and presented him to James. The king warmly thanked the naval hero, conferred knighthood on him, and confirmed the grant made by his father of the lands of Largo. Finding himself a knight and a feudal proprietor, Andrew Wood abandoned trade, and marrying Elizabeth Lundin, a lady of ancient family in Fifeshire, confined his naval operations to the defense of the commerce and coasts of Scotland.

But Sir Andrew Wood was not allowed to enjoy leisure, or repose content with the laurels he had won. Mortified at the defeat of his seamen and the loss of his ships, Henry the Seventh summoned a number of seafaring worthies, and offered rewards to any one who would take the sea against Sir Andrew Wood, and bring him, dead or alive, to London. Tempted by the king's offers, Stephen Bull accepted the commission of admiral, took three large ships under his command, sailed from the Thames, entered the Frith of Forth, anchored under shelter of the Isle of May, and, capturing some sailors, compelled them to give information as to Wood's movements.

The intelligence elicited was not unsatisfactory. Indeed, fortune seemed to be about to throw Wood in Bull's way, and to give Bull an opportunity of conquering Wood. At that time Sir Andrew happened, with his two ships, to have convoyed a fleet of merchantmen to Flanders, and he was daily expected to return to Scotland. Bull therefore resolved to lie quietly in wait for King James's admiral.

It was the 10th of August, 1490, and day was just breaking, when Sir Andrew Wood's two ships came in sight of the English. Bull's heart beat high at the approach of his formidable adversary; and, eager to try conclusions with so renowned a foe, he instantly made preparations for battle. Having distributed wine to his men to rouse their courage, he ordered them to make ready to do their duty against the foes of their king and country.

In the mean time, Sir Andrew Wood, not aware of the peril to which he was exposed, pressed gallantly on toward the Scottish coast. Suddenly, however, he observed Bull's three vessels under sail, coming toward him, and had no difficulty in perceiving that their intent was hostile. Without delay, therefore, he ordered the wine-cups to be filled, and, while each man pledged his neighbor, he exhorted them to fight with their wonted determination.

"My men," said the Scottish hero, "I beseech

you to take courage against your enemies of England, who have doubtless sworn and vowed to make us prisoners to their king. But, God will, they shall fail of their purpose. Therefore, set yourselves in order, every man in his own room. Let the gunners charge their artillery; and the cross-bows make them ready, with the lime-pots and fire-balls in our tops, and two-handed swords in your fore-rooms. And let every man be stout and diligent for his own part, and for the honor of this realm."

As Sir Andrew Wood concluded his address, he gave the signal for an engagement, and with sound of trumpets on both sides, the English and Scottish ships approached each other. Wood, however, contrived to get to windward of the enemy, and, with this advantage on his side, began a deadly conflict, which lasted from sunrise to sunset, while crowds of men, women, and children, standing on the coast of Fife, watched the operations with breathless interest. Darkness, however, interrupted the proceedings; and the combatants parting, drew off from each other till the return of daylight.

No sooner, however, did the morning of the 11th of August dawn, than Wood and Bull roused their men to exertion; once more the sound of trumpets gave signal for a renewal of the strife, and the fleets encountered with even more fury than on the previous day. Indeed, the

SIR A. WOOD ADDRESSING HIS CREW.

men are said to have "fought so cruelly" that
neither skippers nor mariners took heed of their
vessels, but, contending hand to hand, drifted
away with the tide and wind till they were opposite the mouth of the Tay.

As day drew to a close, fortune declared for
Sir Andrew Wood; and Bull, having done all
that a brave admiral could to avert defeat, found
himself forced to yield, carried to Dundee, and,
some days later, presented with his surviving officers to King James. It was not a pleasant position for an admiral who had been sent expressly
to conquer; but Bull soon found that he had fall-
en into the hands of a sovereign very different
from his own. Actuated by that chivalry which
made him aspire, amid the stern realities of life
in an unscrupulous age, to the reputation of a
hero of romance, James not only treated Bull
and his comrades with hospitality, but signalized
his generosity by sending them, with their vessels, as a present to their king.

After the victory over Admiral Bull, which
gratified the pride of the Scottish nation, and
made Sir Andrew Wood's reputation higher than
ever among his countrymen, the hero became the
person whom, of all others, the king delighted to
honor. Being a man of experience, commercial
knowledge, and financial skill, he exercised great
influence over James, and contributed much to
the prosperity which Scotland for a season enjoy-

ed. But the appeal of a foreign princess to the chivalry of the Scottish king changed the whole aspect of affairs, and involved the country in carnage and calamity.

In the year 1513, when war was desolating Continental Europe, when Louis of France was in arms against the Pope and the high-flying republic of Venice, when Ferdinand of Spain was wresting the little kingdom of Navarre from the great family of D'Albret, and when Henry the Eighth of England was, in alliance with the Emperor Maximilian, invading the dominions ruled over by the house of Valois, there reached the Scottish court a cunningly-devised epistle from the Queen of France to the Fourth James, in which he was described as the royal lady's "dear knight," and implored, for her sake, to raise an army, and "march three steps on English ground." The distressed dame, it may be stated, was far too old to inspire feelings of tenderness, and Margaret Tudor, the spouse of James, was sister to the King of England; but the code of chivalry, to which the Scottish monarch professed allegiance, forbade him to resist the appeal from such a quarter; so he assembled the forces of his realm, and prepared to cross the Tweed in hostile array.

It is unnecessary to narrate the events of that ill-starred expedition. Suffice it to say that, after marching over the border, after taking the cas-

tles of Wark, Etal, and Ford, after wasting many
precious lives in insignificant enterprises, and
making love to Lady Heron, King James encountered the Earl of Surrey on the ridge of Flodden;
that he fought, in the hour of agonizing disaster,
with a heroic courage which has half redeemed
his character from the reproach of indiscretion;
and that, when the shades of evening were falling,
and the remnant of the Scottish army was en-
compassed by the conquering foe, the king and
his immediate followers, throwing themselves into
a circle, struggled for a while with desperate val-
or against fearful odds, and with no hope save
that of selling their lives dearly; and that at
length the king, seeing his standard-bearer fall,
and disdaining the thought of captivity, rushed
headlong among his enemies, and fell pierced with
many wounds, within a spear's length of the English general.

Next morning, while traversing the slippery
field, Lord Dacre recognized the body of the royal warrior, and had it conveyed to Berwick; but
the Scots, being by no means ready to believe
that James had stained the purple heath of Flodden with his heart's blood, explained his disappearance in a far more romantic way. The king,
it was notorious, had, in order to perplex the
enemy's sharp-shooters, allowed several of his
knights to array themselves in armor similar to
his own, and it was believed that the body of

H

Lord Elphinstone, a gallant nobleman, who much resembled James in stature and appearance, had been mistaken for that of the monarch. One circumstance favored this theory. James was known to have habitually wore around his waist a chain, by way of penance for participating in the rebellion that led to his sire's untimely death, and to have added thereto a link every year. This penitential belt the English could not produce; and it was confidently averred that the royal hero, fatigued with state, and horrified at the carnage caused by his expedition, had wandered forth to secure absolution by a pilgrimage to the Holy Land.

But while his faithful subjects regaled their fancies with the pleasing delusion that James would, ere long, return to take possession of his throne, there was one person who would seem to have turned a deaf ear to such rumors. In fact, his queen, ere a year elapsed, weary of widowhood, gave her hand to the young Earl of Angus, and sacrificing, by this step, ambition to love, forfeited the Scottish regency.

A new scene was forthwith opened. The Duke of Albany, an exiled prince of the blood, who resided at the court of Paris, was fixed upon to preside over the destinies of Scotland, and Sir Andrew Wood, whose patriotism and sagacity all recognized, was sent as embassador to invite the expatriated prince to assume the reins of

government. The Scottish maritime hero, now
sixty, and gray with years, met with a gracious
reception at the court of Francis the First; and
Albany, embarking under Wood's auspices, left
France with eight ships, and landed safely at
Dumbarton.

The expedition undertaken to bring Albany
from France appears to have been the last piece
of active service rendered by Sir Andrew Wood
to Scotland. In his old age he lived quietly on
his lands at Largo, inhabiting the castellated old
jointure-house of the queens of Scotland. Though
no longer occupied with naval affairs, he retained
his early love of the sea, and still had such a relish for the water that between his house and the
church at Largo he formed a canal, on which he
was rowed by his old boat's crew.

At length time did its work. Worn out with
toil and trouble, Sir Andrew Wood went the way
of all flesh. His mortal remains were laid with
all honor in the church of Largo, and his name
was long remembered with affectionate regard
by his countrymen.

SIR FRANCIS DRAKE.

AT the close of the eighteenth century, there stood on the borders of Devon and Cornwall, not far from Tavistock, a cottage of considerable antiquity and high historical interest. At the time of the Reformation in England, this cottage was inhabited by a man named Drake, who was the father of nine sons. Drake would seem to have been a clergyman by profession, though it has not been clearly proved that such was the case. But it does appear that on religious subjects he was prepared to hold fast his opinions at some personal inconvenience, and that, during the persecutions consequent on the "Six Articles Act," he was under the necessity of escaping from Devonshire and taking refuge in Kent.

Francis Drake, one of the sons of this worthy, was born in the cottage near Tavistock about the year 1539, and was still in childhood when his father fled to Kent. At that time the circumstances of the Drake family must have been narrow, and, doubtless, the prospects of the nine young Drakes were sufficiently gloomy. But, ere long, matters in some slight degree brightened. After King Henry's death, the father emerged safely from his place of concealment at Upmore, on the Medway; and afterward, perhaps in consideration of his sufferings for conscience' sake, he was appointed to read prayers to the seamen of the king's navy.

Being one of a large family, without any of the advantages which wealth commands, young Drake did not enter upon life under the most brilliant auspices. In early boyhood he was sent to sea as an apprentice to the master of a little vessel engaged chiefly in the coasting trade, and held hard to business; but, being a youth of an "aspiring vein," with courage to endure and determination to excel, Drake gradually won so high a place in the opinion of his master, that the worthy skipper, when dying, bequeathed his little bark to his meritorious apprentice.

Fortune having proved so far favorable, Drake began the world on his own account. It appears that, for the next few years, he made good use of his time, and that he gained much knowledge of maritime affairs. He had already undertaken voyages to France, to Zealand, and to the Spanish Main, and acquired considerable experience, when, in 1567, he joined Captain John Hawkins in an expedition to the New World.

It seems that in this enterprise of Hawkins the chief part of the cargo consisted of negroes caught in Africa and carried for sale to the Spanish Main. The voyage proved the reverse of prosperous. Though trading under the protection of a treaty between England and Spain, Hawkins, on reaching Rio de la Hacha, found that commerce was prohibited by the Spanish governor. Indignant at this, he stormed the town, and proceeded, in defiance of the authorities, to bargain with the natives. The Spaniards, however, not relishing this mode of doing business, determined on strong measures. Accordingly, the Viceroy of Mexico, having decoyed the English squadron into the port of San Juan de Ulloa, set several of the ships on fire, killed many of the seamen, took others as prisoners, tortured them cruelly to discover their ulterior designs, and even went so far as to hand over two of them to the Inquisition to be burned alive.

Drake was fortunate enough to escape alive from this disaster, but every thing that he had acquired in the way of property was gone. Not brooking his losses quietly, as another man might have done, he endeavored by diplomatic means to obtain redress from the Spanish government. All his efforts, however, proved futile; and, with an idea of righting himself, he consulted a divine as to what steps he might, as a Christian man, take in the way of retaliation.

"What," he asked, after stating his case, "may I lawfully do under the circumstances?"

"Undoubtedly," answered the divine, "you may lawfully recover from the King of Spain, and repair your losses upon him wherever you can."

Fortified with this high authority, Drake purchased a ship, and, to render himself perfectly acquainted with the coasts he intended to attack, made two preliminary voyages to the Spanish possessions in America. Having formed a plan of operations, he prepared for an expedition of a more important character, and sailed from England with the deliberate intention of making the Spaniards feel his vengeance.

It was not, however, with any formidable armament that Drake furnished himself when leaving the shores of England to make war on that potent personage known as Philip, King of Spain and the Indies. With one bark of seventy tons, under his own command, and with another of twenty-five tons, commanded by his brother John, and with a crew of seventy-five men, the English sea-captain fared forth to attack the possessions of the most powerful of European monarchs. In a small way, however, Drake was well prepared. On board he had a year's provisions, as much ammunition and artillery as he judged necessary for the expedition, and three pinnaces in pieces, but ready framed, and in a condition to be put rapidly together whenever required.

All arrangements having been made, Drake, availing himself of the first fair wind, sailed from the shores of England. About midsummer, 1572, the high land of America appeared in sight, and he began to scent the gold as the bloodhound does the fugitive. Directing his course to the east of Nombre de Dios, at that time the depôt of the treasure brought from Peru, he landed at Port Pleasant, put together his pinnaces, and prepared for operations.

While affairs were at this stage, Drake was unexpectedly re-enforced. A trader from England, with some forty men on board, happened to reach Port Pleasant; and the skipper, after hearing Drake's designs, consented to take part in the enterprise and share the danger. With this accession of force, which at the time must have been welcome, Drake put to sea.

After a short voyage, the little fleet approached Nombre de Dios. It was night, however, and Drake resolved on keeping close to the shore, and refraining from any attack on the town till the break of day. But, learning that his crew were alarming each other about the strength of the place and the number of the inhabitants, he perceived that delay would be dangerous. No sooner, therefore, did the moon rise, than he ordered his men to their oars, and intimated his purpose of at once proceeding to business.

The attempt on Nombre de Dios proved easier than had been anticipated. Drake and his hardy comrades effected a landing without encountering the slightest opposition. But scarcely were the adventurers in possession of the quay, when an alarm was given, and the town in commotion. Drums beat; bells rang; and the populace shouted. Drake, however, was undismayed. Rapidly forming his slender force into two columns, he caused his trumpets to sound, and dauntlessly pressed forward. At first nobody appeared to oppose the entrance of the seamen into the town, but on reaching the market-place they were saluted with a volley of shot. Almost ere this hasty fire took effect, the adventurers, bending their bows, scattered the Spaniards in all directions. Drake, however, was wounded in the leg; but, though suffering severe pain, he concealed the fact, lest his men should make his wound a pretext for returning to their ships.

Having driven the Spaniards from the market-place, the English proceeded to inspect the town; and Drake, seizing one of the inhabitants, compelled him to show the way to the governor's house. Finding the door of this edifice open, the adventurers entered without ceremony; and, making their way to the rooms in which was deposited the silver carried from Panama by mules, they discovered bars piled up in such quantities as well-nigh exceeded belief. At the sight of so much wealth every eye glistened, and every tongue uttered an exclamation of wonder.

" But now," they said, after a pause, " we must carry this to our ships."

"Nay," said Drake, who apprehended that the Spaniards would rally, "we must not meddle with a single bar; but come, and I will lead you to the king's treasury, where are jewels and gold —not only easier carried than this, but nearer to the shore."

The mariners, with visions of gold and jewels before their eyes, expressed their readiness to follow; and Drake, forcing the captive Spaniard to conduct them, proceeded toward the treasury. On arriving before the place, however, they found the gates carefully secured, and a cry of disappointment broke from the party. But Drake was in no mood to relinquish the object on which his heart had so long been set.

"My men," said he, "I have brought you to the mouth of the treasure-house of the world: if ye gain not the treasure, none but yourselves are to be blamed."

"We will gain it!" shouted the adventurers.

"Courage, then," continued Drake; "for if so bright an opportunity once setteth, it seldom riseth again."

After this address, Drake grasped his pike, and made a step forward to force the gate. But he had scarcely done so when he fell fainting on the ground. He was quite speechless, and his companions could not for some moments comprehend the cause. At length they perceived the wound in his leg, and became apprehensive of his dying

of exhaustion. The loss of blood had been excessive. Each print of his foot from the market-
place was red. However, while they bound the
wound with a scarf and administered cordials, he
gradually recovered; and he was so reluctant to
abandon the attack on the treasury, that he only
yielded when the seamen evinced their determination to remove him to his ship by force, if necessary.

Matters were not now quite pleasant. Not
only had the attack on Nombre de Dios failed,
but it had rendered any idea of Drake and his
friends remaining where they were out of the
question. Aware that, if they did not make the
best use of their time, the Spaniards would discover their weakness and adopt measures for
their destruction, they sailed to a small island
hard by, anchored their vessels, rested their
limbs, and refreshed themselves with fruit.

But Drake was not a man to be disheartened
with a mishap. In spite of the severity of his
wound, he panted for the excitement of action,
and, resolving to attack Carthagena, made for
that port. On entering the mouth of the harbor,
however, he found a frigate, on board of which
was an old man, who informed the daring navigator that a pinnace with sails and oars had passed
an hour before, carrying tidings of his coming.
The truth of this statement was evident. In
fact, Drake soon perceived that the castle was

manned, that the shipping was drawn up in hostile array under the walls, and that any attempt would be madness. But he consoled himself by seizing a large ship and two pinnaces, which he found had been dispatched with letters from Nombre de Dios to alarm the coast.

Drake, finding that he had now more ships than crews, caused the "Swan" to be set on fire; and, while the wound in his leg was healing, he opened communications with the Maroons, who were negroes escaped from slavery, and settled on the Isthmus of Darien, under a chief who in the hour of danger could rally around him as many as seventeen hundred fighting men. With the Maroons Drake at once formed an alliance, and, with some of them as guides, set out to intercept the mules bearing treasure from Panama to Nombre de Dios.

While on this adventure Drake reached the summit of a high hill, on which grew an immense tree, in which steps were so cut as to render an ascent easy. Guided by the Maroons, he climbed to the top, where he found a kind of arbor sufficiently large to accommodate twelve men. It was while seated in this tree, and looking around with keen curiosity, that Drake caught his first view of the Pacific; and the idea of exploring that great South Sea, on which no English ship had up to that time sailed, took possession of his imagination. Fired with enthusiasm, Drake fell on his knees, and "implored the Divine assistance that he might, at some time or other, sail thither and make a perfect discovery."

But, meanwhile, the great point was to seize the mules laden with treasure; and having registered a vow to attempt the navigation of the Pacific, Drake, guided by the Maroons, came in sight of Panama. Caution, however, was necessary; and, in order to procure intelligence about the mules, he caused the Maroons to disguise themselves and go into the town, while he and his comrades lay concealed in a grove. Returning, the Maroons brought tidings that the treasurer of Lima would pass during the night on his way to Europe, and that nine mules laden with gold and jewels would accompany him. Drake, on hearing this, leaped with joy, and marching his men some miles on the road to Nombre de Dios, formed them into two companies, and made them lie down to await the treasurer's approach among the long grass that grew on either side of the path.

Drake found that the intelligence brought by the Maroons was quite correct. Indeed, the adventurous seamen had not lain in ambush for an hour when the tinkling of bells intimated that mules were coming in both directions. Drake instantly gave orders that the mules traveling from Nombre de Dios should be allowed to pass without molestation, and that his companions should reserve all their courage to capture the gold and jewels from Panama. He was, however, doomed to disappointment. One man, happening to be intoxicated, rose from the ground at a critical moment; and the horseman who rode in advance of the treasurer's party, seeing there was danger in his way, hastily spurred back to give the alarm. The consequence was fatal to Drake's anticipations. The treasurer sent back the nine mules to Panama; and when Drake rushed out on the cavalcade, hoping to secure boundless wealth, he found, to his mortification, that the gold and jewels had escaped.

But fortune soon after proved less tantalizing. While still watching among the long grass, Drake again heard the tinkling of bells, and ere long he had the gratification of seeing two companies approach. These, being unaware of any danger of their being attacked, manifested the utmost surprise, and without a struggle yielded up their valuable treasure. Drake, taking what he and his comrades could carry, buried the remainder, with the intention of returning; but one of the party loitered behind, and, being taken by the Spaniards, confessed, under the influence of torture, where the treasure was buried. Drake returned to the spot; and, finding that the treasure had been removed, submitted to the disappointment with what patience he could exercise.

At this stage of the enterprise, however, Drake

was torn with anxiety. A new danger had presented itself. Drake had ordered his pinnaces to await him on the coast; but, on his return, they were nowhere to be seen; and the appearance of seven Spanish vessels, evidently on the watch, caused him great alarm. Drake probably feared the worst; but, feeling the absurdity of giving way to despair at such a moment, he collected some trees brought down by the current of a river, formed one into an oar, another into a rudder, constructed a raft of several others, and, converting a biscuit-sack into a sail, ventured out to sea. After being for six hours on the raft, with the water sometimes up to his waist, he caught sight of the pinnaces, which had run for shelter behind a headland. Forcing his raft on shore, Drake crossed a narrow point of land and hailed the pinnaces. Having sailed round to the river, he received his comrades and the treasure on board, took leave of the Maroons, and, having rejoined his ships, availed himself of a favorable wind, sailed from Cape Florida, and in August, 1573, after a voyage of twenty-three days, reached Plymouth.

After arriving in England, Drake occupied his mind with his great project of exploring the Pacific. But it would appear that circumstances were rather unfavorable to his aspirations. Queen Elizabeth, still at peace with Philip of Spain, seems to have regarded Drake's enterprise with disapproval; and finding himself under the dis-

pleasure of the crown, Drake fled to Ireland, and
fought as a volunteer under Walter Devereux,
Earl of Essex. While serving under that nobleman, the hero is said to have made the acquaintance of an officer, named Thomas Doughty, who,
when Essex was dead and when the Irish war
was at an end, introduced the bold sea-captain to
Sir Christopher Hatton; and this wrought such
a change in Queen Elizabeth's opinion, that Drake
was received into her favor and taken into her
service.

But, however that may have been, Drake, in
1577, appeared at court, and met with decided
success. Elizabeth treated him with high distinction, and presented him with a magnificent
sword.

"Receive this sword, Francis Drake," said the
queen, "and wear it till we require it of thee
again; and we do account, Drake, that he who
striketh at thee, striketh at us."

Years had, by this time, passed since Drake
vowed to explore the Pacific, and the period had
now arrived when he was to fulfill his vow. On
the 13th of November, in the "Pelican," better
known as the "Golden Hind," Drake, with
Doughty as second in command, embarked at
Plymouth, attended by several vessels, manned
by a hundred and sixty-four gentlemen and sailors, having on board several pinnaces in frames,
a store of provisions for a long voyage, and arti-

cles of luxury, musical instruments, rich furniture, vessels of gold and silver, to convince foreigners of the wealth and civilization of the English nation. Thus prepared, Drake, under the queen's patronage, sailed from Plymouth, carefully concealing his destination, but steering in a southerly direction.

After a voyage of twenty-one days Drake reached a cape off Barbary, and then sailed along the coast of Fago. Having turned off two of his ships, Drake, with the "Golden Hind" and two others, reached the Straits of Magellan, and happily escaping all dangers, he early in September, 1578, entered the Pacific, of which Balboa, at an earlier period, had taken possession in the name of the King of Spain.

Drake was in no humor to pay any particular respect to the exclusive claims set up by Balboa, when that romantic adventurer " walked up to his middle in the water, in the presence of many Indians and Spaniards, with his sword and target, and called upon them to bear testimony that he took possession of the South Sea and all which pertained to it for the King of Castile and Leon." The elements, however, proved most hostile to the English explorer. For two months he had to contend with a gale which blew fiercely from the east, and his ships were dispersed. One of them was borne away by the tempest, and never heard of again ; another, of which John Winter

I

was captain, returned to England; and the "Golden Hind," commanded by Drake, was left to pursue her voyage in solitude. After being driven to the south, the "Golden Hind" anchored off Cape Horn, and Drake thus, by accident, became discoverer of the uttermost part of the land toward the south pole. Delighted with the idea, he landed, laid himself flat on the ground, and stretched himself as far as was consistent with safety over the promontory.

"Where have you been?" asked one of the officers as he returned to the ship.

"Why," answered Drake, solemnly, "I have been farther south than any other man living."

Drake, still hoping to fall in with his lost ships, now sailed along the coast, plundering as he went. While thus occupied, he landed on an island off Peru, and, while taking in water, found himself in some danger. The natives at first appeared so friendly and harmless that the adventurers were under no apprehensions. One day, however, when Drake went ashore, they suddenly assumed the attitude of hostility, and sent a flight of arrows among the boat's crew. The consequence was most unpleasant. Almost every man was wounded; and Drake, while receiving one arrow in his head, was wounded by another under the eye, and pierced almost to the brain.

"Let us set upon them!" cried the crew, highly exasperated.

"Nay," said Drake, calmly, "the poor creatures have doubtless mistaken us for Spaniards, and as, in that case, they would have been justified in making an attack, let us not punish them for the offense."

It was now late in November, 1578, and Drake was in want of provisions. One day, however, while off the Isle of Moucha, the "Golden Hind" fell in with an Indian in a fishing canoe; and the Indian, having been made to comprehend the navigator's position, accompanied the boats ashore, and prevailed on the natives of the island to bring a supply of eggs, fowls, and a fat hog. At the same time, an Indian of rank, who could speak Spanish, appeared on board the "Golden Hind."

"If you will accept my guidance," said he to Drake, "I will pilot you to the port of Valparaiso, where you will find a Spanish vessel richly laden with treasure."

"Willingly," said Drake; and the "Golden Hind" setting sail, soon came in sight of the Spaniard. No difficulty was experienced in making a capture; and Drake, taking possession, found that his prize contained a quantity of pearls, sixty thousand pieces of gold, and about two thousand jars of Chili wine.

Having liberally rewarded the Indian and put him ashore at the point he wished, Drake sailed onward. Before reaching the equator he captured two other Spanish vessels, but did not value them very highly, as he was impatiently looking out for a large Spanish ship richly laden, of which he had received intelligence. In order to encourage the vigilance of his crew, he promised his gold chain to the man who should first descry her, and the look-out was consequently keen and constant. At length, on St. David's day, a sailor cried out that the Spaniard was in sight, and the " Golden Hind" immediately gave chase. But it soon appeared that there was no danger of the prize attempting to escape her destiny. In fact, the master of the treasure-ship mistook the " Golden Hind" for a Spaniard, and, instead of resisting, made a signal to come on board. Drake, promptly accepting the invitation, placed the Spaniards under the hatches, and found in the ship gold and silver in abundance.

Drake now considered that for one voyage he had done " excellently well," and proposed, without delay, to make for England. This, however, he confessed, was not so easy. He knew that, the whole coast of Chili being in alarm, it would be madness to attempt the Straits; and he formed a plan of sailing northward, and endeavoring to discover between Asia and America a northern passage from the Pacific to the Atlantic. But, after making the experiment, Drake abandoned this project, and, following the example of Magellan, steered direct for the Moluccas. After sailing for two months without seeing land, Drake reached some inhabited islands. At first the islanders showed a wish to traffic, and brought the navigators fruit, potatoes, and various articles of food; but suddenly changing, the savages attacked the "Golden Hind" with large stones. Drake immediately ordered a gun to be fired over their heads, and, alarmed at the sound, they leaped into the water; but, perceiving that nobody was hurt, they became bolder than ever, and attacked so furiously that Drake ordered a shot to be fired into the midst of them. This brought them to their senses; and the "Golden Hind" left the islands in safety, the crew emphatically describing them as the "Islands of Thieves."

At length Drake came in sight of the Moluccas. While passing one of the little islands, the king came off in a boat, and invited Drake to go to Ternate. Before that place, accordingly, the "Golden Hind" anchored; and Drake, having sent a rich cloak as a present to the king, requested a supply of provisions and permission to trade. The requests were both granted; and soon after, the king, with his ministers, attired in white lawn cloth of Calicut, paid a ceremonious visit to the ship. Drake welcomed his royal visitor with sound of trumpet and a salute of cannon; and his majesty, after remaining for some time on board, left, highly delighted with his reception and entertainment.

After taking provisions on board, Drake, sail-

ing in a westerly direction, reached the Celebes,
small islands so surrounded with shoals that he
was fain to change his course. While steering
southward, he met with an interruption which
caused much dismay. Early one morning in
January, the "Golden Hind," while scudding
along with all her sails set, suddenly touched a
rocky shoal, and instantly ran aground. All efforts to get her off proved vain. Luckily, however, the ship did not leak. Nevertheless, the
prospect was dismal, and the crew looked around
with feelings of despair. However, after remaining till next evening, when the wind slackened,
the ship, to the joy and surprise of every one on
board, slid down into the water and floated
gently and safely away.

Meanwhile the voyage so far had not been
accomplished without unpleasant occurrences.
Drake, it seems, was not a man to be trifled with ;
and when Doughty, his chief officer, and Francis
Fletcher, the chaplain, incurred his displeasure,
the bold captain dealt with them after a somewhat summary fashion.

It appears that at an early part of the voyage
Doughty was accused of inciting the seamen to
mutiny. The affair is involved in some mystery.
But it is certain that Doughty was charged with
conspiracy, and that on being tried by an irregular kind of tribunal, he was found guilty. Drake
then offered him the choice of being forthwith

executed, of being put ashore on a desolate island, or of being brought to England to stand his trial. Doughty is said to have chosen immediate execution; and after having partaken with Drake of the Communion in token of mutual forgiveness, the ill-starred officer was beheaded, and buried close to the remains of a wooden frame, on which Magellan had, about fifty years earlier, hung certain mutineers.

At a much later date—indeed, after coming off the rock—Fletcher appears to have been guilty of offense, and Drake is said to have taken the extraordinary step of excommunicating the chaplain. Having fastened Fletcher by one of the legs to a staple knocked into the hatches in the forecastle, Drake summoned the ship's company, and, sitting cross-legged on a chest, with a pair of pantoffles in his hand, he proceeded with the solemn ceremony.

"Francis Fletcher," said he, "I do here excommunicate thee out of the Church of God, and from all the benefits and graces thereof; and denounce thee to the devil and all his angels."

After having charged Fletcher, on pain of death, not to come before the mast, and threatened to hang him in case of disobedience, Drake caused a posy to be written and bound on the chaplain's right arm, on which were the words, "Francis Fletcher, the falsest knave that liveth."

Before the "Golden Hind" still lay a long voy-

age. It was performed, however, without any
such dangers as had hitherto beset her. After
touching at Java, Drake made for the Cape of
Good Hope, which excited the admiration of the
sailors; and after landing at Sierra Leone, he at
length, on the 26th of September, 1580, after a
voyage of more than two years and ten months,
arrived in safety at Plymouth.

Drake's return to England was hailed with enthusiasm. The voyage was regarded as the most
glorious ever accomplished, and, at the same time,
the most profitable. The "Golden Hind" was
said to have brought home treasure to the value
of a million pounds sterling. It seems, however,
that Queen Elizabeth expressed serious scruples
as to the way in which so much wealth had been
acquired. But means were devised to soften her;
and, after giving Drake a gracious reception at
court, she ordered the "Golden Hind" to be
drawn into a creek near Deptford, paid the ship
a visit, partook of a banquet on board, and rendered the occasion memorable by bestowing
knighthood on the great sea-captain.

"Francis Drake," said the queen, when the
feast was over, "we intrusted a sword to thy
keeping till we demanded it of thee again. We
now require thee to deliver it up in the manner
in which thou didst receive it from our hands."

Drake, kneeling before the queen, presented
the weapon in the scabbard; and Elizabeth took

it, glanced carelessly at the sheath, drew it slowly, and examined the blade.

"This, Drake," she said, "is a sword which
might serve thee yet, though thou hast carried it
round the globe. But, ere we return it to thee,
it must render us a service."

While speaking, Elizabeth stepped back a pace,
and when the expectation of the spectators was
raised to the highest pitch, the royal lady, laying
the sword on the great captain's shoulder, said,
"Rise up, Sir Francis Drake!" A burst of applause instantly indicated the joy felt by all present at the honor done to England's maritime
hero, and the queen went ashore with a con-
sciousness of having immensely added to her
popularity. After this the "Golden Hind" remained at Deptford till quite decayed. The ship
was then broken up, and from the soundest plank
a chair was made, and presented to the University of Oxford.

Meanwhile the achievement of Drake was regarded by the people of England with boundless
amazement. In truth, the man who had circumnavigated the globe was thought to possess powers more than human; for, in those days, the
earth was supposed to be flat, and it was not
deemed possible to make a voyage round the
world by plain sailing. It was said that the sole
passage to the other side was a great gulf, and
that Drake, having, with preternatural aid and

by some miraculous process, got access to this,
asked if any of his crew knew where they were.

"Yes," said a boy, "we are now just under
London Bridge."

"What!" Drake exclaimed, throwing the boy
overboard, "hast thou too a devil? If I let thee
live, thou wilt one day be a greater man than myself!"

Nor, according to the popular notions, were
Drake's powers as a magician limited to the
place in which he happened to be present. It
seems that the great navigator, though spending
so much of his time on the sea, twice ventured on
matrimony, and that, during his voyage in the
"Golden Hind," Madam Drake, despairing of his
return, gradually began to consider him as one
dead. Being rich, and not burdened with children, her hand was in request, and at length she
consented to take a second husband. But just
as the bridal party were on the way to church,
one of Drake's familiar spirits carried him the intelligence; and instantly loading one of his great
guns, he fired right through the globe with so
true an aim that the ball came up on the other
side, crashing through the church and interrupt-
ing the ceremony.

"That comes from Drake," cried madam.

"From Drake!" exclaimed the bridegroom in
much amazement.

"Yes," she said; "and while he lives there

must be neither troth nor ring between thee and me."

While such stories were interesting lovers of the marvelous in cottage and in grange, work was found for Drake to do. In 1585, Queen Elizabeth concluded a treaty with King Philip's revolted subjects in the Netherlands; and England being thus brought into collision with Spain, an embargo was laid on English ships and merchandise. It was evident that a war would be the consequence, and in both countries preparations were begun. Philip, who had recently seized the kingdom of Portugal, commenced the construction of a mighty armament for the conquest of England, and Elizabeth appointed Drake to the command of a fleet to attack the Spanish settlements in America.

Sir Philip Sydney manifested much eagerness to accompany Drake in this expedition. But the chivalrous knight had no opportunity of associating his fame with that of the great sea-captain. The queen, without ceremony, prevented Sydney from taking part in the adventure. "I will not," she said, "risk the loss of the jewel of my time."

On the 14th of September, 1585, Drake set sail with twenty ships, carrying above two thousand men. From the expedition important results were anticipated, and a rumor soon reached England that six thousand Maroons had repaired to Drake and crowned him king. Philip of Spain became greatly alarmed. "We hear," wrote Lord Burghley to the Earl of Leicester, "that Sir Francis Drake is a fearful man to the king, and that the king could have been content that Sir Francis had taken the last year's fleet, so as he had not gone forward to the Indies."

In the mean time, Drake was wreaking his vengeance on the Spanish settlements. St. Jago, St. Domingo, and Carthagena were successively attacked. At St. Domingo, having demanded a ransom from the city of twenty-five thousand crowns, and met with a refusal, he set fire to the suburbs till the money was paid; and at Carthagena he pursued the same plan, burning house by house till his demand of a hundred and ten thousand crowns was complied with. Yellow fever, however, made havoc among the crews, and rendered this expedition less distinguished than that in which Drake had formerly taken part. Nevertheless, when he returned to Plymouth in July, 1586, he brought sixty thousand pounds of prize-money, and two hundred and forty guns captured from the Spaniards.

The time was approaching, however, when Drake was to render England services of a far higher character. In 1587, accounts of Philip's preparations for invasion constantly arrived, and created no inconsiderable alarm. At this crisis it was determined to dispatch Drake with a squadron to ascertain the actual state of affairs in

Spain and Portugal. In command of this expedition, for which the queen furnished five ships and London adventurers twenty, Drake embarked in her majesty's good ship the "Elizabeth Bonaventure," and soon signalized the enterprise by a desperate dash at the harbor of Cadiz. Never was a naval warrior more successful. In one day he captured, burned, and destroyed from sixty to a hundred vessels, and, in spite of Spanish fire-ships, Spanish ships at sea, and batteries on shore, made himself master of the roadstead. After this exploit, Drake, returning to Cape St. Vincent, took the forts; and then sailing toward the Azores, he encountered and seized a large Portuguese carack, named the "St. Philip," one of the most valuable prizes ever brought into an English port.

The execution done by Drake at Cadiz had the effect of delaying Philip's attempt at invasion, and giving the English time to prepare. But the King of Spain had no idea of abandoning his project. Preparations went on; a hundred and fifty ships, twelve of which were named after the twelve apostles, were gathered in the Tagus, and described as the Invincible Armada; the Duke of Medina Sidonia left St. Marie Port and his orange groves to figure as admiral; Martin Recalde, a Spanish seaman of renown, appeared as second in command; and Alexander Farnese, Duke of Parma, the most distinguished captain

of the age, was then at Bruges, and expected to
join them with some thirty thousand troops, who
were to be landed at the mouth of the Thames.

But, meanwhile, England was on the alert, and
preparing for the crisis with spirit and energy.
Lord Henry Seymour, with forty ships, was dispatched to the coast of Flanders to keep Parma
in check. Charles Howard, Lord Effingham,
was, in the capacity of Lord High Admiral of
England, nominated to the command of the fleet
fitted out at Plymouth to fight the Spaniards on
their putting to sea; Drake, with Sir John Hawkins and Sir Martin Frobisher, were appointed to
act with the lord high admiral; and Sir Francis,
who hoisted his flag in the "Revenge," far from
showing any fear of his ancient enemies, proposed
to attack the armada on the coast of Spain, or
even in the Tagus.

Drake was the hero of the crisis. His name
was on every tongue, and his power was believed
to be preternatural. It was rumored throughout
the country that, when first made aware of the
national peril, he was playing at skittles on the
Hoe of Plymouth; that, without any change of
countenance, he played out his game; that then,
taking a block of wood, and calling for a hatchet,
he bared his arm, chopped the block into small
pieces, and cast them into the sea; and that, at
his word, each chip was, by some magical process, metamorphosed into a man of war, ready to
guard the coasts and encounter the foe.

But it was not on her navy alone that at this crisis England relied. From Kent to Northumberland almost every county was in arms. Twenty thousand men were posted along the southern coasts; one army was appointed to guard the queen, and another was encamped at Tilbury under Robert Dudley, Earl of Leicester. Elizabeth acted on the occasion as if inspired, for a while, by the soul of the first Edward. With the object of sustaining the national spirit, she proceeded to Tilbury, appeared at the camp mounted on a white steed, the emblem of sovereignty, rode through the ranks to animate the soldiers, called upon them in heroic language to defend their country, and intimated that she, weak woman as she was, would arm and fight for her native soil rather than it should be trodden by the foot of an invader.

"I know," said the high-spirited queen, "that I have but the body of a weak and feeble woman, but I have the heart of a king, and of a king of England too; and I think foul scorn that Parma, or Spain, or any prince of Europe should dare to invade the border of my realms; to which, rather than any dishonor shall grow by me, I myself will take up arms—I myself will be your general, and rewarder of every one of your virtues in the field."

Events hurried onward. On the 29th of May, 1588, the armada left the mouth of the Tagus, and

about the same time the English fleet sailed from
Plymouth. But next day the elements interposed to prevent an immediate encounter. The
wind rising, swelled into a storm of such violence
that the Spaniards, finding the armada crippled
and disabled, were under the necessity of returning to refit at Lisbon; and the naval heroes of
England, driven back to Plymouth, were fain to
put into port, and console themselves with the
idea that, for the present, at all events, the danger
had passed.

But Philip had too much confidence in his
monster armament to be daunted by an adverse
gale. No sooner was his damage repaired than
the Duke of Medina had orders to put to sea, to
proceed directly to the coast of Flanders, and
take Parma and his troops on board. But accident led the Spanish magnate to disobey orders.
Learning from a fisherman that the English fleet
was in port at Plymouth and unprepared for action, he resolved to sail thither with the idea of
annihilating his adversaries at a blow.

It was the close of a day in the month of July
—and at Plymouth so little apprehension was entertained of an early attempt at invasion, that
most of the crews had been disbanded, and many
of the sailors had been sent ashore—when a Scottish pirate, with every sail set, dashed into the
bay with intelligence that he had descried the
armada off the Lizard Point. Not an hour was

then lost. All was bustle and excitement; the seamen were recalled; the ships were hauled out of port, and the fleet had just time to get to sea, when the armada appeared in sight in the form of a crescent, the Spanish vessels, like castles in height, sailing slowly along, and stretching over a distance of seven miles.

The lord high admiral and the English captains were not dismayed by the bulk of their enemy. Indeed, when they saw how heavily the Spanish ships sailed, and how ill built, unwieldy, and unmanageable was the hostile armament, they felt more confidence than ever in their own little fleet. In order to have the wind in their favor, they allowed the enemy to pass; and, having thus freed their small vessels from the danger of being run down by the heavy Spaniards, they resolved upon action. Accordingly, on the 21st of July, the lord high admiral sent forward a pinnace, called the "Defiance," which fired a shot by way of challenging the Spaniards to fight; and a signal for battle having been given, Drake boldly attacked the squadron commanded by Recalde. The Spanish vice-admiral soon found his position so much the reverse of pleasant that he consulted his safety by joining the main part of the Spanish fleet, and nothing like a general engagement took place. But Drake was not without his trophies. At the close of the day a huge Biscay ship, which carried the king's treasure, took fire; and amid

K

the confusion which was the consequence, the galleon of Don Pedro de Valdez hastened to the rescue. But scarcely had the Spaniards succeeded in extinguishing the fire when Drake was upon them. Resistance proved vain. Don Pedro's galleon, with the Don on board, was taken and sent to Dartmouth; and the Biscay ship, seized at the same time by the English, was conveyed in triumph to Weymouth. The sum of fifty-five thousand ducats, seized on board the galleon, was the only valuable capture made during the memorable campaign.

After this encounter, English vessels poured out from every port to join the fleet; and the armada made its way heavily up the Channel, exposed to perpetual attacks from the light squadron of assailants, "like a whale attacked by the harpoons of a flotilla of boats." At length, on the 27th of July, the armada, harassed but not yet broken, anchored off Calais; and while the Duke of Medina was sending off post-haste to summon Parma to his aid, the English fleet, now joined by Seymour from the coast of Flanders, anchored at a short distance from his ships.

While such was the state of affairs, the English resolved upon a bold attack. On the night of the 28th of July, eight vessels filled with combustibles were during the darkness sent with the wind right into the midst of the enemy. Apprehensive that these fire-ships might contain murderous engines of destruction, the Spaniards gave way to terror, cut their cables, hauled up their sails, and took to their oars. Seeing the enemy disperse in alarm, Drake pushed forward, made a furious attack, and, being joined by Effingham, captured twelve Spanish ships and wrought fearful havoc. Nor was there now any hope of Parma coming to the rescue. Aware of the disaster suffered by the armada, that famous captain refused to hazard his troops; and the Duke of Medina, seeing that every thing was against him, resolved upon returning to the Tagus.

Rescued from the sands of Flanders by a sudden change of wind, the armada sailed northward and made the circuit of Scotland. But the English still pursued, and, but for want of ammunition, would probably have taken every ship. So far as the Spaniards were concerned, fortune proved most unpropitious. The weather becoming tempestuous, many ships were wrecked on the coasts of Ireland and Scotland; and of the mighty armament that had left the Tagus, only sixty vessels, and all of them in a most shattered condition, returned to the ports of Spain. Philip was doubtless deeply mortified at the result of his ambitious attempt at conquest. He endeavored, however, to meet the terrible mishap with serenity. When informed that his ships and men had so signally failed him, he took refuge in a simulated resignation. "I did not," he remarked, "send them to fight against winds and waves."

The news of the dispersion of the armada caused great joy in England. The queen, having ordered thanks for the national victory to be offered up in all the churches in the kingdom, went in great state, and attended by a multitude of knights and nobles, to St. Paul's, and there, with the banners taken from the Spaniards hanging around, evinced her gratitude to God for the triumph vouchsafed to her arms. Even in Scotland, the victory over Philip was hailed with delight. "I desire to have sincere and perfect amity with your queen," said James the Sixth to the English embassador. "As for the King of Spain, I expect no other courtesy from him but such as Polyphemus promised Ulysses, that he should be the last whom he would devour."

Drake had scarcely time to recover from his fatigues, when his services were again demanded by his country. Signal, indeed, as had been the discomfiture of the Spaniards, the English were not quite satisfied. The nation was thoroughly aroused. While many proclaimed their disappointment at the escape of the armada from before Calais, all expressed eagerness to see Philip bearded on his own territory. The wish was earnest and the cry loud. An expedition against Spain was consequently projected; and government, with the aid of private adventurers, fitted out a formidable armament. Seamen and soldiers were forthcoming to the number of twenty thousand. Drake, as England's hero, was placed at the head of the naval force; Sir John Norris, a military officer of skill and experience, was intrusted with the command of the troops; and Robert Devereux, the young Earl of Essex, then high in Elizabeth's favor, stole away from the apron-string of the amorous spinster to take part in a patriotic adventure from which much glory was anticipated. Portugal was selected as a vulnerable point of Philip's dominions; and Don Antonio, prior of Crato, an illegitimate heir of the old kings of Portugal, who had been an exile in England, accompanied Drake in the character of pretender to the crown.

Every preparation having been made, and all obstacles overcome, Drake, on the 5th of April, 1589, sailed from Plymouth. The enterprise, however, was not destined to be so successful as was anticipated. Quarrels are supposed to have taken place between Drake and Norris; and when one proposed to attack Corunna, the other opposed such a step. At length, however, they did land at Corunna, and after wasting many days in hard fighting, they re-embarked. Landing next at Peniche, Norris and Essex marched toward Lisbon, Drake promising to go up the Tagus with his ships and the ordnance to their aid.

On reaching Lisbon, which was situated on seven hills, and defended by an old wall, Norris and Essex, who imagined the Portuguese would immediately rise for Don Antonio, occupied the suburbs. They soon had reason to believe that the Don had deceived himself and them. A few unarmed Portuguese did indeed raise the cry of " God save King Antonio," but the people generally showed no inclination to move for the Pretender, and his presence rendered it impossible, without indecency, to plunder the suburbs. Finding that nothing was to be done, having no artillery, and despairing of Drake coming to their assistance, Norris and Essex, after repulsing a sally of the Spanish garrison, commenced a retreat.

It would seem that Drake, considering that the Castle of St. Julian was in the way, had given up his plan of going up the Tagus with his ships as impracticable. However, he seized Cascaes, a little town at the mouth of the river, and subsequently captured a squadron of ships with corn intended for the equipment of a new armada. By this time sickness was making sad havoc among the men; and Drake, Norris, and Essex, no longer hoping to accomplish any thing great, embarked. After some insignificant exploits off the Azores, they, having lost six thousand men during their unfortunate expedition, sailed, somewhat crestfallen, into Plymouth.

Drake had now reached his fiftieth year; and perhaps, after the expedition to Lisbon, which contrasted somewhat unfavorably with others in which he had enacted a part, he felt little inclination to tempt the seas any more. At all events, he remained at home for six years. He possessed the means of making life pleasant to himself and useful to others. Having been careful of his fortune, he had purchased the beautiful abbey and abbey-lands of Buckland Monachorum, near Plymouth, and not only founded "the chest at Chatham," a fund for the relief of worn-out seamen, but constructed the famous aqueduct which conveys water to Plymouth, a remarkable piece of engineering for the period, and so rapidly executed as to give rise to the tradition that, by virtue of a compact with the devil, the water followed the heels of the old hero's horse as he galloped from the spring to the town.

But, while Drake was living in retirement at Buckland Monachorum, occupying his attention with "the chest at Chatham" and the waterworks of Plymouth, four galleys one day anchored off the coast of Cornwall, and a band of Spaniards, after landing without opposition, burned a church and set fire to three fishing villages. The idea that King Philip meditated a second attempt at invasion at that time prevailed in England, and news of the inroad into Cornwall, when carried over the country, confirmed every rumor that had been spread. In consequence, two fleets were fitted out. One of these was designed for the Channel. The other was intended to attack the

Spanish settlements in America, and Drake was appointed to the command. Sir John Hawkins, who had seen nearly fourscore years, resolved to share the voyage of his old naval comrade.

Drake sailed from Plymouth in August, 1595, and late in September his fleet reached the West Indies. But he soon discovered that the Spaniards were somewhat better prepared to defend themselves and hold their own than they had been in the days of his youth. Every place into which he looked was armed to the teeth, and frowned a stern defiance. Attacks were made on several Spanish forts in the Gulf of Mexico, but without success. Every where the Spaniards were on the alert, and prepared to welcome Drake back to the scenes of his celebrated exploits with discharge of cannon. One of his vessels was taken by the Spaniards off Porto Rico; and, while Drake sat one day in his cabin drinking a cup of beer, a ball killed two of his officers before his eyes, and knocked the stool on which he sat from under him.

This change of fortune saddened the soul of the old sea king. Ere long Hawkins died of a broken heart; and Drake, growing quite desperate, made an attempt to march to Panama. The attempt utterly failed, and he suffered grievously from mortification. While he was in this state Drake was attacked by a fever, which rapidly overpowered his constitution, and compelled him to keep his cabin. On the morning of the 28th of January, 1596, however, he insisted on rising and dressing himself. But his condition was feeble; his language was incoherent; and death was written on his face. His officers, shocked, doubtless, at the spectacle of a man who had been the pride of the proudest of nations, and the terror of an empire on which the sun never set, reduced to such a plight, recognized the necessity of carrying the old hero back to bed, and within an hour he breathed his last.

The corpse of Drake was placed in a leaden coffin, and his obsequies were performed with ceremonies befitting the occasion. The seamen were assembled; the service of the Church was read; the appointed signal was made; and, amid a volley of musketry and a discharge from all the guns of the fleet, the mortal remains of England's maritime hero were committed to the deep.

SIR WALTER RALEIGH.

One day, in the eighth decade of the sixteenth century, when Queen Elizabeth, in her splendid barge, surrounded by ladies of honor, lords of high degree, and officers of the household, was taking an airing on the Thames, the weather suddenly broke, and a shower of rain fell. After landing at Westminster, and proceeding from the wharf toward Whitehall, the queen found the ground somewhat moist, and at length her path was crossed by a pool of water, at which she hesitated and halted.

It was an awkward moment for the courtiers of the haughty princess, and each stood irresolute. But at the instant a young man of a most noble aspect stepped forward, and, taking off his richly-embroidered cloak, spread it, with singular grace, on the spot of ground that was wet. Elizabeth, both surprised and pleased at so loyal and chivalrous an action, slightly colored, walked over the mantle, and proceeded to the palace. But the comely face, the handsome figure, and the courtly air of the young gallant had caught her eye and captivated her fancy. Without delay, therefore, she summoned him to her presence and took him into her service. It then became known that his name was Walter Raleigh, and that he was of the ancient gentry of Devon, a body of whom the queen used to remark "that they were all born courtiers with a becoming confidence."

In Devon, during the year 1552, about the time when Edward the Sixth was on his death-bed, and at a place named Hayes, Raleigh first saw the light. The father of Raleigh having figured with some distinction as a naval officer during the reign of Queen Mary, the embryo hero is supposed to have inherited a love for the sea; and the circumstance of Hayes being within a short distance of the coast is believed to have fostered his hereditary passion for the salt water.

It does not appear, however, that Raleigh was destined by his father for maritime affairs. After having been initiated into ancient learning, either at home or at a school in the vicinity, he was sent, when still very young, to pursue his studies at Oriel College, Oxford, and there attracted notice by the wit and brilliancy he displayed. But Raleigh soon tired of the cloisters of a college; and, prompted by an ardent genius, he, at the age of seventeen, buckled on his armor and sought distinction in military life.

Nor was there at that time any lack of opportunity. It was the year 1569, and the war then raging in France between Catholics and Huguenots excited considerable interest in England.

The struggle enlisted the sympathy of the pious, and roused the spirit of the adventurous. Elizabeth, though at that time struggling with many difficulties, showed her sympathy with the French Protestants; and while advancing them money, and taking the jewels of the Queen of Navarre as security, she authorized Henry Champernon to lead a troop of horse, consisting of a hundred gentlemen volunteers, to their assistance.

It was in France, as one of this body of gentlemen volunteers, that Raleigh became familiar with scenes of war, and won a place among men of courage. After having fought for years in France, he enlarged his experience by serving against Spain in the Netherlands; and then, returning from the Continent, took part in the suppression of a rebellion in Ireland. When little more than five-and-twenty, Raleigh appeared in London with laurels on his brow, and with a reputation for valor and experience, but with little prospect of having any early opportunity of realizing his ambitious aspirations.

Fortune, however, proved more favorable than such an adventurer could have anticipated even in his most sanguine moments. After the sacrifice of his gorgeous cloak, Raleigh rose rapidly at court; and when Lord Grey de Wilton was sent to Ireland as lord deputy, Raleigh accompanied him to fight against the Spaniards, who had effected a landing. After signalizing his prowess against the enemy, he had the honor of being sent home by the lord deputy as the bearer of dispatches, and admitted, at Christmas, 1581, to the royal presence, to deliver them into the queen's hands.

But Raleigh derived from the rebellion in Ireland advantages more substantial than the pleasure of fighting and the honor of carrying dispatches. In 1582, the last Fitzgerald who figured as Earl of Desmond, after making himself formidable to the government of Elizabeth, was caught hiding in a cottage, and slain on the spot. His head was brought to England to be placed over London Bridge, and his immense possessions were confiscated. Large grants were made out of the Desmond estates to Edmund Spenser, the poet, and to Raleigh. While Spenser obtained the castle of Kilcoleman and three thousand acres of the adjacent country, Raleigh obtained the castle of Inchequin, and the domain in which stood that feudal pile.

It was shortly before this time that Drake, having "circumnavigated the globe" in the "Golden Hind," returned to England; and Raleigh, like most adventurous Englishmen of that day, began to indulge in dreams of gold. Accordingly, he fitted out an expedition at his own cost, and sailing from Plymouth in 1584, discovered that important part of America bounded by the Potomac, the Atlantic, Carolina, and the Appalachian Mountains. Finding this territory fertile, Raleigh proposed to establish a colony; named the province Virginia, in compliment to Queen Elizabeth; and having obtained letters patent for forming a plantation, appointed Ralph Lane as governor. But the experiment proved quite unsuccessful; and, in 1586, when Drake was on that celebrated voyage during which he took St. Jago, St. Domingo, and Carthagena, he received on board Governor Lane and the remnant of Raleigh's unfortunate colony.

From Virginia Lane brought "that Indian plant called tobacco;" and Raleigh, who by this time had been honored with knighthood, enriched with the estates of the ill-fated Anthony Babington, and granted Durham House as a residence, began to smoke the weed in a silver pipe. As the luxury was at that time wholly unknown in England, his domestics were greatly puzzled as to the purpose for which the article was intended. One day, however, while Raleigh was poring over a book, and regaling himself with a pipe, an old servant, entering the study with a tankard of ale, perceived with horror that smoke was issuing from his master's mouth. Not doubting that Raleigh was on fire, the servant dashed the ale in his face, rushed down stairs, alarmed the household, and loudly proclaimed that his master was in danger of being reduced to ashes.

In spite of such discouragements, Raleigh remained faithful to his pipe, and the subject frequently furnished him with the opportunity of displaying his wit to the queen. On one of these occasions, while Raleigh was expatiating on the properties of his favorite weed, Elizabeth appeared somewhat incredulous, and Sir Walter became emphatic.

"I can assure your majesty," said he, "that I have so well experienced the nature of the plant, that I can even tell the exact weight in any quantity I consume."

"I doubt it much, Sir Walter," replied the queen, "and I will wager twenty angels that you do not solve my doubt."

The bet was taken, and the quantity of tobacco to be thoroughly smoked was agreed upon. Elizabeth thought only of the impracticability of weighing smoke in a balance; but Raleigh, carefully preserving the ashes, weighed them with scrupulous exactness, and gave what was deficient in the original weight as the result.

"Your majesty," he said, "can not deny that the difference hath been evaporated in smoke."

"I have heard of many laborers turning their gold into smoke," said Elizabeth, turning to her ladies, and alluding to the alchemists, "but," continued she, handing the knight twenty angels, "Raleigh, I think, is the first who hath turned smoke into gold."

Raleigh now appeared to enjoy so large a

measure of Elizabeth's favor that the Earl of
Leicester, who was in the Low Countries, became
jealous of the influence he exercised at court.
But, ere long, a formidable rival in the person of
Robert Devereux, Earl of Essex, contrived to
turn the queen's displeasure on Raleigh to such
a degree that, after having taken a conspicuous
part in the operations that ruined the Spanish armada, he was under the necessity of paying a
visit to Ireland till the cloud of royal anger passed over.

While in Ireland Raleigh paid a visit to Spenser at Kilcoleman, and at this time made the
acquaintance of Katherine Fitzgerald, that old
Countess of Desmond who, having figured more
than a century earlier at the court of the conquer-
or of Barnet and Tewkesbury, still lived, in Raleigh's castle of Inchequin, to tell, when the Stuarts were on the English throne, that in her youth
she had danced with Richard the Third when
Duke of Gloucester, and that Richard was the
handsomest man in the room except his brother
Edward. "I knew the old countess," writes Raleigh, "who lived in the year 1589, and many
years since, and who was married in Edward the
Fourth's time, and held her jointure from all the
Earls of Desmond since then."

But Raleigh's exile was not of long duration.
Restored to his former place in the queen's affections, he was, in 1592, intrusted with the com-

mand of fifteen ships, and sailed, with Sir Martin Frobisher as his lieutenant, to attack the Spanish settlements in America. The fleet, delayed and baffled by contrary winds, did not reach its destination. But the result was not altogether unsatisfactory.

When near the Azores, Raleigh happened to fall in with a huge Spanish carack, built with seven decks, carrying six hundred men, and named "The Mother of God." Raleigh thanked his stars for the good fortune that threw such a chance in his way, and, without delay, made an attack. The Spaniard, after a slight struggle, was forced to yield, and was found to contain treasure and merchandise to the value of a hundred and fifty thousand pounds.

Having brought his prize to England, Raleigh for some time stood high in Elizabeth's esteem, occupying a great position, and exercising much influence with benevolence and charity. One day he interceded for a minister of religion, whose zeal had prompted him to incur the anger of bishops and judges; another day he interceded for an officer who, having been wounded in the service of his country, had been unjustly treated by government; and his petitions became so frequent, that Elizabeth at length appeared inclined to remonstrate.

"When, Sir Walter," she demanded impatiently, "when will you cease to be a beggar?"

L

"I will cease to be a beggar," was Raleigh's answer, "when your majesty ceases to be a benefactor."

But, firmly as Raleigh seemed fixed in the queen's favor, a mortifying reverse was at hand. One of Elizabeth's foibles was to insist on the courtiers concentrating their whole admiration on herself; and, though verging on sixty, she encouraged them to address to her compliments which a sensible girl of sixteen would have treated as ridiculous. Any courtier who forgot the queen's claim to admiration, or any maid of honor who was the cause of a courtier forgetting the queen's claim to admiration, was sure to be visited with the royal displeasure in the severest shape. In spite of all this, Raleigh had the indiscretion to fall in love with Elizabeth, daughter of Sir Nicholas Throgmorton.

Raleigh's attachment soon became known to the queen; and the aged spinster, in her jealous wrath, set all propriety at defiance. The lovers were at once committed to the Tower, and there left to repent, at leisure, of the attachment they had rashly formed. Raleigh, however, perfectly understood Elizabeth's weakness, and employed a stratagem which he felt sure would regain him his liberty. When the queen was about to pass the Tower, he insisted on being allowed to see her; and, knowing that his whole conduct would be reported, he was no sooner denied this privi-

lege than he pretended to give way to despair,
and fought like a madman with the governor of
the fortress. At the same time, he wrote to Sir
Robert Cecil that he was full of woe; that he
could not live without seeing her whom he was
"wont to behold riding like Alexander, hunting
like Diana, walking like Venus, the gentle wind
blowing her fair hair about her pure cheeks like
a nymph, sometimes sitting in the shade like a
goddess, sometimes singing like an angel."

Nor had Raleigh exaggerated the royal weakness. His gross flattery had precisely the effect
which he intended it to produce. Elizabeth's
vanity was gratified, and she relented so far as
to order the captive knight to be released from
the Tower. But he was exposed to the inconvenience of being attended by a keeper, and
probably felt the company of such an individual
somewhat irksome.

"I congratulate you on having recovered your
liberty," said one of his friends.

"I am still the queen's poor captive," was Raleigh's reply.

For some time after his imprisonment in the
Tower, Raleigh continued, as it were, under a
cloud. Banished from the court, excluded from
the competition for royal favor, and sneered at
by successful rivals, he soon became weary of inaction. In these circumstances, he resolved on a
voyage to Guiana, the fabled El Dorado, or land

of gold, whose capital city, Manoa, had been described by Spanish writers as " one vaste palace
of Aladdin—a congeries of precious stones and
precious metals."

In the month of February, 1595, while Drake
and Hawkins were preparing for that voyage
from which neither of them was to return, Raleigh set sail from Plymouth, and in good time
reached Trinidad. With great hopes he seized
the town of St. Joseph's, probably expecting to
find some such treasure as Drake had seen at
Nombre de Dios. But, being disappointed in
this respect, he took to his boats, and, with a hundred of his men, made his way for hundreds of
miles up the Oronoco. Nothing of any consequence in the shape of treasure rewarded the adventurous knight's exertions. However, he found
the country fertile and beautiful, and near the
banks of the river discovered some signs of a
gold mine, which for the next twenty years
haunted his imagination, and finally tempted him
on that expedition which sealed his fate.

Meanwhile Raleigh, returning to England, was
the means of accommodating a quarrel that had
taken place between Essex and Cecil. His good
offices on this occasion were not unrewarded.
Received again at court, and restored to the
queen's favor, he was established as captain of
the guard, and admitted to the Privy Council.

About this time King Philip was engaged in

operations, and busy with preparations which the people of England regarded with extreme jealousy; and Elizabeth, unwilling that her coasts should again be menaced by an armada, resolved on attacking those of Spain. With this object, she fitted out an armament not quite so large, but rather more formidable than the Invincible Armada, and giving the command of the land forces to Essex, appointed Raleigh admiral of one of the four squadrons into which the fleet of a hundred vessels was divided. About the beginning of June the armament sailed from Plymouth, and, three weeks later, anchored on the west side of the island of Leon, on which stands the town of Cadiz.

It happened that the harbor of Cadiz was at that time crowded with galleys, merchantmen, and men-of-war; and the English, rejoicing in the thought of striking another shattering blow at the power of Spain, held a council of war. After some deliberation, they decided on an immediate attack, and Essex was so affected at the decision that he tossed his hat in the air for joy.

No time was lost in commencing operations. But the road was so shallow that the larger ships could not come to close quarters with the enemy, and the duty devolved on the smaller vessels of the fleet. Perceiving their danger, the Spanish galleys made off, crept along the shore, and contrived to get away; but the ships that lay at anchor turned their broadsides, and at break of day commenced an obstinate engagement. The English, however, were completely victorious. At noon, the "St. Philip," the Spanish admiral's ship, was set on fire, with two vessels near her, and burned to ashes; and most of the others ran ashore.

After this engagement, which had been long and stubborn, Essex, with eight hundred soldiers, landed at the Puntal, a fort on the island near Cadiz, and advanced to attack the city. But the Spanish troops now deemed it time to strike a blow for the place, and both cavalry and infantry issued from the gates. Repulsed after a sharp conflict, they fled back to the city; and Essex, pursuing them closely, climbed up a newly-built bulwark, leaped thence into the place, while Sir Francis Vere, knocking down the gate, rushed in. After a fierce struggle had been made by the Spaniards in the market-place, the city yielded, and next day the castle followed the example.

While Essex was taking the city of Cadiz, Raleigh was by no means idle. The duty assigned to Sir Walter was to burn the merchantmen at Port Real, and he performed that duty like a man who hated the king and the kingdom of Spain, and every thing which to them belonged. In vain the Spaniards implored him to forbear, and offered an immense ransom.

"If you will spare our ships," said they, "we will give you two millions of ducats."

"No," exclaimed Raleigh, sternly, "I can not listen to such a thing. I was sent to destroy the ships, not to dismiss them on composition."

After the sack of Cadiz and the demolition of the forts, the English, much to the discontent of Essex, returned home. But the chivalrous earl had ere long an opportunity of winning fresh laurels. In fact, Philip's desire for vengeance, which seemed to survive each disaster, prompted him, in 1597, to prepare an armada for the conquest of Ireland; and Elizabeth encountered this new danger by fitting out a fleet of a hundred and twenty ships to destroy this armada in the harbors of Corunna and Ferrol, and then proceed to the Azores to intercept the galleons, which were all then on their way to Spain, laden with the treasures of Mexico and Peru. This fleet was divided into three squadrons. Of these, one was commanded by Essex, who figured as chief of the expedition; the second by Lord Howard of Effingham; and the third by Sir Walter Raleigh.

On the 9th of July, the English fleet weighed anchor and sailed from Plymouth. But the adventure opened inauspiciously. Twice driven back by contrary winds, the ships did not leave the English coast till the middle of August, and then, misled by false information, they made for the Isle of Flores. Not finding any enemy, the commanders resolved on dividing their force, and making simultaneous attacks on several Spanish forts; and Essex, bearing away for Fayal, sent a summons for Raleigh to follow. Raleigh, who was in the act of going ashore to supply himself with water, instantly obeyed, and, steering a straight course, came in sight of Fayal. But Essex had not appeared, and Raleigh determined to land and fill his water-casks.

No sooner did the boats approach the shore than the Spaniards appeared in the trenches, waved their colors, brandished their weapons, and uttered shouts of defiance. This was more than Raleigh's proud spirit could bear. Increasing his party to the number of two hundred, he ordered his pinnaces to fire upon the Spaniards; and, leading the way in his own barge amid a shower of shot, ordered his men to make for the shore as fast as oars would carry them. On nearing the land, he leaped out, waded through the water, clambered up the rocks, cut his way at the head of his party through the narrow entrance, and made an attack so determined that the Spaniards, throwing down their arms, fled into the town.

Raleigh's blood was by this time up, and he had no idea of letting the enemy so easily off. Resolving to take the town, he ordered some sergeants to view the enemy's lines. But they looked at the batteries with alarm, and declined the service as one not to be expected of mortal man.

"It would be certain destruction," they said.

"Bring me my cuirass and my casque," cried Raleigh, "and, albeit this is rather the duty of a common soldier than a commander, I myself will ascertain the approaches to the hill."

Accordingly, he placed himself at the head of his men, and proceeded to make observations. While thus engaged, stones and shot from the walls flew thick around him. But he persevered; and, though his clothes were cut in many places, he remained unhurt. Nor did the Spaniards, with the fate of the Invincible Armada and the sack of Cadiz in their memories, feel much inclination to maintain their ground. Indeed, they were already so disheartened, that when Raleigh and his men prepared to attack, they at once abandoned the fort; and the English, on penetrating into the town, found the place deserted.

Scarcely, however, was Raleigh's victory complete—scarcely had he, with the loss of ten men, taken Fayal, when Essex sailed into the road. The jealousy of the earl was immediately aroused; and Raleigh, being sent for, went on board, and was "entertained with a grim look."

"I can not understand, Sir Walter," said Essex, in an angry tone, "how you could think of landing. Know you not that none may, on pain of death, do that without the general's leave?"

"Indeed, my Lord of Essex," answered Raleigh, calmly, "I know full well that captains, masters of ships, and the others, are within com-

pass of law, but not the three prime commanders, of whom I am one. For the rest," he added,
"I waited long for your coming, and would have
longer waited but for being provoked by the islanders."

The explanation of Raleigh was so plausible,
and the absurdity of a quarrel so apparent, that,
after some mediation on the part of Lord Howard of Effingham, matters were accommodated,
and the fleet sailed for Gratiosa. At this island
Essex proposed to wait the Spanish galleons,
which were now daily expected; but, a pilot
having persuaded him that the harbor was dangerous, he gave orders for sailing to Villa Franca,
where he remained for some time, and found
much booty. But fatal, so far as concerned the
plunder, had been the pilot's advice; for scarcely
had the English fleet disappeared from Gratiosa
when the Spanish treasure-fleet came in sight.
Warned, however, of the enemies that were on
the watch, the galleons fled with all speed, and
soon made themselves secure in the harbor of
Terceira.

It does not appear that the English commanders had hitherto put themselves in the way of
meeting the Spanish armada destined for Ireland.
Nevertheless, they deemed themselves justified in
sailing homeward. But their voyage was the reverse of prosperous. A fearful storm dispersed
and shattered the fleet, and it was with difficulty

that the ships, tossed and weather-beaten, found their way back to Plymouth.

But Philip's armada had meanwhile been on the sea, and had been treated by the elements with still less ceremony than Elizabeth's fleet. In fact, the same wind and waves that had frustrated the aspirations of Elizabeth's commanders, had utterly destroyed the prospects of Philip's enterprise. The only Spanish ship that reached the territories of England's queen was a ship cast by the waves into Dartmouth; and Philip, no longer hoping for success in his attempt on England, abandoned the idea on which he had expended so much blood and treasure.

From the time of his adventure at Fayal to the end of Queen Elizabeth's reign, Raleigh, freed by a melancholy catastrophe from the rivalry of Essex, continued to flourish. As captain of the guard, he attended Elizabeth to the tilt-yard and on her visits to the great nobles, and gratified the royal lady by the magnificence of his attire. At tournaments he wore splendid silver armor, and a sword-hilt studded with rubies, pearls, and diamonds; and on state occasions his shoes glittered with precious stones, and his dress was covered with jewels valued at the enormous sum of sixty thousand pounds. In 1600, when appointed governor of Jersey, his life was brilliant and prosperous; but dark and troublous days were fast approaching.

One morning in the month of March, 1603, Queen Elizabeth died at Richmond, and James, King of Scots, hastened to leave the impoverished north for the fairer and wealthier dominion which he had inherited. Raleigh, who aspired to the highest offices which James had to bestow, soon found himself deprived of Durham House and the posts he had occupied under Elizabeth. In fact, Cecil, who was all powerful, regarded Raleigh with extreme jealousy; and, though in other days associated in many a political enterprise with the brilliant adventurer, had now no scruple in ministering to his ruin. At all events, it happened that James had not been three months on the English throne ere Raleigh was accused of participating in a conspiracy with the King of Spain to place the crown of England on the head of James's cousin, the Lady Arabella Stewart. After a long trial at Winchester, Raleigh was found guilty, and sentence of death was pronounced.

For a month Raleigh remained at Winchester, expecting each day to be his last. At one time he was even warned to prepare for execution. But James, changing his mind, suddenly sent a reprieve, and the captive knight was removed as a state prisoner to the Tower of London.

Among Raleigh's possessions were the castle and estate of Sherborne, in Dorset, and in Sherborne he had taken considerable pride. With fine taste, and at a lavish expense, he had deco-

rated the castle and laid out the grounds; and
he had beautified the place "with orchards, gardens, and groves, of much variety and great delight." At the beginning of his troubles he had,
as a matter of prudence, conveyed Sherborne to
his eldest son, Walter. But, unfortunately, a legal flaw was discovered in the deed of convey-
ance, and the king availed himself of the circumstance to bestow the property on one of his miserable minions.

At a tournament at Westminster, a Scottish adventurer, named Robert Carr, of humble origin,
but of singular beauty, appeared as page to Lord
Dingwall. During the chivalrous pageant, Carr,
having to present the shield of his lord to the
king, was, while doing so, thrown from his horse
with such force that his leg was broken. James,
struck with the handsome appearance of Carr, at
once metamorphosed him into a favorite; and
the Scottish adventurer, whose pedigree was sufficiently obscure, and whose intellect was still
more obscure than his pedigree, entered upon
that part which led to his being Earl of Somerset, and one of the most atrocious criminals who
ever breathed English air.

Raleigh learned while in the Tower that James
intended to bestow Sherborne on Carr, and from
prison addressed a letter warning the young favorite not to accept of the inheritance of children
who were as unprotected as the fatherless. "Sir,"

wrote the captive, "seeing your fair day is now in the dawn, and mine drawn to the evening, your own virtues and the king's grace assuring you of many favors and of much honor, I beseech you not to begin your first building upon the ruins of the innocent, and that their sorrows, with mine, may not attend your first plantation. . . . I therefore trust, sir, that you will not be the first who shall kill us outright, cut down the tree with the fruit, and undergo the curse of them that enter the fields of the fatherless."

This letter failed to produce any effect upon Carr, and Lady Raleigh, the Elizabeth Throgmorton of old, and a woman of high spirit, resolved to make an attempt to move the heart of the king. Obtaining access to the royal presence, and holding her children by the hands, she threw herself on her knees, and implored him to spare the remnant of their ruined fortunes. But the unfortunate lady, instead of satisfaction, got an answer which roused the bitterness of her spirit.

"I maun hae the land," replied James, in a conclusive tone, "I maun hae the land for Carr."

"And may God," exclaimed the lady, as she rose, no longer able to restrain her wrath, "may God punish those unjust men who have brought ruin on my husband and on his house."

It would seem that the misfortunes of Raleigh proved exceedingly inconvenient to his old acquaintance, the Countess of Desmond. Raleigh's estates in Ireland were granted to Richard Boyle, Earl of Cork; and the venerable dowager, who had hitherto been allowed to remain in peace at Inchequin, was forthwith ejected from the castle. But the countess, though she had seen about a hundred and forty summers, and twice renewed her teeth, had still spirit enough to determine on obtaining redress. According to tradition, she embarked for England, landed at Bristol, and traveled on foot to London to present a petition to the queen. What reception she met with at a court where, more than a hundred and twenty years earlier, she had danced with princes of the great house of Plantagenet, is not recorded; but it appears that, notwithstanding her journey to London, and her fourteen decades of years, she died neither of fatigue nor of old age. Indeed, it is stated that she might have lived much longer had she not, in attempting to climb a tree to gather nuts, met with an accident which brought on a fever that caused her death.

Meantime Raleigh bore his captivity with philosophic calmness. Though precluded from pursuing his career as a man of action, he did not yield to indolence. Reconciling himself to his situation, he occupied his time with study, fitted up a laboratory in the Tower Gardens, commenced his "History of the World," and, as years rolled on, recommended himself to Henry,

Prince of Wales, by writing two pamphlets against the project of uniting that brave and gallant boy to a princess of Savoy.

"It is unfortunate," said some one to Henry, "that Sir Walter Raleigh should be the inmate of a prison."

"Yes," said the prince, in a tone of regret; "no king in Europe but my father would keep such a bird in such a cage."

Raleigh's captivity, however, was not very rigorous. Two men were allowed him as attendants; several of his friends were occasionally admitted to visit him; his wife and eldest son, Walter, were permitted to live with him in the Tower; and his youngest son, Carew, was born within the walls of the metropolitan fortress. With the society of his family and his friends, and the excitement of his chemical experiments, Raleigh's time passed gradually away; and he had been nine years a prisoner, when, in the autumn of 1612, the Prince of Wales died at St. James's, and Sir Walter's last chance of recovering liberty appeared to vanish.

But Raleigh was not a man to hold council with despair. Ambitious, and eager as ever for adventurous enterprise, he determined to be free. Circumstances were not unpropitious. Cecil was dead. Robert Carr, Earl of Somerset, was immured in the Tower for crimes of the deepest dye; George Villiers was in a fair way to become Duke of Buckingham, and the most influential man in England; and James, impoverished by lavish grants to favorites, was at his wits' end for money. Raleigh, by a bribe to Villiers, obtained his liberty; and, by a gorgeous picture of the gold mine of which he had twenty years earlier seen traces in Guiana, tempted James to commission him to undertake an expedition. After having raised above thirty thousand pounds by calling in an old debt and selling Lady Raleigh's estate at Mitcham, and "brought many gentlemen of quality to venture their estates and persons upon the design," he hoisted his flag on board the "Destiny," and set sail, in the spring of 1617, with a fleet of fourteen ships. With him went Walter Raleigh, his eldest son, and Captain Keymis, a brave officer, who had accompanied him to Guiana in 1595, and since suffered many hardships as his adherent.

The commencement of the voyage was not such as to elevate the spirits of the adventurers. A storm drove the ships into the Cove of Cork; and, having been detained there till August, they did not pass the Cape de Verd Islands till October, and did not reach Guiana till the middle of November. Meanwhile disease had made fearful ravages. Forty-two men died on board the "Destiny;" and Raleigh, during the voyage, suffered from a violent fever. But his courage was unimpaired; and after landing and meeting with

M

an enthusiastic reception from his old friends the Indians on the coast, he addressed a letter to Lady Raleigh, which rung with his old spirit.

"We," he wrote, "are still strong enough, I hope, to perform what we have undertaken, if the diligent care at London to make our strength known to the Spanish king by his embassador have not taught that monarch to fortify all the entrances against us. . . . . To tell you that I might here be king of the Indians were a vanity. But my name hath still lived among them here. They feed me with fresh meat and all that the country yields. All offer to obey me."

It soon appeared that the Spaniards were up in arms, and prepared to fight desperately for the country. Raleigh's condition was such as to unfit him for action. However willing his spirit might be, his flesh was weak. Indeed, he had been so reduced by fever that he could not even walk. Under these circumstances, he took up his station at Trinidad, and sent Captain Keymis up the Oronoco with five ships in search of gold, with instructions, in the event of the mine proving rich, to establish himself there, and, in the event of its proving poor, to bring away a few baskets of ore, to convince King James that the scheme was not altogether visionary.

In December, Keymis, accompanied by young Walter Raleigh, commenced his voyage up the river; and, not without having to stand the fire of the Spanish forts, arrived off St. Thomas, which the Spaniards had recently built on the right bank. Landing, he took up a position between St. Thomas and the mine, but without any serious intention of attacking the town. During the darkness of night, however, the Spaniards, breaking into his camp, butchered several of his men; and, when morning dawned, the English made an assault. A sanguinary conflict then took place. Young Walter Raleigh, leading the attack, cut down with his own hand one of the principal Spanish officers, but fell when charging courageously at the head of a company of pikemen; and the English, who loved him dearly, became furious at his death, rushed madly forward, slew the governor, set fire to the houses, and chased the Spaniards to the hills and woods.

But, after taking possession of St. Thomas, the adventurers were sadly disappointed. Not finding any treasure to reward their exertions, they became refractory and mutinous. Keymis, pained by the loss of young Raleigh, and confounded by the clamor of the survivors, could form no plan of operations. At first he attempted to conduct his party higher up the river; but his difficulties hourly increased, and after receiving a volley from a body of Spaniards lying in ambush, which killed several of his men, he made the best retreat he could, and hastened to rejoin Raleigh at Trinidad.

The scene which occurred when Raleigh and Keymis met was one which the brave captain could hardly have anticipated. Raleigh, giving way to anger, accused Keymis of cowardice and incapacity; Keymis, yielding to despair, shot himself in his cabin. Immediately all was confusion in the fleet. Several of the captains drew off, and hurriedly sailed for England; and Raleigh, left with only five ships, and overwhelmed with adversity, sailed down the North American coast, refitted at Newfoundland, experienced a fresh mutiny, and after keeping his men together simply by holding out hopes of plundering the Spanish galleons, contrived, in the month of June, 1618, to reach Plymouth.

Meanwhile King James, having been wrought on by the Spanish embassador, and believing at the time that the Spanish court would bestow the hand of the Infanta on Prince Charles, promised that Raleigh should be brought to justice for the affair at St. Thomas. No sooner, therefore, did Sir Walter land at Plymouth, than he was arrested, and conveyed to London to be lodged in the Tower. Feigning to be sick, to be mad, to be plague-struck, he obtained permission to remain for a few days at his own house before being incarcerated, and made a last effort to escape to France. Every thing seemed to promise success. A bark, engaged by Captain King, one of his old officers, was in waiting near Tilbury Fort; a safe-

conduct, privately furnished by the French charge
d'affaires, was in his pocket; and he was quietly
descending the Thames, when a kinsman, who
pretended to be assisting him through the toils,
most basely betrayed him.

Brought back to London, Raleigh was lodged
once more in the Tower. It was already resolved
that he should be executed, and no effort was
omitted to make out that he had been guilty of a
capital crime. This, however, proved most difficult; and, in the end, James ordered that the sentence pronounced fifteen years before at Winchester should be put in force. Accordingly, Raleigh, though suffering from fever and ague, was
made to rise from bed, removed to Westminster,
and, after some formalities, placed in the Gate-
house to await his doom.

It was now the 28th of October, and Raleigh
requested that he might be allowed a short time
to settle his affairs. The answer was that his execution would take place in the Old Palace Yard
at nine o'clock next morning, and he prepared to
meet his fate with the calm courage of a man who
feared not death. That evening he had a last
long interview with his wife; and, as she took
leave of him at midnight, he spoke in a cheerful,
even a jocular strain.

"I may tell you," said the unfortunate woman
at parting, as her tears flowed fast, "that they
have granted me the privilege of disposing of
your body."

"It is well, Bess," said Raleigh, with a smile; "it is well that you may dispose of that dead, which you had not always the disposing of when alive."

Raleigh was now left to the solitude of his prison, and to those reflections which occupy the mind of a man whose soul is about to go to judgment. Early in the morning, however, he was attended by the Dean of Westminster, who administered the sacrament. Raleigh received the consolations of religion with profound reverence, expressed his faith in the mediation of the Redeemer of mankind, and freely forgave all his enemies, even the kinsman by whom he had been betrayed.

Before being led to execution Raleigh breakfasted heartily. After the meal he smoked his pipe, as was his wont, and drank a cup of sack with evident relish.

"Does the sack please you?" inquired the jailer.

"Ay," answered Raleigh, "'tis a good drink, if a man might tarry by it."

"It is sad to die in such a way," some one remarked.

"I would rather thus end my days," replied Raleigh, "than by a burning fever; and I thank God, who hath imparted to me strength of mind never to fear death."

Raleigh now employed himself in changing his

dress. He laid aside his usual attire, donned a plain mourning suit of black satin, and threw over all a black velvet night-gown. A little before nine o'clock he declared that he was ready, and then, attended by the sheriffs of London and the Dean of Westminster, he walked forth to enact the last scene of his remarkable life.

The scaffold was erected in Old Palace Yard, and thither lords, ladies, courtiers, and persons of every degree had crowded to witness the execution. Indeed, the press was so great that, ere reaching the scaffold, Raleigh swooned away. On arriving at the steps, however, he recovered; and mounting with apparent ease, he saluted Lord Arundel and other friends in the crowd with his usual courtliness of manner. Though enfeebled with sickness, his appearance was still noble and impressive; and, silence having been obtained, he addressed the assemblage in a masterly speech, which proved that his intellect was vigorous as in earlier days.

"The morning is cold, Sir Walter," said the sheriff; "would it not be well for you to come down and warm yourself before saying your prayers?"

"No, good Mr. Sheriff," answered Raleigh, "let us dispatch; for within this quarter of an hour my ague will come upon me; and if I be not dead before that, my enemies will say I quake for fear now I am going to God."

"In what faith do you die?" asked the Dean of Westminster.

"In the faith professed by the Church of England," answered Raleigh; "hoping to have my sins washed away, and to be saved by the merits and precious blood of our Savior."

The scaffold was then cleared, and Raleigh, kneeling down, prayed fervently. Rising, he threw off his gown and doublet, and turned to the executioner.

"Show me the axe," he said; and, seeing that this was not immediately done, he exclaimed, "I pray thee let me see it. Dost thou think I am afraid of it? 'Tis a sharp medicine," he added to the sheriff, as he took it in his hand and ran his finger along the edge, "but a sound cure for all diseases."

"I ask your forgiveness," said the executioner, kneeling.

"Be satisfied," said Raleigh, with a smile, laying his hand on the man's shoulder. "I most cheerfully forgive thee, only strike not till I give the signal; and then fear nothing, but strike home."

"Be pleased to place yourself so that your face shall look toward the east," suggested one of the officials, as Raleigh lay down on the block.

"Little matters it," answered he, "how the head lies, provided the heart is right."

After having occupied himself for a while with

prayer, Raleigh gave the signal; and after some hesitation on the executioner's part, the axe fell. At two strokes the head was severed from the body; and the quantity of blood that gushed out showed that, though Raleigh was in his sixty-sixth year, his constitution was still as vigorous as his intellect. After the head had, as usual on such occasions, been held up to the view of the crowd, it was put into a red bag, and, with the body, placed in a mourning coach to be conveyed to Lady Raleigh. The head was embalmed and preserved by the widowed lady with pious care, as a melancholy memorial of the husband whom she had loved so faithfully and so well.

THE EARL OF CUMBERLAND.

One day, when Queen Elizabeth was keeping her court at Whitehall, a remarkable personage of somewhat haughty air and eccentric aspect, with a strong, but agile and exquisitely handsome form, dark hair, black eyes, full cheeks, a proud expression of countenance, and a face that bore the marks of much exposure to wind and sun, was admitted to an audience, after having returned from a long voyage. During the ceremony the queen happened to drop her glove, and the eccentric-looking individual, whom she was evidently in a mood to honor, stepped forward, raised it, and presented it on his knee.

"Nay, cousin," said the queen, "keep the glove for our sake."

"If it so please your majesty," replied he, rising with a grace, and speaking with a courtly ease which showed that he was not the first of his race who had figured at courts. "And I vow that it shall be richly adorned with diamonds, and worn in my hat on all state occasions."

The hero of this little scene was an object of curiosity, both on account of his own exploits and those of his ancestors. He bore a historic name, and could boast of achievements which history was destined to record. He was the head of the great family of Clifford, and one of the bravest of those naval heroes who, in the Elizabethan period, humbled the pride of Spain.

The Cliffords, who came in with the Conqueror, ranked high and fought well among the ancient nobles of England. After taking part in the Barons' wars, in the Welsh wars, the Scottish wars, and the French wars, they ventured into the wars of the Roses, and passionately espoused the Lancastrian cause. In that terrible struggle of thirty years they suffered severely. One Lord Clifford fell at St. Alban's; and his son John, known as "the Black-faced Lord," having in a moment of vindictive fury slain Edmund Plantagenet, the boy Earl of Rutland, was denounced as the "Butcher," and slain without mercy at Towton. The "Black-faced" Clifford left a son, on whom the Yorkists were so strongly inclined to visit the sins of his sire that he was under the necessity of passing his boyhood and youth disguised as a shepherd in Cumberland. After the battle of Bosworth, however, he emerged, at the age of thirty-one, from the "fells," took possession of his ancestral castles, married, and had a son, who betook himself to the life of an outlaw. Being afterward tempted back to regular life, the outlaw was created Earl of Cumberland, and was succeeded at his death by his son Henry, a man of studious and scholarly habits.

At the beginning of his life, Henry, second Earl of Cumberland, being in favor with the Tudors, was furnished by that family with a wife in the person of one of their kinswomen, Eleanor Brandon, daughter of a man who, in defiance of ridicule, ranked as Duke of Suffolk. This lady, whose alliance proved somewhat inconvenient to the heir of the Cliffords, died in 1547; and the earl, afflicted by her death, abandoned court, retired to the Craven, and suffered so severely in health that his life was despaired of. One day, indeed, his physicians thought him dead, and in deference to the fashion observed at that period in the case of men of rank, he was laid on a table and covered with a hearsecloth of black velvet. It happened, however, that some of his attendants, by whom he was greatly beloved, descried symptoms of life; and, having been put to bed, he gradually recovered his health and spirits so far as to think of consoling himself with a second spouse. Accordingly, he, about 1553, ventured again on matrimony. Perhaps the earl had seen enough of court life and court ladies. At all events, he was married at Kirk Oswald; and his bride was Anne, daughter of Lord Dacre of the North, described as "a very domestic woman, who was never at or near London in her life."

It was at Castle Brougham, on the 8th of Au-

gust, 1558, that Anne, Countess of Cumberland,
gave birth to an heir to the house of Clifford.
The boy was named George, and regarded with
pride by his parents. Being, however, of opinion
that "home-keeping youths have ever homely
wits," they sent him to live at Battle under the
auspices of Lord Montagu, who had married his
maternal aunt; and there the heir of the Cliffords
was being drilled into the accomplishments of the
period, and listening to stories of Sir Francis
Drake's voyages, when in 1569 his father died at
a northern castle.

At the time when George Clifford became Earl
of Cumberland he was eleven years of age, and
he was given as a ward to Francis Russell, Earl
of Bedford, whose father had acquired wealth by
plundering the Church, and rank by pandering to
the passions of the Eighth Henry. The young
earl was probably at the time indifferent to such
matters. But in after days he doubtless found,
to his bitter experience, the serious inconvenience
of being connected in such a way with such a
mock patrician.

Meanwhile, Cumberland was fortunate in having a mother eager for his prosperity and welfare.
At an early age he was sent to Cambridge, and
at that seat of learning, with Dr. Whitgift, afterward Archbishop of Canterbury, for his tutor, he
devoted himself with enthusiasm to the study of
mathematics. But the name of Sir Francis Drake

and the adventures of the "Golden Hind" were
soon on every tongue, and Cumberland's mind
was gradually drawn toward navigation and sea
voyages.

But as yet the young earl had not the power
of gratifying his ambition. Indeed, Francis Russell, Earl of Bedford, was not yet done with his
ward. On the 24th of June, 1577, Cumberland,
then nineteen, found himself at Southwark, enacting the part of bridegroom in an important ceremony, in which Margaret Russell, Bedford's
daughter, figured as bride. In the church of St.
Mary's Overy, on that day, the young patrician,
whose ancestors had for six centuries been es-
pousing Bigods and Bohuns, found himself united,
for better or for worse, to a damsel who owed
her position to the fact of her grandfather having
devoted his career to sacrilege and servility.

Of this marriage, two sons, who died early, and
a daughter, who survived her parents, were the
issue. Their existence, for a time, kept matters
tolerable. But a marriage contracted between
such parties, under such circumstances, was not
likely to prove permanently happy. As years
passed over, they not unnaturally had their quarrels; and in 1586, Cumberland, weary perhaps of
domestic strife, resolved on fitting out a fleet,
and sailing on an expedition against the Spaniards. .

But it was no easy matter to undertake such

an expedition. An adventurer had to create his
materials, not merely to place himself at the head
of a force already prepared. Nor when the
queen's ships could be borrowed was the circumstance in all respects advantageous; for so invet-
erate were the scruples of the council, that few
would be fettered with their instructions. Cumberland, on one occasion, when offered a ship
from the royal navy, positively refused to ham-
per himself. "No, I thank you," he said; "such
are your scruples about hazarding her majesty's
cordage and timber in close conflict, and laying
valuable property alongside the enemy, that I
prefer taking merchantmen only."

In spite of many difficulties, Cumberland, in
1587, equipped a fleet for the South Seas. But,
strangely enough, instead of accompanying it, he
sailed with Sir Roger Williams and a party of
volunteers to relieve Sluys, then besieged by the
Duke of Parma. The enterprise proved unsuccessful, and Cumberland returned to England
with the ambition of rivaling the exploits of
Drake.

While Cumberland was maturing his project,
and dreaming of treasure-houses and treasure-
mules, Spanish galleons and Portuguese caracks,
news of the Spanish armada being about to leave
the Tagus roused all England to arms; and the
earl, embarking in the "Elizabeth Bonaventure,"
joined the lord high admiral in the Channel.

During that exciting week when the armada coasted the southern shores of England and made its way up the Channel, assailed by the English squadrons, and in vain expecting Parma to come to the rescue, Cumberland highly distinguished himself by his skill and courage; and when the united fleet anchored off Cadiz, and the English commanders were within an ace of destroying the enemy by the fire-ships, the earl displayed a degree of knowledge in naval affairs that won him honor and excited admiration.

While Drake and Essex were preparing their great armament to beard Philip in his own territories, Cumberland persevered with his preparations for an adventure on his own account; and Elizabeth, no longer keeping on terms with her Continental foe, not only furnished the earl with a royal commission, but lent him one of her own ships, named the "Golden Lion." Every thing being ready in October, Cumberland set sail, with high hopes of success. But the expedition had not a prosperous commencement. Baffled by contrary winds and tossed by tempests, the little fleet was in the utmost danger; and the earl, after having been under the necessity of cutting away the mainmast of his own ship, was at length obliged to return to England, not perhaps without disagreeable anticipations of being sneered at by those who wished him ill, and of being laughed at by those who wished him well.

But Cumberland was not to be put down by the scorn of foes or by the ridicule of friends. In June, 1589, he was again ready for sea. With a ship named the "Victory," borrowed from the royal navy, and three ships of his own, on board of which was Edward Wright, the celebrated mathematician, he again put to sea, and, sailing for the Azores, succeeded in taking Fayal, dismantling the fort, and bringing away fifty-eight pieces of artillery.

Pursuing his success, and attacking the Spaniards whenever he fell in with them, Cumberland took many prizes. Indeed, during the cruise he sent home twenty-eight ships of various burden as evidence of his success. But he did not find all of them an easy prey. Off St. Michael's he encountered a Brazilian ship of formidable proportions, and laid the "Victory" alongside. A desperate battle took place; and the earl, being in the hottest of the conflict, was not only severely scorched, but received several wounds. Nor was this the worst. The change of climate and the want of water produced much disease among the crew, and the adventurers suffered fearful horrors. After having lost hundreds of their comrades, however, they, about the beginning of December, reached the coast of Ireland and anchored in Bantry Bay.

Most men of Cumberland's rank would now have given up maritime enterprise as too perilous

N

and unprofitable to be pursued; but he was not inclined to yield to adverse circumstances. Restless and energetic, he equipped another little fleet, and in May, 1591, again gave his sails to the wind. His success, however, was indifferent, and, after cruising for some months in the Mediterranean, he returned to England.

Notwithstanding his numerous adventures, Cumberland had not yet reached the age of forty, and his spirit soon prompted him to tempt the seas once more. After having, in 1593, been admitted to the Order of the Garter, as a recognition of his services to the queen and the country, he resolved on a new voyage, and fitted out another fleet. Having equipped four ships of his own, and borrowed the "Golden Lion" and the "Elizabeth Bonaventure" from the navy, he embarked at Plymouth, and, hoisting his flag on board the "Golden Lion," set sail. But fortune proved quite adverse. After capturing a convoy of great value, Cumberland's health broke down; and after struggling against sickness, he was obliged to resign the command of the fleet to Monson, and return to Plymouth.

At Plymouth, Cumberland took to bed for a time, overcome with sickness and disappointment; but a favorable change soon occurred; and, recovering gradually, he rose from his bed, applied himself to ship-building, and commenced the construction of a formidable man-of-war.

This vessel, of nine hundred tons, was launched at Deptford, destined for service against the Spaniards, and named by the queen the "Scourge of Malice."

With the idea of capturing Philip's Portuguese caracks and American treasure-fleet, Cumberland now equipped six vessels, obtained the queen's commission, and sailed in search of exploits. For months he incessantly harassed the Spaniards, but without the result which he expected. In fact, the Spaniards were now constantly on their guard; and Cumberland, after waiting long, found the season pass over without the caracks or galleons making their appearance. Under these circumstances, he resolved on a bold dash at some of the Spanish settlements in the West Indies, and sailed to Porto Rico.

The temptation to attack a Spanish settlement was infinitely less than when Drake led his men into Nombre de Dios, seized the mules on their way from Panama, and burned house by house at Carthagena till the ransom he demanded was forthcoming. Events had made Philip fully aware of the danger to which his West Indian possessions were exposed, and he had taken every precaution to guard them against the attacks of the English. "While the King of Spain guarded the head and heart of his dominions in Europe," says Fuller, "he left his long legs in America open to blows; till, finding them to smart, being beaten black and blue by the English, he learned to defend them at last."

Accordingly, Porto Rico was no longer without defenses; and St. John's, its capital town, built, after the Spanish model, on a small island within the harbor, on the north side of the principal island, was defended as well as the entrance of the harbor with forts and batteries. It was at Porto Rico that Drake and Hawkins had met with a reception that broke the hearts of both; and it was while lying at anchor before St. John's that a shot killed two of Drake's officers in his cabin, and knocked from under the conqueror of the armada the stool on which, shortly before his death, he sat drinking a cup of beer. Every where the Spaniards were on the alert; and, as was remarked, "cannon balls were more plentiful than pieces of eight had been on former occasions."

Formidable, however, as might have been the aspect of affairs, Cumberland was not daunted; and as, with eyes flashing fire, he stood upon the deck of the "Victory," he communicated to the companions of his voyage some portion of the ancestral valor that glowed at his heart. Encouraged by his example, the adventurers attacked with such determination that they carried all before them, and Cumberland found himself master of a place which Drake and Hawkins had not even ventured to assail.

But honor was all that Cumberland gained by this achievement. Hardly were the adventurers in possession, when that fever which prevails in those latitudes about the end of summer attacked them with merciless severity. Man after man yielded to the climate. Within forty days, seven hundred sickened and died; and the earl, obliged to abandon his conquest, sailed with the sad survivors for England. In the month of October, 1598, he again set foot on his native shores.

After this Cumberland undertook no more voyages. Accommodating himself to the circumstances of the times, the earl lived at peace and at home. Domestic happiness he could not hope to enjoy, for he was separated from his wife, his daughter lived with her mother, and his sons were dead. But he amused himself with horse-racing and tournaments; and the queen evinced her appreciation of his unbought services by constituting him her champion in the tilt-yard, and by granting him a more substantial privilege in the shape of a patent for the exportation of cloth.

When Elizabeth expired, and King James had the crown of England placed on his learned forehead, Cumberland would appear to have been among the malcontents; and he is mentioned by Sully, who then came to England as embassador from Henry the Fourth, the great King of France, along with Raleigh, Cobham, and Northumberland, as being men who "breathed a spirit of sedition, and were ready to undertake any thing in favor of novelties, even were it against the king himself." But if so, the earl was either more prudent or more fortunate than his confederates. Instead of being implicated in plots and sent to the Tower, he was, besides being nominated one of the new king's councilors, appointed warden of the West and Middle Marches, lieutenant general of Cumberland, Northumberland, Westmoreland, and Newcastle-on-Tyne, keeper of Tynedale and Redesdale, governor of Harbottle, and captain general of the city and castle of Carlisle.

Cumberland did not live long to exercise his extensive jurisdiction. Wounds and fatigues incurred during his voyages had left their impression behind; and after having carried the Golden Rod on the occasion when Prince Charles—afterward Charles the First—was created Duke of York, his health gave way. Finding himself sick unto death, in the autumn of 1605 he made his will, leaving his goods and chattels to his daughter, and his estates and castles to his younger brother; and then, turning his thoughts toward heaven, expressed contrition for his sins. The earl was, during his last hours, attended by his wife and daughter; and in their presence, in the Duchy House, Savoy, he, on the 30th of October, 1605, penitently yielded up his soul.

The body of Cumberland was conveyed to the

north, and interred at Skipton, in Craven, among
the bones of those ancestors who had so often
and so gallantly fought England's battles in the
days of the Plantagenets; and the memory of the
patrician seaman who had taken Fayal and Porto
Rico was long held by the English in affectionate
regard as a man of noble mind and great natural
parts, who, at much private cost, had at critical
periods courageously done his duty against the
enemies of his country.

ADMIRAL BLAKE.

ABOUT the close of Queen Elizabeth's reign, Humphrey Blake, a man of somewhat ancient family, lived in Bridgewater, and carried on trade with Spain. Not being vowed to celibacy, Humphrey Blake espoused a lady of the name of Williams, who brought him a small estate called Plansfield, and made him father of several sons. Of these, the eldest was the renowned admiral of the Commonwealth, and one of England's greatest naval heroes.

Robert Blake was born at Bridgewater in the autumn of 1599, and educated at the Grammar School of his native town. Having a love of books and a turn for learning, Blake was thought likely to excel as a scholar, and was sent at the age of sixteen to the University of Oxford. During his residence at the University he made himself remarkable for regularity and industry, and, after some years, became ambitious of obtaining a scholarship in one of the colleges. Accordingly, on the occasion of a vacancy at Merton, he offered himself as one of the candidates. His ambition, however, was not gratified. In fact, Sir

Henry Saville, at that time warden, had an eccentric dislike for men who were not six feet in height; and the circumstance of Blake wanting several inches of that stature is supposed to have lost him his election.

For some years after being disappointed of a fellowship Blake remained at Oxford. Pursuing his studies, he in due time took the degree of master of arts. But the dream in which he had indulged of passing life within the precincts of a college was not to be realized. About 1625 he was summoned home; and after the death of his father he undertook the duty of bringing up the numerous family of which he was the eldest. Imagine a thick-set young man midway between the ages of twenty and thirty, about five feet six in height, with a fair complexion, an expression which gave dignity to his countenance, simple in his tastes and habits, somewhat austere in manner and blunt in address, with a dauntless determination and an iron will, and you will have some idea of Robert Blake when he left the University of Oxford and returned to his native town in Somersetshire.

Blake would seem to have been by nature a Puritan and by conviction a Republican. When, therefore, the disputes between King Charles and the Parliament began to agitate the country, he appeared in the character of a Roundhead, and had the distinction of being elected member for

Bridgewater; in 1645 he was returned to the Long Parliament as member for Taunton; and when an appeal was made to the sword, he took up arms with alacrity. He was one of the first adherents of the Parliament who brought troops into the field; and he distinguished himself in several of those encounters with which Cavaliers and Roundheads commenced the great civil war.

As events marched on, Blake won high reputation in the struggle raging throughout England. After taking a conspicuous part in the defense of Bristol, somewhat pusillanimously surrendered by Fiennes to Prince Rupert, he threw himself into Lyme, and successfully held that fishing town against Prince Maurice; and then, seizing Taunton, he maintained himself there against the Cavaliers, under circumstances which much influenced the fortune of the war, and raised his reputation high among Roundhead warriors. It was on the sea, however, and against foreign foes, that Blake was destined to perform the exploits which were to make his name immortal.

Blake, though a sincere Republican, appears to have had no sympathy with the violent proceedings of those men who imbrued their hands in the king's blood. Indeed, though opposed to monarchy, he protested strongly against the execution of Charles, and declared that "he would as freely venture his life to save the king as ever he had done to serve the Parliament." It was probably deemed politic by men with ulterior views to get so pure a patriot out of the way, and the necessity for clearing the narrow seas of Cavaliers who had taken to piracy presented a favorable opportunity. Accordingly, Blake was requested to assume the command of the Commonwealth's forces at sea; and, at the age of fifty, he became England's admiral.

At that time the vanquished adherents of the Stuarts had fortified the Channel islands, and made themselves most formidable by piratical excursions. Roaming the seas, they terrified mariners, plundered traders, and conveyed their booty to Scilly, of which they boasted they would make a second Venice. Blake's first enterprises were undertaken against the corsair-cavaliers; and having cleared the narrow seas of the enemies of the new republic, he reduced the Channel Islands to submission with a degree of energy which won him high renown as a naval warrior.

While engaged in operations against the unfortunate Royalists, Blake had reason to take offense at the attitude assumed by the admirals of France, and resolved on seizing an early opportunity of teaching the French government a wholesome lesson. Accordingly, one morning in the spring of 1651, when the English admiral was in the Straits, the look-out man perceived a French sail in the offing. Making a signal for his fleet to follow, Blake bore down upon the strange ship, which proved to be a French vessel of considerable force. At the time it was not generally known that there was war between the two countries, and the Frenchman, on being hailed, suspected no hostile intention.

"Monsieur le Capitaine," shouted Blake, through his speaking-trumpet, "will you come on board my ship?"

"Yes," answered the Frenchman.

"Now," said Blake, after the Frenchman made his appearance and became aware of the state of affairs, "are you willing to lay down your sword and yield at once?"

"No, admiral," replied the Frenchman, gallantly. "It is true I am in your power; but, though unprotected on your deck, I refuse either to give up my sword or my ship."

"Then," said Blake, "you are at liberty to go back to your ship, and defend her as well as you can."

The Frenchman, eager to do his duty, readily accepted Blake's offer, returned to his ship, and prepared to defend himself. But his efforts were vain. After a fight of two hours, he was under the necessity of striking his flag. On being brought on board Blake's ship, he made a polite bow, confessed that he was vanquished, and, after kissing his sword, surrendered it to his conqueror.

For the great service he had rendered the republic in clearing the narrow seas of cavalier-corsairs and in reducing the Channel Islands, Blake received the thanks of Parliament, and probably indulged in the anticipation of returning to peaceful life. But, if so, he was destined to disappointment. England was on the eve of a great naval war, and at such a time the country could not dispense with the energy and enthusiasm of such a hero.

At that period Holland was one of the wealthiest countries in Europe; and the Dutch were so intoxicated with success and prosperity that they deemed nothing was too great for them to accomplish. The men who then ruled England had ministered to Dutch vanity by an unpatriotic proposal to sink English nationality by a fusion with the Dutch republic; and the Dutch, not distinguishing between England and England's rulers, and little calculating on the spirit of the nation which the Plantagenets had governed, began to regard the islanders with some degree of contempt, and to dream of wresting from England the sovereignty of the seas. After some fruitless negotiation, war became inevitable, and Blake was selected as the man to maintain the interests of England and chastise the insolence of England's foes.

Blake did not shrink from the duty; but it was not one which could be described as "boy's play." The Dutch navy was great and powerful, elate with victory over Spain, and boasting of Van

Tromp as a naval hero, who, from his experience and his exploits, was famous as "the most renowned sea-captain of the age."

Martin Harperz Van Tromp was born in the last decade of the sixteenth century, and spent most of his life on the sea. In 1606, when a mere boy, he served in one of the ships which, under Henskerke, burned the Spanish fleet in the harbor of Gibraltar, and shared in the triumph of that memorable day. His career, however, had not been without its misfortunes. A ship in which he sailed having been taken by an English cruiser, he was compelled by his captors to serve for a time in the capacity of cabin-boy, and afterward condemned by fortune to pass years on board of Dutch traders. But he struggled through a hundred difficulties to high command in the naval service of Holland, and in 1639 won great fame by destroying the Spanish fleet destined to attack Sweden. He had now seen well-nigh threescore years; but genius, energy, experience, love of Holland, and hatred of England, indicated him as the man qualified above all others to support the honor of the Dutch and humble the pride of the English.

It was in the month of May, 1652, when Van Tromp, with a fleet of forty ships, sailed up the Channel. Blake, who was then in the Downs on board the "James," with twenty sail, immediately approached, and insisted that the Dutch should

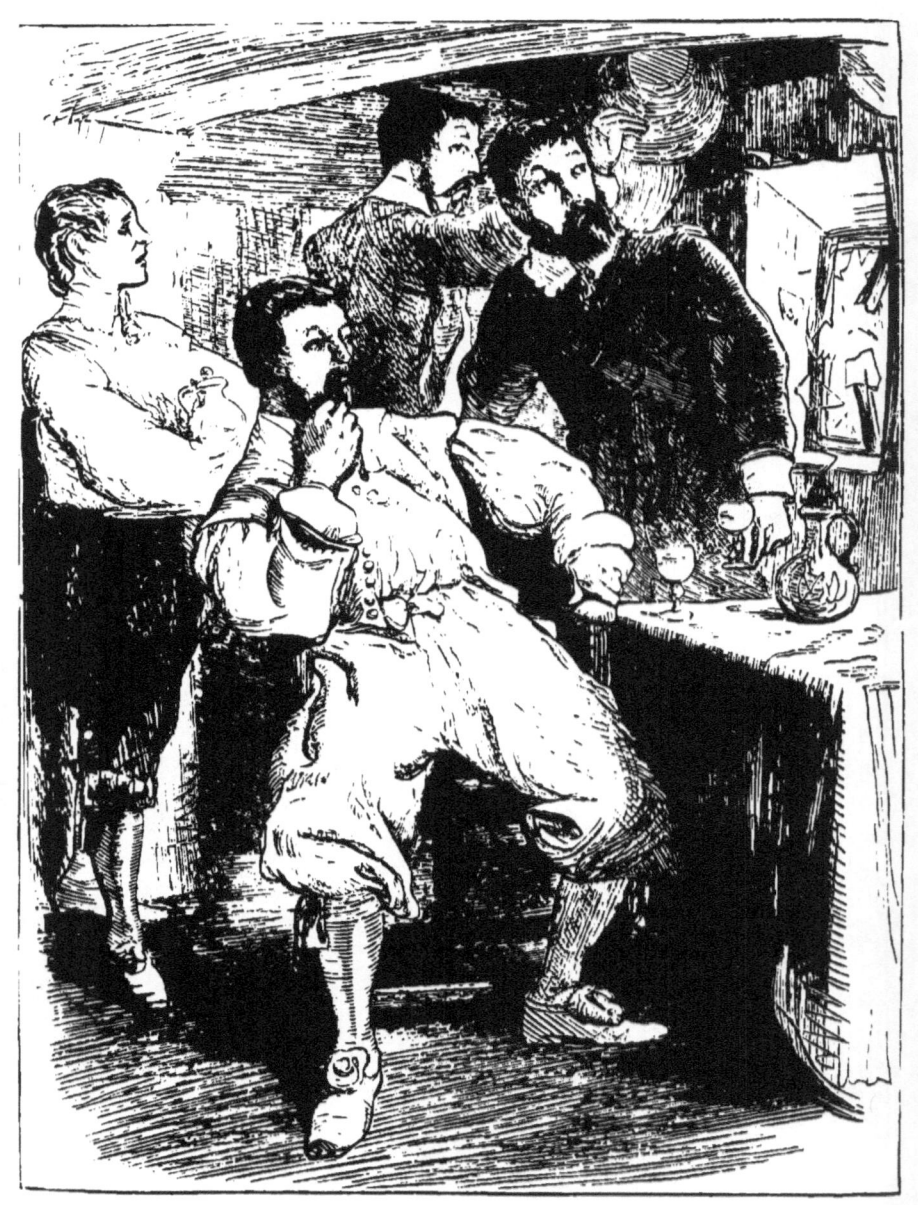

BLAKE SURPRISED BY A VOLLEY FROM VAN TROMP.

strike their topmasts to his flag, in acknowledg-
ment of England's sovereignty over the narrow
seas. Van Tromp, however, declined to show
this courtesy; and Blake, apprehensive that he
would bear away without going through the ceremony, ordered a gun to be fired at the Dutch
flag. Instead of answering this in the way that
was expected, Van Tromp replied with a broadside, which severely damaged the " James," and
smashed all her glass. Blake and his officers, who
at the time were drinking in the cabin, and holding a kind of council, were quite taken by surprise.

"Ho! ho!" exclaimed the officers with one
voice, as they started up in amazement.

"Well," roared Blake, as he curled his whis-
kers, "I take it very ill of Van Tromp to treat
my flag-ship as a brothel and break my windows."

By this time it was three o'clock in the afternoon, and before another hour the battle began.
Ship grappled ship as they chanced to fall in each
other's way, and the conflict was fiercely maintained till nightfall. By that time more than
seventy balls were lodged in the hull of the
" James." The masts were shot away, and the
rigging was torn to rags. But the men fought
on with resolute courage; and the Dutch admiral, aware that Blake's rear-guard had arrived to
take part in the action, sheered off about nine
o'clock, and made such good use of the night

O

that when morning dawned his sails were not to
be seen.

News of the encounter of Blake with Van
Tromp reached London, and the populace were
furious at the conduct of the Dutch admiral, and
eager for a decisive war. It was in vain that the
Dutch embassador attempted to explain. All
evasions and apologies were laughed to scorn,
and the two nations prepared for hostilities on a
large scale. Blake was of course intrusted with
the command of the English fleet ; and, leaving
Sir George Ayscough with a squadron in the
Downs, he sailed northward to intercept a squadron of twelve Dutch ships, acting as convoy to
busses laden with herrings caught among the
northern islands. After a sharp conflict, he sunk
three of the ships, captured nine, and, having
charged the Dutch fishermen on their peril not
to fish in the creeks and islands of England without a formal permission from the Commonwealth,
allowed the herring busses to go home.

When Blake sailed northward, Van Tromp, at
the head of a hundred and twenty sail of ships,
was lying in the Texel. No sooner, however,
did the Dutch admiral become aware of his great
adversary's absence, than he hoisted sail, and soon
appeared in the Downs. Ayscough, unprepared
to cope with the Dutch force, was fain to take
refuge under the guns of Dover Castle, and the
coast was in the utmost alarm. Fortunately a

calm, succeeded by a violent storm blowing from the land, prevented Van Tromp from doing mischief; and, disappointed in this respect, but confident of his superiority, the Dutch admiral went northward in search of Blake's squadron.

On the evening of the 5th of August the Dutch and the English fleets came in sight of each other, and Van Tromp and Blake prepared to do battle on the morrow. But the elements interfered to prevent the engagement; the wind, rising during the night, swelled into a gale; the gale became a hurricane; and the hostile admirals found themselves in no plight for action. Van Tromp was fain to run with the shattered remains of his fleet to Scheveling; while Blake, thanking God for his escape from the fury of the winds and the waves, found his way to Yarmouth.

The Dutch were in no humor to say to Van Tromp as Philip of Spain had said to the Duke of Medina Sidonia, "We did not send you out to fight the winds and waves." In fact, their indignation against their admiral was high, and their language so insulting that the veteran laid down his commission in disgust, and retired to digest his mortification in privacy. They still calculated with certainty on ultimate triumph, and, fitting out a new armament, intrusted it to the auspices of the celebrated De Witt, under whom De Ruyter figured as second in command.

Blake was undaunted by the news from Hol-

land of preparations making for his destruction.
When informed by signal, on the 28th of September, that the Dutch admirals were off the North
Foreland, he at once exhibited his characteristic
energy. "As soon," he said, "as some more of
our ships come up, bear in among them." De
Witt, on his part, had no inclination to avoid a
battle; and about four o'clock the action began.
At first the contest was hot on both sides, and
the crash of the broadsides terrific. But gradually the Dutch fire slackened, and night, closing
over the scene, put an end to the carnage. But
the Dutch were decidedly beaten; and when
morning broke De Witt ordered sails to be hoisted, and, without waiting for a renewal of the conflict, bore away for his own coast with all the
speed he could. Blake, after pursuing the Dutch
fleet into the Goree, returned in triumph to the
Downs.

Meanwhile the reception which De Witt met
from his countrymen was not such as to console
him for the castigation he had received from his
country's foes. After being mobbed, hooted,
and accused of cowardice, he offered to lay down
his commission; and Van Tromp, recalled from
retirement, and placed in command of a new fleet,
with De Ruyter as vice-admiral, appeared suddenly in the Downs.

The yr 1652 was drawing to a close, and
Blake, wh was on board the "Triumph," had no

expectation of an enemy appearing in winter. He scarcely knew that Van Tromp was stirring, and was cruising about with thirty-seven ships, when in the Downs he was suddenly faced by the Dutch admiral with eighty men-of-war and ten fire-ships. The odds against Blake were overwhelming; but it was not his wont to shirk a foe; and, on a December afternoon, he came close to the enemy off that Essex headland known as the Nase. A fierce action then commenced; and Blake exercised all his skill, while Van Tromp encouraged his men by words and gestures to exert themselves to the utmost. The "Garland" and "Bonaventure," two English ships, were boarded; and Blake, coming to attempt to recapture them, was surrounded by the enemy. The struggle was fierce. Thrice the Dutch boarded the "Triumph," and thrice they were repulsed with fearful slaughter. But Blake's ship was almost reduced to a wreck, and the whole fleet was in such danger that when night fell he availed himself of the darkness to draw off. The Dutch, meanwhile, had suffered severely. But, in the intoxication of victory, they scarcely counted their losses; and Van Tromp, left master of the Channel, was so elate that, instead of the pendant at his topmast, he hoisted a broom, to intimate his intention of sweeping the English from the seas.

Events ere long proved that such vaunting was premature. Blake vigorously applied his ener-

gies to the collection of such a fleet as would en-
able him to encounter his great foe on something
like equal terms; and early in February, 1653, he
embarked in the "Triumph," and sailed from
Queensbury with sixty men-of-war, having on
board twelve hundred troops, under the command of General Dean and George Monk, a great
soldier of fortune, afterward known to fame as
the hero of the Restoration. Burning to redeem
his defeat and humble his adversary, Blake went
in search of Van Tromp.

It was the morning of a Friday, about the middle of February, when, at break of day, Blake descried the Dutch fleet, consisting of seventy-six
men-of-war, with many merchantmen in convoy.
Immediately Blake made toward the enemy, and
Van Tromp, though surprised at the appearance
of an English fleet, prepared for an encounter.
No time was lost by either party. About eight
o'clock the action was begun by the "Triumph,"
which, being inadequately supported, received
seven hundred shots in her hull. But when the
rest of the English ships came up the fleets engaged on equal terms, and continued to fight furiously until night parted them. On Saturday
morning, Van Tromp, anxious to secure his convoy, disposed his fleet in the form of a crescent,
with the traders in the centre, and, crowding sail,
stood directly up the Channel. Blake, however,
pursued with his whole force, and Van Tromp, in

the afternoon, finding that he must renew the
combat, told the traders to make for the nearest
Dutch port, and then turned fiercely on his pursuers. The battle was now renewed with more
than former fury; but, after some hours of hard
fighting, Van Tromp fell back toward Boulogne.
No sooner, however, did Sunday morning dawn,
than Blake, bearing down upon the foe, again
brought Van Tromp to action; and the conflict
continued till four o'clock in the afternoon, when
the Dutch admiral, completely vanquished, ran in
under the French shore some miles from Calais,
whence he made for Dunkirk, and subsequently
reached the harbors of Zealand.

Blake, after his great victory, sailed for England with his prizes, and the country rang with
admiration of his achievements. It appears that
he had been severely wounded in the engagement. Nevertheless, he was soon afterward dispatched northward with a fleet; and it was in
April, 1653, while he was on the coast of Scotland, that Cromwell surrounded the houses of
Parliament with troops, turned the members out
of doors, ordered the mace to be taken away, and
assumed supreme authority. Blake, who no more
approved of such proceedings than he approved
of cutting off the king's head, received the intelligence when off Aberdeen, called his captains,
and narrated the circumstances.

"And shouldn't we declare against this usurp-
ation?" asked some of the officers.

"No," said Blake, calmly; "for 'tis not our duty to mind state affairs, but to keep foreigners from fooling us."

It was well for England that Blake took such a view of the question. Not doubting that the outrage at Westminster would produce discord and disorder in the English navy, the Dutch hastened to equip a fleet to strike a great blow, and, before the end of May, Van Tromp, De Ruyter, and De Witt, with a hundred and twenty ships, suddenly appeared off Dover.

Intelligence of this new danger was without delay dispatched to Blake by mounted couriers, and meanwhile Dean and Monk, with above a hundred ships, prepared to front the peril. About noon on the 2d of June, the battle began with great fury. Scarcely had it lasted an hour, when Dean, who was with Monk on the deck of the "Resolution," was shattered to pieces. But Monk, throwing a cloak over the mangled body of his comrade-in-arms, shouted to the men to avenge their leader's fall. The fight continued till night with an extraordinary display of courage on both sides, and, when darkness put a period to the slaughter, they parted with the intention of resuming operations on the morrow. Accordingly, next day, the English and Dutch again opened fire; and the combatants were still engaged with energy, when Blake's ships came tilting over the waters, and the sound of his guns

intimated to the Dutch that their terrible foe
had arrived on the scene. Having struggled
desperately for an hour, Van Tromp gave way,
and the Dutch fleet made for Ostend, their renowned admiral, in a swift frigate, heading the
flight.

After cruising off the coast of Holland and taking many prizes, Blake returned to England, but
with health so shattered that he was carried
ashore like one dead. In his absence, the Dutch
made one last desperate effort to retrieve their
disasters, and on a July Sunday a final engagement took place. The English, on this occasion,
completed the ruin of the Dutch navy; Van
Tromp, shot through the heart with a musket
ball, fell never more to rise; and Monk's victory
was so complete, that the Dutch, relinquishing all
hope of coping with England for the sovereignty
of the seas, hastened to make peace with Cromwell.

When Van Tromp fell in his last effort to assert the naval superiority of his country, his great
adversary was gradually recovering from his
wounds and fatigues. Scarcely was Blake restored to health when work was found for him
to do. About the opening of the year 1654, two
fleets were fitted out. One was intrusted to Penn
and Venables; the other was commanded by
Blake. Their destinations were kept profoundly
secret; but Penn and Venables sailed for the

West Indies. Blake, after having anchored off Cadiz, proceeded to Leghorn to obtain redress from the Duke of Tuscany for having allowed cargoes to be sold in his ports by the corsair-cavaliers. The duke, after a stern demand, sent Blake fifty thousand pistoles, with a message that several of the cargoes had been sold in the Roman ports. Blake, to whom the information was welcome, immediately dispatched an officer to Rome to demand reparation; and the Pope, after finding hesitation and remonstrance vain, settled the matter by paying twenty thousand pistoles.

Having thus squared accounts with the Grand Duke and the Pope, Blake proceeded to Tunis, and sent one of his officers to intimate to the Dey that reparation must be made for injury done to England by his corsairs, and that all English subjects held in captivity within his domains must forthwith be restored to freedom. The Dey, however, treated the demand with contempt, and even refused to allow a supply of fresh water to be taken on board.

"What!" exclaimed Blake, when he received the answer, "does he refuse us even water? Tell the Dey," he continued, "that God gives the benefit of water to all His creatures, and that for men to deny it to each other is both insolent and wicked."

Blake's officers returned to the Dey's palace with the admiral's message; but the Dey, with a

look of defiance, pointed significantly to his batteries along the shore, and to his ships formed in
a line under the castle.

"You must not," he said, "think to brave us
with the sight of your fleet."

"Is that your answer?" asked the English officer.

"Yes," replied the Dey. "Here are our castles of Goletta and Porto Ferino, well manned
and furnished with ordnance. Do what you can;
we fear you not."

Blake, who was not the man to be thus trifled
with, at once resolved on inflicting a signal chastisement on the barbarian. Meanwhile he sailed
away toward Trapani, and the Dey thought he
had seen the last of the English admiral. One
April afternoon, however, the fleet once more appeared, and, entering the Bay of Tunis, furnished
the Dey with startling evidence of the indiscretion of which he had been guilty. In vain the
castle guns played upon the ships. Blake's cannon shook the place to its centre, and within two
hours the Dey's castle was defenseless, his guns
dismounted, nine of his ships in a blaze, the stones
of the palace clattering about his ears, and he
himself ready to submit to whatever terms Blake
chose to dictate.

After having paid visits to Tripoli and Algiers,
Blake, aware that a war with Spain was more
than probable, sailed toward the Straits of Gib-

raltar. On the way, being in want of fresh water, he called at Malaga to take in a supply; and,
while lying off that port, some of his sailors got
leave to go ashore. Rambling through the streets,
the sailors met a procession of priests carrying
the Host, and forgot themselves so far as to ridicule the ceremony. The priests, amazed at being
insulted, called on the populace for protection;
and one of them, in the excess of his indignation,
urged the populace to resent the injury.

"Children of the true Church," he cried, "will
you tamely see these heretic dogs mock your Savior?"

"No!" answered the populace, stamping with
fury.

"Up, then," exclaimed the priest, "and resent
the insults offered to the Blessed Host!"

Thus encouraged, the inhabitants of Malaga
fell upon the sailors, and beat them with merciless severity. On returning to their ships, the
sailors so loudly complained of the treatment
with which they had met, that Blake deemed it
necessary to demand redress. Accordingly, he
dispatched an officer to the Viceroy of Malaga
with a request that the priest who had hounded
on the mob should be sent on board.

"I have no authority over the priest," said the
viceroy, "and I can not send him."

"I did not inquire into the viceroy's authority," said Blake, when this answer was brought;

"but if this priest is not on board within three hours, I will burn the town."

The menace proved perfectly effectual. The viceroy had no inclination to try conclusions with the conqueror of Van Tromp; and the priest, however reluctantly, made his appearance on the deck of the "St. George," and gave his version of the story.

"But I want to know," said Blake, "by what right you urged the populace to maltreat my sailors?"

"Remember the provocation given by the seamen," said the priest.

"Yes," said Blake; "but, had you complained to me, I should have punished them severely. I will not allow my men to insult the religion of any country. Nevertheless, let none else assume that power; for I will have all the world to know that an Englishman is only to be punished by an Englishman."

After having treated the priest with great civility, Blake sent him back; and the priest, on going ashore, gave such an account of the interview, that Blake's magnanimity was highly applauded.

Leaving Malaga, Blake passed the Straits, and anchored in the Bay of Cadiz. At first he was treated with high distinction; but, ere long, news reached Madrid that the English fleet under Penn and Venables had seized Jamaica; and Philip of Spain instantly declared war. Blake's presence before Cadiz was then perfectly understood, and it became known that Cromwell intended to strike a great blow at the power of Spain.

At that time Blake became aware that two silver fleets were on their way to Spain—one from Mexico, the other from Peru. With the object of intercepting these fleets, he kept watch before Cadiz; but months having passed without their appearing, and his ships being in a most unsatisfactory condition, he was at length under the necessity of going home to refit and repair his shattered vessels. On reaching England he was in such health as to be almost unfit for farther exertions; but, finding that his services could not be dispensed with, he hoisted his flag on board the "Naseby," and soon appeared once more in the Bay of Cadiz. In spite of wind and weather, he remained before Cadiz, expecting the silver fleets, and even announced his intention of keeping his station during the winter months. The Spaniards ridiculed the idea, and described Blake as a madman. But winter passed, and spring came, and still the English admiral was before Cadiz.

It happened that in the spring of 1657 Blake took a cruise to the coast of Africa, leaving Captain Richard Stayner in command of a squadron to keep watch before Cadiz. During Blake's absence, the fleet laden with silver from Mexico made its appearance; and Stayner, having after a brief struggle captured the ships, sent the bullion home to Portsmouth. Scarcely, however, had Blake returned to the station, when he received intelligence that the fleet from Peru, consisting of six royal galleons, and sixteen other vessels, richly laden, had, on learning the fate of its predecessor, put into the Canary Islands, and run for security into the harbor of Santa Cruz. On learning this, Blake set sail with his whole force, and on Monday, the 20th of April, his red cross became visible from the Spanish galleons. At daybreak, an English frigate, sent forward to look out, returned with intelligence that the silver fleet lay at anchor without the harbor, "barricaded in the bay in a semicircular manner."

The Spaniards, it seemed, were neither frightened nor unprepared. In fact, the harbor of Santa Cruz was strongly defended. At one end stood a castle fortified with ordnance. Round the bay were seven forts, each having six, four, or three guns. Earth-works formed a chain of communication from fort to fort, and afforded shelter to musketeers. Moreover, Don Diego Diagues, the Spanish admiral, caused all the smaller vessels to be moored close to the shore, and placed the six galleons, well manned, farther out, with their broadsides facing seaward; and, thus prepared, he awaited the approach of the foe with courage and confidence.

But there was one person, at least, at Santa Cruz, who did not share the feeling of security experienced by Don Diego. A merchantman belonging to Holland at that time happened to be in the harbor, and the skipper, who retained a vivid remembrance of Blake's victories over Van Tromp, no sooner became aware that the terrible sea-captain was approaching than he became eager to be gone.

"What do you fear?" asked Don Diego, with a smile, as the skipper presented himself. "See you not that, with our castle, our forts, and our galleons, our position is impregnable?"

"Nevertheless," said the skipper, speaking bad Spanish with a Dutch accent, and shaking his head, "I feel sure that Blake will soon be among you."

"Well," said Don Diego, proudly, "go if you will, and let Blake come if he dare."

"They little know Blake who trust to his not daring," muttered the skipper, as he hastened to his vessel, hauled up anchor, hoisted sails, and left Santa Cruz without a moment's delay.

Meanwhile Blake was by no means daunted by the menacing aspect of Santa Cruz. Without hesitation he prepared to attack. Having caused all his men to kneel down and supplicate the aid of God, he arranged his ships in two divisions. One he intrusted to Captain Stayner, to force an entrance into the bay; of the other he himself retained the command, to storm the castle and the forts.

At eight o'clock, Stayner, with the wind in his favor, led his squadron forward, and commenced a destructive conflict with the Spaniards; and Blake, having silenced the guns of the castle, pushed on to Stayner's aid. The conflict was terrific. By two o'clock, however, the English were victors; and Blake, seeing that he could not bring off the galleons, consigned them to the flames. The fire rapidly did its work, and soon not a spar nor sail was to be seen above water. When the destruction of the silver fleet was accomplished, the wind, which had been blowing into the bay, suddenly veered round, and Blake, availing himself of the change, got the English ships out to sea without loss.

When intelligence of the marvelous feat performed by Blake at Santa Cruz reached London, the popular enthusiasm knew no bounds. Bells were rung, bonfires were lighted, and ballads sung in honor of the victory. Parliament, participating in the excitement, voted thanks to the fleet, granted five hundred pounds to buy a jewel for Blake, and set apart a day for returning thanks to God for so signal a triumph over England's enemies.

After his exploit at Santa Cruz, Blake cruised about for some time, and succeeded in compelling the rovers of Salee to restore their Christian captives to liberty. But his career was rapidly approaching its close. Finding his constitution utterly broken, he resolved to return to England,

P

and in the month of August, 1657, approached
the shores which he had so often defended. He
was not, however, destined again to set foot on
English ground, for on entering Plymouth Sound
he breathed his last.

The body of England's great naval hero was
embalmed, conveyed by sea to Greenwich, and,
after lying in state, carried to Westminster for
interment. No ceremony was omitted that could
render the obsequies worthy of the occasion.
Admirals and vice-admirals, the Protector and
his privy councilors, the mayor and aldermen of
London, went in procession to the Abbey; and
in Henry the Seventh's chapel, among the Tudor
sovereigns, Blake's remains were laid, with all the
honors due to an Englishman whose patriotism
had been pure, and whose exploits had added so
immensely to the glory of his country.

PRINCE RUPERT.

ONE day, early in the year 1620, Prague was the scene of consternation and dismay. On the White Hill outside the city, Austrian troops were victorious over the forces of Frederick, the Elector Palatine, who, a few months earlier, had somewhat rashly accepted the crown of Bohemia. Frederick, and his spouse Elizabeth, daughter of James, king of England, despairing of saving their capital, determined to save themselves; and while the fair Queen of Bohemia, long after celebrated as the " Queen of Hearts," rode off on a pillion behind Ensign Hopton, the king and the officers of his household made all haste to escape from danger.

Prince Rupert, third son of the king and queen of Bohemia, who had drawn his first breath at Prague on the 18th of December, 1619, and was now an infant, experienced great danger on this occasion. When the confusion was at its height, he was asleep in his nurse's arms, and the woman, anxious for her own safety, laid him on the floor, ran to see what was doing, and perhaps, in her terror, forgot his existence. At all events, there was a considerable probability of his lying there till the Austrian troops came to take possession of the palace, in which case he would most likely have perished. But Providence had otherwise ordered. Indeed, the royal infant bellowed out so loudly that his father's chamberlain was attracted to the nursery. Rupert consequently found himself picked hastily up, carried to the court-yard, and thrown into the last carriage that dashed out of the palace gate; and he lived to figure as the most dashing cavalry officer of the period, and one of the most daring sea kings who had appeared since the days of Harold Hardrada.

When the royal exiles who fled from Prague had wandered for a time from place to place, they at length found a home at the Hague; and, as years passed on, Rupert was placed with his brothers at the University of Leyden. At that seat of learning Rupert applied himself to his studies, but rather with diligence than devotion. In fact, he had a natural passion for martial affairs; and having early dedicated himself to the profession of arms, he, at the age of fourteen, commenced his apprenticeship at the siege of Rhinberg, and soon after made a campaign under the Prince of Orange, enduring all the hardships of war.

At an early stage of his career, Rupert paid a visit to England, where his uncle Charles the First then reigned, and the prince liked his moth-

er's native country so well that he immediately
began to consider it as his own. But as England
was not a place in which Rupert could find any
suitable occupation, and as he was not a man to
spend his time in lolling listlessly about the palace of Whitehall, he ere long embarked in an adventurous project for the recovery of his father's
dominions, and, near Lippe, fought a stubborn
battle with the Austrians. The enterprise, however, was not destined to succeed; every thing
was against him; and after fighting till he was,
almost forcibly, overpowered and taken, he was
committed prisoner to a castle, where he passed
three years of irksome captivity, spurning all pro-
posals to purchase his freedom by abandoning
the cause of Protestantism in Europe, consoling
himself with the love of a youthful countess, and
diverting himself during many weary hours with
a tame lion, which ultimately placed him under
the necessity of terminating its existence, and a
white dog, which afterward accompanied him
through many a bloody day, and lost its life when
many gallant men died so bravely on Marston
Moor.

Rupert had scarcely recovered his liberty
when he learned that England was on the eve of
a civil war, and, with his brother Maurice, he hastened to aid Charles the First in the contest upon
which that king had entered with the Long Parliament. Rupert's personal courage, and his ca-

pacity as a captain of cavalry, rendered him in many respects a valuable adherent. But his presence in England did not prove altogether advantageous to the royal cause. The evils that had crossed his destiny, and the difficulties that beset his path, had rendered him somewhat reckless in spirit, and want of moderation led to his making enemies of many who might, under different auspices, have been stanch friends of the king.

On fields of fight, however, Rupert's name was of high account; and when, mounted on his black steed, and attended by his white dog, he headed the king's cavalry, the sight of his noble form and conspicuous stature, towering in front of the Cavaliers, might well strike dismay into the sternest hearts in the ranks of the Roundheads. But he was slow in learning that discretion is the better part of valor; and after his hottest charges at Edgehill, at Marston, and at Naseby, he, by riding headlong from the field in pursuit of the Roundheads opposed to him, returned to find that he had given the enemy an opportunity of winning the battle during his absence from the field.

When the war between king and Parliament was at an end, when the Roundheads were elate with victory, and the Cavaliers prostrate with defeat, when the king was in the hands of the Scots, and when the city of Oxford surrendered,

Rupert and his brother Maurice received passports, took shipping at Dover, and proceeded to Paris. At the palace of the Bourbons, where Louis the Fourteenth then reigned, and Anne of Austria enacted the part of regent, Rupert was favorably received; and, though defective in the "transient varnish of a court," he made such an impression on the queen regent that she showed every inclination to advance his fortunes. But Rupert had thrown his whole heart so completely into the war in England that the prospect of renewing it in any form was a temptation which he could not resist.

Accordingly, when part of the English navy went over from the Parliament to the king, Rupert required little persuasion to exert his energies to render the royal fleet terrible to the enemies of the royal cause. Repairing to the Hague, where young Charles Stuart was then in exile, Rupert, on condition of having unlimited control, undertook to restore and enforce discipline. Money, indeed, was wanting. But even this difficulty was got over. The Queen of Bohemia having pawned her jewels, and Rupert having sold the ordnance of the "Antelope" to the Dutch, a sufficient sum was raised to fit out the ships; and having hoisted his flag on board the "Admiral," the prince in January, 1649, sailed from Helvoetsluys.

No sooner was Rupert at sea than he made

himself formidable. Prize after prize was taken,
and the rich merchandise was stored in the Channel Islands. It soon appeared that Rupert intended to carry on his operations on a grand
scale, and he made no secret of his projects. "I
doubt not," he wrote, "ere long to see Scilly a
second Venice. It will be our security and benefit; for if the worst came to the worst, it is but
going to Scilly with this fleet, where, after a little
while, we may get the king a good subsistence,
and I believe we shall make a shift to live in spite
of all factions."

At this time James Butler, the great Marquis
of Ormond, was struggling desperately to maintain the royal cause in Ireland; and Rupert, after
cruising about in the Channel, selected Kinsale
as a convenient port for carrying on operations.
At first he was signally successful. The royal
ships, sallying out, brought prize after prize into
the harbor, and Rupert's hopes rose high. But
a change was at hand. Early in the summer of
1649, the prince's vessels, sent forth on a cruising
expedition, were separated by a storm and involved in a fog. Before they could secure themselves they were attacked by a hostile fleet, and,
while one of them surrendered, the others were
chased into Kinsale. Rupert probably had some
difficulty in believing the fact. But there was no
mistake about the matter. Admiral Blake was
at the mouth of the harbor.

Rupert's position was now unpleasant, and his prospects were the reverse of brilliant. His courage, however, did not fail him, and he proposed to sail forth and give Blake battle. His officers, however, objected so positively to the scheme, that he had to pass the whole summer in inactivity; and in August, the arrival of Cromwell in Ireland made matters more dismal than they had previously appeared. But, in the midst of despondency, such a man could still indulge in hope. Rupert watched Blake as keenly as he was watched; and when autumn came, and the ships of the Puritan admiral had to ride far from the mouth of the harbor, he prepared to escape. It was impossible, indeed, at that moment to man the whole of the royal fleet; but Rupert, leaving several of his vessels behind, embarked with his brother Maurice, and with six ships dashed out of Kinsale.

At sea new adventures awaited the prince. While scudding away from Kinsale, Rupert, in the "Admiral," was separated from his comrades for two days. At the end of that time he espied seven ships, and immediately gave chase. On coming up, however, he found that they were his five missing vessels, with two prizes they had taken. Soon after joining company, he fell in with two large ships, to which he gave chase. After some time the chase terminated in a capture; and these vessels, like the others, proved to be merchantmen of London. Having now four goodly prizes, and anxious to dispose of them, Rupert deemed it necessary to make for some friendly port; and, after deliberation, resolved to sail up the Tagus, and place himself under the protection of John of Braganza, king of Portugal.

In the year 1635, John, duke of Braganza, then about thirty, espoused Louisa, daughter of John Emanuel, duke of Medina Sidonia, and had several sons and daughters, one of whom, Katherine of Braganza, was afterward wife of Charles the Second. But Louisa was not content with being a duchess and a mother. Ardent and ambitious, she desired to see her husband on the throne of Portugal, and so prompted John to assert his claims as heir, through his mother, to the ancient kings, that at length he had the fortune to drive the Spaniards out of Portugal, and find himself crowned as king at Lisbon. Perhaps the new monarch had some romantic ideas about being the legitimate representative of John of Gaunt, and took, on that account, a more kindly interest in the misfortunes of the Stuarts than was felt by other regal personages of that age. At all events, he assured Rupert that, in the Tagus, he should be protected against all enemies.

Accordingly, after entering the river, and passing St. Katherine's, Rupert anchored at Belleisle, and there met with a most encouraging reception. Indeed, the highest nobles of Portugal

were sent to escort him to the palace of Lisbon,
where, having been warmly welcomed by King
John, he succeeded in fascinating Queen Louisa,
as he had formerly fascinated Anne of Austria,
while his ships, with their prizes, sailed up to Lisbon to victual and refit.

It can hardly be doubted that, with festivities
in the palace, and with bull-fighting in the great
square in which the palace of the Braganzas stood,
Rupert spent his time pleasantly enough in Lisbon. But when winter passed, and spring came,
that city of seven hills began to lose its attrac-
tion, and the prince sighed for new adventures.
Eager again to roam the seas, he went on board
his ships, and prepared to bid farewell to Portugal; but, to his dismay, he found that Blake, with
the English fleet, was at the mouth of the Tagus.
Not being strong enough to force his way, Rupert again came to anchor. But he soon perceived that he was in a somewhat awkward predicament. In fact, Blake demanded leave to enter the river, and attack the prince's fleet; and
John of Braganza was so little inclined to drive
matters to extremity with the English Commonwealth, that, instead of returning a denial, he hesitated and paused.

While the king wavered, and while the council
were divided in opinion, Rupert was not idle.
Already he was a favorite in Lisbon. The inhabitants, so long accustomed to the stately gravity

of Spanish grandees, were charmed with his sol-
dierly frankness; and, Protestant as he was, he
contrived so to engage the sympathy of the priests
and the populace, that, instead of wishing to burn
him as a heretic, they displayed the utmost enthusiasm in his cause. With such support, and
with the queen's heart and ambition on his side,
he contrived for a while to stave off the danger.

But affairs ere long reached a crisis. Blake,
indignant at being trifled with, seized the Brazil
fleets; and King John, enraged at the outrage,
ordered his admiral to join Rupert and drive the
English from the waters of Portugal. This, however, proved no easy business. Two attacks were
indeed made, but without the slightest success.
Between the prince and King John's admiral
there was an utter want of concert, and the Portuguese vessels were never ready to take part in
the action till Rupert had failed. After some
wrangling, they returned up the Tagus; and King
John, arriving at the conclusion that he must
yield to circumstances, sent messengers to intimate in polite terms to Rupert that Portugal
could no longer afford him protection.

"It will be impossible," said the king's messenger, "to prevent the enemy from attacking
you at your moorings."

"Well," said Rupert, "it matters not much.
Misfortune is no novelty to us. We plow the

sea for a subsistence, with revenge as our guide, and poverty and despair as our companions."

Accordingly, on Michaelmas day, 1650, Rupert sailed from Lisbon and put to sea, intending to steer for the Straits. While coasting Andalusia, Rupert fell in with some ships, gave chase, fired upon them, and, under cover of night, captured two. Learning at the same time that several English vessels were at Malaga, he steered thither, and burned them in port.

At Cape Palos, near Carthagena, Rupert encountered a fearful storm. Nor was this the worst; for scarcely had he left Malaga when Blake appeared in pursuit. Several of the ships, under press of weather, ran into Carthagena, where, after being ill treated by the Spaniards, they were destroyed by Blake. But Rupert and Maurice, separated from their companions, and driven out to sea, came up with a trader, pursued her to the coast of Barbary, and, after this long chase, succeeded in making a capture. With the trader as a prize, they stood across for Toulon, where they hoped to find security. A fearful storm, however, separated the ships, and while Maurice reached Toulon, Rupert was driven eastward to the coast of Sicily. After remaining there all winter, uncertain as to his brother's fate, he made for Toulon. But he had scarcely anchored in the road to refit his shattered·vessel when Blake arrived, and, as the Admiral of England, protested against the enemies of the English Commonwealth being sheltered in a French port. It was a moment of peril for Rupert. The French admiral hesitated, and avoided responsibility by hastening Rupert's departure. Finding that there was not an hour to lose, Rupert and Maurice refitted in haste, seized a favorable opportunity, escaped from the roadstead, and, passing through the Straits of Gibraltar, sailed for the West Indies.

It was Rupert's intention to land at Barbadoes, where, in defiance of the Parliament, Lord Willoughby, under a commission from King Charles, exercised the functions of governor; but, passing that island in the night without being aware, he made St. Lucia. However, the royal brothers did not fare better in the tropics than they had done in Europe. "The sad strokes of adverse fortune," says a contemporary chronicler, "which had eclipsed the royal throne of England, did, even in these distant parts, pursue this illustrious pair of princes." After preying for some time on the richly-laden merchantmen of Spain, and making themselves terrible to shippers and traders, Maurice and Rupert parted company in one of those hurricanes which occasionally desolate the West India Islands. Maurice was never more heard of with certainty; Rupert, with a sad heart, sailed for Europe.

It was at the close of the year 1652, when

Cromwell had defeated the Scots under David Leslie at Dunbar; when Worcester had run red with Cavalier blood; and when Charles, after hiding in the royal oak, had made his miraculous escape to France, that Rupert, in the "Swallow," reached Nantes with the prizes he had taken in the West Indies. The prince was in no joyous frame of body and mind. Fatigue, hope deferred, and the melancholy disappearance of Maurice, had been too much for his iron frame and haughty spirit. On landing, he became so sick that it seemed as if he were about to close his strange career. Gradually, however, he recovered, and learned that his fortunes were not altogether desperate. An invitation from Louis the Fourteenth summoned Rupert from his chamber of sickness to the court of France; and, going to Paris, he was appointed the young king's master of the horse.

But, as time passed on, Rupert's ears were reached by a rumor that must have disquieted his soul. It was to the effect that Maurice, instead of being drowned, as had naturally been concluded, had been driven by the hurricane as far as Hispaniola; that, as he was sailing from that place to Spain, in a bark laden with silver, he had been taken by a pirate of Algiers, and afterward carried to Africa as a slave. The story would seem to have been without foundation; but it caused Rupert, in 1654, to leave Paris for

Germany, where he remained till the Restoration.

When Charles took possession of Whitehall, Rupert returned to England, and in the spring of 1662 he was sworn a member of the Privy Council. He was no longer the fierce warrior of Edgehill and of Naseby. Experience had cooled the prince's ardor. He acted with a degree of judgment which he had not exhibited in earlier years, and persons most strongly prejudiced against him were forced to admit that he was a changed man.

When, in 1664, a naval war broke out between England and Holland, Rupert was appointed vice-admiral of the fleet, and had actually gone on board; but the cabal about the king contrived by their intrigues to deprive him of his command, and he was under the necessity of returning ashore; while the Duke of York fought that battle with Opedain in which the Dutch fleet was defeated and the Dutch admiral killed. But in 1666, when London had been desolated by the plague, and when the French king, in alliance with the Dutch, declared war against England, Rupert was appointed to command the fleet in conjunction with George Monk, now Duke of Albemarle, and, hoisting his flag on board the "Royal Charles," he put to sea about the end of May.

At that time, De Ruyter, the Dutch admiral, was in the Texel with a formidable fleet. It was not, however, expected that the Dutch would immediately put to sea, and Rupert, after appointing a meeting with Monk at the Gun Fleet, an important anchorage near Harwich, steered westward with the white squadron, consisting of thirty sail, to look after the French, who were expected from the Mediterranean. Early next morning—it was the 1st of June—the English, with surprise, beheld the Dutch fleet lying at anchor half-channel over. Calling a council of war, Monk resolved on fighting before Rupert returned, and gave the signal for an attack.

The attack was made by the English with great spirit; but an hour passed on, and the consequences proved somewhat disastrous. Not only were the English utterly inferior in force, but the wind and the sea prevented them from using their lower tier of guns, and their rigging was fearfully injured by the Dutch chain-shot, then newly invented. The conflict, however, was bravely maintained till nightfall, when darkness came to Monk's rescue.

Next morning Monk found the aspect of affairs still more threatening. The Dutch, re-enforced by sixteen vessels, renewed the encounter with great vigor; and Monk, after several of his ships had been disabled, was obliged to retreat. The destruction of the English fleet seemed inevitable. Fortunately, however, a calm prevented the enemy from following.

Q

On the morning of the 3d of June the battle
was renewed; and Monk, having resolved to
abandon the disabled ships, and given them to
the flames, fought retreating. When the Dutch
advanced, the ships most shattered stretched
ahead, while sixteen of those in the best fighting
order followed, and kept the enemy in check.
But the position of the English was extremely
perilous; and Monk, who closed the rear, was
standing on deck, determined rather to blow up
his ship than yield, when a squadron, crowding
all sail, was seen to the south, and the English,
with a thrill of joy, raised a shout that Rupert
was coming.

In fact, Rupert had not sailed farther westward
than St. Helen's when he received intelligence
that De Ruyter was at sea. The prince immediately put about for Dover, but he did not reach
that point till the evening of the 1st of June,
when the fight had lasted a whole day; and
when he got into the Downs he could neither
see nor learn any thing of the hostile fleets. Eager and anxious, Rupert then made for the Gun
Fleet, where he had appointed to meet Monk;
but there he was disappointed in his hope of intelligence, and from having now the wind against
him, he passed the 2d of June in painful suspense.
Next day, however, while still beating about, he
heard a heavy cannonading; and, spreading his
canvas, he hastened to the scene of action just in

time to save Monk from the destruction that impended.

No sooner did the morning of the 4th of June dawn than the battle was renewed. Rupert exerted all his mighty energies, and De Ruyter began to feel in a situation almost as desperate as Monk had been on the previous day. A thick fog, however, coming to his rescue, interrupted the carnage. Neither fleet had gained a victory. But when the fog dispersed, the Dutch were seen in retreat; and the English, in no condition to pursue, took refuge in their own ports.

Hostilities were speedily resumed. In the month of July, De Ruyter, with a larger fleet than before, put boldly to sea. But this time the issue of the engagement was not doubtful. Monk and Rupert encountered the Dutch admiral at the mouth of the Thames, and, after a severe action, gained a complete victory.

" We must fly," said the Dutch.

" Oh God !" exclaimed De Ruyter; "among so many thousand bullets, is there not one to put an end to my miserable life?"

De Ruyter sailed back to the Texel in rage and despair, and the English were again masters of the sea. Monk then left the fleet to enjoy his laurels on shore; but Rupert remained, in full command, and learning that the Dutch fleet was about to attempt a junction with the French under the Duke de Beaufort, he immediately sailed

to prevent them, and chased the enemy into Boulogne.

But events sadly marred the joy excited by
these naval triumphs. In the autumn, the great
fire, breaking out in London, destroyed nearly
thirteen thousand houses, and the king soon after
sent plenipotentiaries to Breda to treat for peace
with France and Holland, dismantled his fleet,
laid up the ships, and discharged the seamen.
The impolicy of this course of conduct ere long
became evident. In the beginning of June, 1667,
a Dutch fleet dashed into the Downs; and while
De Ruyter entered the mouth of the Thames,
Van Ghent, with the lightest ships, sailed up the
Medway, made himself master of Sheerness, burned the magazines, blew up the fortifications, and
then, proceeding as far as Chatham, burned several vessels of war.

Among the ships given to the flames on this
occasion was the "Royal Oak," commanded by
an officer bearing the noble name of Douglas.
Seeing his vessel on fire, and in despair of saving
her, Captain Douglas lay down on deck to die.

"There is nothing for it but to escape," said
the crew.

"No," exclaimed the brave captain, his eye
flashing with pride, "a Douglas will never live
to bear the reproach of quitting his post."

On leaving the fleet, Rupert, who regarded the
renewal of the alliance with France without the

slightest favor, and who felt no sympathy whatever with the policy of the court, had retired into privacy. On hearing, however, that De Ruyter had entered the Thames, he roused himself to energy, hastened to Woolwich, sunk a number of vessels to block the passage of the Thames, and hastily threw up batteries. When the danger had passed, he returned to Windsor, of which he was governor, and lived much in seclusion, keeping a yacht, riding after his pack of hounds, and diverting himself with philosophical studies and chemical experiments. He held himself so much aloof from political affairs that he was respected by men of the most opposite views; and he rendered himself highly popular with his neighbors, the gentry, yeomanry, and peasantry of Berks.

But, meanwhile, the war between England and Holland had been renewed; and in 1672, when the Duke of York, as lord high admiral, encountered the Dutch fleet at Solebay, and the Earl of Sandwich's ship was blown up with his whole crew, Rupert was summoned from his retirement and appointed vice-admiral. Next year, when the Duke of York, in consequence of Parliament passing the Test Act, resigned his post, Rupert took the command of the fleet, and having in April hoisted his standard on board the "Royal Charles," he put to sea.

About the middle of May the prince got in sight of the Dutch fleet, and in two engagements

of great severity, during one of which Van Tromp
—son of Blake's great rival—had to shift his flag
four times, Rupert performed wonders. But his
fleet was in such a condition that all his exertions
could not secure a decisive victory; and when
the Dutch retreated, he returned to the Nore,
and hastened to London to report the state of affairs.

Rupert, however, was soon recalled to the
scene of his duties, and on the 11th of August,
1673, he once more encountered De Ruyter. A
fierce conflict took place. Rupert and De Ruyter put forth all their strength, but neither could
with justice boast of a triumph. The losses on
both sides were nearly equal, and victory remained dubious.

It was the last time that Rupert fought for England. For several years he survived the terrible encounter, and was idolized in the navy as
"the seaman's friend." But he lived for the most
part in privacy, and doubtless reflected with sadness on the many and strange vicissitudes of his
career. At length, in his sixty-third year, it became evident that Rupert's days were numbered,
and on the 29th of November, 1682, he went the
way of all flesh. He died at his house in Spring
Gardens, and his bones found a resting-place in
the chapel which his maternal ancestor, Henry
Tudor, had added to the Abbey of Westminster.

SIR CLOUDESLEY SHOVEL.

ABOUT the time of the Restoration of Charles the Second, a shoemaker's apprentice from the interior of that county where, in feudal ages, the Bigods held sway, being one day sent on an errand to a sea-port town, stood regarding the shipping with a delighted eye, and vowing that, come what might, he would be a sailor. The name of this boy was Cloudesley Shovel, and he was a native of Cockthorpe, a small parish in Norfolk, where Sir John Narborough is said to have first seen the light.

The surname of Shovel was in ancient days borne by men who figured in Norfolk as lords of the soil. But the parents of the embryo hero appear to have been in very humble circumstances. Indeed, it was from being so poor that they bound their son apprentice to a shoemaker. But, almost from infancy, Cloudesley had a strong fancy for going to sea; and his visit to the sea-port fired his imagination to such a degree that his enthusiasm could not be restrained. Fortunately for young Shovel's aspirations, circumstances threw Narborough in his way, and that eminent admiral agreed to take Cloudesley to sea as one of his cabin-boys.

Once on that element for which he had cherished such a longing, Cloudesley Shovel took an early opportunity of showing his defiance of danger and his zeal for the service. Narborough, while near an enemy's fleet, being anxious to have some documents of importance conveyed to the captain of a certain ship, kept pacing his cabin and expressing his anxiety.

" I wish," said the admiral to his officers, in his own rough style, " I wish I could contrive some way of sending these papers."

"Trust me with them," said Cloudesley, "and I will swim with them in my mouth."

Narborough consented, and young Shovel accomplished the daring feat of swimming through the enemy's fire. This service raised him high in the admiral's good opinion; and in 1674, when Narborough was about to send a remonstrance to the Dey of Tripoli for acts of piracy committed by the corsairs, he selected his protégé as the fittest person to undertake the mission.

Armed with his credentials to the Dey, Cloudesley Shovel went ashore, and performed the duty with much spirit. The remonstrance failed in its object; but while ashore, on two occasions, he projected an attack on the Tripoline ships at their moorings, and under the guns of the town, which seemed so likely to be successful that Narborough readily gave it his sanction.

" And," said the admiral, " I know no person

SIR CLOUDESLEY SHOVEL'S FIRST ENTERPRISE.

more fit to execute such a project than its author."

"Sir," said the brave Cloudesley, "I will do my best."

Accordingly, on the night of the 4th of March, Cloudesley Shovel, having all the boats of Narborough's fleet at his disposal, made for the harbor, commenced operations, seized the guard-ship, entered the mole, burned five large armed vessels, and returned without the loss of a man. Convinced more than ever of his young friend's skill and courage, Narborough did all he could to advance the interests of so promising a sailor, and in May, 1677, Cloudesley Shovel had the gratification of being appointed to the command of the "Sapphire."

At that time Tangiers, which had formed part of the marriage portion of Katherine of Braganza, still belonged to the English crown. It was, however, exposed to the attacks of the Moors; and in November, 1679, the place was besieged by a Moorish army. At that time the "Sapphire" formed one of Admiral Herbert's fleet, and Captain Shovel was among the officers employed ashore, with a party of seamen, to assist in the defense. One day, when the Moors made a desperate effort to carry the place by assault, Captain Shovel exhibited his gallantry in a striking light, and greatly contributed to the repulse of the foe. On that occasion he received a wound, which rendered him for a time unfit for service; but, ere long, he recovered sufficiently to take the command of the "James" galley, and to signalize himself in naval encounters with the cruisers of Barbary.

One day, while in company with the "Sapphire," Captain Shovel fell in with a corsair of Algiers, known as the "Half Moon," which he took after a long and desperate action; another day he attacked a corsair named the "Flowerpot," which he drove ashore, and captured with his boats; and he continued to take his part in the war with great distinction till 1686, when he left the Straits and returned to England.

Having remained in command of the "James" galley till the death of Charles the Second, Captain Shovel, appointed by the last Stuart king to the command of the "Dover," stuck to the service till the Revolution. When that important event occurred, however, he readily gave in his adhesion to William and Mary. Having been appointed to the "Edgar," he displayed such skill and gallantry at Bantry Bay, that when the Dutch king went to Portsmouth to reward the seamen, and gave the earldom of Torrington to Admiral Herbert, he with perfect propriety conferred knighthood on Cloudesley Shovel.

At this period the aspect of affairs in Ireland was such as to alarm the new government; and in 1690, Sir Cloudesley, having removed to the

"Monk," was dispatched in command of a small squadron to cruise in the Channel, and prevent the landing of the French troops. Learning after he had anchored off the coasts that there were several ships-of-war in Dublin Bay, he left his flag-ship, went on board a small vessel, ran several of the enemy aground, and brought off a large ship in triumph.

Soon after this success Sir Cloudesley Shovel was appointed to convey William of Orange to Ireland. His services on the occasion were highly appreciated; and when he was shortly afterward promoted to the rank of Rear Admiral of the Blue, the king, as a mark of royal favor, delivered the commission with his own hand.

In the spring of 1692, when William went to the Continent, Sir Cloudesley Shovel was appointed to act as convoy. On this occasion his services were rewarded with promotion to the rank of Rear Admiral of the Red. Returning from Holland, Sir Cloudesley joined Admiral Russell, who was then in search of the French fleet, which, under the command of Admiral Tourville, had been dispatched by Louis the Fourteenth with peremptory orders not to decline an engagement.

Early in the morning of the 19th of May, 1693, fast-sailing vessels, dispatched by Russell to look out for the French, gave information that they had descried the enemy off Cape La Hogue; and, orders having been immediately given to form in

order of battle, the English, by eleven o'clock,
came face to face with their foes. For two hours
the battle raged furiously. By that time, however, the masts, yards, and rigging of the "So-
leil Royal," Tourville's flag-ship, were fearfully
shattered, and, in this disabled condition, she had
to be towed out of the line. Nevertheless, the
combat was maintained with spirit on both sides
till three o'clock. A thick fog then enveloped
the fleets so closely that they could not see each
other. When the fog cleared off, Tourville was
discovered towing away to the northward, followed by the shattered remains of his fleet.

On the memorable day when the battle was
fought off La Hogue, Sir Cloudesley Shovel had
his flag hoisted on board the "Royal William,"
a new ship of a hundred guns, and contributed,
in a great degree, to the victory that was won.
Availing himself of a change in the wind, he
weathered Tourville's fleet, and, bringing his
squadron to bear on the flying ships, he did terrible execution. But the fog, becoming denser
than ever, forced him to bring his squadron to
anchor; and the honor of giving the last shattering blow to the fleet of the "Grand Monarch"
was reserved for Sir George Rooke.

Rough admiral as Sir Cloudesley was, his ideas
were not wholly confined to the affairs of a man-
of-war. Indeed, he would almost seem to have
been a man of "aspiring vein." As his fortunes

rose, he purchased Stafford's Manor, in Norfolk, from Lord Ashley, lived in a great house in Soho Square, and married the widow of his old patron, Sir John Narborough. By this lady he had two daughters, one of whom became the wife of Sir Narborough Daeth, the other the wife of Lord Romney.

After taking part in several of the naval enterprises which William's wars rendered necessary, Sir Cloudesley was, by the king's express orders, dispatched on an expedition to Dunkirk, which was a nest of privateers. On the 2d of September, 1694, his fleet, armed with a number of explosive machines called "infernals," appeared before the place, and next day he commenced the attack. The operations, however, were not attended with success; and, indeed, upon a close inspection of Dunkirk, the admiral became aware that his forces and appliances were quite insufficient for its reduction. Sir Cloudesley finally left without having succeeded in his object; but, notwithstanding the public disappointment, he was well received in England.

"Sir Cloudesley Shovel," said some, "has taken care to demonstrate that there lay no fault in him; for he went in a boat within the enemy's works, and so became an eye-witness of the impossibility of doing what his orders directed to be done."

"Yes," said others, "he is a man who will

command success where success is possible, and omit nothing in his power where it is not."

Events passed onward; and in 1701, when Europe was agitated with the question whether the grandson of the King of France or the brother of the Emperor of Germany should succeed to the Spanish throne, James the Second died at St. Germain's. Louis the Fourteenth, with more magnanimity than prudence, caused the son of James to be proclaimed King of England, and William of Orange, immediately organizing a great coalition of Continental powers to check the ambition of France, prepared for war. William died before operations commenced; but Anne having been placed on the English throne, the war began vigorously; and in June, 1704, Sir Cloudesley Shovel sailed from England to join Sir George Rooke in the Mediterranean.

Soon after the junction of Sir Cloudesley and Sir George, they resolved on a sudden attack on Gibraltar, and on the 21st of July sailed into the bay. Having landed marines and some sixteen hundred troops, they summoned the governor to surrender; and, being answered that "he would defend his trust to the last," they next day commenced a brisk cannonade. The position of Gibraltar was such that fifty men might have held the place against as many thousands. Nevertheless, the Spaniards ere long began to desert their batteries; and the seamen of the fleet, having embarked in their boats, pulled to the shore, landed rapidly, climbed the fortifications, and took possession.

When Charles Mordaunt, Earl of Peterborough, was sent to Spain with five thousand troops to aid Charles of Austria to wrench the Spanish crown from Philip the Fifth, Sir Cloudesley Shovel was appointed admiral and commander-in-chief of the fleet. Having landed at Lisbon in June, and taken the Archduke Charles on board, the English proceeded to the coast of Catalonia, and laid siege to Barcelona. Sir Cloudesley having, during this siege, furnished not only guns, but men to work them, Barcelona, though defended by a strong garrison, was compelled to surrender, and the whole province of Catalonia soon submitted to the archduke.

In the summer which succeeded that in which the capture of Barcelona occurred, Sir Cloudesley Shovel was again placed in command of the English fleet, and returned to the Mediterranean. In the autumn he reached Lisbon, and found the Portuguese much less earnest in the cause of the allies than he could have wished. When Sir Cloudesley, with his flag hoisted on board the "Association," appeared in the Tagus, his ships were fired upon by the guns of the Castle of Belamy, and some of the seamen, on going on shore, were grossly abused. Having reason to believe that one of the princes of Braganza had instigated

R

these insults, Sir Cloudesley demanded satisfaction from the government.

"It seems," said the ministers, "that the whole affair originated in a mistake. Orders had been given to detain, and, if necessary, to fire upon a Genoese ship, whose master had not paid his port-dues."

"That," replied Sir Cloudesley, "is not a satisfactory answer; and I will not allow the English flag to be so insulted while I have the honor of being intrusted with it."

The government of Portugal had the prudence to apologize; and Sir Cloudesley, having expressed his satisfaction, sailed with a fleet of forty-three men-of-war and fifty-seven transports. At Nice he gave a splendid banquet on board the "Association;" covers were laid for sixty; and among the guests were the Duke of Savoy, Prince Eugene, many general officers, and the English and Dutch embassadors. The banquet was so well conducted, and every thing went off so admirably, that, during dinner, the Duke of Savoy could not refrain from expressing his admiration.

"I am glad," said Sir Cloudesley, "that your highness is pleased with the efforts made to entertain you."

"Pleased, admiral!" exclaimed the duke; "why, if you paid me a visit at Turin, I could scarcely entertain you half so well."

At a council of war held after dinner, it was resolved to attempt the reduction of Toulon, and Sir Cloudesley engaged to assist to the utmost of his power. The enterprise, however, miscarried; and the English admiral, leaving part of his fleet in the Mediterranean, sailed with the remainder toward England.

While sailing homeward, Sir Cloudesley, on the morning of the 22d of October, 1707, struck soundings in ninety fathoms; and as the wind was then blowing strong, with hazy weather, he made signal for the fleet to bring to. At six in the evening, however, he again made sail, and stood away from under his courses, from which it is believed that he thought he saw the Scilly Lights. Soon after, the " Association" made signals of danger, and about eight o'clock she disappeared. She had struck either upon the rocks known as the " Bishop and his Clerks," or upon the Gilstones, but so sudden was the catastrophe that it was never known which. Several vessels shared her fate.

The body of Sir Cloudesley Shovel was washed up by the sea, cast ashore under the rocks of St. Mary, stripped by the natives, and thrown with others into a hole dug in the sands. There it would have remained; but the purser of the " Arundel," hearing of an emerald ring which he knew to be Sir Cloudesley's, instituted inquiries, made the islanders declare where the hero was buried, and, having ascertained the spot, caused the body to be disinterred and conveyed to Portsmouth.

From Portsmouth the remains of Sir Cloudesley Shovel were carried by land to London, and, after remaining for a short time at his house in Soho Square, found a resting-place in Westminster Abbey. His melancholy fate caused profound grief in England. The queen expressed her sense of the merits of the admiral who had so zealously served the crown, and the people bewailed the death of a hero who had so well and so faithfully fought the battles of his country.

ADMIRAL BENBOW.

One day, when Charles the Second visited the Tower of London to examine the magazines, his eye was arrested by the appearance of a brave Cavalier who had fought at Worcester, and aided him to escape from that unfortunate battle.

"Colonel Benbow," exclaimed the king, "my old friend, what do you here?"

"I am here," replied the Cavalier, "because I have a place which brings me fourscore pounds, for which I serve your majesty as cheerfully as if it brought me four thousand."

"Alas!" said Charles, "is that all that can be done for an old Worcester friend?"

The king then promised that Colonel Benbow should be provided for, and left the Tower. But the Cavalier, who had risked and lost all in the royal cause, did not live to benefit by the royal bounty. Profoundly affected by the interview, he sunk down on a bench, and, almost ere the king left the Tower, breathed his last, leaving one son, who was destined to a remarkable career.

John Benbow was born about the year 1650, and was still very young when his father died.

His prospects were the reverse of brilliant. In fact, he is said to have originally been bound apprentice to a waterman. In early life, however, he made the ocean his home, became a thorough seaman, and, as time passed on, began to figure conspicuously as owner of a vessel known as the "Benbow Frigate."

During his voyages in this frigate Benbow encountered pirates on the sea with quite as much courage and rather more success than his father had encountered Roundheads on the land. His naval exploits soon made his name famous, and in the foreign ports to which he sailed he was regarded with curiosity and not without awe.

In the year 1686, when on a voyage to Cadiz, Benbow was attacked by a Salee rover. Though quite unequal in point of numbers, Benbow and his men defended themselves with obstinacy. At length, however, the Moors boarded the frigate, and Benbow perhaps felt that he was in a perilous predicament. Undauntedly, however, he continued the conflict on his own deck, killed thirteen foes, and made the others glad to scramble back to their own vessel. He then ordered the heads of the thirteen dead Moors to be cut off, and thrown into a tub of pork pickle.

On arriving at Cadiz, Benbow prepared to go ashore. Before doing so, however, he ordered a negro, named Cæsar, to lift the Moors' heads out of the tub, to put them in a sack, to take the sack

on his shoulders, and to accompany him ashore.
Cæsar obeyed; and the captain and his negro
had scarcely set foot on land, when the revenue
officers demanded what was in the sack.

"Salt provisions for my own use," replied Benbow.

"That may be so," said the officers, "but we
want to see them."

"Why," said Benbow, in his own rough way,
"I am no stranger here. I am not used to run
goods, and I take it very ill of you to suspect
me."

"Well," said the officers, "we only want to do
our duty. But the magistrates are sitting close
by, and if they are satisfied with your word, you
may carry the provisions where you please."

"Very well," said Benbow, "let us go."

Accordingly, the party marched to the custom-
house, Benbow walking in front, Cæsar in the
centre, and the officers bringing up the rear. On
reaching the building, Benbow was treated by
the magistrates with great civility, but requested
to exhibit the contents of the sack.

"We are sorry," said they, "to make a point
of such a trifle. But the nature of our employment renders it necessary to demand a sight."

"I told you," replied Benbow, "they were
salted provisions for my own use. However,
Cæsar," he continued, "throw them down; and,"
added he, as the Moors' heads rolled on the ta-

ble, "gentlemen, if you like, they are at your
service."

"Astonishing," cried the Spaniards, as they recovered from their surprise and listened to the
story of Benbow's adventure, "that a man with
so small a force should have been able to defeat
so many of the barbarians."

When intelligence of Benbow's exploit reached the court of Madrid, Charles, king of Spain,
was so interested that he said, "I must see this
man." Benbow, it would seem, went to Madrid,
and, after having been treated with great respect,
was dismissed with handsome presents. Moreover, the King of Spain wrote to James the Second, paying Benbow high compliments, and
strongly recommending him to the royal favor.

In May, 1687, while Benbow was in command
of a ship named the "Malaga Merchant," he was
attacked near the mouth of the Straits by a Salee
rover of considerable force. After discharging a
broadside, accompanied with small shot, the pirates endeavored to board; but the attempt cost
them many lives, and they found their reception
so hot that they sheered off. Benbow then,
pouncing upon them, made a vigorous attack;
but the rover, being a faster sailer than the "Malaga Merchant," contrived to escape without farther loss.

By this time Benbow's praise was on every
tongue, and his valor was so highly extolled that

government became desirous of having his services. Accordingly, on the 30th of September, 1689, without having previously served in the Royal Navy, he was nominated to the command of the "York."

After seeing something of the king's service, Benbow was in 1693 appointed to the "Norwich," and dispatched with a squadron of frigates and bomb-ketches to bombard St. Maloes. Having performed this business with ability and success, he was next year appointed by Sir Cloudesley Shovel to cover the attack on Dunkirk with the "infernals." Soon after this, Benbow, appointed to the "Northumberland," a ship of seventy guns, was employed under Lord Berkeley; and early in 1696 he went with the squadron under Sir Cloudesley Shovel to bombard Calais.

During the operations at Calais Benbow was wounded; but he soon recovered, and pursued his nautical career with such success that William of Orange, in recognition of his capacity and courage, promoted him to be a Rear Admiral of the Blue. Benbow then hoisted his flag on board the "Suffolk," and sailed with a squadron to block up the port of Dunkirk, where Du Bart then lay.

In this position, and while watching Du Bart, Benbow showed remarkable activity, and had the satisfaction of saving the English fleets on their way from Virginia and the West Indies from fall-

ing into the hands of French privateers. He was
less successful in the main object of his vigil, but
from no fault of his own. It is said that, had the
Admiralty listened to his representations as to
the proper time for sending home ships to refit,
Du Bart could hardly have escaped. As it was,
the ships were at Dunkirk when they should have
been in the Downs, and consequently in the Downs
when they should have been at Dunkirk; and Du
Bart, availing himself of the circumstance, put to
sea with the spring tides. Benbow afterward
pursued, but Du Bart, by superior sailing, contrived to elude the English admiral.

After returning from Dunkirk, Benbow was
appointed by Sir Cloudesley Shovel to protect
English commerce in the Channel, and, hoisting
his flag on board the "Shrewsbury," he occupied
himself with that kind of service until the Peace
of Ryswick. Being then appointed to the command of a small squadron equipped, notwithstanding the peace, to keep guard over English
interests in the West Indies, he, in 1698, proceeded to Jamaica. Returning from that station, he
was ordered to shift his flag to the "Winchester," and dispatched with a squadron to Dunkirk,
where the French were supposed to be fitting out
an armament for a descent on England. But all
apprehensions of danger in that quarter having
vanished, Benbow sailed back to England; and,
having been promoted to the rank of Vice Admi-

ral of the Blue, probably considered that he had, by his long and arduous services, entitled himself to a little leisure.

But, if Benbow indulged such ideas, his disappointment must have been considerable. At that time England was on the eve of a new war. In fact, Louis the Fourteenth, by placing his grandson on the throne of Spain, and proclaiming the son of James the Second as King of England, roused Europe to arms, and William of Orange perceived the necessity of sending a naval force to cope with the French in the West Indies. A squadron was accordingly fitted out; but such was the prejudice then entertained against the tropical climate, that every gentleman sailor to whom the command was offered by government shrugged his shoulders, and declined the appointment with evident horror.

"It is clear," said the king's ministers, "that Admiral Benbow is the proper man."

"No," said William, "it is unreasonable to ask a man to return to the West Indies who only came from Jamaica last year, and who has since been at Dunkirk."

"But no other man will go," urged the ministers.

"Well, then," said William, yielding, "I suppose we must spare our beaux, and send honest Benbow."

"For my part," said Benbow, when the subject

was mentioned to him, "I know no difference of
climates, and I don't think an officer has a right
to pick and choose a station. I myself will always be ready to go to any part of the world
where his majesty thinks proper to send me."

Benbow now hoisted his flag in the "Breda,"
and, sailing from Spithead with the squadron,
reached Barbadoes as the autumn of 1701 was
expiring. Finding the Leeward Islands in no
danger, the admiral proceeded to Jamaica, and
anchoring off Port Royal, made such arrangements for defense as rendered any attack upon
that place utterly hopeless. This done, Benbow
found himself master of the seas in which his fleet
lay.

In the spring of 1702, however, intelligence
reached Port Royal that the French had a much
stronger naval force at Martinique than the English had at Jamaica. Moreover, rumors ran
that Admiral Du Casse was coming from Europe
to re-enforce the French fleet, and, as commander-in-chief, to make the flag of the Bourbons supreme in the West Indies. Benbow, who was
not in the least daunted by this intelligence, prepared to put to sea; and learning, while cruising
about, that Du Casse had sailed for Carthagena,
and was to steer from Carthagena to Porto Bel-
lo, he without delay went off in pursuit.

For some time Benbow's search after Du Casse
proved futile. On the evening of the 19th of

August, 1702, however, he descried some tall ships to the westward, and standing toward them, found to his joy that they were French men-of-war, and Du Casse's fleet. Immediately he made a signal to form in line of battle, and next morning the action began ; but, to Benbow's astonishment and dismay, two of the English ships, after firing their broadsides, got out of the line, and the admiral began to perceive that some of his captains were either cowards or traitors.

Nevertheless, Benbow, in the "Breda," stuck to the French ; and, though sometimes unattended save by the "Ruby," kept the enemy company for days, and attacked whenever a favorable opportunity presented itself. At length, on the evening of the 23d of August, after the chase had continued for days, Benbow found that his whole squadron was up ; and as the French were within two miles, he congratulated himself on the prospect of doing something that would be talked of in England. But no sooner did he indicate his intention of attacking the enemy than his captains again showed the white feather, and almost every ship of his squadron fell astern.

Notwithstanding this desertion, Benbow, early in the morning of the 24th of August, came up with the sternmost ship of Du Casse's fleet, and instantly gave battle. The Frenchman quickly returned the fire, and a severe conflict commenced. As the firing became hot, a chain-shot, striking

Benbow, broke his right leg, and he was carried
below faint and bleeding; but, quickly recovering his spirits, he ordered that he should be taken
to the quarter-deck, and, seated there in a cradle,
he urged his men on to the encounter.

"Sir," said one of the officers of the "Breda,"
approaching, "we are all so sorry that you've lost
your leg."

"I'm sorry for it too," said Benbow; "but
confound me if I would not rather have lost both
legs ten times over than have seen this dishonor
brought on the English nation! Do you hear?"

"Yes, sir," said the officer.

"Well, then, look you," continued Benbow,
"if another shot should take me off, behave like
brave men and fight it out."

Resolved to make a last appeal to the honor
and patriotism of the captains, Benbow requested them to come on board the "Breda," and implored them to keep the line and behave themselves like Englishmen. But his appeal was vain.
Nothing could be made of the recreants; and
Benbow, reluctantly compelled to abandon all
idea of a victory over Du Casse, made up his
mind to return to Jamaica.

In his distress, Benbow derived some slight degree of satisfaction from a letter which he received from a quarter whence, perhaps, he least
expected expressions of sympathy. It was from
the admiral whom he had been so eager to en-

gage. "Sir," wrote Du Casse, "I had little hope
on Monday last but to have supped in your cabin.
However, it has pleased God to order it otherwise, and I am thankful. As for the cowardly
captains who deserted you, hang them up, for
they deserve it!"

When the English fleet reached Port Royal, a
court-martial was held, and Wade and Kirkby,
two of the captains, were tried for cowardice and
breach of orders. They were then sent to England; but, on reaching Portsmouth, they were
ordered to be shot without being allowed to set
foot in the country on whose flag they had
brought dishonor.

Meanwhile Benbow, on arriving in Jamaica,
had his shattered leg cut off, and for a time entertained hopes of recovery. Fever, however,
followed the operation; and, after struggling for
weeks, his strong constitution yielded. On the
4th of November, 1704, the brave admiral expired; and his body, having been brought to England, was buried in a church-yard at Deptford.

LORD RODNEY.

AT a levee held by George the Second toward the middle of the eighteenth century, an Admiral of the Blue, who was also a Lord of the Admiralty, presented a naval captain, who was then approaching his thirtieth year, and probably looked much younger than he was.

"I did not imagine," said the king, speaking with a strong German accent, "I did not imagine that I had so young a captain in my navy."

"Sire," was the reply, "young Rodney has been for six years a captain; and, without reflecting on any one, I most heartily wish your majesty had a hundred such captains."

The Admiral of the Blue was Lord Anson, then fresh from his victory over the French; and the juvenile captain was George Brydges Rodney, who, by his behavior, had in various actions won reputation for courage and resolution, and son, moreover, of a naval officer who had commanded the yacht kept to convey George the First to the Continent when that personage left his new kingdom to visit his old electorate, and exchanged St. James's Palace for the delights of Hernhausen.

Rodney was born on the 19th of February, 1718, and soon after baptized by the names of George and Brydges, in honor of his sponsors, who were no less important personages than the King of England and the Duke of Chandos. At an early age he was sent to Harrow. But he did not sit long on the benches of that celebrated seminary. At twelve, indeed, he left school and his juvenile comrades to enter upon that career which was to conduct him to influence and fame.

It was about the year 1730 that Rodney first went to sea. The king having given him a "letter of service," he commenced his professional duties, and roughed it out for several years on the Newfoundland station. As time passed on, he was appointed lieutenant of the "Dolphin," in which he sailed with the Mediterranean squadron; and having spent three years between that vessel and the "Essex" and the "Royal Sovereign," he in 1742 found himself in command of the "Plymouth." With this ship of sixty-four guns Rodney brought three hundred merchantmen through the French fleet, then cruising in the chops of the Channel; and, having been removed by the Admiralty into the "Ludlow Castle," he had the distinction of capturing the "St. Maloes," a great privateer.

This was, indeed, a period when an English officer of Rodney's spirit could hardly fail to win honor. The death of Charles, the last German

S

emperor of the house of Hapsburg, had thrown
Europe into confusion; for Charles left no son,
and the hereditary claims of his daughter, Maria
Theresa, wife of Charles of Lorraine, were fiercely disputed by the Elector of Bavaria. The
princes of Christendom were drawn into the
quarrel; and, as George the Second espoused the
cause of Maria Theresa, while Louis the Fifteenth
took the side of the Elector, England and France
were speedily at war. Blood was soon shed.
The King of England vanquished the French at
Dettingen, while his son, the Duke of Cumberland, was defeated at Fontenoy; and matters
were embittered by the adventure of Prince
Charles Edward Stuart, who, while King George
was in Hanover, landed in Scotland, rallied the
Highlanders to his standard, and attempted to
enforce the claims of his father James to the sovereignty of Great Britain.

At this crisis, Rodney was appointed captain
of the "Eagle," a new ship of sixty guns; and,
after distinguishing himself against the enemy
while cruising on the Irish station, he sailed with
that squadron which, in the spring of 1747, was
sent to seize a hundred and seventy French merchantmen on their voyage from St. Domingo. In
this expedition Rodney displayed his wonted energy, and in the scramble that ensued had the
satisfaction of taking six prizes.

Soon after this achievement, Rodney, in the

"Eagle," joined the squadron which, in the autumn of 1747, sailed from Plymouth to intercept a fleet of trading vessels which nine French ships-of-war were convoying. After a long watch, the English, on the 1st of October, caught sight of the enemy; and the French admiral, having directed that one ship of the line and several frigates should make the best of their way with the merchantmen, drew up his ships, and intimated his intention of giving battle.

In the action that ensued Rodney took a conspicuous part. During the engagement, the "Eagle," after passing through a raking fire all down the French line, commenced a desperate struggle with two of the enemy. Her position exposed her to a fearful hazard; her wheel was shot away, all her braces and bowlines were gone, and she was for a time quite ungovernable. Rodney, however, persevered with the combat, and had just boarded and taken his principal adversary, when Hawke came to the rescue. Not content with his prize, Rodney hastened to repair the damage which the "Eagle" had sustained, and went in pursuit of the French admiral.

The chase proved unsuccessful; but soon after Rodney consoled himself for his disappointment. Being one of a small squadron that fell in with a Spanish fleet of twelve sail of the line with a rich convoy from the West Indies, he took part in an attack, and the Spaniards, notwithstanding the

superiority of their force, saw six of the merchantmen carried off as prizes.

At length, in 1748, the struggle that had for
years agitated Christendom was terminated by
the peace of Aix-la-Chapelle; and the "Eagle"
being paid off, Rodney returned to England. But
he did not remain long unoccupied. Almost ere
the peace was signed he was appointed Governor
of Newfoundland, and commander-in-chief on the
Newfoundland station. In that position he continued till the close of 1752, when he came to England, married a lady named Compton, who was
sister of the Earl of Northampton, and found his
way into the House of Commons as member for
Saltash.

While Rodney occupied a seat in Parliament,
Europe was again threatened with war. In fact,
the limits of territory in North America, not having been well defined by the treaty of Aix-la-
Chapelle, gave rise to controversy; and in 1755
England and France were closely watching each
other, when encroachments led to bloodshed. In
consequence, the English seized some French
vessels; and the demand of the French government for restitution having been rejected, hostilities on a great scale became inevitable, and the
two nations prepared, with all their old antipa-
thies in full force, for that terrible struggle celebrated in history as "The Seven Years' War."

At the beginning of the war, which opened inauspiciously for England with the loss of Minorca and the execution of Admiral Byng, Rodney does not appear to have had any opportunity of signalizing himself. It is true that, appointed to the "Dublin" in 1757, he sailed with Hawke in the expedition against Rochefort, and in the spring of 1758 joined the squadron sent under Boscawen to reduce Louisburg. But it was not till 1758, when promoted to the rank of Rear Admiral of the Blue, that his energy and talent were fully displayed.

About that time the French, ever vaporing about invading England, had collected a number of flat-bottomed boats at Havre de Grace. Against this place it was thought fit to send a small squadron of ships-of-war and bomb-ketches. Rodney was appointed to the command of this force; and, sailing from St. Helen's, he, on the 3d of July, anchored in the road of Havre, and immediately prepared to execute his orders by placing the bomb-ketches in the narrow channel of the river, and stationing the ships-of-war so as to protect them.

Early in the morning of the 4th of July, every thing was in readiness, and the bombardment commenced. For more than fifty hours operations went on, the French replying briskly, and making every effort to defend the place. Nevertheless, the town was repeatedly in flames; and for six hours the magazines burned furiously, in spite of extraordinary efforts to extinguish the fire. At length, the French flotilla having been utterly destroyed, the inhabitants of Havre fled in consternation, and the place, completely ruined as a naval arsenal, was left wholly incapable of causing annoyance to England.

After this achievement Rodney continued on the French coast, displaying all the zeal and energy for which he was remarkable. In 1761, however, he was appointed to the command of an expedition fitted out to reduce Martinique, and, hoisting his flag on board the "Marlborough," he in October sailed from Spithead with four ships, three bomb-ketches, and a sloop-of-war.

Martinique was the most important of all the French settlements in the West Indies, and the seat of the governor general of the French Caribbee Islands. The acquisition of the place was for many reasons regarded as of great importance to England, but the reduction of it was deemed a matter of no small difficulty. Indeed, when, during the previous war, the English made a descent with that object, they had found it so well fortified as to defy their efforts.

About the beginning of January, 1762, Rodney, who had been re-enforced at Barbadoes by two ships, with troops fresh from the conquest of Belleisle, arrived off Martinique. Having anchored in St. Peter's Bay, and silenced the forts there, the admiral proceeded to land his troops. This was accomplished without loss; but formidable difficulties still lay before the English. In fact, four miles had to be traversed before siege could be laid to Fort Royal; the country, mountainous in the centre, was intersected with deep ravines, through which flowed streams the fords of which were rendered difficult by the rocks that had rolled into them from the sides of the mountains. Moreover, the French had batteries erected and guards posted wherever practicable, and improved the natural fortifications of the island by every means in their power.

In spite of the formidable array of difficulties that beset his path, Rodney hastened to land the artillery, and, while regular troops and marines marched along the shore toward the town to storm the redoubts, a thousand seamen, in flat-bottomed boats, rowed close in-shore to assist the operations. The attack was made on all hands with courage, and succeeded in every quarter. Indeed, the French were panic-stricken as redoubt after redoubt fell, and abandoned their citadel almost without a blow; St. Pierre, the capital of Martinique, and the whole island, ere long surrendered; Grenada, St. Vincent, and St. Lucia were soon after reduced; and the whole of the French Caribbees were in the hands of the English.

By this time, indeed, the genius and vigor of

the first Pitt had wrought wonders, and his very
name was terrible to his country's foes. Every
where the English were triumphant; the shattered remains of the fleets of France were shut up
in ports, and the coasts of France were at the
mercy of the squadrons of her victorious foe.
But in 1763, soon after George the Third ascended the throne, the war was closed by a treaty
which, while restoring some of the conquests to
France, left England undisputed mistress of the
seas.

At the peace Rodney returned to England.
In recognition of his services he was created a
baronet, and thanked by both houses of Parliament. In the following year he was appointed
Governor of Greenwich Hospital, and in the winter of 1765 entered upon that post.

It would seem that when Rodney became governor of Greenwich Hospital the out-pensioners
were not allowed great-coats except under pecul-
iar circumstances, and by order of the governor.
Rodney had the usual applications; and as he
could not say "No" to an old sailor on a cold
day, the demands became so numerous and the
great-coats so general, that, at the next meeting,
the lieutenant governor took upon him to repre-
sent the matter to the Board.

"I must say," he observed in conclusion, "that
the indulgence shown by the governor is extremely reprehensible."

"Sir," said Rodney, rising and addressing the
lieutenant governor, "I have the greatest respect
for you as a man who, by the greatest merit, have
risen from the station of a foremast man to the
rank of admiral, a circumstance which not only
does you the highest honor, but would have led
me to expect you as an advocate rather than an
opponent of such an indulgence. Many of the
poor men at the door have been your shipmates,
and once your companions. Never hurt a broth-
er-sailor; and let me warn you against two
things more: the first is, not to interfere between me and my duty as governor; and the
second is, not to object to these brave men having great-coats, while you are so fond of one as
to wear it by the side of so good a fire as that
by which you are at present sitting."

In 1771, Rodney, having meanwhile embarked
in a ruinous contest as candidate for the borough
of Northampton, resigned his post as Governor
of Greenwich Hospital, and for some time was
commander-in-chief of the West India station.
After returning home, he found his affairs so em-
barrassed, and his creditors so importunate, that
he was under the necessity of going to France
and living in obscurity. While in this plight,
the admiral attracted the attention of the French
Minister of Police, who recommended the Duke
de Brion to offer him a liberal supply of money
on condition of his taking command of the French

fleet in the West Indies. The duke accordingly
invited Rodney to visit him, and one morning,
when they were walking in the garden of the
chateau, delicately broached the question. Rodney, however, quite failed to perceive at what his
host was driving, and the duke, at last, had to re-
fer to his guest's debts, and to speak in somewhat plain terms.

"I am empowered on the king's behalf," such
were Brion's words, "to offer you any sum of
money you require on condition that you will
take the command of his majesty's fleet in the
West Indies."

"Sir," said Rodney, after a painful pause, during which he mastered his emotions, "it is true
that my distresses have driven me from my country, but no temptation whatever can ever es-
trange me from her service. Had this offer been
a voluntary one on your part, I should have
deemed it an insult; but I am glad to think that
it proceeds from a source that can do no wrong."

After this memorable scene, no farther attempt
was made; but in 1778, when war between England and France again appeared inevitable, Rodney was enabled, with Brion's kindly aid, to accommodate matters with his creditors and come
to England. Some time before leaving Paris he
met the Duke of Chartres, who afterward, as
Duke of Orleans, rendered himself so notorious.

"Do you know," said Chartres, "that I am to

have a command in the fleet that is to oppose
your Admiral Keppel?"

"Indeed!" said Rodney.

"Yes," replied Chartres; "and," asked he, in
an insulting tone, "what do you think will be the
result of our meeting?"

"I think," answered Rodney, "that my coun-
tryman will carry your grace home with him to
learn English."

Rodney's reception in England was by no
means such as he might reasonably have anticipated. For some time the heroic admiral's offers
were coldly treated by government. At last,
however, his ambition to serve his king and country was gratified. About the end of the year
1779 he was appointed to the command of the
Leeward Island station; and having been promoted to the rank of Admiral of the White, he
hoisted his flag on board the "Sandwich," and
sailed from Spithead with eighteen sail of the
line, transports with stores for Gibraltar, and a
large fleet of merchantmen for the Mediterranean.
Prince William Henry, afterward Duke of Clarence and King of England, went as a midshipman
on board the "Royal George."

For some time after sailing from Spithead Rodney met with no adventures worthy of record.
On the 8th of January, 1780, however, when west
of Cape Finisterre, he had the good fortune to
capture a valuable Spanish convoy; and, while

proceeding with this prize along the coast of Portugal, he obtained information that the Spanish admiral, Don Juan de Langara, was cruising off Cape St. Vincent with fourteen ships of the line. Rodney, placing his convoy in the rear of his fleet, ordered that his ships should sail abreast in line of battle, and about noon on the 16th of January the enemy appeared in sight.

When first descried the Spaniards were under easy sail, and some of the ships were standing toward the English. Indeed, it seemed probable that, from the English line being much extended, and the weather hazy, Don Juan de Langara had no idea of Rodney's force. Soon, however, the Spaniards, as if suddenly aware of their danger, began to retreat. But, not having the least intention of allowing them to escape, Rodney made the signal for giving chase, and issued orders for his ships engaging as they came up with the enemy.

An hour or two passed over; the pursuit became more and more exciting; and at four in the afternoon Rodney perceived that the most advanced ships were near the Spaniards. Immediately he made the signal to close and engage, and soon the action became general. For many hours the conflict was maintained with vigor on both sides, and the fire was kept up constantly till after midnight. Meanwhile one Spanish ship having blown up, every man on board having perished, and the " Minorca," which led the Spanish van, having struck to the " Sandwich," the conflict ceased, and the defeat of the Spaniards was complete.

After proceeding to the relief of Gibraltar, Rodney pursued his voyage, and, arriving in the West Indies, found himself in command of twenty-one sail of the line and several frigates. Hearing, while in this position, that the Count de Giuchen had left Fort Royal under cover of night, the English admiral got under way and sailed in pursuit, and on the evening of an April day he came so near to the French as to ascertain that their exact force was twenty-three ships of the line, besides frigates and corvettes.

Rodney now exercised all his ingenuity to bring De Giuchen to battle, and the Frenchman used his utmost efforts to avoid an engagement. A whole day was spent in the manœuvres of the admirals. But, on the morning of the 17th of April, Rodney, seeing that the English fleet was favored by the wind, gave the signal for close action, and, having ordered that every ship should bear down and steer for that in the enemy's line which was opposite to her, he set the example by riding gallantly down upon that which bore the flag of the French admiral. De Giuchen was by this movement forced out of the line, and two of his ships coming to his aid, rendered the position of the " Sandwich" somewhat critical. In fact,

Rodney had to maintain the contest against fearful odds for nearly an hour. But the English seamen fought with characteristic resolution; and such was the spirit with which the admiral inspired his crew, that a woman on board fought a twenty-four pounder gun. It soon appeared that Rodney's captains had imperfectly understood his orders. But at length Sir Hyde Parker came to the admiral's rescue; and De Giuchen, leaving the "Sandwich" almost a wreck, drew off. It was found impossible that night to pursue the French. Moreover, every subsequent attempt to make them renew the engagement proved futile; and the re-enforcement of De Giuchen by a Spanish squadron at Guadaloupe rendered the French admiral so infinitely superior in most respects that Rodney was fain to remain inactive.

In the autumn of 1781, Rodney — who meanwhile had sailed to the American station, attempted without success to take St. Vincent, and succeeded in reducing St. Eustace—found his health so impaired by hard and harassing service that he deemed it necessary to repair to England. Scarcely had he arrived when he was, on the death of Hawke, nominated Vice Admiral of Great Britain, and soon after he was reappointed to his command in the West Indies. Hoisting his flag in the "Formidable," Rodney sailed early in 1782, and, having formed a junction off Antigua with Sir Samuel Hood, he prepared to conquer.

It was, indeed, essential at that period to the interests of England that a great blow should be struck. At Fort Royal, under the Count de Grasse, the French had prepared a formidable armament for the reduction of Jamaica, which in 1656 had been wrested by Penn and Venables from the Spaniards, and had ever since been held by the English. With a fleet of thirty-three sail of the line, numerous frigates, corvettes, and armed brigs, more than five thousand troops, and a heavy train of artillery, De Grasse made ready to embark; and he indulged the hope, without hazarding a battle, of forming a junction at Cape François with a force which, when added to his own, would give him the command of nearly fifty ships of the line, and some twenty thousand troops. Elate with anticipations of a triumph likely to be long remembered among the glorious achievements of France, De Grasse sailed from the Bay of Fort Royal, his flag flying on board of the "Ville de Paris," which had, at an earlier date, been constructed at the expense of the city as a gift to Louis the Fifteenth, and which had since been celebrated as the largest ship in Europe.

But Rodney was awake to the importance of the crisis, and ready, at the earliest opportunity, to pounce upon the French as his prey. On the 8th of April, 1782, having previously been informed that troops were embarking at Fort Royal, he

received intelligence that De Grasse was coming
out of the bay. Instantly he made the signal to
weigh, and without delay the English fleet got to
sea. Stretching over to Fort Royal, and finding
the French gone, he gave the signal for a general
chase, and at night the lights of the French ships
became distinctly visible.

Early next morning, when De Grasse seemed
to be turning to bay, Rodney made the signal for
forming line. But by this time the fleet was becalmed under the high lands of Dominica, and
the ships could not get into their stations. Ere
long, however, a breeze reached the van; and
Hood, who, in the "Barfleur," commanded that
division, standing in, closed with the enemy's
centre. De Grasse had still no desire to fight.
Indeed, a battle was what he least wished to hazard; but the temptation of crushing the van of
the English, while their centre and rear lay becalmed, proved too strong for his resolution.
Forming, he received the fire of Hood's squadron; and the action having commenced, Hood
had the honor of maintaining the conflict for a
whole hour in the most gallant style, the "Barfleur" being frequently engaged at the same time
with three adversaries.

Meantime, however, the wind began to fill the
sails of Rodney's centre and rear, and as the English ships gradually crowded up to support their
van, the aspect of affairs changed. Repenting of

his rashness, and observing that matters were proving serious, De Grasse, followed by his fleet, withdrew, and, favored by the wind, defied Rodney's efforts to bring him to an engagement. But, induced by the signals for assistance thrown out by some stragglers, which were in imminent danger of being captured, the French admiral bore down to their relief; and Rodney, promptly availing himself of the circumstance, speedily placed De Grasse in such a position that the struggle could no longer be avoided. Accordingly, on the morning of the 12th of April, the action commenced, and the guns blazed and thundered along both lines.

It was now that Rodney put in practice a manœuvre, the consequences of which he had well considered. This consisted of breaking the enemy's line, to which his own ran obliquely. After having received and returned the fire of half the French force, he resorted to this famous expedient, and the "Formidable," followed by the ships in her rear, and continuing her course, broke through De Grasse's line about three ships from the "Ville de Paris," wore and doubled upon the enemy, and kept up a fire so destructive that the French were not only divided, but thrown into utter confusion.

At this stage Hood's division, which had been becalmed, appeared, and, coming up where the fire was hottest, completed the rout. For a con-

T

siderable time several of the French ships held
out gallantly; but at length, just as the sun was
setting, De Grasse, seeing that all was lost, and
that the "Ville de Paris" was disabled by foes
and deserted by friends, hauled down his colors.

Meanwhile government, in their wisdom, had
sent an admiral named Pigott to the West Indies with orders to supersede Rodney. When,
however, news of the important victory reached
London, a swift cutter was dispatched to recall
Pigott, but it was too late; and the new admiral,
on reaching Fort Royal, took the command of
Rodney's victorious fleet.

Rodney immediately shifted his flag, and sailed in a seventy-four gun ship for England. The
welcome he met must in some degree have consoled him. The populace were enthusiastic in
their applause; Parliament voted thanks to him
and to his officers and seamen; and the king
raised him to the peerage with the title of Baron
Rodney of Rodney Stoke, in Somerset.

After this Rodney never accepted of any command; nor, indeed, though he long survived his
victory, did he live even to hear of that great
war with France during which England produced
so many naval heroes. In the spring of 1792,
while Louis the Sixteenth was still residing at
the Tuileries, and while Pitt was still hesitating
in Downing Street, Rodney's last hour drew nigh.

On the 24th of May, while in London, the old admiral departed this life, leaving a name worthy of being mentioned with affectionate pride so long as Englishmen continue to admire heroic courage and to appreciate patriotic devotion.

EARL HOWE.

In the year 1744, when England and France were commencing that war which was terminated by the peace of Aix-la-Chapelle, an English merchantman was one day taken by a French privateer under the very guns of St. Eustace, one of the Caribbee Islands subject to Holland. The Dutch governor permitted the capture without even an attempt at interference, and an English officer, not yet out of his teens, was dispatched, at his own request, to claim the merchantman. His mission, however, proving unsuccessful, he begged to be allowed to cut her out of the harbor; and, disregarding all warnings as to the danger of such an attempt, he entered with the boats, brought away the vessel, and returned her to the owners. The brave officer was Lieutenant Richard Howe, younger son of the second Viscount Howe, a peer of Ireland.

Richard Howe was born in the year 1725. Being the son of a man of rank, and of a lady whose father, Baron Kielmansegge, figured as Master of the Horse to the first of the Georges, he entered upon life under auspices somewhat brighter than most of those heroes who have add-

ed to the glory of the English navy. At the age
of fourteen, however, he left Eton to go on board
the "Severn," and from that day showed no inclination to shirk the duties devolving upon him
as an English sailor.

At the time when Howe entered the navy, Lord
Anson was on the point of commencing his voyage round the world, and the "Severn" was one of
the squadron destined for the enterprise. Howe
was not, however, privileged to accompany Anson to the end of his adventurous voyage. In
fact, the squadron, while passing through the
Straits of Le Maire, was dispersed by a storm;
and the "Severn," after having been separated
from her companions, and tossed by winds and
waves, was fain to make for Brazil.

After this somewhat disastrous opening to his
career, Howe went on board the "Burford," and
served under Commander Knowles in the squadron sent to the coast of Curacoa to attack Laguy-
ra. During the expedition the "Burford" suffered severely, and the captain dying of his wounds,
Howe had the honor of being appointed acting
lieutenant. In this capacity he brought the ship
to England; but, finding that the Admiralty
did not confirm his commission, he returned to
Knowles in the West Indies, and, becoming lieutenant of a sloop of war, performed his celebrated
exploit at St. Eustace.

With the fame of this achievement associated

with his name, Howe returned to England; and in 1745, when Fontenoy was fought, and when Prince Charles Edward landed in Scotland to raise the Stuart standard, he was promoted to the rank of commander, and appointed to the "Baltimore." While cruising in that sloop off the coast of Scotland, Howe fell in with two vessels. On making them out to be French frigates carrying arms and ammunition to the young chevalier, he immediately ran the "Baltimore" between them, and made an attack of the most vigorous kind. While urging on his men with courage and calmness, Howe was wounded in the neck, taken up for dead, and carried from the deck. At first he showed no signs of life. Soon, however, he began to move, and gradually regaining the use of his faculties, cried out to fight on. His wound was then dressed; and no sooner was the operation over, than he made his appearance on deck, and, amid the loud shouts of his men, continued the conflict with such energy that the French frigates sheered off and made for their own coast.

During this action the "Baltimore" was so crippled that all attempts to pursue the French proved vain. But Howe's services did not pass unrewarded. On hearing of his display of zeal and valor, the Admiralty immediately raised him to the rank of post-captain; and he pursued his professional career with distinction, commanding various ships, and serving in different parts of the world.

It was at this period that Howe was one night roused from his slumbers by a first lieutenant, who, in great alarm and agitation, informed him that the ship had taken fire near the powder magazine.

"If that be the case, we shall soon know it," said Howe, rising leisurely to put on his clothes, while the lieutenant hurried away to make farther investigation.

"You need not be afraid," said the officer, returning; "the fire is extinguished."

"Afraid!" exclaimed Howe. "What do you mean, sir? I never was afraid in my life. How does a man *feel* when he is afraid? I need not ask you how he *looks*."

In 1754, Howe, having seen much service, returned to England, and was next year nominated to command the "Dunkirk," a new ship, fitted out in anticipation of that rupture with France which appeared inevitable. Accordingly, the "Dunkirk" formed one of the fleet which sailed for North America under Boscawen. A French fleet sailed from Europe about the same time; and Boscawen, hoping to obstruct the passage into the Gulf of St. Lawrence, took his station off Newfoundland. But a fog came to the assistance of the French admiral, and, availing himself of the advantage, he contrived to escape Boscawen's squadron.

While such was the posture of affairs, the fog, one June day, cleared away, and two French ships, separated from their comrades, appeared in sight. The "Dunkirk," followed by the "Defiance," was then in advance of Boscawen's squadron; and Howe, having borne down on the Frenchman, requested the commander to go immediately under the English admiral's stern.

"Is it peace or war?" asked the Frenchman.

"Come," said Howe, who, being in no humor to be trifled with, repeated his order, "you had better comply at once, for every moment I expect to see a signal to commence the attack."

"Commence when you please," cried the other.

"Very well," replied Howe. But, seeing the quarter-deck covered with ladies and other passengers, he took off his hat, and politely begged them to leave the deck. "You can have no part in the action," said he, "and I only await your retiring to begin."

Ere this the ships had come close to each other, and at the same moment their guns opened. An hour of fierce strife succeeded; and when it was over, one French ship had struck to the "Dunkirk," the other to the "Defiance." Many prisoners and an immense sum of money fell into the hands of the English.

Time passed on; and in 1758, when Europe was excited and agitated by the Seven Years' War, Howe, then in command of the "Essex," on the 6th of August anchored with a squadron in the Bay of Cherbourg with the intention of attacking the port. At night a few shells were thrown into the town, and the troops, having landed next morning, took possession of the fortifications, levied a contribution on the inhabitants, ruined the celebrated basin, destroyed twenty-seven vessels in the harbor, rendered useless two hundred iron guns and mortars, took twenty pieces of brass cannon on board the ships, and, sailing in triumph toward England, anchored off Weymouth.

Soon after this successful exploit Howe was instructed to proceed with his squadron toward St. Maloes, to make frequent descents, and keep the French coast in alarm. The town of St. Maloes, however, was the point at which he chiefly aimed, and troops were landed to make an attack. Every thing seemed to promise success; but, at the last moment, the officers in command of the land forces hesitated, deliberated, and finally declaring that victory was not to be hoped for, determined that the troops should re-embark. This, however, was no such easy operation. In fact, they had to march overland to St. Casse; and in getting into the boats, they had to stand a murderous fire from the French guns.

In the midst of this fire, which daunted the bravest, and cost more lives than it would have cost to take St. Maloes, Howe's courage shone conspicuously. Ordering his boat to be rowed into the thickest of the fire, he stood up, and both by words and gestures encouraged the men to persevere. Animated by his voice and example, they made every possible exertion, and he had the satisfaction of saving hundreds, who, without his aid, must have perished.

In 1759, Howe, who had just married a lady named Hartop, and succeeded his brother as fourth viscount, was stationed in the Channel, of which Hawke then had the command. In this position he took part in the great action between Hawke and the naval force of Louis the Fifteenth under De Conflans, which resulted in the defeat of the French admiral and the destruction of the French fleet. Next year Howe reduced the French fort on the island of Dumet; and having continued at sea till the peace of 1763, he was appointed to a seat at the Board of Admiralty, and gradually promoted to the rank of Vice Admiral of the Blue. His promotion appeared so rapid as to occasion some discussion in the House of Lords; but Hawke, then First Lord of the Admiralty, answered in the most conclusive tone.

"I advised his majesty to make the appointments," said Hawke; "I have tried my Lord Howe on very important occasions, and he never asked me how to execute any service—he went and performed it."

"My lord," observed King George, when Howe

was presented at court, "your life has been a continued series of services to your country."

Howe's services had indeed been arduous. His career, however, was not yet closed. In fact, he was destined to associate his name with three great events. These were the struggle between England and the American colonists, the war of England with the French and Spanish Bourbons, and that long contest on the sea and on the land between England and revolutionized France, which was brought to a close at Trafalgar and Waterloo.

When Parliament, under the auspices of George Grenville, prime minister of England, passed an act imposing a stamp act on the American colonies, the colonists, indignant and irritated at the idea of being taxed by an assembly to which they sent no representative, resolved on resistance; and when government made formidable preparations to enforce submission, Howe was appointed to the command of the fleet on the American station. Hoisting his flag on board the "Eagle," Howe, in July, 1776, about the time when blood was shed at Lexington, arrived at Halifax, and signalized his term of command by taking New York, Rhode Island, and Philadelphia.

At one period of the war, indeed, the cause of the colonists appeared hopeless. But the aspect of affairs suddenly changed. France, eager by any process, however impolitic, to gain some tem-

porary advantage over the foe by whom she had
a hundred times been castigated and humbled,
formed an alliance with the Americans; and in
1778, the Count D'Estaing unexpectedly appeared with a large fleet. Howe's ships were in no
condition to carry on an offensive war. He con-
tented himself, therefore, with standing on his defense, and, in spite of countless disadvantages,
contrived to baffle the foe and to close the campaign with honor.

Meanwhile France and England had declared
war, and France, having doubled her naval strength
by an alliance with Spain, threatened England
with a descent. The menace resulted in nothing;
but in 1782, the Duke of Crillon having seized
upon the island of Minorca, laid siege to Gibraltar, of which Sir Gilbert Elliot was then governor,
and erected floating batteries opposite those of
the town, while the combined navies of France
and Spain, under the command of Don Louis de
Cordova, were prepared to prevent relief from
England reaching the garrison. Nevertheless,
government mustered a fleet to relieve the be-
leaguered strong-hold, and Howe, who had recently been created a peer of Great Britain, took
the command.

It was the autumn of 1782 when Howe left the
shores of England with thirty-four sail of the line.
Entering the Straits on the 11th of October, he
anchored off the Bay of Gibraltar. A storm hav-

ing dispersed the French fleet, two of Howe's vessels without delay passed in with the store-ships and tenders under the guns of the fort, while the English admiral, with the remainder of his force, defied the French to a combat. Don Louis de Cordova, however, declined the challenge; and Howe, having relieved the garrison without firing a shot, dispersed the squadron to their various stations, and returned to England.

Next year, when Lord Shelburne became prime minister, and Pitt, then twenty-three, became Chancellor of the Exchequer, peace was concluded, and Howe, whose services were not required at sea, undertook the duties of First Lord of the Admiralty. In this position he continued during Pitt's first administration till 1793, having in the interval been advanced to the dignity of earl, and promoted to the rank of Admiral of the Blue.

Meanwhile the French Revolution had startled Europe. In 1789, the financial embarrassment caused by the interference of France in the American war led to the assembling of the States-General at Versailles, and to the beginning of the Revolution. Soon after, the States-General formed themselves into the National Assembly, and Paris became the scene of sanguinary insurrections. Events hurried rapidly onward. The Bastile was taken; the princes of the blood and the French nobles were under the necessity of leav-

ing the country; Louis the Sixteenth, brought
forcibly from Versailles to the Tuileries, was
forced to accept the Declaration of the Rights of
Man; monastic institutions and titles of nobility
were suppressed; the king, intercepted at Varen-
nes in endeavoring to escape, was brought back
a prisoner; the palace of the Tuileries was forced
by an armed mob; the king and his family, having taken refuge in the National Assembly, were
incarcerated in the Temple; the National Convention having been constituted, abolished monarchy, proclaimed France a republic, decreed fra-
ternity and assistance to all nations in the recovery of their liberty, brought the king to trial,
condemned him to death, and sent him to execution.

While these events were occurring, England
looked on without attempting to interfere; but,
after the execution of Louis the Sixteenth, the
government of England declined to recognize the
French embassadors, and the Convention retali-
ated by a declaration of war. The English then
entered on the struggle with confidence; and
Howe, invested with extraordinary power, left
the Admiralty to take the command of the Channel fleet.

For some time after going on board the "Queen
Charlotte," Howe occupied himself with watching a formidable French fleet, which, under the
command of Admiral Villaret Joyeuse, lay in the

port of Brest. The watch was long, and doubt-less somewhat wearisome to the English sailors, burning with that eagerness natural in the cir-cumstances to the fighting men of "an old and haughty nation, proud in arms." At length, ear-ly in May, 1794, the French admiral did pluck up courage to venture out of Brest, and, concealed by a fog, passed, without being discovered, within earshot of the English fog-signals. On the 21st of May, however, Howe received information that the force under Villaret Joyeuse was twenty-six ships of the line and five frigates, and set out in pursuit. On the morning of the 28th of May, while the wind was blowing fresh with a rough sea, he had the gratification of learning that the enemy was in sight; and the first shot having been fired about two o'clock that day, the fleets for the next two days kept up a running fight, the French getting the worst in every encounter.

On the night of the 29th of May, however, a dense fog put a stop to all operations; but on the 31st of May the fog cleared away, and the French were descried about seven miles to the north-ward. Howe immediately bore up and formed, but Villaret Joyeuse held off, and night fell with-out an action taking place. During the night the French kept up a press of sail, to take advantage of any negligence on the part of the English; but Howe, who had been apprehensive of their weathering him in the darkness, exercised the ut-

most vigilance, and when morning dawned the
hostile fleets drew up in order of battle.

It was Sunday morning—the morning of the
1st of June, 1794, a day indissolubly associated
with the memory of Howe, and worthy of being
long remembered with pride by Englishmen.
At half past seven Howe made a signal that he
should attack the French centre, passing through
the enemy's lines, and engaging them to leeward.
Villaret Joyeuse, in the "Montaigne," awaited
the attack with firmness, and the French guns
were the first to open, but at too long a range to
provoke reply. At length, however, when the
fire had continued for a quarter of an hour along
the line, Howe's guns answered heavily, full, and
rapidly. After this, little regard was paid to position. Some of the English ships cut through
the French line and engaged to leeward; the
others hauled to windward; but all fought desperately, each ship bringing her guns to bear on
the nearest Frenchman, and rapidly dismantling
the fleet of the new republic.

About eleven o'clock, indeed, the conflict was
virtually at an end, and Howe's victory was as
complete as he could have anticipated. When a
lull took place and the smoke cleared away, the
French line was hopelessly broken. Many ships
were totally mastless, six were in the hands of
the English, and Admiral Villaret Joyeuse, in the
"Montaigne," was making sail ahead with all the
vessels in a condition to fly.

Howe, having thoroughly done his work, returned to England, and on the 19th of June the victorious fleet appeared off Portsmouth. Seldom has that town presented a scene more exciting. Crowds occupied the beach and the ramparts; a salute from the batteries hailed the "Queen Charlotte" when she came to anchor; and a round of artillery, mingled with mighty shouts of applause from the multitude, greeted the conquering hero as he stepped ashore.

The House of Lords and the House of Commons voted Howe thanks for the exertions which had resulted in "the glorious 1st of June;" and on the 26th of that month George the Third, with the queen and three of the princesses, arrived at Portsmouth to visit Howe's ship. Next morning the royal party proceeded in barges to Spithead, where the "Queen Charlotte" lay; and the king, having dined on board, held a naval levee, when he presented Howe with a sword of great value, and a gold chain, to which was appended a medal that had been struck for the occasion.

"My lord," said King George, "you have rendered your country the most invaluable of services."

"Not I," said Howe; "but," he added, turning toward the seamen, "those noble fellows who gained the victory."

Howe continued for twelve months longer to command the Channel fleet. During the spring

U

of 1795, however, his health was in such a state
that he was obliged to resign. In the year 1796
he was appointed Admiral of the Fleet, and undertook the command of the western squadron.
But early in 1797, when beyond the age of threescore and ten, he finally left the pine plank for the
peaceful hall.

Even when he had thus struck his flag Howe's
career was not quite closed. In the very last
year of his naval life he rendered to his country
a memorable service. When the spirit of insubordination which was abroad found its way to
his majesty's ships of war, and when mutinies at
Portsmouth and the Nore disgraced the navy and
alarmed the nation, Howe exerted all his sagacity
and influence to save England from the disaster
with which she was menaced, and to restore the
honor of that profession of which he had long
been the pride and the ornament.

Intent upon allaying the spirit of mutiny, Howe
suggested several measures to the government
of the day, and exerted all his personal influence
to expel the disloyalty which began to prevail
among the seamen of England. Having contributed by every means in his power to bring back
the good old temper of the English navy, he retired from public life.

On the 2d of June, 1797, Howe was invested
with the insignia of the Garter; but he did not
long survive his admission into "the noblest of

European orders." On the 5th of August, 1799, a few months before Bonaparte was declared First Consul, Howe breathed his last. His name was long of high account with the people of England, and his memory, to which a monument was erected in St. Paul's Cathedral, was long held by them in affectionate regard.

EARL ST. VINCENT.

One day, early in the year 1748, a few months after the victory achieved by Hawke over the French fleet, and shortly before the peace of Aix-la-Chapelle, a little boy, about thirteen years of age, in a garb somewhat grotesque, arrived at Portsmouth, and went on board the "Gloucester," then fitting out for the West Indies. His prospects can not be said to have been brilliant. He had no money except the few pounds carried in his pocket; and, though his blood was better and more ancient than that of most aristocrats, he had little or no aristocratic influence on which to rely for aid in fighting the battle of life. But he had, as the result proved, the spirit of a man, the resolution of a hero, much hope, founded on an instinctive confidence in his own capacity, and enough, at all events, of that energy which is hope in action to struggle upward to distinction, fame, wealth, and an earldom, and to leave a memorable example to aspiring youth of industry, perseverance, courage, and self-denial, elevating their possessor from obscurity and neglect to renown and rank.

John Jervis was descended from a family which

had occupied a position of some consideration in Staffordshire while the Plantagenets ruled England, and he was born on the 20th of January, 1735, at Meaford, in the parish of Stone. In the neighborhood of that market-town Jervis passed the years of his childhood. At an early age, however, he was deemed fit to go from home, and sent to be educated at Burton-on-Trent.

The school at which Jervis was placed does not appear to have been quite to his liking. The temper of the master was the reverse of mild; the temper of the master's wife was not celestial; and the former, being kept in a state of perpetual irritation by his shrewish dame, treated his pupils with a degree of severity well-nigh intolerable. Jervis, however, applied himself to his studies with diligence, and with such success that he ere long enjoyed the reputation of knowing more of Greek than any boy of whom the seminary could boast. He was, in consequence, put forward on great days, and exhibited as "a show scholar."

This distinction was not without inconveniences. It happened that on one occasion a rich London distiller, paying a visit to Burton, and feeling an interest in the institution, expressed a desire to ascertain the proficiency of the boys. The master readily consented; and Jervis was, as a matter of course, selected for the honorable duty of reading a passage from Homer. This

task he undertook with ardor, and entered upon
with courage. But he had been particularly
taught "to sing out," as it was expressively
termed, and consequently read in so loud a tone
that the metropolitan distiller could not refrain
from indicating his surprise.

"I am not deaf," he said.

"What, sir?" stammered Jervis, in confusion.

"I am not deaf, sir," cried the distiller; "but
you read, sir, as if you spoke through a speaking-
trumpet."

Completely discomfited by this cruel interruption, Jervis, with all his natural resolution, could
scarcely restrain his tears. But the distiller cool-
ly took snuff without evincing any regret for the
pain he had caused, and the master had the mortification of perceiving that his chosen performer
was effectually silenced.

Jervis was still learning Greek and Latin at
Burton when Prince Charles Edward landed in
Scotland, mustered the Highlanders, defeated Sir
John Cope at Prestonpans, took possession of
Edinburgh, crossed the Border, and carried his
standard on English ground as far as Derby.
The excitement pervading the country was great,
and plaids were sent to most of the boys at school
from their homes to wear in honor of the young
chevalier. But Jervis and Meux, afterward the
opulent brewer, declined to display the slightest
sympathy with the Jacobite cause, and their pol-

itics proved somewhat inconvenient. Indeed, Jervis was pelted at Burton-on-Trent for being a Whig as mercilessly as Gibbon at Kingston-on-Thames was persecuted for being a Tory.

Almost ere Jervis emerged from early boyhood and entered his teens, his father, Swynfen Jervis, who was a barrister, became counsel for the Admiralty and auditor of Greenwich Hospital. This led to the family, of which the embryo hero was a member, moving from Staffordshire and settling at Greenwich; and Jervis, who had been destined for the legal profession, no sooner exchanged the banks of the Trent for those of the Thames than he began to take new views of life.

It seems that, after being removed to Greenwich, Jervis was placed to pursue his studies at a seminary known as "Swinden's Academy," where his associates, one of whom was Edward Wolfe, destined to become so celebrated as the conqueror of Quebec, were for the most part sons of naval officers, and Jervis, being much in their company, conceived an earnest desire to go to sea. Circumstances, however, might have proved stronger than his aspirations after a naval career, had he not met with decided encouragement from a worthy who figured as his father's coachman.

"What line of life are you going to follow, Master Jacky?" asked the coachman, as the boy, musing dreamily of sea-fights, sat on the box, or stood by while the horses were groomed.

"I believe I am to be a lawyer," answered Jervis, simply.

"Oh! don't be a lawyer, Master Jacky," exclaimed the coachman; "all lawyers are rogues."

"What should I be?" asked Jervis.

"If I were you, I would be a sailor," replied the coachman.

Jervis was doubtless glad to get so much encouragement from any person connected with his father's household. But it would seem that the counsel to the Admiralty was by no means of his coachman's opinion. The boy's determination, however, growing day by day, became much too strong to be restrained; and at length, availing himself of his father's absence on the Northern Circuit, he formed an adventurous project with a comrade, who told marvelous stories of sea life, took the daring step of running away from school, and, with the resolution never more to expose himself to Swinden's birch, concealed himself on board a ship at Woolwich. At the end of the third day, however, he left his lurking-place, made up his mind to return to Greenwich, and reached home after nightfall.

"Oh," said his sisters, "you have behaved so improperly! Won't Mr. Swinden give it you for running away from school!"

"No," replied Jervis, "he'll certainly have no chance, for I don't intend to go back to school any more."

"Not go back to school?" exclaimed the young ladies.

"No," said Jervis, conclusively; "I intend to be a sailor."

It now became evident that the resolution of Jervis was too strong to be overcome, and his father reluctantly yielded to his will. Seeing that it was no whim, but an earnest aspiration by which the boy was animated, the lawyer wisely endeavored to smooth his son's path; and Jervis, after having been recommended by a lady of rank to Captain Townshend, had the gratification of hearing that officer consent to receive him on board the "Gloucester," which was then at Portsmouth fitting out for Jamaica.

"And," asked the captain, who at the time wore his night-cap and slippers, and spoke in the roughest of voices, "how soon will you be ready to join your ship?"

"Directly," was the reply.

"Then," said Captain Townshend, "I will give you a letter to the first lieutenant, and you can go to-morrow."

Accordingly, Jervis, having received the blessing of his parent, and the sum of twenty pounds to pay for outfit and to serve as pocket-money, found his way to Portsmouth. "My equipment," he afterward said, "was what would be called rather grotesque. My coat was made for me to grow to; it reached down to my heels, and was full large in the sleeves. I had a dirk and a gold-laced hat."

About the autumn of 1748, Jervis, when little more than thirteen years of age, sailed for Jamaica; and in good time the "Gloucester," reaching her destination, anchored in the harbor of Port Royal, then slowly recovering from the effects of the terrible hurricane of 1747, and deemed by Englishmen the very reverse of healthy. The climate, the unwholesome water, tropical fruit, rum punch, sharks, and barracudas, caused the death of English seamen by hundreds. Moreover, boys were under strong temptations of indulging in idleness and dissipation, luxuriating in "Jamaica baths," and frequenting dignity balls and cock-fights. Jervis, however, by the exercise of marvelous prudence, altogether avoided the many perils that beset him.

In fact, it would seem that a circumstance which at the time must have been most discouraging, secured Jervis against a too free indulgence in the pleasures of the colony. A bill which he had drawn for twenty pounds was returned protested; and he not only vowed never to draw another bill without the certainty of its being paid, but determined meanwhile to save sufficient money to take up that which had been dishonored. With this view, he completely changed his mode of living: he quitted his mess, washed and mended his own clothes, and at one time even submitted to the sacrifice of selling his bed, and sleeping on the bare deck. But his heart did not sink under hardship and poverty. On the contrary, severe experience strengthened his faculties, and helped to form the boy into the hero he became. It created a high spirit of independence, taught him to rely on his own resources, and proved of inestimable advantage to him in the struggles of after life.

Finding himself without money, and perceiving that his time might be better occupied than on board a guard-ship, Jervis became most alert to volunteer into any vessel that was going to sea, especially if any thing of importance was to be done, instead of lolling lazily on deck, or carousing over the punch-bowl, or betting at cock-fights with hospitable planters, or perambulating Kingston with an eye to the favor of fair Creoles or fascinating Quadroons.

While on the West India station, Jervis, during one of his cruises, made the acquaintance of an old quarter-master, who in other days had been mate of a merchantman. Struck with the young midshipman's intelligence, this worthy offered to teach him navigation. Jervis accepted the offer with gratitude, and in this way came by the only instruction of the kind he ever received. But, meanwhile, he never ceased to teach himself. When unavoidably in port and unoccupied, he devoted himself to books; and by reading and so exercising his intellectual faculties as to profit by his studies, he greatly added to his professional and general knowledge.

After having seen six years' service in the West Indies, Jervis, by this time nearly twenty, returned in the "Sphinx" to England. The vessel was shortly afterward paid off. But Jervis, being transferred to the "William and Mary" yacht, completed the term required for the rank of lieutenant, and having passed his examination with great credit, received his commission, with orders to repair to Chatham, and assist in fitting out the "Prince," commanded by Captain Saunders, and intended for Lord Anson's flag.

No sooner did Captain Saunders set his foot on board the "Prince" than Jervis hit his fancy. Nor did experience of the young sailor belie the captain's first impressions. In fact, Saunders formed the highest opinion of Jervis, and became eager to advance his interests. The approbation of so distinguished an officer proved of high value; and in the spring of 1755 Jervis was removed to the "Nottingham," which was to form part of the fleet dispatched from Portsmouth, under Admiral Boscawen, against the French force collected at the Isle of Rhée.

Meanwhile Saunders was mindful of the high qualities Jervis had exhibited on board the "Prince." When, therefore, during the Seven Years' War, General Wolfe was assigned the duty of wresting Quebec from the French, and when Saunders, now an admiral, was appointed to command the naval force ⌐ , to co-operate, Jervis was immediately select⌐d as first lieutenant of the "Prince," which was to bear the admiral's flag. The fleet, consisting of twenty-two line-of-battle ships and an equal number of frigates, set sail early in February, 1758, and, after much unavoidable delay, entered the St. Lawrence in June. During the expedition Jervis was promoted to the command of the "Porcupine" sloop, and after the capture of Quebec and the death of Wolfe, who fell in the hour of victory, he was dispatched to England with intelligence of the great triumph that had been achieved.

After his return from Quebec, Jervis was, about the time when George the Third began to reign, promoted to the rank of post captain in the "Gosport." But the war soon after came to a close, and the "Gosport" having been paid off, he did not again serve for six years. At the end of that time, however, Jervis was appointed to the "Alarm," and, while commanding that frigate on the coast of Barbary, had a controversy with the Bey of Tunis. It happened that when the "Alarm" was in the waters of Tunis, and one of her boats was one day ashore, two runaway slaves swam to the boat, and, after concealing themselves to escape observation, sought protection under the English flag. When the circumstance

became known in Tunis, the Bey was informed
of what had happened, and demanded in peremptory language that they should be sent ashore.

"No," answered Jervis, "I must decline to
comply; for the moment men take refuge under
the British flag they are free."

"In that case," said the messenger, "the Bey
will certainly fire on your ship."

"Tell him," said Jervis, "that in the event of
a single shot being fired, the castle shall be level-
ed with the ground."

Having sent this message to the Bey, Jervis
prepared to execute his threat, and placed the
"Alarm" abreast of the Castle of Tunis. It was
not, however, found necessary to proceed to extremities. The Bey, seeing that the English captain was not a man to be trifled with, and daunted by the attitude of the frigate, refrained from
taking any steps likely to provoke hostilities, and
Jervis had the satisfaction of bringing off the escaped slaves without molestation.

Fortune, hitherto favorable to Jervis, now
amused herself by playing him a trick. Soon
after being the means of liberating the slaves, he
was shipwrecked in the Bay of Marseilles. But,
appointed ere long to the "Foudroyant," he was
present at the drawn battle with the French off
Ushant, and, in consequence, examined as a witness before the court-martial held at Portsmouth
on Admiral Keppel.

But England, weary of a long struggle, was on the eve of peace, and Jervis was soon to figure in contests very different from those connected with naval warfare. In 1783 he was nominated commodore of an expedition against the Spanish West Indies; but when the American war subsided into what was termed the "armed neutrality," the project was abandoned, and Jervis, instead of going to the West Indies, was returned as member of Parliament for East Yarmouth. While occupying a seat in the House of Commons, he took an earnest and active interest in political affairs. A Whig by nature, he admired Fox, disliked Pitt, and held fast by the creed for which he had been beaten by the schoolboys at Burton. On subjects connected with the navy he was listened to with respect, and considerably increased his reputation by the facility with which he engaged in discussions relating to his profession.

While such was the position of Jervis, now a knight, and holding the rank of Admiral of the Blue, the States-General assembled at Paris in May, 1789, and commenced that revolution in France which caused the exile of the nobility, the overthrow of the monarchy, and the execution of the king. At first Pitt did not interfere. Indeed, that minister, whose influence was then supreme, struggled hard to keep England out of the contest that was agitating Europe. Events and public feeling, however, proved too much for his

potent will and imperial mind; and in 1793, the
government of England having declined to recognize the embassadors of the French Republic,
the Convention declared war.

When events hurried England into that contest destined to continue for nearly a quarter of
a century, Jervis was one of the first officers called into active service. After having been sent
with a squadron to attack the French West Indies, he was appointed to the command in the
Mediterranean. While cruising about, Jervis had
his indignation aroused by the Emperor of Morocco, and sent a threatening message to that po-
tentate.

"Why, what harm can he do me?" asked the
emperor, in amazement.

"He can destroy a number of your forts along
the coast," was the answer.

"Is that all?" said the emperor. "Tell him I
will destroy them for half the money."

But Jervis soon had to contend with an adversary of more importance. The King of Spain, at
the beginning of the Revolutionary war, had
ranked among the enemies of France, and even
gained some slight successes on his frontier; but
in 1794, the Republican generals, marching thither, and speedily repairing the early reverses sustained by the French, penetrated into the Penin-
sula, and took possession of St. Sebastian, Fonta-
rabia, and a number of other places. Alarmed,

the King of Spain signed a peace with France, and, soon after doing so, formed an offensive alliance against England. It was this circumstance which gave Jervis the opportunity of winning that great battle with which his name is inseparably associated.

It was the 5th of February, 1797, and Don Joseph de Cordova, the Spanish admiral, sailing from Carthagena to Cadiz, was informed by an American that the English fleet on the station off St. Vincent consisted only of nine ships. Not doubting the accuracy of the information, and being at the time in command of twenty-seven ships, besides ten frigates and a brig, Don Joseph could not help deeming the opportunity of securing an easy victory much too favorable to be lost. Instead, therefore, of proceeding to Cadiz with a view of forming a junction with the fleets of France and Holland, he determined upon seeking the enemy, and, owing to the report given by the American, felt so certain of conquering that he allowed his ships to remain somewhat dispersed and in disorder. At daybreak on the morning of the 14th of February, however, the English fleet appeared in sight, and when the fog that for some time concealed the number of the ships cleared away, the captain of the Spanish vessel appointed to look out saw that the odds against the English were not quite so large as had been anticipated. Fancying that his first signal had

X

been disregarded, and anxious at such a crisis to rouse his commander, the Spaniard made another signal to the effect that the English fleet consisted of forty sail of the line; and this not only attracted attention, but sadly perplexed the Spanish admiral, while alarming each of the officers under his command.

It would seem that Jervis, when seen by the American, had only nine ships, but that he had subsequently been re-enforced by an arrival from England. It happened, therefore, that when, on the 13th of February, Commodore Nelson, in the "Minerve," reached the station with information that he had seen the Spanish fleet off the mouth of the Straits, Jervis had in reality under his command fifteen ships of the line, with four frigates, a sloop, and a cutter. No time was lost. It was late in the day when Jervis received the information off St. Vincent, and before sunset he gave the signal to his ships to prepare for action, and to keep during the night in close order.

Every preparation was made, and next morning, when day dawned, and the fog dispersed, and the fleet of Don Joseph de Cordova came in sight, Jervis, who was on board the "Victory," commenced operations with his wonted spirit. Ere the Spaniards had sufficiently recovered from the alarm caused by the signal from their look-out ship, or found time to form in regular order of battle, Jervis, carrying a press of sail, came up

with them, passed through their fleet, and then
tacking, contrived to cut off nine of their ships
from the main body. Astonished at the manœuvre which had separated them from their companions, the nine ships attempted to form on the
larboard tack with the object of rejoining their
fleet. The effort proved unsuccessful. One of
them, indeed, favored by the smoke, which so
covered her that the intention was not perceived
till too late, accomplished her object; but the
others, in endeavoring to pass through the English lines, met with a reception so warm that
they deemed it prudent to put about, take to
flight, and not again to interfere with the action.

Having thus dexterously freed himself from
eight formidable adversaries, Jervis had still to
deal with a force infinitely superior to his own in
numbers, and still more in weight of metal. However, he knew that his officers and seamen had
every advantage in skill and discipline; and with
little doubt as to the issue of the conflict, he made
the signal to his ships to tack in succession.

But Nelson, who had shifted his pendant on
board the "Captain," and taken his station in the
rear of the English line, was not satisfied with
the expediency of this order. The movements
of the Spaniards filled that hero's mind with suspicion. "It is clear," he said to himself, "that
the enemy are bearing up before the wind with
an intention of forming their line, going large.

and joining their separate ships, or else getting off without an engagement; it is necessary to frustrate their purposes." Accordingly Nelson, disobeying the signal, ordered the "Captain" to be wore, and this bold manœuvre at once brought him into action with a four-decker called the "Santissima Trinidad," and six other vessels, among which were the "San Nicholas" and the "San Joseph." The position occupied by the "Captain" was of course somewhat perilous; but the "Culloden," coming up, lent powerful support; and after the struggle had lasted an hour, the "Blenheim," passing between the combatants, gave the English a respite, and poured her fire into the Spaniards. At the same time, two of the Spanish ships, dropping astern, were fired into and forced to strike by Captain Collingwood in the "Excellent," who, observing that Nelson was in a critical situation, ranged up, and hauling up his mainsail just astern, passed close to the "San Nicholas," gave her a tremendous fire, and then went on to deal with the "Santissima Trinidad."

By this time the "Captain" had been rendered incapable of farther service. Every sail, every shroud, every rope was gone; her wheel was shot away, and she had lost her fore-topmast. Nelson therefore directed the helm to be put a-starboard, called for the boarders, pointed to the "San Nicholas," and ordered them to board.

This was done; and a marine having broken the window of the upper quarter galley, leaped in, followed among others by Nelson, who, disdaining all danger, burst open the door of the cabin, pushed on to the poop, hauled down the Spanish ensign, and made the Spanish officers surrender their swords.

While this was taking place, a fire of smallarms opened from the admiral's stern-galley of the "San Joseph;" but Nelson, giving orders to board her from the "San Nicholas," led the way with the exclamation, "Westminster Abbey or victory!" and soon reached the quarter-deck, where he took possession of the prize, and received the swords of the Spanish officers. At the same time the "Victory," passing with Jervis on board, saluted Nelson with three cheers, and the example was followed by every ship of the fleet.

A pause now took place, and the action was discontinued; but Don Joseph de Cordova felt not yet quite content to yield to his fate. Having no decided opinion of his own as to the condition and prospects of the fleet, he assembled his captains, and asked whether the battle ought to be renewed or not.

"Let us fight it out," said two of these officers, braver or more desperate than their comrades.

"No," said nine, "it is not expedient."

"At any rate," said the others, "it will be well to delay the business."

The opinion of the majority prevailed; and the contest being at an end, Jervis received Nelson on the deck of the "Victory," took the hero in his arms, and exclaimed, "I can not sufficiently thank you." Nelson presented to Jervis the sword of the Spanish rear admiral, but Jervis insisted on Nelson keeping the weapon which he had won in a way so heroic.

In England the probability of the Spanish admiral forming a junction with the French and Dutch fleets had been much dreaded, and the news of the victory off St. Vincent was peculiarly welcome. Nor was the nation slow to evince gratitude to the men who had freed England from such a danger. For his distinguished services, Jervis was created a peer with the title of Earl St. Vincent, and for some time after he employed himself in the blockade of Cadiz. But old age was now coming rapidly upon him, and his health giving way, he, in the month of August, 1799, resigned his command, and with the prospect of quietly enjoying repose and his laurels, landed at Portsmouth.

But it soon appeared that there was still much life in the old sea king, and in 1800 he took the command of the Channel fleet. At that time, however, he was called upon to serve his country in another sphere. When, in 1800, Addington became prime minister, Lord St. Vincent accepted office as First Lord of the Admiralty. In that position he figured with credit. Being frugal of time and money, and having a most systematic notion of affairs, he rectified many abuses, and proved an admirable man of business.

After the retirement of Addington and the death of Pitt, Lord St. Vincent resumed command of the Channel. But he had now passed the age of threescore and ten, and doubtless felt his energies somewhat decayed since the days when he had defied the Bey of Tunis and threatened the Emperor of Morocco. Accordingly, he, in 1807, resigned his command, and passed much of his time in retirement. In the course of his career he had married his cousin Martha, daughter of Chief Baron Parker, and he had acquired an estate named Rochetts. In this place Lord St. Vincent took great delight, and he had it ornamented in a style that did credit to his taste. In his retirement, he regularly commenced the business of the day with sunrise, and during summer was sometimes in his grounds as early as two o'clock.

Lord St. Vincent survived the king whom he had so long served, and the close of the maritime war in which he had enacted so conspicuous a part. He lived to receive from George the Fourth a commission as an admiral of the fleet, and his last public appearance was on board the royal yacht on the occasion of the king's embarkation for Scotland. Soon after, on the 15th of March, 1823, when nearly ninety years of age, Lord St. Vincent breathed his last at Rochetts, and subsequently a monument was erected to his memory in St. Paul's Cathedral.

LORD DUNCAN.

ABOUT the time when Prince Charles Edward was making his marvelous escape to France, and when the Jacobite lords were dying on the scaffold for the house of Stuart, a stripling of sixteen, tall for his age, and inclining to be handsome, left Dundee, under the auspices of a carrier, to go on board a man-of-war, and push his fortune at sea. He traveled in a somewhat unostentatious style, but not from any lack of pretensions to gentility; for he was cadet of a family that had for centuries flourished with respectability at Lundie, in Perthshire.

It was at Dundee, on the 1st of July, 1731, that Adam Duncan drew his first breath. He was educated in his native town, and passed his time very much like other boys of his station in life, till he reached the age of sixteen, and dedicated himself to the naval profession. Leaving Dundee with the carrier's cart, walking part of the way, riding part, he reached Leith, took his passage in a smack, sailed from Scotland, and, reaching London in safety, found his way on board the "Shoreham."

After serving two years in the "Shoreham,"

and growing to the height of six feet four inches,
Duncan, at the age of eighteen, removed as midshipman into the "Centurion," then fitting out
to carry the broad pendant of Commodore Keppel, who had been appointed to the command of
the Mediterranean. This exchange was destined
to exercise no inconsiderable influence on Duncan's career. In the tall young Scot, whose countenance was so mild, and whose manners were so
simple, Keppel recognized an embryo hero of extraordinary ability and energy; and, during the
three years that Duncan remained in the "Centurion," he won the commodore's friendship by
the diligence which he displayed in the discharge
of his duties.

At length Keppel found an opportunity of advancing Duncan's fortunes. In 1755, when the
government of England, alarmed at the encroachments of the French in North America, resolved
on sending out a strong military force, the commodore was appointed to convoy the transports.
Anxious to reward Duncan's zeal, Keppel strongly recommended him to the Admiralty; and, at
the opening of 1756, Duncan was promoted to
the rank of lieutenant, and appointed to the "Norwich," which sailed as one of Keppel's squadron.
Fortune proved favorable to Duncan in this expedition. The armament had scarcely reached
Virginia, when the promotion of some officers
from the "Centurion" made room for Duncan;

and, removing to Keppel's ship, he had the advantage of pursuing his career under the eyes of his friend and patron.

After the return of Keppel's squadron to England, the commodore removed to the "Torbay," and Duncan accompanied him to that ship. After taking part in an expedition against the French settlements of Goree, on the coast of Africa, during which he was wounded, and figuring as first lieutenant of the "Torbay," Duncan returned to England, and rose to the rank of post-captain.

At this period the Seven Years' War was raging; and Keppel, having been intrusted with the duty of attacking Belleisle, Duncan, appointed to the "Valiant," took part in the enterprise. The operations were crowned with triumph, and the whole island fell into the hands of the English.

Soon after the capture of Belleisle, an expedition was projected against Havana, and Duncan accompanied that division of the fleet which, under Keppel, was appointed to protect the troops while landing. The expedition was attended with complete success; and Duncan, who greatly distinguished himself during the siege, had the honor, when the place surrendered, of being sent to take possession of the Spanish ships.

In the beginning of 1763, however, the Seven Years' War, so glorious for England, came to a close; and Duncan, returning home, remained long without employment. While ashore he married a lady of the family of Dundas, daughter of the President of the Court of Session. But soon after this, the war consequent on the league between the French king and the American colonists recalled Duncan to his professional duties.

It was in 1778 that hostilities commenced between England and both branches of the house of Bourbon; and Duncan, appointed to the "Monarch," was sent as one of the fleet with which Rodney went to the relief of Gibraltar, then besieged by the Spaniards. In this expedition Duncan had an opportunity of exhibiting his ardor and his courage.

One day, early in the year 1780, Rodney was informed that fourteen Spanish ships of the line, under Don Juan de Langara, were cruising off Cape St. Vincent. The intelligence was welcome, and Rodney, ordering his fleet to sail abreast, came, about noon on the 16th of January, in sight of the enemy. Unaware at first of Rodney's force, the Spanish admiral showed no wish to shirk an encounter; but no sooner did the English fleet appear fully in view than the Spaniards began to retreat. Rodney, however, not to be baffled, gave the signal for close chase; and, ordering each ship to engage on coming up with the enemy, approached the Spanish fleet about four o'clock with a determination to conquer.

It was now that Duncan showed his skill and energy. In spite of the "Monarch" being the reverse of a swift ship, he contrived to get into action before any other of Rodney's fleet, and, indeed, manifested such ardent eagerness to come up with the Spaniards, that he was warned of the danger of dashing so hastily into the hostile fleet.

"There are three of the enemy immediately ahead of you," was the warning cry.

"So I see," answered Duncan; "and to be among them is precisely what I wish."

Ere a few minutes passed, Duncan's aspiration was so far gratified that he found himself within gunshot of three antagonists. The "Monarch" immediately opened fire, and while one of the Spaniards, named the "St. Augustin," ran alongside, the two others, lying within musket range, rendered his situation most dangerous; but Duncan, undismayed by the odds against him, calmly maintained his position till the approach of the English fleet freed him from two adversaries, and left the "Monarch" to fight it out with the "St. Augustin." Nor did Duncan find this a matter of very great difficulty. In fact, the Spaniard soon hauled down her colors; but, owing to the rigging of the "Monarch" being completely shattered, and the wind blowing hard, Duncan found it impossible to take possession of the "St. Augustin," and was fain to leave his beaten enemy to be seized as a prize by the ship that next came up astern. Doubtless this was mortifying; but the gallant captain had the ennobling conscious-

ness of having done his duty, and the consolation
of having contributed to a great and glorious
victory.

After having taken so heroic a part in Rodney's victory, Duncan returned to England; and
having for some time been attached, in the "Blenheim," to the Channel fleet under Lord Howe, he
was, at the peace of 1783, removed to the "Edgar," one of the guard-ships stationed at Portsmouth. In 1787, however, he became Rear Admiral of the Blue; in 1793, Vice Admiral of the
Blue; in 1794, Vice Admiral of the White; and
in 1795, Admiral of the Blue. But during that
long period all his efforts to obtain employment
proved futile; and, baffled in his wish to serve
his country on the sea, he was abandoning
dreams of farther distinction, and contemplating
a civil appointment connected with the navy,
when, at the age of sixty-four, he found himself
favored with an opportunity which he turned nobly to account.

At the opening of the Revolutionary War, the
French Convention reckoned Holland as an enemy, and a French army invaded the United
Provinces. In order to save the Dutch from being conquered, the Duke of York was sent with
an army from England to aid them in their struggle; but, after having found his efforts vain, he
was obliged to retire, and the French, pursuing
their success, overran Holland. Imbued with

revolutionary principles, the Dutch patriots seconded the efforts of the invaders, and the Stadtholder having taken refuge in England, they gave the United Provinces the title of the Batavian Republic, and formed a close alliance with France.

It now became necessary for the government of England to guard against the maritime power of Holland, and in 1795, Duncan was summoned from retirement, and appointed to the command of the North Seas. Hoisting his flag on board the "Venerable," the admiral for some time fulfilled his functions without the excitement of a conflict. Indeed, he had to perform duties the reverse of agreeable; for the state of feeling in the navy was such as severely to try officers in high command, and Duncan had his share of the troubles of the period.

In 1797, the mutiny which broke out at Portsmouth and the Nore speedily made its influence felt in the North Sea fleet. Duncan, as might have been expected, showed himself equal to the crisis, and by firmness and sagacity contrived for a time to keep down discontent. But the spirit of insubordination was too strong to be long suppressed; and one day, when the admiral, about to sail from Yarmouth Roads, made a signal for a frigate called the "Trent" to get under way, he found that he was not obeyed.

Duncan was doubtless mortified, but he acted with characteristic courage and decision. Issuing orders without delay that all the men of the "Venerable" should assemble on the quarter-deck, he presented himself before them with that tall stature, that athletic and finely-formed person, and that countenance which expressed such frankness of heart and such benevolence of mind.

"It is my intention," said Duncan, after informing them of the insubordination of the crew of the "Trent," and expressing his indignation at their conduct, "it is my intention to-morrow morning to go alongside the frigate and compel the men to return to their duty. And," asked the admiral, in conclusion, "who is there, who, on such an occasion, would desert me?"

"None!" was the answer that rose loud and high from the quarter-deck.

But the danger was not overpast. The crew of the "Trent," indeed, warned by the spirit displayed on board the "Venerable," promptly returned to a sense of their duty. But in May, a few months after the victory off St. Vincent, when Duncan was about to leave Yarmouth for the Texel, two ships of his fleet positively refused to put to sea; and their example was too readily followed. In fact, the admiral found that of all the ships of his fleet, only the "Venerable" and the "Adamant" recognized his authority.

Nor was this the worst. In a short time it appeared that even the "Venerable" had been infected with the spirit of mutiny; and Duncan found, to his horror, that a plot had been formed for carrying the ship to England. On being informed of this, the admiral instantly ordered all hands on deck; and after addressing them on the folly of being disloyal, told six men, whom he knew to be the ringleaders, to stand forward.

"My lads," said the admiral, " I am not the least apprehensive of any violent measures you may have in contemplation; and though I assure you I would rather have your love than your hatred, I will shoot with my own hand the first man who displays a symptom of rebellious conduct."

"Tush!" muttered one of the ringleaders.

"What, sir," exclaimed Duncan, turning suddenly and fixing his eye upon the mutineer, "do you really want to take the command of the ship out of my hands?"

"Yes, sir," replied the man, boldly.

Exasperated at the mutineer's audacity, Duncan drew his sword, and, raising the weapon, was about to slay the man where he stood. Luckily, however, the chaplain interposed, arrested the admiral's arm, and prevented the blow being struck. Recovering his presence of mind, Duncan, in a voice still agitated, appealed to the crew.

"Hearken!" he said. "Let those who will stand by me and my officers pass over to starboard, that I may see who are my friends and who are my enemies."

"Yes," cried the crew, with a loud voice; and

Y

every man, except the six ringleaders, rushed to the starboard side.

Inexpressibly relieved, Duncan sheathed his sword, and ordered the culprits to be seized, put in irons, and confined in the gun-room. These orders were promptly executed; and the ringleaders, having time to repent of their folly, expressed such remorse that they were one by one liberated.

While Duncan was contending with desertion and mutiny, the Dutch fleet, consisting of fifteen ships of the line, six frigates, and five sloops, was ready for action, under the command of Admiral De Winter, a man of high courage, great ability, and of a stature which almost equaled that of Duncan. Moreover, when, with his two ships, Duncan appeared in the Texel, the wind was favorable for De Winter putting to sea; but, by a variety of signals, as if to ships in the offing, Duncan managed to convey the impression that he was in command of a force superior to that of the Dutch; and De Winter, completely deceived, refrained from coming out.

Availing himself of the success of his stratagem, and of the channel through which the Dutch fleet had to pass only admitting one vessel at a time, Duncan brought the "Venerable" and the "Adamant" to anchor at the entrance. While in this position, he had the satisfaction of seeing ship after ship of his fleet appear, and of being joined by so many that he no longer looked forward to an engagement as an affair to be avoided.

But Duncan soon found that De Winter was in no hurry to put to sea, and week after week the English lay off the Texel, in vain awaiting the foe. De Winter still tarried; and Duncan, at length compelled to go into port to refit and revictual, determined to return to Yarmouth. Before doing so, however, he sent orders to have every thing in readiness, that he might lose no time in returning to his station.

No sooner did De Winter hear of Duncan having sailed, than he resolved to make a movement. Going on board the "Vryheid," therefore, he put to sea, but rather to gratify the vanity of his countrymen than with any idea of emulating the exploits of Van Tromp. Indeed, De Winter knew too well the prowess of the enemy to feel any eagerness for a battle; and he hoped that the same breeze which brought the English fleet from Yarmouth would waft that of Holland back to port.

De Winter found, ere long, that he had not sufficiently estimated the prescience and activity of the adversary with whom he was contending. At the earliest possible moment, Duncan had intelligence of De Winter having come out of port, and within eight days of his arrival at Yarmouth the old admiral was at sea. With every sail set, and every faculty in full exercise, he went tilting

over the water to resume his post, and found his
exertions rewarded when, one morning, a little
after sunrise, the headmost ship of his fleet made
a signal that the enemy was in sight.

It was the 11th of October, 1797, when, about
nine o'clock, the Dutch fleet became visible to
leeward. Duncan stood toward them, and by
midday came in sight of the land between the villages of Camperdown and Egmont. De Winter
was gradually making toward his own shores,
and it was apparent that, in the event of the
Dutch ships getting within a certain distance of
their own coast, there would be no possibility of
following them with any prospect of advantage.

Duncan, however, was determined that De
Winter should not escape without an engagement, and about twelve an order was given " to
pass through the enemy's line and engage then
to leeward;" soon after, the signal for close action was made, and kept flying on board the
" Venerable." All was now excitement; and at
half past twelve, while the weather was variable
and rain fell in showers, the action was begun by
the " Monarch," which broke the line of the
Dutch, and passed under the stern of their vice
admiral.

When affairs reached this stage, Duncan pressed eagerly on to engage De Winter, and there
was every prospect of the " Venerable" coming
to close quarters with the " Vryheid." But an

obstacle presented itself in the shape of the "States-General," a Dutch ship of seventy-six guns. The "Venerable," however, put helm to port, ran under the Dutchman's stern, engaged him close, and, compelling him forcibly to get out of line, fell alongside the "Vryheid."

The two admirals now engaged in close conflict, and while the action became general around them, a desperate struggle took place between the "Venerable" and the "Vryheid." De Winter, who was well supported, kept up a heavy fire, while Duncan was gallantly aided by the "Ardent," by the "Triumph," and by the "Powerful," which, having taken her antagonist, ran up and rendered the admiral effectual assistance when surrounded and struggling with enemies. Meanwhile the starboard broadside of the "Venerable" was doing fearful execution among the rigging of her chief adversary; and, finally, De Winter, no longer deluding himself with the hope of fighting with advantage, struck his colors and surrendered.

It was nearly three o'clock when the weather cleared, and the aspect of affairs was gratifying to the British admiral. By that time, nine of the enemy's ships and two of their frigates had struck; and about four, De Winter, conducted by the captain of the "Circe," came on board the "Venerable," and stared to find that his conqueror was a still taller man than himself.

"Ha!" exclaimed the Dutch admiral, in surprise.

"Yes, upon my soul, sir," said Duncan, interpreting his prisoner's look and exclamation, "I do wonder how you and I have escaped the balls in this hot battle!"

In the conflict at Camperdown, the "Venerable" was so much injured that she was with difficulty brought into port. Duncan therefore shifted his flag into the "Kent," a ship newly launched, and continued in command of the North squadron. But meanwhile the news of the victory caused London to be lighted up; his praise was on every tongue; he was eagerly voted the thanks of Parliament and the freedom of the city, with a sword valued at two hundred guineas; and he was raised to the peerage of Great Britain under the titles of Viscount Duncan of Camperdown and Baron Duncan of Lundie.

It was not, however, till the spring of 1800, when apprehensions were no longer entertained of the hostility of the Dutch fleet, that Duncan again set foot on the shores of England. His work appeared to be done; and, returning to Scotland, he passed several years in his native country. His career had been crowned with success; but of all men he was the least dazzled with the triumphs he had achieved, and exhibited the same modesty of demeanor and simplicity of mind as he had done half a century earlier.

At the age of seventy-four, however, Duncan
was seized with a desire to devote what remained of his life to the service of his king and country. With this view, in the summer of 1804,
when the peace of Amiens was at an end, when
Pitt reappeared at the head of the English government, and when Bonaparte became Emperor
of the French, the venerable hero journeyed to
London and presented himself at the Admiralty.
But he had been severely tried by the loss of
several children, and his health was more seriously impaired than he himself believed.

It was ordered that Duncan should not again
meet his country's foes. One day, while attending at the Admiralty, the brave old admiral was
seized with apoplexy. He recovered sufficiently
to set his face northward, and had even crossed
the Border on his way home. At Kelso, however, he had a second attack; and in that town,
hard by the spot where the Tweed and the Te-
viot form a junction, in the month of August,
1804, the hero of Camperdown gave up his soul
to God.

LORD NELSON.

ABOUT the time when George the Third ascended the English throne, and when the war in which England regained the empire of the seas came to a close, there might have been seen about the village of Burnham-Thorpe, in Norfolk, a somewhat delicate little boy, with a heart full of enthusiasm, and an eye brilliant with genius, sailing his miniature ship in the nearest pond, watching the brindled cows cooling their hoofs in the water, throwing stones at the pigeons perched on the barn-tops, casting wistful eyes toward the apples that reddened on the boughs of the orchard, or climbing trees to the·destruction of his clothes, and seeking for young hawks at the hazard of his neck. The name of this boy was Horatio Nelson, and he was son of the Reverend Edmund Nelson, Rector of Burnham-Thorpe.

The immediate progenitors of the rector of Burnham-Thorpe appear to have moved in the ranks of the yeomanry. His pedigree, however, did not stop with his immediate progenitors. The Nelsons, it seems, claimed descent from men of Anglo-Danish origin, who had occupied a place among the gentry of Norfolk, and ancient monu-

ments to the memory of various magnates of the
name were to be seen about churches and church-
yards of the county. At all events, the rector
had been deemed of sufficient gentility to espouse
a lady named Suckling, connected with the Wal-
poles; and she proving, if any thing, inconven-
iently prolific, made him father of eleven children.
One of these, the little boy whom we have seen
sailing his miniature ship, was destined to make
his name known to fame as that of the greatest
naval hero the world has ever seen.

It was on the 29th of September, 1758, at the
parsonage house of Burnham-Thorpe, that Nelson
first saw the light. Having been cradled and
swaddled with the usual ceremonies, he was
named Horatio after his godfather, the first Lord
Walpole. Of all the rector's sons, however, he
seemed the least likely to play a great part in the
world's affairs. From the first, his constitution
was the reverse of vigorous, and at an early age
an attack of ague much reduced his natural
strength. But his courage and high spirit were
early conspicuous, and almost in childhood he
gave indications not to be mistaken of the char-
acteristics he was to exhibit in after years.

One day, when a mere child, Nelson happened
to be on a visit to his grandmother. Straggling
from the venerable dame's house in search of
birds' nests, in the company of a cowboy, he became so absorbed in his adventures that he parted

company with his comrade, and allowed the din-
ner-hour to pass without returning. Alarmed at
his absence, his grandmother gave way to fearful
apprehensions, and exclaimed that doubtless he
had been carried off by gipsies. Diligent search,
however, was made, and the embryo hero was
discovered sitting by the side of a brook which
he had found some difficulty in crossing, and
quietly diverting himself by dropping pebbles
into the water.

"I wonder, child," cried his grandmother, when
he appeared at the house, " that fear did not drive
you home."

"Fear?" said Nelson, inquiringly.

"Yes, fear!" cried the grandmother, probably
in no gentle accents.

"Fear?" repeated Nelson, thoughtfully. "I
never saw fear. What is it?"

When Nelson reached his ninth year, his mother departed this life, leaving eight out of her
eleven children to the care of her husband. Soon
after this melancholy event, her brother, Maurice
Suckling, a captain in the navy, visited the be-
reaved rector, and promised to provide for one
of his nephews at sea. It does not appear that
Horatio was the one intended. The young hero,
however, seems to have concluded that he was to
be the man, and no doubt began to pant for the
hour when he was to exchange the green fields
of Norfolk for salt water, and to regale his imag-

ination with visions of such sea-fights as he had
heard of by the fireside, or read of in some odd
volume among the theological works in his father's bookcase.

But, however that may have been, Nelson was
still too young for a man-of-war, and he was sent
with his brother William to a school at North
Walsham. The boys boarded with the master,
but they went home during the holidays, and did
not always, on such occasions, manifest particular
impatience to return. In this way it happened
that, being one day after Christmas sent off from
Burnham-Thorpe on horseback, they considered
a fall of snow as a capital excuse for turning the
horse's head, and rode back to the parsonage
house.

"Why have you come back?" asked the rector, as they appeared at the door.

"We are afraid the snow will be too deep for
us," answered William.

"In that case," said the rector, "you certainly
shall not go. But make another attempt, and I
will leave it to your honor."

"Very well," said the boys.

"If the road is dangerous you may return,"
repeated the rector. "But remember, boys, I
leave it to your honor."

The young Nelsons again took the road for
North Walsham, and found as they advanced
that the snow was quite deep enough to justify

them in turning back a second time. In fact, William, who had no very eager desire to resume his studies, and therefore no relish for the journey, was strongly inclined to rein round.

"The snow is far too deep," he said; "we must go home again."

"No, brother," said Horatio, "we must go on if possible. Remember, it was left to our honor;" and William no longer objecting to proceed, they trotted on, and safely reached North Walsham.

When months passed over—when spring succeeded winter, and summer succeeded spring, and autumn succeeded summer, some pears in the schoolmaster's garden attracted the eyes of the boys. None, however, ventured to gather them. The pears, indeed, were considered lawful booty, but they grew against the wall of the house, and in such a position that the strongest and hardiest quailed at the idea of climbing.

"It is impossible to get them," was the conclusion expressed after a long discussion.

"No," said Nelson, "it is not impossible. I will get the pears."

Accordingly, when Nelson went to his room that night he prepared for the desperate venture. Having taken the sheets from his bed, and caused himself to be let down by them from the window, he possessed himself of the pears, all of which, after having ascended by the same process, he handed to his companions.

"Why," they exclaimed, "you have not kept any to yourself! You should have the largest share."

"No," said Nelson, pouting his lip proudly, "I only took the pears because every other boy was afraid to do it."

In the year 1768, while the rector of Burnham-Thorpe, who now suffered severely from paralytic and asthmatic affections, was at Bath, the young Nelsons went as usual from North Walsham to spend their holidays at the parsonage house. Reading in a newspaper that Captain Suckling had just been appointed to the "Raisonable," a ship of sixty-four guns, Horatio perceived that his opportunity for going to sea was now come.

"Do write to my father, William," he said, "and tell him I should like to go with Uncle Maurice."

"What," asked Captain Suckling, when his request was conveyed to him, "what has poor Horatio done, who is so weak, that he, above all the rest, should be sent to rough it out at sea? But let him come, and the first time we get into action a cannon ball may knock off his head, and provide for him at once."

It was a dark night in spring when a servant from Burnham-Thorpe arrived at North Walsham with a summons for Horatio Nelson to leave school and join the "Raisonable," then in the Medway. Nelson forthwith bade farewell to his

youthful comrades, and, this ceremony over, proceeded to his father's house. Accompanying his
son to London, the rector placed him in the coach
for Chatham, and on arriving there, Nelson was
set down with the other passengers; but, being
in a strange place, and utterly unaccustomed to
travel, he was quite unable to find the ship. However, while he was wandering sadly about, an officer, remarking his forlorn appearance, spoke to
him, and finding that he was Captain Suckling's
nephew, gave him something to eat, and conducted him to the " Raisonable."

But Nelson's preliminary troubles were not yet
ended. On going on board, he found that Captain Suckling was not there, and that no one had
been apprised that the captain's nephew was
coming. In consequence, Nelson paced the deck
during the remainder of that day, and it was not
till the second day that any notice was taken of
his presence, and that he was recognized as belonging to the profession in which he was ere
long to win immortal fame.

The dispute with Spain about the Falkland Islands had led to the "Raisonable" being commis-
sioned, and when the dispute was settled the ship
was paid off. Captain Suckling was then removed to the "Triumph," stationed as a guard-
ship in the Thames. Nelson would have accompanied his uncle, but the life in a guard-ship was
considered too inactive for a boy like Nelson.

The young sailor was therefore put on board a merchantman bound for the West Indies, and during the voyage acquired considerable knowledge of seamanship, and imbibed a strong dislike to the royal navy. On the merchantman's return to England, however, Captain Suckling received his nephew into the "Triumph," and contrived gradually to reconcile him to the king's service.

While Nelson was on board the "Triumph," studying navigation, and acquiring confidence among rocks and shoals under the auspices of his gallant kinsman, he learned that two ships, the "Race-horse" and the "Carcass," were fitting out for a voyage of discovery to the North Pole, and expressed an eager desire to take part in the expedition. Some difficulties presented themselves; but at length he was admitted as coxswain, and in the summer sailed from the Nore. The ships encountered fearful obstacles, and when they made the land off Spitzbergen the ice rendered their position perilous in the extreme. Throughout the expedition Nelson conducted himself with great courage, and, after having had the honor of saving a boat's crew from a number of exasperated walruses, he figured as hero of a daring adventure.

One night, during the mid-watch, Nelson, with a youthful comrade, stole from the ship, and, taking advantage of a fog, set out on the ice in pursuit of a bear. The chase was keenly urged, and at length became so close, that when, in the morning, Nelson's powder was exhausted, and his musket flashed in the pan, a chasm in the ice alone saved him from the bear's embrace.

"Come on," cried his companion.

"Stop a minute," said Nelson in reply. "Do but let me get a blow at this devil with the butt-end of my musket, and we shall have him."

Meanwhile the absence of Nelson and his comrade from the ship had been remarked, and the captain, becoming seriously alarmed, endeavored to learn what had become of them. For a time all was doubt. Ere long, however, the fog cleared away, and the two boys were seen at a distance in close conflict with the bear. A signal to return to the ship, which was immediately made, failed to attract Nelson's attention. But the danger appeared such that the captain ordered a gun to be fired, and this had some effect. The bear, hearing the report, ran away; and Nelson, perhaps a little afraid of the consequences of his escapade, hastened over the ice to the ship.

"I can't understand," said the captain, after a severe reprimand, "what motive you could have for hunting the bear."

"Sir," answered Nelson, pouting his lip as he was in the habit of doing when excited, "I wished to kill the bear, that I might take home the skin to my father."

When the adventurers in the " Race-horse" and
the " Carcass," baffled in their attempt at discovery, returned to England, Nelson was placed by
Captain Suckling in the " Sea-horse," and in that
vessel he sailed for the East Indies.   The climate,
soon proving too much for his constitution, reduced him to a skeleton, and he was carried on
board the " Dolphin" to return to England.   But
he scarcely hoped to live through the voyage.
Mental despair accompanied physical depression,
and he long afterward spoke of the misery he experienced.

"I felt impressed," he said, " with a feeling
that I should never rise in my profession.   My
mind was staggered with a view of the difficulties I had to surmount, and the little interest I
possessed.   I could discover no means of reaching
the object of my ambition.   After a long and
gloomy reverie, in which I almost wished myself
overboard, a sudden glow of patriotism was kin-
dled within me, and presented my king and country as my patrons.   ' Well, then,' I exclaimed, ' I
will be a hero; and, confiding in Providence, I
will brave every danger!' "

After landing in England, Nelson discovered
that he was not so destitute of influence as he
had supposed.   During his absence, Captain
Suckling had been appointed Controller of the
Navy; and when, in the spring of 1777, Nelson
presented himself to the Board, and with great

credit passed his examination for a lieutenancy, his gallant kinsman presided.

"Gentlemen," said he, after Nelson had acquitted himself to admiration, "this is my nephew."

"Indeed!" exclaimed the examiners, in surprise; "and you did not tell us of your relationship before."

"No," said Captain Suckling, "I didn't want the youngster to be favored. I knew, however, that he would pass a good examination, and I have not been disappointed."

After so creditably performing the ceremony of passing his examination, Nelson was appointed to the "Lowestoffe." In that frigate he sailed for Jamaica, and while on the West India station took part in the capture of an American letter of mark. The captain ordered the first lieutenant to board the American; but the officer went below for his hanger, and not finding the weapon quite readily, he remained so long that the captain's patience wore out.

"What!" he exclaimed, "have I no officer who can board a prize?"

"I will go," said the master.

"No," said Nelson, who hitherto had awaited the first lieutenant's return, but no sooner heard the master volunteer than he sprang into the boat; "it is my turn now, and if I come back it is yours."

The high spirit displayed by Nelson on this and

many similar occasions recommended him to the captain's favor, and after having been transferred to the "Bristol," the admiral's flag-ship, he was, when twenty-one, appointed commander of the "Badger." But from that vessel he was soon removed, and, as post-captain in the "Hinchenbrook," dispatched to aid in taking Fort San Juan.

The expedition against Fort San Juan proved unsuccessful, and most of those engaged fell victims to the climate. Nelson, on being appointed to the "Janus," escaped with life; but he reached Port Royal so weakened that he was fain to resign his command, and embarked in the "Lion" to return to England. The probability of reaching his native shore alive was somewhat slender; but Cornwallis, who commanded the "Lion," treated him with great kindness, and almost amazed at having survived the voyage, Nelson repaired to Bath to recruit his health. His condition was so feeble that for a time he had to be carried to and from bed. Gradually regaining his strength, however, he hastened to London, applied to the Admiralty, and ere long found himself appointed to the "Albemarle."

Nelson's health was still in a precarious state. Nevertheless, he was ordered to the North Seas, and kept there a whole winter. It was during this period that he acquired that knowledge of the Danish coast which, years after, and on a memorable day, he turned to good account. On returning to the Downs, he sailed in the "Albemarle" for Canada.

After cruising about for some time, the "Albemarle" was ordered to convoy a fleet of transports to New York, and, on arrival at Sandy Hook, Nelson waited on Admiral Digby, the commander-in-chief.

"You have come to a fine station for prize-money," remarked the admiral.

"Yes, sir," said Nelson; "but I would rather be on the West India station. The West Indies is the station for honor."

Fortunately for the fulfillment of his desires, Lord Hood, who had been intimate with Captain Suckling, happened at that time to be at Sandy Hook with a detachment of the fleet which under Rodney had defeated the Spaniards. At Nelson's request, Hood used his influence with Digby to get the "Albemarle's" company; and Nelson, having obtained Digby's reluctant consent, gladly sailed for the station where honor was to be won. There Nelson became acquainted with Prince William Henry, afterward Duke of Clarence and King of England. Lord Hood, who introduced them to each other, took the opportunity of paying Nelson a high compliment, and the royal sailor expressed his surprise at the hero's appearance.

"He was the merest boy of a captain I had

ever seen," said the prince, "dressed in a full-
laced uniform, an old-fashioned waistcoat with
long flaps, and with his lank unpowdered hair
tied in a stiff Hessian tail of extraordinary length,
making altogether so remarkable a figure that I
had never seen any thing like it before. Nor
could I imagine who he was, nor what he had
come about. But his address and conversation
were irresistibly pleasing, and when he spoke on
professional subjects, it was with an enthusiasm
that showed he was no common being."

Soon after Nelson's introduction to Prince William Henry, the peace of 1783 was signed, and
the "Albemarle," returning to England, was paid
off. Nelson remained for a time without employment, paid a visit to France, and resided for a
while at St. Omer's; but, falling in love without
being in circumstances to indulge in matrimony,
he determined to overcome his attachment, left
France with the resolution of applying for a ship,
and made his appearance at the Admiralty, where
Lord Howe then presided as first lord. The result was his appointment to the "Boreas," in
which he went to the Leeward Islands, and occupied himself with enforcing the provisions of the
Navigation Act against the Americans. At the
same time, he became enamored of a young widow; and the circumstances on this occasion being such as seemed to justify a dash at matrimony, he married in the spring of 1787, and

Prince William Henry, then in the West Indies, was present by his own desire to give away the bride.

After having been three years on the West India station, the "Boreas" was ordered to Europe. Nelson, who was again in wretched health, sighed for the green fields of his native county. However, the "Boreas" was kept for months at the Nore; and he was so much mortified at this circumstance, that when at length, in November, orders came for paying off the vessel, he could not refrain from expressing his indignation at the treatment with which he had met.

"I hear that orders have come for the 'Boreas' being paid off," said an officer of the "Medway."

"Yes," said Nelson, "it will release me forever from an ungrateful service, for it is my firm determination never again to set foot on board a king's ship."

"Really!" said the officer.

"Yes," continued Nelson. "Immediately on my arrival in town I shall go to the Admiralty, wait on the first lord, and resign my commission."

Being a man of sense, the officer of the "Medway" refrained from remonstrating; but he privately communicated with Lord Howe; and Nelson was immediately, by a letter from the first lord, politely requested to call as soon as he reached London. Going to the Admiralty, he held a satisfactory conversation with Lord Howe, and,

on being presented to George the Third on a
levee day, met with so gracious a reception from
the king that his discontent evaporated.

With his feelings soothed and his mind more
at ease, Nelson repaired with his wife to Norfolk,
and took up his quarters at Burnham-Thorpe.
For some time he cheerfully occupied himself
with rural affairs, assisted to cultivate his father's
glebe, amused himself with digging in the garden, sometimes went bird-nesting like a boy, and
at others indulged in greyhound coursing and
partridge-shooting. But he was no shot, and
coursing was his favorite sport.

While enjoying rural leisure, however, Nelson
began to pant for the salt water; and, when the
French Revolution came to a height, and England appeared on the eve of war, he lost no time
in offering his services. In consequence, he was,
on the 30th of January, 1793, appointed to the
"Agamemnon," a ship of sixty-four guns. It was
nine days after the head of Louis the Sixteenth
had fallen on the scaffold, and two days before
the French Convention declared war with England. But Nelson went not the less readily
that there was a prospect of fighting the ancient
enemies of his country. He hated the French,
and he was at no trouble to conceal his hatred.

When Nelson took the command of the "Agamemnon," he was ordered to the Mediterranean,
and, after some severe service under Lord Hood,

he was detached with a small squadron to Corsica to aid General Paoli against the French. At the siege of Calvi, where he highly distinguished himself, a shot happened to strike the ground near him, and drove sand and gravel into his eye. Nelson treated the accident lightly, and did not allow it to confine him for more than a single day. Even when writing to Lord Hood he merely mentioned that he had got a little hurt. But it was nevertheless serious, for the sight was lost forever.

After the fall of Calvi Lord Hood sent Nelson's journal to England for the perusal of the government. Nevertheless, his services were overlooked, and his name was not even mentioned in the "Gazette." Nelson was naturally annoyed; but he consoled himself with the thought that he would find a way of making ministers of state treat him with more respect. "They have not done me justice," he said; "but never mind, I'll have a 'Gazette' of my own one day."

When Sir John Jervis took command of the fleet in the Mediterranean, Nelson, who was then at Leghorn, hastened to present himself, and met with a reception which was such as to excite envy.

"The 'Agamemnon' is to go home," said Jervis; "but you can have either the 'St. George' or the 'Zealous.'"

"If the 'Agamemnon' is ordered home," said

Nelson, "I should, on many accounts, like to return to England."

"But we can not spare you," said Jervis, conclusively.

Nelson now hoisted his broad pendant on board of the "Minerva." He soon after signalized his prowess by the capture of a Spanish frigate, and on this occasion had an opportunity of showing his chivalry. Finding that the commander was Don Jacobo Stuart, a descendant of the famous Duke of Berwick, Nelson, with a respect due to a brave man whose ancestors had been kings of England, returned the Don's sword, and sent him with a flag of truce to Carthagena.

But a great event was on the wing. At this time Nelson became convinced that an important battle would ere long be fought, and had no fears of the result, except, indeed, that he might not be present to share the glory. Fortune, however, proved more favorable than he anticipated. One day in February, 1797, having just made his way with a convoy from Porto Ferrajo to Gibraltar, Nelson proceeded westward in search of Jervis, and at the mouth of the Straits fell in with the Spanish fleet. Reaching the station off St. Vincent, he immediately communicated the intelligence, and having shifted his broad pendant to the "Captain," greatly contributed to the victory. The sword which the Spanish rear admiral surrendered to Nelson on the occasion, and

which Jervis insisted on his retaining, he presented to the mayor and corporation of Norwich.
His provincial pride was strong; and there was
no place, he said, where it could give him and his
family more pleasure to have such a trophy kept
than in the capital city of the county where he
was born. Jervis, for this great victory, was
created an earl, with the title of St. Vincent; and
Nelson, who had previously been promoted to
the rank of rear admiral, was rewarded with the
Order of the Bath.

After the battle of St. Vincent, Nelson hoisted
his flag on board the "Theseus," and took the
command of the inner squadron in the blockade
of Cadiz. Making an attack by night, his barge
was encountered by an armed launch, and a struggle of extraordinary ferocity took place, the English and Spanish fighting hand to hand. The
odds against Nelson were fearful, but nothing
could withstand his courage and that of his men.
Eight of the Spaniards having been killed, the
others surrendered with the launch. Nelson was
repeatedly in danger of being cut down; and he
was twice saved by John Sykes, his coxswain,
who not only parried blow after blow, but interposed his own head to save that of his commander.

After this adventure Nelson received orders to
proceed to Santa Cruz, and to make a sudden assault on that town. Accordingly, he sailed with

four ships of the line, three frigates, and the "Fox" cutter, and on the 24th of July, having previously attempted in vain to gain the heights above the fort, he brought his ships to anchor about two miles to the north of the town, with the intention of attacking. About six on the evening of that day a signal was made, and at eleven all the boats, with six or seven hundred men, and the "Fox" cutter with a hundred and eighty men, made for the town. After rowing for more than an hour without being observed, they got within gun-shot of the landing-place. But at that point they were descried by the enemy; and Nelson ordered the boats to cast off from each other, give a loud hurrah, and row for the shore.

Scarcely, however, had the cheer subsided when the bells of Santa Cruz rang, and the enemy's guns opened fire. The courage of the men was proof against the danger; but the night was unfortunately so dark that most of them, not seeing the mole, went ashore through the raging surge; and the "Fox" cutter, which received a shot under water, began to sink rapidly.

Meantime Nelson, in the act of stepping out of his boat and drawing his sword, received a shot through his right arm. The shock threw him back into the boat, and his sword fell into the water. Recovering himself, he groped in the water for the weapon, and grasped it firmly in the left hand, while the companions of his peril placed him in the boat, and bound the wound with a handkerchief. But, roused at that moment by a cry of distress from the cutter, he forgot his wound, and exerted himself so energetically that eighty of the men were saved.

The attack on Santa Cruz having utterly failed, Nelson allowed himself to be rowed to the "Theseus," and a chair was brought that he might be taken easily on board. But he was so anxious to send the boat back to the aid of the cutter that he refused to wait. Catching hold of a rope with his remaining hand, he twisted it round his arm, and sprang boldly up the side of the ship.

"Now," said Nelson, as he reached the deck, "tell the surgeon to make haste with his instruments. I know I must lose my right arm, so the sooner it is off the better."

Nelson, after this unfortunate adventure, was compelled to return to England, and in September he reached London, dejected at the failure of his enterprise and the loss of his arm. For three months he suffered acutely; and he was staying in Bond Street and experiencing much pain, when the metropolis was illuminated in honor of Admiral Duncan's victory over the Dutch fleet, and a violent knocking was soon heard at the door.

"Why don't you illuminate?" roared the populace.

"Admiral Nelson is here," replied the servant;

"he is in bed, and so ill that the least disturbance may be fatal."

"Admiral Nelson!" said one of the leaders; "that alters the case. You'll hear no more of us to-night."

The leader of the populace kept his word; and Nelson, gradually recovering, found himself, about the spring of 1798, in a condition to return to sea. Accordingly, he sailed in the "Vanguard" to re-join Lord St. Vincent. Almost immediately he was dispatched with a squadron to ascertain the object of the armament which Bonaparte was then preparing for the East. While Nelson was in the Gulf of Lyons a severe gale dispersed his ships, and about the time the French fleet passed within a few leagues; but, owing to the thick and stormy weather, his shattered squadron was not observed by the foe.

Unaware of the danger he had almost providentially escaped, Nelson rapidly refitted, and having been re-enforced by twelve of Lord St. Vincent's best ships, among which was an old acquaintance, the "Culloden," Nelson set out in pursuit of the French. Having no instructions, he acted on his discretion, and sailed for Alexandria; but, not finding an enemy to encounter, he returned to Sicily. Believing, however, that the French were bound for Egypt, he resolved to seek them once more at the mouth of the Nile. "Be assured," he wrote to Sir William Hamilton, the English embassador at Naples, "I will return either crowned with laurel or covered with cypress."

It was the morning of the 1st of August, 1798, when Nelson came in sight of Alexandria. From intelligence received during the voyage he had little doubt of this time finding the enemy, and he was not disappointed. The port, which at his former visit had been solitary, was now crowded with ships, and the tri-color flag was waving haughtily from the walls.

Admiral Brueys, who commanded the French fleet, was of that great Norman family which in another age had produced the hero King of Scots. Much superior in force to Nelson in ships, guns, and men, and somewhat confident of victory in case of a conflict, Brueys had already delivered it as his private opinion that the English admiral had made a point of missing him, from not deeming it prudent to try conclusions with such a foe. Not being able to enter the port of Alexandria, which was ruined, the French admiral had moored his ships in Aboukir Bay, and formed them in so strong and compact a line that the French believed they could bid defiance to a force more than double their own.

For several days before that on which Nelson's eye was gladdened with the sight of the French fleet, his anxiety had been so intense that he could neither eat nor sleep. Now, however, his mind was easier, and, while preparations were being made, he ordered dinner to be served, and seated himself at table with his officers.

"If we succeed," said one of them, "what will the world say?"

"If!" exclaimed Nelson; "there is no if in the case. That we shall succeed is certain, though who may live to tell the story is a very different question. Before this time to-morrow," he exclaimed, as they rose from table, "I shall have gained a peerage or a place in Westminster Abbey."

It was four o'clock when the fleet advanced amid showers of shot and shells from the island of Begniers. At the same time, a steady fire was opened by the enemy; but this was received in silence. The men on board each of Nelson's ships continued to furl their sails and prepare to anchor.

At this critical moment a French brig endeavored to decoy the fleet to a shoal which lay off the island, but the attempt was vain. The English moved gallantly onward. The "Goliah," leading the advanced ships, doubled on the French vessels at anchor between them and the shore, while the main body, led by Nelson in the "Vanguard," with six colors flying at different parts of his rigging, lest one should be shot away, took their station outside the enemy. Veering round half a cable, the "Vanguard" suddenly,

just as the sun was going down, opened fire, under cover of which the other ships sailed on ahead.
The play of cannon·was soon terrific. In a few
minutes every man at the first six guns in the
forepart of the "Vanguard's" deck was killed or
wounded, and these guns were three times cleared. Ere seven o'clock night closed over the
scene, and the darkness was unbroken save by
fire that flashed incessantly from the guns of the
hostile fleets.

At the commencement of the battle four of
Nelson's ships were at a considerable distance.
They had endeavored to come up, but the darkness immensely increased the difficulties of the
navigation; and the "Culloden" ran aground in
such a way that every exertion to get her off to
take part in the action proved vain. This accident, however, prevented farther mischief. The
other vessels, warned of the danger, and guided
by the "Culloden," which served as a beacon, escaped her fate, and took up their station in a
manner that excited admiration.

By this time the French had suffered severely.
Indeed, the action had not lasted a quarter of an
hour ere their two first ships were dismasted.
Before long the three next were in the hands of
the English, and the battle wore such an aspect
that the French could no longer hope for victory.
Brueys, on board the "Orient," received three
wounds, but would not leave his post. A fourth

cut him almost in two; and he desired to be left
to die on deck. Scarcely was Brueys dead when
a fire broke out on board the "Orient." The
ship had been newly painted, and the oil jars and
paint buckets fed the flames, which rapily mastered the ship; and such was the conflagration, that
the hostile fleets were now distinctly seen, the
colors of both being quite visible.

Meanwhile Nelson was not unscathed. A piece
of langridge shot, striking him on the head, in-
flicted a ghastly wound, and a large piece of skin,
cut from the forehead, fell over his eye, and left
him in total darkness. One of his captains caught
the hero in his arms, and, alarmed at the effusion
of blood, hardly doubted that the wound was
mortal. Nelson was instantly carried below; and
the surgeon, leaving the seaman whose wound
he was dressing, hastened to attend the admiral.

"Not yet," said Nelson, pushing him away.

"Why not?" asked the surgeon, in surprise.

"Because," answered Nelson, "I will take my
turn with my brave fellows."

After a time Nelson's turn did come, and great
was the joy displayed when the surgeon, removing the skin from the eye, announced that the
wound was superficial, and declared that only
quiet was necessary. But at that instant a cry
arose that the "Orient" was on fire; and Nelson,
forgetting his wound, rushed on deck, and ordered his boats to the relief of the imperiled crew.

A A

Only eighty of them could be saved. The flames rapidly overpowered the ship, and about ten she blew up with a tremendous shock.

After this explosion, which was felt to the bottom of every ship in both fleets, and succeeded by an awful silence on both sides, the firing was renewed, and continued till three o'clock. But the defeat of the French was at that time complete. At daybreak two of the French ships had colors flying, and, cutting their cables, they stood out to sea, accompanied by two frigates. None of the others escaped.

"What a victory!" said the English.

"Victory!" exclaimed Nelson; "victory is not a name strong enough for such a scene. It is a conquest."

When news of the battle of the Nile reached England, Nelson was created a peer, with the title of Baron Nelson of the Nile and of Burnham-Thorpe. Many thought his title should have been higher, and in the House of Commons General Walpole expressed his opinion to that effect; but Pitt treated the question as not worthy of discussion.

"Admiral Nelson's fame," he said, "would be coequal with the British name; and it would be remembered that he had won the greatest naval victory on record, when no man would think of asking whether he had been created a baron, a viscount, or an earl."

After defending Naples from the French, and taking, under Lady Hamilton's influence, a part in the affairs of that kingdom, which can not be said to have added to his fame, Nelson was created Duke of Bronte by King Ferdinand. Early in the year 1800 he returned to England; but he was not allowed to enjoy repose. Up to that date Russia had, of all powers, been hostile to revolutionary France. But the Czar Paul, an eccentric sovereign, declared himself the champion of Bonaparte, and formed with Denmark and Sweden what was called the " Northern Confederacy" to destroy the maritime supremacy of England. This project roused the Addington cabinet to energy, and an armament was fitted out. Sir Hyde Parker was appointed commander-in-chief; but Nelson, who appeared as second in command, was in reality the soul and right arm of the expedition.

About the middle of March, 1801, the English fleet set sail from Yarmouth, and in nine days reached the Cattegat. Anchoring there, they learned from Mr. Vansittart—who, in the capacity of English embassador, had left the fleet at Scaw and proceeded to Copenhagen — that the Danes were entirely disinclined to negotiate. Nelson, on hearing this, was opposed to any delay in commencing hostilities. But Sir Hyde Parker hesitated, and it was not till much precious time had been lost that the fleet passed the

Sound, regarded by the Danes as "the key of the Baltic," and anchored between Copenhagen and the island of Huen.

It was the afternoon of the 30th of March when a council of war was held to decide on the course to be pursued. So great appeared the difficulty of attacking the Danes, that while Sir Hyde Parker sat irresolute and Nelson kept pacing the cabin, several officers expatiated on the dangers to be encountered in the event of an attack.

"We must," said they, "bear in mind the number of Swedes and Russians whom we shall afterward have to engage."

"The more numerous the better," cried Nelson, pouting his lip and moving the stump of his right arm. "I wish they were twice as many; the easier the victory, depend upon it. And," he continued, still pacing the cabin, while his breast swelled with a valor that knew no fear, and his brain flashed with an eccentric genius far more valuable than the wisdom of others, "I offer my services for the attack. Only give me ten sail of the line and the small craft."

"I will give you twelve ships and all the small craft, and leave every thing to your judgment," said Sir Hyde Parker, inspired for a moment by the hero's enthusiasm.

The council having arrived at a decision, it was determined that the attack on Copenhagen should be made from the north; and Nelson busied himself night and day, making soundings and laying down buoys. Every thing being in readiness, on the morning of Wednesday, the 1st of April, the fleet moved to an anchorage within two leagues of the Danish capital, and off the end of a shoal known as the Middle Ground, lying exactly before the city, and extending along the whole sea-front.

News of the arrival of an English fleet off the Sound produced the most intense alarm at Copenhagen. The Danes, however, met the crisis with a courage worthy of men whose forefathers had been led by Sweyn and Canute. People of all ranks volunteered to serve their country in the hour of her need. A mighty force was rapidly mustered; twelve hundred youths, furnished by the University, were constantly employed in the management of the guns; and the line of defense, consisting of nineteen ships and floating batteries, flanked by two formidable forts at the mouth of the harbor, and manned indiscriminately by soldiers, sailors, and citizens, was arranged in the King's Channel, between the Middle Ground and the city.

But Nelson was no whit dismayed by the formidable preparations made for resistance. From anxiety, indeed, he could not be free; but his soul panted for the strife, and his brain glowed with anticipations of a signal triumph. At half past nine o'clock on the morning of the 2d of April,

the ships under his auspices weighed anchor and
stood on toward Copenhagen. Three of them,
owing to the indecision of the pilots, grounded,
and disasters more fatal might have followed.
But Nelson, in the "Elephant," quitting the order of sailing, exerted himself to guide the fleet
safely forward; and, though only one of the gun-
brigs got into action, all of the remaining ships
anchored as they arrived, and presented their
broadsides to the Danes. A little after ten, when
the Crown Prince of Denmark took his station
on one of the batteries to witness the conflict
and issue orders, the battle began with a roar of
guns.

Nelson had naturally been disconcerted by the
accident that deprived him of three ships and so
many gun-brigs. But no sooner did the battle
fairly commence, than his countenance cleared,
his eye glistened, and the remnant of his right
arm began to move. But Sir Hyde Parker did
not share the hero's elevation. Being at such a
distance as only to observe the mishaps of the
ships, and overestimating the disadvantages under which the English fought, he suffered the
most painful anxiety, and, after the action had
lasted three hours without slackening, his suspense became intolerable.

"I will make the signal of recall for Nelson's
sake," he said. "If he is in a condition to continue the action successfully, he will disregard the

signal; if he is not, it will be a good excuse for his retreat, and no blame can be imputed to him."

"But," urged a captain, "would it not be well to delay till you communicate with Nelson?"

"No," said Sir Hyde, "the fire is too hot."

At this stage of the operations, Nelson, with a flaming eye and a determination to conquer, was pacing the quarter-deck of the "Elephant." A shot through the mainmast knocked about the splinters. But he only smiled, and had just expressed the gratification he felt in being where he was, when the signal for discontinuing the action was observed.

"No. 39 is thrown out by the commander-in-chief," cried the signal officer. "My lord," he repeated, as at the next turn he met Nelson, who had paid no attention to the information, "No. 39 is thrown out; shall I repeat it?"

"No—acknowledge it," answered Nelson, as he continued his walk, and raised his glass to his blind eye. "I really do not see the signal. Keep mine for closer battle flying! That's the way I answer such signals. Nail mine to the mast."

Along the line the action continued with unabated vigor; and while the English fought with characteristic courage, the Danes displayed a desperate resolution which elicited admiration from their foes. A boy of seventeen, named Villemoes, highly distinguished himself in the strife. Villemoes had obtained the command of a floating

battery, which was a mere raft. But he got under the "Elephant's" stern, and made a display
of juvenile heroism which caused Nelson to exclaim that he ought to be an admiral.

But the conflict was too hot to last; and about
two o'clock the Danes began to slacken their fire
and to strike their colors. Half an hour later the
contest became so irregular, and was carried on
in such a way, that the Danes were not only shed-
ding English blood, but slaughtering hundreds
of their own countrymen. Nelson, whose humanity was aroused, retired to the stern galley of the
"Elephant," and penned a brief epistle to the
Crown Prince.

"Vice Admiral Lord Nelson," he wrote, "has
been commanded to spare Denmark when she no
longer resists. The line of defensé which covered her shores has struck to the British flag; but,
if the firing is continued on the part of Denmark,
he must set on fire all the prizes that he has taken,
without having the power of saving the men who
so nobly defended them. The brave Danes are
the brothers, and should never be the enemies of
the English."

"What is the object of Lord Nelson's note?"
inquired the Crown Prince.

"Lord Nelson's object in sending this flag of
truce," wrote the hero, "was humanity. He
therefore consents that hostilities shall cease, and
that the wounded Danes may be taken on shore."

Hostilities were accordingly suspended, and the Danes had leisure to count their slain. Almost every house in Copenhagen was a house of mourning. Mothers bewailed their sons, sisters their brothers, and wives their husbands. Indeed, so severely had the Danes suffered that the members of almost every family had to lament the loss of some whom they had held dear.

After the victory Nelson landed, proceeded to the palace of Copenhagen, and had an interview with the Crown Prince. Not without reluctance, the Danish government consented to a treaty; and Nelson, appointed to the command of the fleet on Sir Hyde Parker's recall, was preparing to deal with the other Northern powers, when the assassination of the Czar Paul dissolved the confederacy. Nelson then returned home, where he was welcomed with enthusiasm, and elevated to the rank of viscount in the peerage of England.

At the time that Nelson, with the laurels won at Copenhagen, set his foot in England, Bonaparte was busy with his mysterious preparations at Boulogne. Much alarm was the consequence, and Nelson was requested to undertake a command which extended on both shores from Orfordness to Beachey Head. Hoisting his flag in the "Medusa" frigate, he went to reconnoitre Boulogne, and planned a boat-attack on the flotilla. The attempt, however, failed; and Nelson was about resigning his command, when, in the spring of 1802, he found himself relieved by the Peace of Amiens, and retired to Merton, in Surrey, where he had purchased a house, and where he intended to pass his life peacefully under the shadow of his own vine and fig-tree.

But the Peace of Amiens proved brief. The ambition and insolence of Bonaparte speedily disgusted the people of England; and in May, 1803, the English embassador left Paris. A renewal of the war forthwith took place; and Nelson, appointed to the command of the Mediterranean, blockaded Toulon, where was the French fleet under Villeneuve, a man of talent and a seaman of skill. So vigilantly did Nelson do his duty, that for two long years he was only ashore three times, each time on the king's service, and on no occasion for more than an hour.

In the mean time, Spain was forced into a declaration of war with England, and the French, with the co-operation of the Spanish navy in prospect, plucked up courage. One day, in the middle of January, 1805, Villeneuve ventured on putting to sea. At that time, Nelson, on board the "Victory," was at anchor off the coast of Sardinia. But he received prompt intelligence of the French fleet having left Toulon, and instantly sailed with the hope of an encounter. The fates, however, were not propitious. Bad weather enabled the French to elude his search;

and, utterly at a loss whether they were bound
for the West Indies or for Ireland, he scarcely
knew on which side to turn. After experiencing
much misery, he received information that the
French were bound for the West Indies; he pursued them thither, frightened them back to Europe, and, after having chased them half round
the globe without the satisfaction of bringing
them to an engagement, he landed at Portsmouth.
There Nelson learned that Villeneuve, having
been engaged by Admiral Calder to the west of
Cape Finisterre with success, indeed, but without
a decisive victory, had deemed it prudent to bear
away. Fatigued and worn with anxiety, Nelson
retired to recruit his health and energies at Merton.

But the work of England's hero was not yet
done. One morning in the autumn of 1805, when
Nelson had not been long in retirement, Captain
Blackwood, on his way to London with dispatches, looked in at Merton. It was five
o'clock; but, early as was the hour, Nelson, already dressed, immediately appeared, and welcomed his visitor with a countenance eager with
expectation.

"I am sure, Blackwood," he exclaimed, "that
you bring news of the French and Spanish fleets."

"Yes," Blackwood answered; and explained
that, after the indecisive action with Calder, Villeneuve had refitted at Vigo, then gone to Ferrol,

brought the squadron from that port, and with it entered the harbor of Cadiz.

"I think, Blackwood, I shall yet have to beat them," said Nelson. "Depend upon it," he added, "I shall have to give M. Villeneuve a drubbing."

Nevertheless, the idea of leaving Merton was not altogether pleasant, and, after Blackwood's departure, Nelson seems to have wavered. But, after restlessly pacing the walks of his garden, he resolved to offer his services; and his services having been readily accepted by the government, over which Pitt once more presided, the "Victory" was refitted to carry his flag. The nation was in raptures when intelligence went through the land that Nelson was going to fulfill his threat of "teaching Bonaparte to respect the British navy;" and, when he reached Portsmouth, an immense crowd was assembled to witness his embarkation.

On the 29th of September, 1805, the "Victory" arrived off Cadiz, and Nelson's reception by the fleet was such as to gratify his heart. But, fearing that if the French knew his force, Villeneuve would not venture out, he desired Admiral Collingwood neither to hoist colors nor to fire a salute, and refrained from going within sight of land.

It happened that, on the very day of Nelson's arrival, Villeneuve resolved to take the earliest opportunity of putting to sea with the combined fleets. But, on hearing a rumor of Nelson having resumed the command, the French admiral hesitated; and a council of war which he summoned decided that, unless assured of the French force being stronger than the English, it was inexpedient to leave Cadiz. At that time, however, an American arrived from England, and treated with ridicule the idea of Nelson having left home.

"Lord Nelson is in the Mediterranean," people said to him.

"Impossible," answered the American; "I saw him in London only a few days ago, and then there wasn't a word about his going again to sea."

While Villeneuve was thus led to doubt the rumor of Nelson's arrival, Nelson was forming his plan for "giving Villeneuve a drubbing." The fleet was to sail in two lines, with a squadron of fast-sailing two-deckers in advance, and the order of sailing was to be the order of battle. Collingwood, as second in command, with the full direction of his own line, was to break through the enemy at the twelfth ship from the rear.

About three weeks after Nelson's arrival, a signal was made that Villeneuve was coming out of Cadiz. The fleets of France and Spain consisted of thirty-three sail of the line and seven large frigates, and, both in point of size and weight of metal, they had a still greater advantage than in

numbers over the English. Moreover, they had
on board four thousand troops, and among these
were the best riflemen that could be found in
Europe. Villeneuve, tacking to the northward,
and bringing the shoals of Trafalgar under the
lee of the English, while keeping the port of Cadiz open for himself, formed his fleet in a double
line.

At daybreak on the morning of the 21st of October Villeneuve's fleet became distinctly visible
from the deck of the " Victory," and a signal was
made for the English to bear down upon the enemy. Accordingly, the fleet advanced; the lee
line of thirteen ships being led by Collingwood,
the weather line by Nelson in the " Victory,"
which carried several colors, lest one should be
shot away.

At an early hour Captain Blackwood came on
board the " Victory," and found Nelson, who was
dressed in his admiral's frock-coat, and decorated
with badges of four of the orders to which he
had been admitted, in high spirits, but calm, conscious that his life would be aimed at, and with
an anticipation that he was destined to purchase
victory with his life. He was, however, paying
the utmost attention to the enemy, and predict-
ing that the issue of the encounter would be a
triumph for England.

" Blackwood," he suddenly asked, " what
should you consider a victory ?"

" Well," answered Captain Blackwood, " considering the handsome way in which battle is offered by the enemy, I think it would be a glorious result if fourteen were captured."

" No," exclaimed Nelson, " I shall not be satisfied with less than twenty."

" Don't you think," said Nelson, after a pause, " don't you think there is a signal wanting ?"

" It seems to me," replied Blackwood, " that the whole fleet clearly understand what they are about."

But scarcely were the words spoken when that signal was made, so well remembered, and never without a glow of patriotic ardor,

" England expects that every man this day will do his duty."

" Now," said Nelson, " I can do no more. We must now trust to the great Disposer of events and to the justice of our cause. I thank God for this great opportunity of doing my duty."

By this time a long swell was setting into the Bay of Cadiz, and the English ships, crowding all sail, were majestically moving onward. Villeneuve, viewing them from the deck of the " Bucentaure," and unable to repress his admiration, involuntarily exclaimed to his officers that such conduct could hardly fail of success. A few minutes before twelve o'clock the French opened fire, at first with single guns, to ascertain the range ; and Nelson, perceiving that the shot passed over the "Victory," desired Captain Blackwood to repair to his frigate.

"My lord," said Blackwood, as he left the "Victory," "I hope soon to return and find you in possession of twenty prizes."

"God bless you, Blackwood," said Nelson; "I shall never see you again. See," he exclaimed, "how that noble fellow Collingwood carries his ship into action."

After the French had continued to fire for some time, they observed a shot pass through the main topgallant sail of the "Victory," and hoping to disable her before she could close with them, they aimed at her rigging, keeping up a raking fire, which quickly wounded many of her men, and sent several of them to their last account. Nevertheless, for some considerable time after the French opened fire the "Victory" did not return a single shot. A few minutes after twelve, however, her guns thundered forth on the enemy from both sides of her deck.

"It is impossible," said Captain Hardy, addressing Nelson, "to break the enemy's line without running on board one of their ships. Which would you prefer?"

"Take your choice, Hardy," answered Nelson; "which it is does not matter much."

Captain Hardy, exercising his discretion, ordered the master to put the helm to port, and the "Victory" ran on board the "Redoubtable."

This ship, the tops of which were filled with riflemen, received the "Victory" with a broadside, and, for fear of being boarded, let down her lower deck ports, and did not again fire a great gun during the action. Nelson, supposing from this circumstance that the "Redoubtable" had struck, issued orders to refrain from firing. But, though her great guns were silent, the riflemen who filled her tops continued to deal destruction around.

It was a quarter past one o'clock, and Nelson was standing on the deck of the "Victory," when a ball fired from the mizzen-top of the "Redoubtable" struck the epaulette on his left shoulder, and prostrated him on his face. Three sailors instantly rushing forward, raised him to his feet; and Captain Hardy, turning round and seeing what had happened, hastened to their assistance.

"They have done for me at last, Hardy," said Nelson.

"I hope not," cried Hardy.

"Yes," replied Nelson; "my backbone is shot through."

But at this moment the hero's presence of mind did not desert him. Covering his face and his stars, that the crew might not be aware that he was wounded, he allowed himself to be carried to the cockpit, and placed in a midshipman's berth. The wound was found to be mortal; but this circumstance was concealed from all except the chaplain and the surgeons. Nelson, though in great pain, feeling certain that nothing could be done for him, requested the surgeons to attend to those to whom they might be useful. But they continued to fan him, and gave him lemonade to assuage his thirst, which was intense. Nevertheless, at each cheer from the crew, which announced that a French ship had struck, his eye brightened, his tongue uttered an exclamation of joy, and he became more and more anxious to hear of the battle from Captain Hardy, who was absent more than an hour before he could again leave the deck.

"Well, Hardy," said Nelson, when the captain appeared, "how goes the day with us?"

"Very well," replied Hardy; "ten ships have struck; but five of the van have tacked, and seem to be bearing down on the 'Victory.' However, I have called two or three of our fresh ships round, and have no doubt of giving them a drubbing."

"I hope," said Nelson, "that none of our ships have struck."

"No fear of that," replied the gallant captain.

"Hardy," said Nelson, for the first time speaking of himself, "I am a dead man. I am going fast. Come nearer to me," he continued; "let my dear Lady Hamilton have my hair and all other things belonging to me."

"I trust," said Captain Hardy, "that the doctor can still hold out hope."

"Oh no," replied Nelson, "my back is shot through. He will tell you so."

But the battle still raged fiercely, and Captain Hardy was under the necessity of hastening back to the deck. For fifty minutes he was absent. At the end of that time, however, he returned to the cockpit, and, taking Nelson's hand, congratulated the dying hero on having won a complete victory.

"I do not know exactly how many of the enemy we have taken," he said, "but fourteen or fifteen at least."

"'Tis well—'tis excellent!" exclaimed Nelson; "but yet," he added, thinking of his conversation with Captain Blackwood, "I had bargained for twenty. However, anchor, Hardy, anchor."

"Don't you think," suggested Hardy, "that Admiral Collingwood will take the direction of affairs?"

"Not while I live," said Nelson, making an effort to raise himself. "Obey my orders, and anchor. And," he continued, "don't fling me overboard. I wish to repose with my family in the church-yard of my native village. Unless," he added, thinking of Westminster Abbey, "my king and my country should be pleased to order otherwise. Now kiss me, Hardy!"

Nelson now seemed to sink, and after a few

moments Hardy stooped down and kissed his forehead.

"Who is that?" asked Nelson.

"It is Hardy," was the answer.

"God bless you, Hardy! God bless you!" exclaimed Nelson, and they parted.

"Turn me on my right side," said Nelson to those around; "I wish I hadn't left the deck, for I shall soon be gone." However, he continued to exclaim repeatedly, "Thank God, I have done my duty!"

But death was now rapidly approaching. Nelson's articulation gradually became more difficult and less distinct. At half past four, just after the last guns fired at the flying enemy sounded in his ears, and proclaimed that the victory was complete, the hero breathed his last, and sank in death.

The mortal remains of Nelson were brought in the "Victory" to England. A public funeral was decreed; and after lying in state in a coffin long before made of the mast of the "Orient," the corpse was laid with all honors in St. Paul's Cathedral. Never had warrior been more highly venerated or more sincerely lamented. By his sailors he was regarded as a saint. The leaden coffin in which he had been brought from Trafalgar was cut in pieces, to be distributed as relics of St. Nelson; and the flag with which he was lowered into the grave was rent to fragments by the sailors who assisted at the ceremony, that each, while he lived, might preserve a memorial of the man who had fought triumphantly, and died gloriously, in vindicating England's claim to the sovereignty of the seas.

LORD COLLINGWOOD.

ABOUT the time when the people of England were lighting bonfires to celebrate the victory of Admiral Boscawen over the French off Gibraltar, and that of Admiral Hawke over the same enemy at Belleisle, and when watchmen at midnight bawled through the streets of London the news of General Wolfe's triumph at Quebec, there might have been observed among the Northern juveniles at the grammar-school of Newcastle a pretty and somewhat gentle boy, who rejoiced in the name of Cuthbert Collingwood. There was little in the dress, or position, or prospects of the lad to give him an advantage over the sons of tradesmen and coal-fitters with whom he associated; but his sentiments must have been somewhat different. He bore a name which had been renowned in centuries that were past, and which he was to render famous for centuries to come.

The Collingwoods long maintained territorial state and formed high alliances in Northumberland. Indeed, through the Greys, they derived descent from Joan Plantagenet, known in history as "The Fair Maid of Kent," as wife of the Black Prince, and as mother of Richard the Second.

Moreover, they displayed their prowess in the old Border wars, and suffered for their loyalty in the wars of the Jacobites. One of them, Cuthbert Collingwood, described by the old ballad-maker as "Collingwood, that courteous knight," fought in the Raid of the Red Swire; and another of them, George Collingwood, celebrated in song as the friend of Lord Derwentwater, took part in the insurrection of 1715, lost his estates, and laid his head on the block for the house of Stuart. After such an event, the Collingwoods naturally came down in the world; and in the eighteenth century, Cuthbert Collingwood of Ditchburn, one of the representatives of the family, who inherited little beyond the name and surname of the "courteous knight" taken at the Red Swire, "finding himself reduced to a very moderate fortune," settled at Newcastle about the time when the inhabitants were in dread of the Highland host under Prince Charles Edward, married Milcha, daughter and co-heir of Reginald Dobson, of Barwess, in Westmoreland, and, as years passed on, became the father of several sons and daughters.

It was on the 26th of September, 1750, that Cuthbert Collingwood, eldest son of the heir of Ditchburn and the co-heiress of Barwess, drew his first breath. He was born in Newcastle, and appears to have been, when a month old, baptized at St. Nicholas's church in that town. But noth-

ing that occurred to him during his childhood
has been deemed worthy of record. After being
carried about the quays and streets of his native
town, taught to run about the margin of the
Tyne, and taken on fine afternoons to buy short-
cake at the neighboring village of Chester-le-
Street, he was sent to be educated at the grammar-school, and placed at that time-honored seminary with other boys of his age, among whom
were the two Scotts, sons of a coal-fitter, and destined to be celebrated in after years as Lord
Stowell and Lord Eldon.

Fortunately, when Collingwood took his seat
on the benches of the grammar-school of Newcastle, that institution, which a few years earlier
had been well-nigh deserted, was flourishing under the auspices of the Rev. Hugh Moises, who
exercised his functions with great dignity, appeared every morning in a gown which reminded his pupils that he had taken a degree at Cambridge, conducted the business of the school with
signal vigor and success, instilled into the minds
of the boys during the week wholesome ideas of
reverence and obedience, taught them to fear
God and honor the king, and on Sunday marched
them to church in a body under his own eye.
Moises, it seems, was a teacher of the old stamp,
who never spared the rod when punishment was
likely to do good; but he was inclined to treat
his scholars with kindness, and disinclined to

withhold praise when praise was likely to encourage exertion. Such was the training under
which were cherished in Collingwood's heart the
sentiments of chivalry and piety which he inherited from his ancestors, and which, during a long
and arduous career, he exhibited to his contemporaries.

But the scholars of Moises were not those "de-
mure boys," who, as Falstaff hath it, never come
to any proof. Many anecdotes have been related
which vindicate them from any such charge as
being deficient in the spirit of mischief. They
engaged in frays with boys belonging to the other schools, mobbed old ladies in the street, rode
during play-hours on the tomb-stones in St. John's
church-yard, and even on one occasion, according
to Lord Eldon, went the length of plundering an
orchard. Whether Collingwood was the rival
of the embryo chancellor in those pranks does
not appear; but it is certain that, like the legal
sage, he profited by the tuition of Moises, and
that he left the seminary with a considerable
knowledge of Latin, and with the faculty of writing English with correctness and propriety.

At an early age Collingwood was dedicated to
that profession of which he became so useful a
member and so bright an ornament. A naval officer named Braithwaite, who had married Collingwood's aunt, was then in command of the
"Shannon," and the young Northumbrian was

got ready to go to sea under his kinsman's protection. Accordingly, his chest having been
packed, and his mother having placed therein a
plum-cake as a token of maternal affection, he
took leave of his friends, and, when scarcely more
than eleven years of age, left home to " rough it
out at sea."

No sooner was Collingwood on board the
"Shannon," and surrounded by unfamiliar faces,
than he was overcome by a sense of solitude.
During his first days at sea he experienced the
utmost sadness, and sat on deck, his eyes filled
with tears, which flowed the faster as he looked
at the shore, and thought of the friends he had
left. But the first lieutenant, perceiving that the
comely little sailor was downcast, and perhaps
remembering his own feelings under similar circumstances, considered that a few words of com-
fort would not be wasted. Approaching, therefore, he laid his hand on Collingwood's shoulder,
and addressed him in a tone of kindness.

" Cheer up, youngster," he said; " this is all,
no doubt, very strange to you; but keep a good
heart, and you'll soon get used to it."

Looking up through his tears, and seeing sympathy in the speaker's face, Collingwood felt particularly grateful. Indeed, he led the first lieutenant to his chest, and gratefully presented the
officer with a large piece of the plum-cake which
his mother had given him when parting.

For one so young as Collingwood was when he went on board the "Shannon," the life on which he had entered was doubtless harsh; but, experiencing much kindness from Captain Braithwaite, he soon got over his feeling of loneliness, and afterward acknowledged the obligations which, as concerned professional knowledge, he owed to his gallant kinsman. Meanwhile his own sagacity and energy stood him in good stead, and he was far from trusting to the aid or inspiration of others in his brave struggle for fame and fortune.

In the ordinary course of events, Collingwood parted with his friend, Captain Braithwaite, and sailed for some time under another officer. Between these two services the young Northumbrian passed thirteen long years of his life without promotion. But, cheerless as might have been the circumstances, and distant as might have been the prospect of brighter days, he turned his time to good account, and arduously prepared to avail himself of the chances in store. While working diligently, he studied earnestly. Not only did he peruse books on naval affairs, but he devoted much time to historical works, and made a point of never neglecting the cultivation of his intellect. He strongly recommended to others the steadiness and self-culture which he practiced. "A man," he said, "should, before arriving at his twenty-fifth year, establish for himself a character and reputation of such a kind as he would have no cause to be ashamed of in after life."

At length, when Collingwood had reached the age of twenty-five, Fortune, which had previously been so coy, condescended to favor him with a chance. In 1774, when the War of Independence was commencing in America, and when the soldiers of England and the exasperated colonists were about to cross bayonets, Collingwood sailed in the "Preston" under Vice Admiral Graves, landed at an opportune period at Boston, and took part in the battle fought in June, 1775, at Bunker's Hill. On that occasion Collingwood commanded a party of seamen sent to assist the troops. The Americans, exhibiting high courage, convinced their adversaries that they were no contemptible foes. Victory, however, remained with the English; and Collingwood, promoted for his exertions on the field to the rank of lieutenant, joined the "Somerset" in that capacity.

Collingwood returned with Admiral Graves to England. But his stay was brief. Appointed to the "Hornet," he sailed in that sloop to Jamaica, and on the West India station formed an intimate friendship with Nelson, which lasted to the day of Trafalgar. At the same time, Sir Hyde Parker, commander-in-chief, recognized both as officers of remarkable promise, and did his best to advance their fortunes; and so managed that whenever Nelson got a step, Colling-

wood came in for a share of promotion. When
Nelson was removed into the " Bristol" flag-ship,
Collingwood succeeded Nelson in the "Lowestoffe ;" when Nelson became commander of the
" Badger," Collingwood succeeded Nelson in the
" Bristol ;" when Nelson was transferred to the
" Hinchenbrook," Collingwood was appointed
commander of the " Badger ;" and when, during
the siege of San Juan, Nelson was nominated to
the " Janus," Collingwood, as post-captain, took
command of the " Hinchenbrook."

But, notwithstanding these frequent promo-
tions, the position of Collingwood was at this period the reverse of enviable. The climate at St.
Juan proved most fatal to the English. Of eighteen hundred men sent upon the expedition, not
four hundred returned. The " Hinchenbrook's"
complement consisted of nearly two hundred
men. Eighty-seven took to their beds in one
night; and of the whole crew, not more than a
score survived. "My constitution," says Collingwood, " resisted many attacks, and I survived
most of my ship's company, having buried in four
months a hundred and eighty out of the two
hundred who composed it."

After escaping from the pestilential climate of
San Juan, Collingwood was appointed to the
" Pelican." In this vessel he fell in with a French
ship, which had seized a richly-laden merchantman belonging to the port of Glasgow. Making

an attack, he captured the Frenchman and liberated the prize. But his connection with the
"Pelican" was not destined to have a lucky ter-
mination. On the 1st of August, 1786, the frigate was driven by a tremendous gale on the rocks
of the Morant Keys. "The next day," says Collingwood, "the ship's company with great difficulty got ashore on rafts made of the small and
broken yards, and upon these sandy islands, with
little food, we remained ten days, until a boat
went to Jamaica, and the 'Diamond' frigate came
and took us off."

After the wreck of the "Pelican," Collingwood,
gradually rising in his profession, was appointed
to the command of the "Samson," a ship of sixty-
four guns. But in this position he had no opportunity of distinguishing himself. At the peace
declared in 1793 the "Samson" was paid off, and
Collingwood was dispatched in the "Mediator"
to the West Indies.

By this time the Americans, headed by General Washington and aided by the French, had
been so successful in their struggle with England
that George the Third had been reluctantly compelled to acknowledge their independence. On
that point there was now no dispute; but the
Americans, having severed their connection with
England, were still much disinclined to abandon
the privileges which they had enjoyed as subjects of England's king, and, taking advantage of

the ships' registers they had obtained in other days, they attempted to trade as before with the West India Islands which belonged to the English crown. Nelson, who was then in the "Boreas," perceiving the illegality of such commerce, expressed strong objections, and Collingwood perfectly agreed with his old friend.

Accordingly, Nelson, accompanied by Collingwood, went to the commander on the station, and represented the necessity of enforcing the provisions of the Navigation Act. No encouragement, however, did that functionary afford to the daring captain of the "Boreas." Nevertheless, Nelson held resolutely to his purpose; and Collingwood, in the "Mediator," with his brother Winifred, who commanded the "Rattler," lent all the aid in their power. The steps taken by Nelson, and the energy shown by the Collingwoods, proved successful; and the Treasury transmitted thanks to the commander-in-chief for his zeal in protecting English commerce. "Had they known all," said Nelson, "I do not think they would have bestowed thanks in that quarter and neglected me."

In 1786 Collingwood left the West Indies and returned to England. It was the year of the celebrated treaty of commerce between England and France; and perhaps, with half the country indulging in dreams of perpetual peace, Collingwood thought his occupation gone. However, he climbed to the top of the coach, turned his face northward, and consoled himself with the prospect of making the acquaintance of his relatives, of whom he had hitherto seen very little.

At this period Collingwood was in his thirty-sixth year, and was a man of whom his friends might well be proud. He was of middle stature, with a slender but well-formed person, a sagacious countenance, and a full, dark eye, that shone with resolution and beamed with intelligence. His manner and his heart were equally admirable: his heart was one of the kindest that ever beat in a human bosom; and his manner was characterized by an antique kind of politeness, which was gradually disappearing from society. Imagine such a man with excellent conversational powers, lively wit, and a propensity to speaking on most subjects with interest, and not without a smack of that Danish burr which the Northumbrians have inherited from their northern ancestry, and you will have some idea of what Collingwood was when, after a long absence, he returned to the banks of the Tyne, leaped from the coach, and stood in the streets of his native town.

After reaching Northumberland, Collingwood appears to have spent four years in quiet and peace. At the end of that time, however, disputes with Spain led to an idea that war was inevitable; and Collingwood, nominated to the command of the "Mermaid," hastened at the call of duty to his post. But the dispute was speedily accommodated; and the "Mermaid" having been paid off, the gallant captain again made for his native north.

In fact, Collingwood had now a more powerful motive in going to Northumberland than even the desire of making the acquaintance of his kindred. During his four years' residence he had become attached to a lady of that great province named Blackett; and being now turned of forty, an age at which, according to the poet, there is no dallying with life, he probably considered that he had little time to lose. At all events, he resolved without delay to venture on matrimony; and at Newcastle, one day in the month of June, 1791, received the hand of his bride in St. Nicholas's Church.

His marriage solemnized, Collingwood took up his residence at Morpeth, an ancient and interesting town, with an old church dedicated to St. Mary, and a castle which calls to memory the feudal grandeur of the Merleys, as the doorway of the conventual church at Newminster reminds visitors of the magnificent abbey which long commemorated their piety. In his retreat at Morpeth, where he had a garden situated on the banks of the beautiful Wansbeck, Collingwood appears to have spent three happy years; and with two daughters, who soon appeared to claim his paternal affection, he looked forward to a long sea-

C c

son of domestic enjoyment. But he was disappointed.

When, in 1793, war was declared with France, Collingwood was appointed to the "Prince," the flag-ship of Admiral Bowyer. As the Northumbrian captain hated the French, and believed that every Englishman was in duty bound to consider every Frenchman as an enemy, he had no scruples about the contest in which he was going to take part on that element where he was destined to spend so many years, and to acquire so great a name. Ere long, however, Admiral Bowyer shifted his flag, and Collingwood, removing with the admiral to the "Barfleur," was on board that vessel when she formed part of the fleet with which Lord Howe encountered the French off Ushant.

It was Sunday, the 1st of June, 1794, and the French having appeared in sight, the English fleet drew up and dressed ranks. About eight o'clock the signal for action was given. Every vessel then bore down upon her adversary. About ten o'clock Lord Howe began the battle, but Admiral Bowyer and Collingwood, who, before firing a gun, had to go through the fire of three of the enemy, in one of which was the French admiral, were somewhat later in getting into action.

"Warm work," remarked Bowyer, as they received the Frenchman's broadsides.

"And at home, about this time, the church bells will be ringing, and our wives will be going to church," said Collingwood, as his thoughts strayed to the abode of his family, to the Wansbeck flowing through a succession of fertile valleys, and to the green woodlands and the blue mountains of Northumberland. "But," he added, turning from the scene conjured up by his fancy. "I think the ringing of the church bells will not be quite so loud as the peal we are going to ring about the Frenchman's ears."

At length the "Barfleur" opened fire, and in the battle that ensued Collingwood bore himself with singular gallantry. Nevertheless, when the victory was won, his services were not acknowledged by Lord Howe; and when medals were distributed, he was unaccountably passed over. This circumstance caused much surprise in the fleet; and the officers who had fought by Collingwood's side, and witnessed his exertions, expressed their amazement.

"Collingwood without a medal!" they exclaimed.

"I'm sure," said Captain Pakenham, of the "Invincible," "if Collingwood has not deserved a medal, neither have I, for we were together the whole day."

Collingwood could not, of course, overlook this injustice. But he had too much pride and too much sense of propriety to waste words on the subject. A man of real merit can afford to bide his time under such circumstances; and Collingwood, no doubt, felt certain that ere many years passed over an opportunity of obtaining redress would occur. Meanwhile he was removed from the "Barfleur," appointed to the "Excellent," and sent to join Sir John Jervis, who had taken the command of the Mediterranean. Nelson, who had previously joined the fleet, hailed the arrival of his old friend with a shout of joy. "Here," he exclaimed, "comes the 'Excellent,' and she is as good as two added to our number."

At the battle off Cape St. Vincent, where Jervis won his earldom, Collingwood gained high honor. When Nelson, in the "Captain," was maintaining a desperate contest with several of the Spaniards, and when the "Salvador del Mundo" and the "San Isidro," two of the "Captain's" adversaries, dropped astern, Collingwood fired into them in masterly style. The "San Isidro" struck, and some thought the "Salvador" struck also. "But Collingwood," says Nelson, "disdaining the parade of taking possession of beaten enemies, most gallantly pushed up with every sail set to save his old friend and messmate, who was to all appearance in a critical situation."

After the victory off Cape St. Vincent, Sir John Jervis, in writing to the First Lord of the Admiralty, mentioned Collingwood in terms of praise; and he soon after announced that the captain of the "Excellent" was to receive one of the medals distributed to commemorate the event. The time thus came when Collingwood could, without loss of dignity, speak of the injustice done him by Lord Howe, and he expressed his sentiments with characteristic firmness of tone.

"I must decline to receive this mark of distinction," he said, as his eye flashed with pride and his heart swelled with emotion; "I must decline to receive this medal while the former one is withheld."

"Such is your answer?" asked Lord St. Vincent.

"Yes," replied Collingwood; "I feel that I was improperly passed over; and to receive such a distinction in this case would be to acknowledge the propriety of that injustice."

"That," said Lord St. Vincent, with admiration, "is precisely the answer I expected from you, Captain Collingwood."

After this conversation Collingwood had the gratification of receiving two medals from the Admiralty, and with them an apology for the former one having been kept back. But man at his best estate can not readily forget what appears a deliberate injury, and it may be doubted whether the high-spirited Northumbrian, with all his goodness of heart, ever mentioned the name of Richard Lord Howe, or "Black Dick," as that distinguished personage was called by the sailors, without a feeling of antipathy.

But the reputation of Collingwood as a naval officer did not rest entirely on his exploits on the 1st of June, 1794, and the 14th of February, 1797. The influence he exercised over men under his command was too remarkable not to attract notice. His nature, indeed, rendered him averse to severity and opposed to harsh measures, but he had a way of his own of governing men, and , never failed in enforcing discipline. Accordingly, when the spirit of mutiny, displayed at Portsmouth and the Nore, agitated the navy, and excited men to insubordination, his talent for maintaining order was highly appreciated.

"What in the world is to be done with these men?" officers would say to Lord St. Vincent.

"Send them to the 'Excellent,' " Lord St. Vincent would answer; "Collingwood will soon bring them to order."

It thus happened that when men proved unmanageable they were drafted into the "Excellent;" and such was Collingwood's kindness, so evident his anxiety for their health and welfare, and so scrupulous his old-fashioned politeness, that even the most refractory mutineers became in his hands model seamen.

Having remained in the "Excellent" till January, 1799, when that ship was paid off, Collingwood was in February promoted to the rank of Rear Admiral of the White, and ordered to hoist his flag on board the "Triumph," and join the

Channel fleet under Lord Bridport, one of the Hoods. However, he was soon after dispatched with a re-enforcement of twelve sail of the line to Lord Keith in the Mediterranean, where the chief naval force of France and Spain then lay. In June, 1800, he removed to his old ship the "Barfleur," and having, about the opening of 1801, been advanced to the rank of Rear Admiral of the Red, he remained at sea till relieved from duty by the peace of Amiens.

It was late in March, 1802, when the treaty was signed, and in May Collingwood found his way to Morpeth. Having passed his fiftieth year, he doubtless sighed for rest from his labors, and he appears to have much relished the repose he had so well earned. He was fond of company, and among his friends he could talk admirably and well. He read, wrote to improve his style, superintended the education of his daughters, indulged his fancy for drawing, walked about the pleasant paths that curve along the margin of the Wansbeck, and spent much time in gardening, which, like Lord Bacon, he seems to have considered " the purest of pleasures."

One day, at this period, a naval officer came to visit Collingwood. Learning that the admiral was about his grounds, the visitor went to look for him. After searching some time without seeing any body, however, he manifested symptoms of impatience.

"Where the deuce," he exclaimed, "can the admiral be?"

"Here," cried a well-known voice.

The naval officer, guided by the sound, renewed his search, and soon discovered Collingwood. In fact, the hero of a hundred fights, and the patrician of twenty descents, was busily engaged, with an old gardener named Scott, digging at the bottom of a trench.

This kind of life, however, was abruptly terminated. In May, 1803, the peace with France came to an end, and Collingwood, summoned once more from his tranquil and happy retreat, went forth to guard the coasts of England from the foe, who was earnestly planning her destruction. Domestic quiet, social enjoyment, health, life itself, were not in the eyes of a hero, with Plantagenet blood in his veins, to be compared with the duty of preserving the shores and independence of England, and he left, without a murmur, the home where were those he held most dear. Having been appointed to the "Venerable," he sailed to rejoin the squadron under Cornwallis, off Brest.

"Here is the 'Venerable,'" was the cry.

"Yes," said Cornwallis, gladly; "here comes Collingwood, the last to leave, and the first to rejoin us."

Month after month Collingwood devoted himself to the blockade, shifting his flag from ship to

COLLINGWOOD IN RETIREMENT.

ship, so as never to leave the harbor even for victualing or repairs. "I am lying off the entrance of the Brest harbor," he wrote, "to watch the motions of the French fleet. Our information respecting them is very vague, but we know that they have four or five-and-twenty great ships, which makes it necessary to be alert, and keep our eyes open at all times. I therefore bid adieu to snug beds and comfortable naps at night, never lying down but in my clothes."

The duty of blockading an enemy's port was not one which Collingwood relished. But grand and stormy scenes were at hand. In the beginning of 1805, the Toulon fleet, under the command of Villeneuve, ventured out of port. Nelson then went off in pursuit, and Collingwood, who had in the previous year become Vice Admiral of the Red, was detached with a squadron, and took his station off Cadiz. In this position his talent as a naval tactician was conspicuous. Left with four ships of the line, he made his dispositions with such skill as to delude the enemy into a belief that he was at the head of a formidable force, and that the ships visible from the harbor were merely a small part of his fleet. When Villeneuve, after having been chased by Nelson "from hemisphere to hemisphere," appeared with the combined fleets of France and Spain, Collingwood found it necessary to retire ; but in the autumn he resumed his post in the

"Dreadnought," and continued to watch the foe with the utmost vigilance, sometimes passing the night on deck, seated on a gun.

At the close of September, however, Nelson came to perform his threat of "giving M. Ville-neuve a drubbing," and "teaching Bonaparte to respect the British navy;" and on the 9th of October, 1805, Collingwood received what was called "the Nelson touch." "I send you my plan of attack," wrote Nelson, "as far as a man dare venture to guess at the very uncertain position the enemy may be found in; but it is to place you perfectly at ease respecting my intentions, and to give full scope to your judgment for carrying them into effect. We can, my dear Coll., have no little jealousies. We have only one great object in view, that of annihilating our enemies, and getting a glorious peace for our country. No man has more confidence in another than I have in you, and no man will render your services more justice than your very old friend, Nelson and Bronte."

Expectation now sat on every face; and when, without much delay, Villeneuve came out of Ca-diz, Collingwood, who meanwhile had shifted his flag from the "Dreadnought" to the "Royal Sovereign," hastened on board the "Victory" to hold a last conference.

"Coll.," asked Nelson, "where is your captain?"

"The fact is," answered Collingwood, "we are not on good terms with each other."

"Terms!" exclaimed Nelson; "not on good terms with each other! I'll soon arrange that."

Accordingly, a boat was dispatched to the "Royal Sovereign," and Captain Rotherham was brought on board the "Victory." As soon as Rotherham came on deck, Nelson led him to Collingwood.

"Look," said Nelson, "yonder is the enemy."

"Yes," said they.

"Well," he added, "shake hands like Englishmen."

Matters having been arranged and plans discussed, Collingwood and Nelson parted; and on that memorable morning, when the hero of the Nile and of Copenhagen came on the deck of the "Victory" decorated with stars, and prepared for glory and death, Collingwood, more calmly, but not less courageously than his illustrious compeer, prepared to take his part in the impending conflict. Generally, he gave little attention indeed to his dress, which even on state occasions consisted of a small cocked-hat, a square-cut blue coat with tarnished epaulettes, blue waistcoat and small-clothes, and boots guiltless of blacking. But he perhaps felt that the day of Trafalgar was to be the most important day of his life, and he arrayed himself with extraordinary care.

"Clavel," he said, meeting his favorite officer as he left the cabin, "are you ready?" .

"Quite ready, sir," answered the lieutenant, doubtless somewhat surprised at the admiral's attire.

"But," said Collingwood, "you had better pull off your boots, and put on silk stockings, as I've done; for, if we should get a shot in the leg, the stocking would be so much more manageable for the surgeon."

Having given this prudent advice, Collingwood went among the seamen and officers, and enjoined them, with a dignity worthy of the first great Edward or the "stout Earl of Warwick, to perform their duty as Englishmen and freemen, and to do something that would be talked of in time to come. Having thus encouraged the companions of his peril, he awaited the moment which was to bring him into action against his country's foes.

As the hour of battle approached, the fleet, as had been arranged, advanced in two lines, Nelson leading one, and Collingwood the other; and the ships, crowding all sail, moved gallantly forward, with a light wind from the southwest. The sun shone on the sails of the French and Spaniards, and so formidable appeared the armament that it would have daunted meaner adversaries. But the English sailors, confident in the genius of their chiefs and the justice of their cause, when looking upon the hostile fleet only thought of the beauty of the ships, and loudly expressed their admiration.

"What a fine sight!" cried some.

"Yes," said others. "What a sight yonder ships would make at Spithead!"

Meanwhile Collingwood, leading the lee line in the "Royal Sovereign," steered right for the centre of the enemy's line, and cut through it astern of a Spanish three-decker named the "Santa Anna."

"See," cried Nelson at that moment, as he stood on the deck of the "Victory," "see how that noble fellow Collingwood takes his ship into action!"

"Rotherham," said Collingwood, delighted at being in the heat of the fire, and at no loss to imagine the feelings of his friend at such a moment, "what would Nelson give to be here?"

But this was no time for prolonged speculations as to the feelings of others. The "Royal Sovereign," having engaged the "Santa Anna" at the muzzle of her guns on the starboard side, poured a broadside and a half into her stern. The two ships were soon so close that their lower guns were locked together. Nor was it with a single antagonist that Collingwood had to contend. A second vessel was placed on the "Royal Sovereign's" lee quarter; three others bore down upon her bow; and thus she was at once engaged in deadly strife with five of the enemy. But the "Royal Sovereign" held her own, and dealt destruction about her in a way that caused astonishment among her assailants.

At length, after a severe struggle, the "Royal Sovereign" compelled the "Santa Anna" to strike, and the Spanish captain, coming on board, surrendered his sword and seated himself on one of the guns.

"What is the name of this ship?" he asked in broken English.

"Royal Sovereign," was the answer.

"Royal Sovereign!" he exclaimed, patting the gun with his hand; "I think she should rather be called 'Royal Devil.'"

When Nelson fell, a messenger was sent to Collingwood with intelligence that the admiral was wounded, but not dangerously. Collingwood, however, suspected that the case was more serious than the message intimated, and, ere long, he found his saddest forebodings realized. About the close of the action, Captain Hardy presented himself on the deck of the "Royal Sovereign," and announced to Collingwood that Nelson was no more.

The brilliancy of the triumph achieved by the English at Trafalgar was in some degree diminished by the fall of the conqueror. Nevertheless, it was almost as complete a victory as could have been wished, and one of the most glorious in the annals of maritime warfare; and Collingwood, on whom devolved the command of the fleet, appointed the following day for a general thanksgiving to Almighty God.

"It was well," said George the Third, when Collingwood's dispatches reached England, "that the command devolved on an officer of Admiral Collingwood's sense and experience. I was surprised," remarked the old king, "how a naval officer could write so excellent a dispatch. But I find he was educated by Moises."

"I know not where Admiral Collingwood got his style," said an eminent diplomatist, "but he writes better than any of us."

For his share in the victory of Trafalgar Collingwood did not go unrewarded. The king created him a peer of the realm; Parliament voted him thanks and a pension; and many of the chief cities in the kingdom marked their appreciation of his career by granting him their freedom. But leisure, for which he sighed, was what neither Parliament nor his country could grant. True it was that the English fleet had so thoroughly done its work at Trafalgar that the navy of England's enemies had vanished from the seas, and the maritime war was virtually at an end. But the post which Collingwood occupied was still highly responsible, and to none could it be intrusted save to the man who had shared Nelson's glory. Besides commanding the fleet, Colling-

wood had the duty of conducting the political re-
lations of England with the countries bordering on
the Mediterranean; and, his political penetration
being keen, he was peculiarly fitted for the post.

At sea—with the soul of a hero, the heart of a
patriot, and the spirit of a martyr—Collingwood
remained, performing his duty to admiration, exhibiting undeviating devotion to the service, and
saving government immense sums by the old-
fashioned economy he practiced.   He was strict
with his officers, especially if they owed their position to rank and wealth, and not to merit.

"I like," he said, "to see a man get in at the
port-hole, not at the cabin-window."

It was not wonderful, of course, that a man
who, with the blood of princes and cavaliers in
his veins, had served for fourteen long years without promotion, should have looked with little favor on the spectacle of modern aristocrats being
put over the heads of their superiors in ancestry
and intellect.   But it would appear that, when in
duty bound to find fault, Collingwood did so
calmly and with point.

On one occasion, when anxious to take in provisions and to sail without delay, he ordered that
all the boats should be sent on shore, and that
not a minute should be lost.

"Are the boats all gone ashore?" he inquired
of the captain, soon after issuing his instructions.

"All but my barge," was the reply.

"Oh, of course," said Collingwood, "a captain's barge must never be used for such a purpose. But I hope they will have no scruple in making every possible use of mine."

On another occasion, when a captain in the fleet, whose ideas were somewhat grand and whose ship was rather gay, displayed new sails, Collingwood ordered the old ones to be brought to him for inspection. Finding them in better condition than his own, he caused his mainsail, which was much the worse for wear, to be taken down, and that which had been brought for inspection to be hoisted instead. Having then invited the gay captain to dinner, he introduced the subject.

"What do you think of my mainsail?" he carelessly asked.

"In fair condition, my lord," unwarily answered the guest.

"Well," said Collingwood, "if it's in fair condition for an admiral's ship, I think it might have done for a captain's."

In this way Collingwood passed several years, endeavoring faithfully to serve his country and his God. He was ever vigilant, and sometimes, even when torrents of rain poured through the shrouds, he appeared on deck without a hat, his gray hair floating in the wind, and his eye like the eagle's on the watch. It was his general rule in stormy weather to sleep on his sofa, only taking off his epauleted coat and donning a flannel gown. Throughout, he was unpretendingly pious, and never neglected his religious duties; and on Sundays, when the weather was such that the crew could not assemble on deck, he was in the habit of retiring to his cabin and reading the service for the day.

At length Collingwood's constitution began to break down. Colds, ague, and rheumatism he had been in the habit of setting at defiance. But they left their traces, and constant toil and exposure in the end brought on a disease that could hardly fail to prove fatal. But still he was held at his post by a sense of duty, and remained racking his brain and shattering his frame. At last his legs began to swell; and, perceiving that he must yield, he made up his mind to resign his command and proceed to England.

Collingwood's last service was directing preparations which resulted in the destruction of two French ships of the line on their own coast. On the 3d of March, 1810, having well-nigh reached the age of threescore, he embarked on board the "Ville de Paris;" and feeling quite convinced that his end was approaching, he, when at Minorca, ordered on board a quantity of lead with which to make a coffin to convey his corpse to England. But when informed that he was again at sea, he slightly rallied, and expressed some hope of recovery.

"I may yet," he said, "live to meet the French again. And yet," added he, "if I could but see my family, I should die happy."

A relapse, however, occurred; and next morning, when the captain of the "Ville de Paris" entered the cabin, Collingwood had but very little hope of either once more meeting the French, or again seeing the faces of those he best loved on the banks of the Wansbeck.

"I fear," said the captain, scarcely able to conceal his emotion, "that the motion of the vessel disturbs you."

"No," said Collingwood, "I am now in such a state that nothing in the world can disturb me. I am dying; and I'm sure it will console you, and all who love me, to see how comfortably I meet my end."

On the 10th of March no hope remained. Evident it then became to the least observing that the hero's body and soul must part. During his last sufferings Collingwood bore himself with the resignation of a Christian and the dignity of a gentleman; and at six in the evening, after having taken an affectionate farewell of those who stood by his couch, he committed his soul to God. His body was brought to England, and laid, with befitting ceremonies, beside the bones of Nelson in St. Paul's Cathedral.

THE END.

Miss Sedgwick's Works.

Miss Sedgwick has marked individuality; she writes with a higher aim than merely to amuse. Indeed, the rare endowments of her mind depend in an unusual degree upon the moral qualities with which they are united for their value. Animated by a cheerful philosophy, and anxious to pour its sunshine into every place where there is lurking care or suffering, she selects for illustration the scenes of every-day experience, paints them with exact fidelity, and seeks to diffuse over the mind a delicious serenity, and in the heart kind feelings and sympathies, and wise ambition, and steady hope. Her style is colloquial, picturesque, and marked by a facile grace, which is evidently a gift of nature. Her characters are nicely drawn and delicately contrasted; her delineation of manners decidedly the best that have appeared.—*Prose Writers of America.*

MEMOIR OF JOSEPH CURTIS. A Model Man. By the Author of "Married or Single?" "Means and Ends," "The Linwoods," "Hope Leslie," "Live and Let Live," &c., &c. 16mo, Muslin, 63 cents.

MARRIED OR SINGLE? By Miss Catharine M. Sedgwick, Author of "Hope Leslie," "The Linwoods," "Means and Ends," "Live and Let Live," &c., &c. 2 vols. 12mo, Muslin, $2 19.

LIVE AND LET LIVE; or, Domestic Service Illustrated. By Miss C. M. SEDGWICK. 18mo, Muslin, 56 cents.

MEANS AND ENDS; or, Self-training. By Miss C. M. SEDGWICK. 18mo, Muslin, 56 cents.

A LOVE TOKEN FOR CHILDREN. Designed for Sunday-School Libraries. By Miss C. M. SEDGWICK. 18mo, Muslin, 56 cents.

THE POOR RICH MAN AND THE RICH POOR MAN. By Miss C. M. SEDGWICK. 18mo, Muslin, 56 cents.

STORIES FOR YOUNG PERSONS. By Miss C. M. SEDGWICK. 18mo, Muslin, 56 cents.

WILTON HARVEY, AND OTHER TALES. By Miss C. M. SEDGWICK. 18mo, Muslin, 56 cents.